NO LAUGHING MATTER

Carlow's left hand shot toward the bartender's outstretched arm and held it. Instinctively the man tried to pull away but couldn't. Carlow's grip was prison steel. Raising his right leg, Carlow drew the knife from his leggings with his free hand and placed the blade against the wild-eyebrowed bartender's throat. Carlow's eyes drove their way into the man's soul.

As if it had been yanked offstage, the laughter jerked to a tense quiet and the saloon quit breathing. Even the old singing Rebel hesitated and stopped in the middle of "The Girl I Left Behind Me."

Carlow's intense gaze and the closeness of the sharp knife took away what little courage the bartender had as the young Ranger growled, "I didn't come this far to listen to some silly fools jabber. The man I'm after killed my best friend. It sounds to me like you boys are trying to hide him. You wouldn't want me to think that, would you…?"

STANDS A RANGER

COTTON SMITH

LEISURE BOOKS NEW YORK CITY

*To those American heroes
who fought and died serving our country
so that I might have freedom.*

A LEISURE BOOK®

March 2006

Published by

Dorchester Publishing Co., Inc.
200 Madison Avenue
New York, NY 10016

ISBN 0-8439-5539-2

The name "Leisure Books" and the stylized "L" with design are trademarks of Dorchester Publishing Co., Inc.

Printed in the United States of America.

Visit us on the web at www.dorchesterpub.com.

Stands a Ranger

Chapter One

Guessing wrong now would mean death. This was a good place for an ambush. Too good. Just ahead, a narrow pony trail disappeared into a maze of jagged hills, annoyed by petulant autumn weather.

Immediately ahead were thickets of loblolly pine, sage, and pickerel weed holding tight to a reddish knoll. Dark clouds were recruiting others, emboldened by the thunder's growling orders. Rain wouldn't be too far away, but he couldn't stop. Not now.

On the left side of the crowded trail, the land bottomed out into a dry creek that had lost its way years before. On the right, boulders were strewed around the hillside, making it difficult for a horse or a man to pass. His superstitious uncle, a longtime Ranger, would tell him this was a land where faeries, leprechauns, and wind spirits lived. His own instincts warned a dozen men could hide easily in this squeezed gathering of earthen knobs and ravines.

But there was only one man Texas Ranger Time Carlow was worried about. The outlaw Silver Mallow should be more than a day ahead of him.

If he was wrong, the young Ranger wouldn't see the sun set.

Off to Carlow's right was a cluster of trees. Overhead a hawk waltzed on a strong wind that was bringing rain fast. The sun had been kidnapped by huge gray clouds before it could settle at the edge of the world. The air was cool and had been warning him of an oncoming storm for two hours now.

He had ignored it too long, knowing rain would wash out the escaped outlaw's faint trail. His tracking skills were more the result of the guidance given by a Mescalaro Apache years before than of his Ranger uncle's teaching. Carlow and the Apache, Kayitah, had become friends after the young Ranger whipped three white men who were beating on Kayitah in a nameless town along the western edge of Texas.

Deciding cover was important, from either the certain storm or possible gunfire, he cut his tiring horse hard toward the trees. Scraggly bushes grabbed at the Kiowa leggings encasing Carlow's lower legs and worn boots as the black horse moved to obey. Branch fingers played with his large-roweled Mexican spurs and rubbed on the bone handle of a Comanche war knife carried in his right legging.

Fresh streaks on his horse's chest and flanks, layered over dried sweat marks, told the story of pushing hard. Too hard. Carlow couldn't remember being so tired; he'd been in the saddle for two days and three nights. He had slept only in short, fitful spurts, usually in the saddle. Stops were limited to brief rest, relieving himself, and giving canteen water to his fine black horse, Shadow, and the same for himself and his wolf-dog companion, Chance.

Occasionally, he would swallow bites of corn

dodgers and jerky, offer some to Chance, and hold handfuls of grain from the sack in his saddlebags for Shadow to down. The horse was too hot to be eating at all and feeding him might knot his intestines in colic, but Carlow felt he had to risk it to give the animal strength to keep on.

Three strides behind him now came Chance, panting heavily. The dark beast's tongue was long and dancing from his mouth. Anyone seeing them together would have feared a large prairie wolf strangely stalking its prey, not a loyal pet following its master.

Right now, Carlow's attention was elsewhere, trying to fight through weariness to be alert. Silver Mallow wasn't insane, as some said; Mallow was cunning, with a gift for disguise. Only his love of music and jewelry seemed out of place with his evil ways. Any other man would just keep running, especially if he thought he was being followed. Mallow would assume he was. But it would be like him to turn unexpectedly and kill, when he had the chance. Carlow knew the outlaw leader was wounded, and that only made him more dangerous.

As Carlow's black horse scrambled up a steep embankment of hard clay and tall grasses, the young Ranger's chiseled face was tense. Smoothly he drew his cut-down Winchester, carried as a handgun, and levered it one-handed with the sawed-off stock against his thigh. He swung the hand-carbine toward movement on his left. His light blue eyes were cold, expecting danger. For the moment, weariness was forgotten as body and mind shifted to his natural inclination to fight. His fingers tightened around the trigger before his mind ordered it.

A lost calf! His trigger finger eased as he realized the small animal was watching him curiously from the middle of an uneven thicket of misshapen bushes.

Shaking his head, he muttered sarcastically, "You're a little jumpy, Ranger. Or do you think Silver's going to disguise himself as a cow? Or one of those rain clouds?"

Reining his horse, he relaxed and waved the gun at the calf to get it started back toward a herd in the valley below. Instead of running, the small animal cocked its head to the side and bawled loudly.

"Oh, go on, boy. Your mama is going to think we're hurting you." Carlow looked around but saw no cow anywhere near.

He waved his arms again without any reaction from the calf. He couldn't help thinking his uncle, Ranger Aaron "Old Thunder" Kileen, would have announced that it was a sign of death in the family if a cow wandered from the field into one's garden. Carlow would have pointed out this wasn't a garden, but that wouldn't matter to Kileen. In honor of him, the young Ranger cursed out loud, an Irish curse his uncle often spat.

Chance took Carlow's swearing as a signal to get involved and ran at the calf growling and nipping at its heels. The calf wanted none of this nastiness and took off, running in gangly strides that made Carlow laugh. He yelled at Chance to return. The wolf-dog needed no such restriction, too tired to chase the animal more than a few steps.

Years in the Texas sun had browned Carlow permanently, and more than one person had mistaken him for a Comanche. But he was pure Irish. Black Irish, to be exact. Born of an Irish warrior who died sailing with his pregnant wife to the New World. Kileen was the only father he had ever known, helping raise him and caring for Carlow's mother until she, too, died when the boy was twelve.

Texas Ranger Kileen would not have been many people's idea of a model father. His past was clouded with questionable deeds and superstitious ways, having been a bare-knuckle prizefighter and worse to keep his sister and her child in food and shelter in New York and, later, in Texas. That didn't stop Kileen from serving in the Confederacy with Captain McNelly—and now serving Texas as a Ranger. But he loved Carlow unconditionally and was very proud his nephew had joined him on the state police force.

Long black hair brushed against Carlow's shoulders, matching his tailored dark mustache and brooding eyebrows. He was a deceptively strong young man with a solid chest, heavily muscled arms, a boyish grin that could charm women of any age and disarm most men, and an ability to use a gun that men like Silver Mallow feared.

"What say we find some cover for a while, Shadow?" Carlow patted the sweating neck of his black horse. "There's no need to get soaked. Besides, I'm so tired, I'm seeing Silver Mallow everywhere."

Lightning pushed through the hole between the rapidly darkening clouds. Thunder followed. A few raindrops splattered on the rim of his hat with its wide brim pushed up permanently in front. The proud black was suddenly alert, his ears cocked; Carlow reasoned Shadow was trying to determine the extent of the advancing storm. He may have overreacted to the threat of an ambush here, but already the rain was becoming serious, pounding the earth into a soaked surrender. His voice calmed the big horse. Rolling his neck to relieve his own tension, he leaned back to untie his trail coat from its rolled-up position behind the cantle.

The knots were tight, instead of their normal quick-pull tie. As the rain sought him, he lowered his shoulders and head to get a better angle on loosening the wet rawhide string. A naughty breeze flipped up the kerchief tied loosely around his neck and momentarily blocked his vision. He yanked the cloth sideways so it would lie out of the way on his right shoulder.

At first, Ranger Carlow thought it was thunder as the sound of a rifle reached him. His head jerked sideways, followed by a red line popping across his left temple. His hat went flying. The impact spun him halfway around as if yanked by a rope. A second bullet ripped across his upper right coat sleeve. A third burned Shadow's right flank. He lost the reins, along with his balance, and fell flailing from the saddle. His hand-carbine tried to fly by itself. One of his two canteens joined the flight.

Terrified, the black galloped away, leaving Carlow dazed and disoriented in a swale beside the rain-darkening trail. The disruption of the horse passing between him and his ambusher hidden in the rock lodge far to his right—and the blurring rain—momentarily kept him from being a helpless target. He frantically searched the rain-soaked ground for his hand-carbine. A short-barreled Colt was also holstered on the left side of his gunbelt, its walnut handle tilted forward for a right-handed draw. But his favorite weapon was the cut-down Winchester.

Rain pelted at his eyes, but the water was keeping a line of blood from reaching them. Strands of long black hair stuck against his chiseled face. A coat sleeve was ripped, and he thought his arm was hit. He fought off the shock of his head being grazed, found the gun, and fired a random shot. Return fire snapped angrily two feet from his shoulder. Wildly, he looked for somewhere to hide.

A downed oak tree twenty yards away was the closest cover. He scrambled toward it, firing once more. His head thudded with each step, as if his brain were being jolted first one way, then another. Around him sickening thumps of bullets striking trees were matched by the sounds of lead ripping through branches. Another shot bounced off the oak tree as he stumbled for cover within its uneven shadows. Thickening rain was saving his life, giving Silver Mallow only a flickering target.

After sprawling behind a fallen tree, Carlow levered his gun into readiness. The Winchester's barrel and stock had been carefully cut down by a Waco gunsmith, who had also created the unusual belt holster of rawhide bands and thick leather backing tied to his leg. On its shortened walnut stock was carved a Celtic marking, an ancient war symbol for victory, or so his superstitious uncle declared.

An enlarged circular lever increased cocking speed. So the weapon gave him the quick handling of a pistol combined with a rifle's punch and accuracy. But not quite its full distance. Handling the gun one-handed, like a pistol, came easily to him. Or he could brace it against his hip and lever shots faster than most could fan a pistol.

Right now, though, he would have traded it for the long-barreled 1863 Sharps rifle on his saddle. Converted to centerfire cartridges, it was a standard arm for post–Civil War Rangers. Silver Mallow was positioned far enough away to make it difficult to reach him without such firepower. Was that just luck, or had the outlaw been smart enough to realize the cut-down carbine didn't have the same range as a rifle?

Carlow realized Mallow's injured shoulder—from the gunshot when he was captured—should be tender enough to keep him from holding the gun effectively. His blackened eye and battered face and ribs might have played a role, too; they had come from the fists of Carlow's uncle. Or was it just by chance the young Ranger had moved his head at the right time?

If he were there, Kileen would nod and mutter, "By me sister's honored grave, 'tis the luck of a mad Welshman." It wouldn't matter that Mallow wasn't Welsh. Then Kileen surely would have added, "I should'a killed hisself when I be havin' the chance. Him right in front o' me fists an' all. 'Tis only a few ribs I be breakin'."

Within the protection of the tree, Ranger Carlow gulped for air that wouldn't come fast enough. The shooting had stopped. Where was his wolf-dog? Had Chance been hit? He surveyed the open land in all directions. Within the wall of rain, he saw the blurred image of his black horse standing off to the side of the trail. Or was it a tree broken in half by fierce weather?

Chapter Two

Squinting again into the torrent of rain, Carlow decided it was definitely Shadow, standing quietly with the loosened end of Carlow's long trail coat draped over his rear. The young Ranger wasn't surprised; the great mount was too steady to leave him.

Still, he didn't see Chance. He frowned and tried to concentrate. At the moment there were no signs of the escaped outlaw. Mallow was either moving to a new location along that yellowish hill to the Ranger's right or waiting for Carlow to show himself, or closing in. All Carlow could see was rain.

Maybe it was smart to be superstitious like his uncle. Carlow wished the gruff Irish Ranger were with him right now. Kileen would confidently tap his rifle three times on a tree, yell out some strange-sounding Celtic plea, and proudly announce that the land's faeries, "gods of the land," would be helping them soon. Then he would warn Carlow to speak carefully about them, always calling the "wee people" as "gentry," for they were easily offended and might leave on the merest

9

sense of being slighted. Not many people believed in them anymore, he said, and that was why they were so rarely seen. Then he would remind Carlow that they lived in places such as this.

That would bring a laughing comment from Carlow that believing in such creatures was helped if a person drank a lot, which his uncle did. Undismayed, Kileen would describe the little people at length, even if they were under fire, as he was now. How their form would change on a whim, and so would their interest. With his huge head cocked, he would state the only hardworking faery was the leprechaun. The rest spent their time in combat or feasts, making love or beautiful music.

The young Ranger decided he could use a few faeries right now, if they carried rifles and could shoot. Or knew how to stop the rain. He had heard those stories and others like them a hundred times from his bear-sized uncle. But right now Kileen was part of a Ranger force trying to break up a band of Mexican rustlers fifty miles away. No closer than his uncle's so-called wee people.

Captain McNelly assigned Carlow to bring in the escaped outlaw. Alone. It was definitely a compliment to the young Ranger. His first solo assignment. McNelly had initially considered sending three lawmen but decided he couldn't spare that many. Kileen had tried to talk McNelly into letting him go with his nephew, but the hard-nosed leader wouldn't listen.

In the past, Carlow had always ridden with others, including his uncle and his best friend, Shannon Dornan, who died in an ambush by Mallow's gang. Sometimes, Kayitah had joined them as a tracker, but he, too, had left this world. Regardless, it was an affirmation of Carlow's abilities that McNelly sent him by himself. He wouldn't let the Ranger captain down. Or his uncle. Or his best friend's memory.

Apparently a saloon singer, infatuated with the outlaw leader, had orchestrated Silver Mallow's breakout from the Bennett, Texas jail. There was no proof, only a lot of coincidence. None of Mallow's arrested gang escaped with him, and Bennett Marshal Moore proudly took credit for their retention, although he had nothing to do with it. Mallow simply decided to leave them behind because it would make his personal escape easier.

The outlaw had showed remarkable recuperative powers, acting so quickly after the beating received from Kileen and the gunshot from Widow Beckham that had saved both Rangers' lives. Her surprise use of Carlow's hand-carbine had delivered a cut along the top of Mallow's shoulder, forcing him to drop his hidden pistol. His arrest for murder and cattle rustling followed.

Afterward, the local newspaper had referred to the Ranger-led town posse's victory at Silver Mallow's hideout as "The Bennett War"—but only five gang members remained when the posse arrived. Out of town during Mallow's subsequent breakout, Carlow discovered the outlaw had managed to get away undetected by disguising himself as an old woman, most likely with clothes from the same saloon singer. Trying to help, Widow Beckham recalled seeing an older lady in eyeglasses and long gray hair ride out of town in a buggy. She hadn't recognized the woman but didn't think anything of it until she learned of Mallow's escape.

Thinking about his uncle made him remember the acorn in his vest pocket. Kileen had given it to him with the observation that carrying an acorn would give him good luck and a long life. Impulsively, he reached into his wet vest pocket to touch the acorn where it was jammed alongside extra cartridges, two pieces of hard candy, and an old silver watch.

Also in his pockets were two tiny flat stones, darkly stained with long-ago blood, a memory possession. One stone had belonged to Dornan. A large chip was gone where it had deflected a bullet. The other flat pebble was his. They were from a childhood ceremony based on their version of an Indian blood brother ceremony mixed with an ancient Gaelic rite. His Ranger badge was there, too; he never wore it on the trail. Reflection could easily indicate his location.

Smoke from Mallow's rifle, followed by the retort, brought him back to the trouble at hand. The white cloud was an instant, quickly smothered by the rain. Almost like it didn't happen. Mallow was dug in behind a wall of fallen timber several hundred yards away on that yellow hillside. It was a solid position twenty feet above him with a good field of fire. *A lot better than mine,* thought Carlow. At least his adversary wouldn't be able to move in easily. The hard crack of a rifle bullet tore through the branches near his elbow, reminding him that closing in wasn't necessary to ending his life.

Maybe the outlaw would make a mistake. Carlow felt weak and defenseless. He couldn't even fire without exposing himself foolishly. His head wound was making it difficult to concentrate, and even the simplest task took immense willpower. He squeezed his eyes to keep the swell of unconsciousness from advancing. To pass out now was to die. As he considered the situation, two slugs bit into the ledge above him and broke up his moment of wishful thinking. The trailing sounds followed by a count. This time Carlow didn't see the gunsmoke at all. The rain that had helped save him was working against him now.

But he could tell Mallow had moved. Twenty yards to the right. Carlow's answering fire was probably not close; Mallow would have rolled away as soon as he shot.

Another bullet clipped a rock beside his arm. Screaming its metallic song, the slug disappeared in the opposite direction. Carlow crawled frantically away from the tree and alongside a rain-swollen knoll for cover. Every advance pounded at his brain, and he bit his lower lip to keep from yelling out. He could only wait for the white smoke from Mallow's continued firing to know where he was. If the rain took that knowledge away, he could only hope Mallow didn't become lucky. An eerie silence wrapped around the area as no more shots came.

"I rode into an ambush," Carlow snarled angrily, "just like some damn greenhorn." *Captain McNelly—and Thunder—would be ashamed*, he thought.

Only his movement toward the rolled-up trail coat had saved his life. The thought sent a shiver through his body. He was the one who was lucky. Very lucky. Maybe Kileen was right. Maybe he did have invisible helpers protecting him. Somehow he had never wanted to challenge the idea by thinking about it too much. There were many things a person didn't understand in this world, especially things of the spirit. Certainly he had seen things that couldn't be explained by anything that made any sense. At least not to him. Maybe it was smart to be a little superstitious. Kileen said this feeling came from seeing miracles that occurred in everyday life and not recognizing them as miracles. Maybe so.

He was soaking wet and dizzy. His head swam with an ache that wanted to send him to sleep. Staying put wasn't a good idea. Eventually Mallow would close in and finish him. Or try to. Darkness was only hours away, and it would help the outlaw, not him. Carlow wished Kileen were here, right now. What would he do? The answer was obvious: the savvy old street-fighter would figure out some way to take the fight to his enemy.

Kileen's booming, joyful voice came again to his mind with the same advice he'd given so often: "Me lad, be fakin' the jab, fakin' the jab—and movin', always movin', then when he's come to expect yer journey—boom, ye let 'im have it with yer bloomin' right. From the tips o' yer toes, it does come. Oh, 'tis not a sight for the women or the troubled, aye, 'tis not." Kileen was right. It was time to change the fight.

Four more shots clipped along the top of the knoll, each about two feet from the other, as if someone were lining up rows to plant. The shots weren't close to Carlow. Maybe Mallow didn't know where the young Ranger was and just sprayed the area for "possibles." Or was it a way to lull Carlow into exposing himself? If he wanted to put Mallow on the defensive, Carlow's only real option was to get the Sharps from its saddle sheath.

Shadow stood, grazing, only fifty feet away. It seemed like fifty miles. Was it possible to get there unseen? The northern edge of the thicket might protect him for the first twenty feet, if Mallow didn't happen to move into a position where he could see where Carlow was going. That was certainly possible. But if Mallow did, he would then be in a position to shoot Carlow regardless. The last thirty feet would be open, flat land. Maybe Mallow wouldn't be expecting him to go there. Maybe. The rain would help him. This time.

The best way to get the rifle would be for Shadow to come to the young Ranger. Normally the black horse would do so eagerly when he called, but this wasn't normal. Carlow figured his violent dismount, coupled with the gunshots and the storm, had scared the animal. Horses were skittish by nature; as a species, they had survived centuries by running. Whether imagined adversaries or real, it didn't make any difference; they ran. Shadow was also inclined to be stubborn when he was very tired. Still, it was worth trying—and better than exposing himself to Mallow's likely gunfire.

Anything was better than staying where he was and letting Mallow make all the decisions for him. Carlow drew his Colt and used three rocks to prop the gun against the top of the knoll with a bit of the barrel showing. Just enough that it might look as if he remained there, at least from a distance. The trick probably wouldn't fool Mallow long, but it might keep him thinking for an extra minute or two. That might be enough. He slid new cartridges into the hand-carbine and began his ascent along the edge of the knoll toward Shadow.

Only the song of rain trailed him as he crawled, staying close to the vertical slope of the land swelling and then along the back side of the bunched-together thicket. Sweat mixed with rain splatters streaked the young Ranger's tanned face. His brain wobbled and ached. A stray blood finger from his forehead salted his eye. If Mallow guessed his actions, he would be an easy target just on the other side of this last bedraggled bush, where the land opened up. The closer he got, the more apparent it was he couldn't get to Shadow. Even if he surprised Mallow, the outlaw had plenty of time to adjust and kill him as he ran. His hopes for getting the big gun lay with Shadow's inclination to obey his command. But would Mallow guess the significance of the movement and kill his horse before Shadow could return to cover?

Carlow's faded shirt sleeves were becoming stiff with clay smudges from the soggy ground as he crawled. So were his pants and Kiowa leggings. The bottom fringe on the lower leg wraps was tangled up with moist clay. Even the two eagle pinfeathers that dangled from the top of each legging were streaked with mud. His knife carried an elongated clump of mud that covered all of the bone handle exposed above the leather's end. His right fist held the readied hand-carbine, using the stock as support in his advance and to keep his hand away from the mud so his shooting wouldn't be hindered by its stickiness. His left hand was a fist against the ground; it was just a little better than using his open hand.

Nightfall was slowly taking command of the land, flowing unabated from the west. The rain had lost some of its anger after the initial rush, settling into a steady shower. Shadows were swallowing the earth as fast as the storm had charged across the land. Their growing blackness offered patches of momentary protection, along with the blurring of the rain itself. Protection he would need as soon as he left the thicket. Everything around was heavily silent, except for the rain's chatter. A crease between the last two bushes offered a good place to observe the distant wooded area without revealing himself.

Through the hazy rain, Carlow studied Mallow's last position for signs. Where was he? Lots of men had died simply by being too eager to assume their enemy hadn't expected a certain move. That thought was pure Kileen. Patience was one of the traits of a great Celtic warrior, his uncle said. Carlow had learned the lesson well. He thought of this as he stared at a dark shadow seeping toward his horse. Should he try to make a run for it?

No, it was time to believe in his horse. Clearing his throat of the anxiousness that had settled there, he whispered, "Shadow, come here, boy. Come here."

Shadow's head came up and looked in Carlow's direction. Talking quietly to the tired horse so the animal wouldn't shy away, he called once more to Shadow. First, the horse's ears became alert, and that was followed by his black head shaking up and down. Carlow held his breath. He wanted to yell his command but knew he could not. Every sound would carry in the wet twilight; even his whisper might be heard farther than he wished. His fear returned that Mallow might shoot his great horse.

"Come on, Shadow, come on, boy," he whispered, and glanced away at the ridge where Mallow had been. Should he fire several rounds in that direction to keep the outlaw pinned down? He dared not. Shadow had bolted once; more gunfire surely would send him away for good.

With reins dragging on the muddy ground, the animal hesitated, and for an instant, Carlow thought the horse was going to run farther away. But a soft whinny preceded his turn and Shadow trotted toward him. Forgetting the danger, he jumped up and grabbed the loose reins with his left hand, holding the hand-carbine with his right. He glanced furtively at the hillside, leading the horse behind the bushes and back far enough to keep him away from Mallow's possible line of fire.

In the relative safety behind the knoll, Carlow took a deep breath, patted Shadow's neck, thanking him, and holstered the sawed-off Winchester. With a determined scowl, he moved swiftly to the saddle sheath. Too swiftly. He became dizzy and fell to the ground. The rain followed, creating a small puddle around his face.

Chapter Three

Moments later, Carlow refound his equilibrium and returned his attention to the big gun. He loaded the single-shot rifle from a pouch of ammunition tied to the trigger guard. He tried to keep the rain from reaching the cartridges by holding his hat over the loading. Cocking the big hammer was an important statement in the thickening gray. Everything around him was soaked with heavy air and tension. Pushing his hat back on his head, Carlow wrapped Shadow's reins around a big rock and returned to the bushes. The hat's return made his head ache even more.

Mallow hadn't fired for almost a half hour. Was he moving closer?

There! Movement. The rain hid specifics but couldn't cover up the sensation.

Through the wetness, Carlow picked up motion more than definitive shape. Mallow was on horseback and escaping over the hillside. Carlow could only guess the outlaw had lost his nerve once his ambush attempt had failed. Maybe Mallow didn't realize how close he had come. Surely he hadn't seen him get his horse and the big gun. No, that would have brought immediate gunfire. Maybe he thought Carlow was dead.

Carlow's anger swelled within him, and he flicked up the sight on the Sharps and aimed at the distant movement passing like blurred vision against the lighter ground. He would shoot for the man's middle, but not his horse. He didn't have any intention of tracking an unhorsed man in this darkness, especially this man. He wiped away the water reaching his eyes and the action made him stagger. He swallowed and steadied himself.

Slowly his finger tightened on the steel trigger. The boom of the Sharps was hard against the silence. And harder against his shoulder. Carlow always liked the angry action of this weapon. The hostile kick was smothered by practiced placement against his shoulder. Even so, he felt the impact and the biting jump in his hands. He missed, and the dark shape continued its path.

Mallow was nearly to the top of the ridge.

Carlow ejected the large shell and entered another. He fired once more at a place where the movement danced lightly against a row of oak trees. The distance was beyond logic but he had to try. Nothing. Carlow knew he had missed again. The blur of horse and rider became only black rain as Mallow disappeared over the ridge.

Carlow fired again, more out of frustration than for any tactical advantage. It just felt good to shoot. Nothing in the dark land moved now. All was still, except for the rain telling him "you missed, you missed, you missed." He began to retrieve the empty cartridges for reloading later. At least he had given Mallow a scare. The outlaw would know he had failed to kill him.

Behind Carlow came a noise. He whirled to meet it. The suddenness brought dizziness to his head, and he thought he was going to retch. He grimaced to stay alert, pointing his Sharps in the direction of the sound. Had Mallow fooled him into thinking he was leaving? Should he drop the empty rifle and grab his hand-carbine?

Chance appeared from around a low rock formation, his long tail wagging happily. The wolf-dog was thoroughly soaked

"Well, howdy, boy, I thought you might've run off," Carlow managed to mutter.

Weakness flooded his mind and body and he slumped to the ground. The wild wolf-dog came to him and licked his face. Carlow patted the animal. "We'd better find a place to hide for the night, my friend. We'll backtrack. Mallow might try again." He rubbed his hand over the happy beast's nose and across his dark head, bringing water with the movement. Chance licked Carlow's other hand, the one holding the Sharps. "Yeah, I'd better start thinking that way, shouldn't I? Almost rode us into one. Good boy. Let's go get Shadow. He's ready to get out of here, too."

A shiver ran down Carlow's back. He remembered his uncle saying that meant someone had stepped on his grave. He looked around and tapped his rifle three times on a large, square rock, then muttered thanks to the "gods of the land" and acknowledged to himself that this wasn't the moment to be skeptical about things unseen. Was there anything else he should say or do? For the first time, he noticed the moon in the soaked sky was heading toward its full circle. If his uncle were here, Kileen would declare, "Much to be wary about with the moon, me lad, ye be knowin' that. Don't be pointin' at it. The man there gets angry—at bein' pointed at."

Carlow's usual response would be that he didn't like being pointed at either. His grin would follow.

But that wouldn't be the end of it. Kileen would rub

his unshaven chin and announce, " 'Tis a good time to be killin' the pig. When the moon is becomin' her full se'f, makes the fryin' bigger." He would then take a long breath as if preparing himself for a most serious statement. " 'Course, the moon in her full can make a man crazy, ye know. Best not to tempt her."

With the recollection in his eyes, Carlow looked up at the moon again, half a grin on his tanned face. His uncle was the most superstitious man he knew. Many Irish had tendencies to believe in, or at least talk about, things beyond their control, but Kileen was certain of every one of them. Sometimes, Carlow wondered how he made it through the day with all the interlocking and contradictory superstitions he followed.

After returning the Sharps to its sheath, he untied the other saddle strings from his long coat and eased into it. There was something comforting in the action, even though the garment was thoroughly wet. Readied for riding again, he pulled loose the reins, slipped a boot into the stirrup, and tried to pull himself into the saddle. His body rose, and dizziness again swirled through his head, robbing him of balance and momentum. He fell backward as if pushed and thudded against the rain-soaked ground.

Dark and blurred images danced within his mind. Silver Mallow was chasing his mother, and Carlow was a small boy trying to stop him with a stick for a gun. Tiny people sprung from out of the mist. They urged the young Carlow onward. When he looked down, his toy was a real weapon.

Something touched his cheek. It was warm and wet.

He blinked and was awake. Chance stood over him; the wolf-dog's tongue across his face had brought him from a netherworld of sickening sleep. He didn't know how long he had been there, but the swimming in his head had lessened. Rising slowly, he patted the wolf-

21

dog and thanked him. For the first time he was aware that he still held the reins. And the rain had stopped. Completely.

"Sorry, Chance, Shadow. Guess I wasn't quite ready for all that." He stroked the neck of his waiting horse. "Yeah, I was lucky. Old Thunder would be telling both of you that, wouldn't he?"

Shadow whinnied and shook his head. Carlow tried to chuckle at the response and couldn't help but wonder if the horse actually understood. A trickle of blood slid down his eyelid. He wiped the salty moistness away with his coat sleeve, unsure whether it was blood or just water dripping from his hat. He didn't look; he didn't want to know.

A more cautious mount was successful, and he rode back to retrieve his propped revolver and then headed toward a location he'd noted in passing, a half hour before the ambush. It was an unforgiving, elevated rock shelf. The possible camp was nearly hidden from the main trail below by a circle of stunted pines wrapping the base of the rock ledge. He had noticed the shelf because it was a possible place for Mallow to hide. Not finding the outlaw there had reinforced the faulty notion that Mallow was not going to turn and wait.

As he approached the shelf once more, he realized that it would be preferable to find an area where he could have seen anyone approaching from a greater distance. But it was far safer than camping anywhere near the trail, and he was too weak to look further. Struggling to stay conscious, he managed to picket Shadow in an opening at the back of the rock shelf, a giant vertical crack along the fault of the ridge. No one on the trail below would be able to see the horse. Grass was sufficient to keep him content and quiet through the night. A large natural bowl in the rock held ample rainwater as well.

But Carlow still felt the need to give Shadow water from his remaining canteen and poured liquid into his hat from which to refresh his horse. It had more to do with assuaging his guilt for pushing the animal so hard than anything else. The hat shook in his hand as he held it for the animal to drink. Vaguely, he recalled having a second canteen but couldn't remember what had happened to it.

Chance barked and Carlow filled the hat again to let the wolf-dog share in the water's goodness as well.

Apparently this thin shelf hadn't been used recently. Not even by the unshod ponies whose tracks he had seen earlier the day before. A faint path wandering away from the flattened rock most likely had been created by animals. For the first time in three days, Shadow's saddle came off. It felt like a boulder in Carlow's weakened arms, and he dropped it at his feet and let the gear remain there, as if that had been his intent.

Forcing himself to stay alert, he rubbed the great animal's back with the damp saddle blanket, pleased to see there were no raw spots. Next he checked Shadow's legs. Definitely a tenderness in the long tendons in both forelegs. He grimaced at the discovery and knew he had pushed the horse too hard. Hooves were examined for rocks and bruises. He found neither. Carlow's face was dotted with sweat, yet he was cold. Very cold. Each task wallowed in slow motion in his aching mind.

Satisfied, Carlow stepped away to an open space and crumpled. He was asleep in seconds, staying awake only long enough to pull the hand-carbine from his holster. Sleep came too quickly for a man who lived with danger, but the bullet crease along his head robbed him of any options. His shoulder, too, was reminding him of the second bullet's cut.

Minutes later, his wolf-dog nestled against the young

Ranger's back, having assured himself that the area was safe.

Cruel, festering dreams descended upon Carlow, resembling his minutes of unconsciousness back at the ambush. They rushed him mentally to a world of strange conflicts and stranger presentations of people known and unknown.

Sometime during the night, a lone rider retraced Carlow's trail. He stopped his horse where the ascent to Carlow's encampment began. Listening for long minutes without moving, he started to dismount. An unseen growl from the shelf above made him hesitate. Silver Mallow rubbed his aching shoulder and touched his swollen face, recoiling at the pain. He thought the young Ranger had to be dying but wasn't certain enough to move closer. After all, Mallow had expected to find Carlow's body when he circled around to come up behind him. The anticipated enjoyment of putting more bullets into Carlow became a bitter disappointment as he discovered Carlow had been strong enough to ride away.

Facing that wolf-animal with Carlow in the dark wasn't a good idea, either. Cursing softly, Mallow assured himself that his adversary could no longer be a danger and disappeared into the night, returning along the same trail. He wanted to laugh but the ache in his face wouldn't let him. He cursed again; this time it was directed at the big Ranger. Then he wondered why Kileen wasn't with Carlow, and that did prompt a tight-mouthed snicker. It was all he could do without pain.

A breeze nudged Carlow awake, but only briefly. Did he sense something on the trail below? Chance had moved away from him. Only his low growling defined his presence. The beast stood at the edge of the shelf, staring down into the night. The soothing, rhythmic sounds of his horse grazing nearby encouraged Carlow's tired mind to continue its rest.

In the pinkish sky, a weakening, but nearly full, moon was defending its position but could not last much longer. Dying leaves sang their morning songs. Tiny things whispered. An owl was making a dawn search for small animals making their last mistake. A prairie sparrow welcomed the young lawman from its perch on a low tree branch.

Only part of him knew he lay on a wide rock ridge away from the trail; the rest was down in the dream life. It was not the thick sweetness of deep sleep, rather just the relaxation of guardian nerves. He was awake yet not alert; he was alert yet not awake. His head and shoulder ached, and he wondered why. Disoriented, he had no idea of where he was or what day it was. He was weak, dizzy—and ravenous.

Warmer winds pushed the dampness away, at least for now, but his body was chilled, even with his long trail coat on. He didn't remember going to sleep wearing it—or his boots. Rubbing his hand across his mouth, Carlow sat up and was surprised to see he held his sawed-off Winchester. Had it sneaked into his hand during the night? A sickening dizziness revisited, and he reholstered the gun and lay back down to let the disabling spell have a chance to leave.

Slowly he tried again to sit up. He studied the horizon for signs of a rider he didn't expect to see and didn't. Was there a man at the base of the ridge last night? His mind refused to remember and didn't connect the thought with Silver Mallow. After a few minutes of clouded contemplation, of trying to get his mind focused, Carlow finally stood. Darkness swooped across his eyes. He swallowed repeatedly to hold back the urge to vomit. His body began to shake uncontrollably, and he struggled to retain his balance. He turned to run away from the awful trembling and fell.

When he awoke once more, the day was well along; the sun had taken a commanding position in a sky inclined to deliver more rain. For the first time, he discovered his pants and leggings were more mud-covered than not. Staring at the mostly dried marks, he recalled the ambush for the first time and looked around frantically, swinging his gun in each direction. Then he remembered where he was and why.

Tentatively he tried to stand again, thought better of it, and crawled toward his saddle and gear. He pulled his remaining canteen from beneath the rig. Where was his other canteen? Why wasn't it with his gear? After taking a long, slow drink, he removed his kerchief, wet the cloth, and tied it around the thundering wound on his forehead. Chance wandered over to him, more concerned about breakfast than his master. Shaking slightly, Carlow took off his hat, rumpled from sleeping with it on, and poured water into the crown for the wolf-dog. Chance lapped it eagerly. He looked around to see Shadow had water in the rock bowl and that grass remained.

From a squatting position, he emptied his filled saddlebags to determine what food might be there. He pushed aside a backup Smith & Wesson revolver, a bent tin cup, a box of cartridges, three pieces of rock candy, and a rolled-up strip of leather. He wasn't interested in the tin plate or the small pot for making coffee or cooking, either, at the moment. In the pile were other things: a well-used cleaning kit for his weapons, a leather bag jammed with tinder and matches to help assure the starting of a fire. The set of army binoculars he'd bought from a green army lieutenant in Waco. One tightly rolled collarless shirt. A leather sheath with paper and a pencil. A rapidly depleting grain sack for his horse was there, too.

Foodwise, his supplies yielded a can of peaches, another of peas, half a potato and an onion, a fat sack of coffee and a thin one of dried beans, and a rolled-up cloth containing strips of jerky. His Apache friend, Kayitah, had taught him to pack away any edible or medicinal wild plants he came across as he traveled, but he hadn't done so in his hurried need to catch up to Mallow. Only a fistful of crumbled cattails remained.

He turned his head to retrieve the jerky and around him everything was suddenly blurry. Someone put a hand on Carlow's shoulder. It was his uncle, and the big Ranger wanted to show his nephew something across a mist-laden Irish moor. Carlow saw a long walkway lined with stone walls wandering toward the sea and fading eerily into the mist rising from its green waves. Clumps of fog broke off and drifted toward him along the passage. Or were they ghosts of Celtic warriors? Kileen pointed out a leprechaun outside his stone-and-thatch cottage. Before Carlow could ask a question, his uncle left to talk with the young Ranger's mother at the far end of a dissolving mist. A yell to them to help him didn't get their attention. Instead they strolled further into the mist.

He jerked awake.

Carlow gradually realized he had passed out on top of his food and gear. Slowly and carefully he stood, allowing his head to adjust to the movement. This time the dizziness was less intense. He tried walking toward his grazing horse and the steps became easier. His hat again was a container for canteen water his horse gratefully accepted, even with the rock water so close. Chance didn't wait for another turn, lapping up some of the rainwater instead. Once again, Carlow realized he had lost one of his canteens. However, this time, his mind told him it probably flew off when he was ambushed. Maybe it would still be there.

Shadow needed rest more than food, Carlow knew. A renewed wave of guilt passed through him as his eyes took in the horse's flank and saw the red searing of a bullet. "Damn!" he muttered out loud. "How did I miss that?"

Shadow's head rose to determine the concern.

No wonder Shadow had run, he thought, and patted the horse's neck to reassure him. After the horse finished drinking, Carlow pulled the kerchief from his head to wet it again with canteen water. Only a few drops remained so he staggered to the pool of rainwater and soaked the cloth. Returning to the quiet horse, he carefully cleaned the mount's bullet burn. There was no sign of infection. Shadow flinched when he first touched the wound but quickly understood what his master was doing and returned to grazing.

"I'm sorry, Shadow, I pushed you too far. Too far. You need rest—but I can't give it to you just yet. I'm sorry, but I can't."

Chapter Four

After returning the wet kerchief to his head without worrying about its being clean, he decided to build a small fire. Dry tinder from his pouch immediately became a tiny, rich blaze. Thanking Kileen for the savvy, he laid a pattern of gathered small twigs and branches upon the small flames. Smoke would disclose his location. But hunger and the cold within his body had taken away any such worry. Gradually the small fire took hold and warmed his body; so did coffee from his small cooking pot.

Hot food sounded mighty good. He hadn't eaten since he'd gnawed a little jerky at midday the day before. After pouring the remaining coffee into his cup, he drew the Comanche war knife carried in his legging and sliced the remaining potato half into small chunks. He decided to add the onion and peas to the mix. With a little water, he began frying the assembly in the same pot used for the coffee. He laid slices of jerky on top to warm them. It felt good to busy himself with the cooking, even if he wasn't particularly good at it. A jab of the knife into the wet ground served to clean it, and he wiped it off on his leggings and returned the blade to its sheath tied inside.

Memories of his late friend and fellow Ranger, Shannon Dornan, seeped into his mind unexpectedly. Dornan was the one who always handled the cooking chores, preparing food as meticulously as he did most things. Of course, his late friend was greatly influenced by the immigrant Irish family that raised him in matters of perfection. Everything counted; everything was counted. His real family died in a Kiowa raid when he was four. His meticulous approach led to a fascination with superstitions and myths and, therefore, to keen interest in everything Kileen had to say. Carlow shook his head, recalling the concerns and rituals Dornan— and Kileen—had about certain foods. His best friend had been killed during a Mallow gang ambush and that fact alone was enough to drive Carlow after the escaped leader. Silver Mallow would pay; he would not be allowed to escape.

Bread, butter, salt, eggs, milk, onions, cabbage, and even Christmas pudding came to his mind as he pushed the collection of frying food around in the pot. He remembered Kileen and Dornan admonishing him not to break a Christmas pudding into parts when it was taken from the oven. Such a breakage was an evil omen and meant death to one of the heads of the household. Vaguely he recalled teasing them that the way around the bad luck was to announce—before taking out the pudding—that the dessert was already separated for eating. Neither seemed convinced.

There were many more superstitions about food, but he couldn't recall them at the moment. Or didn't want to make his mind work that hard. Occasionally he had questioned both men about how they were able to get through the day with so many restrictions. Right now he would have listened to anything just to hear Dornan's voice again. But that wasn't to be—and the man responsible rode ahead, hoping to kill him, too.

Of course, Dornan would never have put food in the cooking pot without cleaning it first. Carlow figured since he liked the taste of coffee, it shouldn't affect the meal negatively. Besides, it was quicker. He was also certain Dornan never would have cooked this mixture for breakfast—nor any other meal, for that matter. But he was hungry, and it seemed like a reasonable approach.

Dornan and Carlow had grown up together. The hatred toward the Irish didn't register on them until they were in their early teens. Then it hit hard—but they hit harder. Few who knew them as wild youngsters would have guessed they would both eventually become lawmen. But everyone knew they could fight. And liked fighting.

Carlow missed his friend greatly, and that loss gnawed at him when he least expected it. The image of a dead Shannon Dornan lying in a pool of his own blood followed the warm memories, and he jerked backward, almost knocking over the pot. He stood, shaking and trying to put the horrible picture back into the hole in his soul where it was kept.

As hungry as he was, food was quite hard to keep down, and he decided the mixture wasn't one he would make again. Even Chance avoided everything given to him on Carlow's plate, except the jerky. The young Ranger saw the can of peaches among his gear and decided it would taste better than his cooking. The can was opened with his Comanche knife; its contents downed in minutes. Half of a peach was offered to Chance, who sniffed it cautiously, then devoured the sweet fruit.

Carlow decided the heaviness in his stomach was best handled by keeping busy. With his fork, he squashed the cattails from his saddlebags into the same pot, added some water, and worked to turn the plant heads into a poultice. He couldn't remember if Kileen added anything to them or not but poured in some remaining coffee from his cup for good measure.

Applying the warm mixture to Shadow's wound was more about comforting himself than about helping to heal the wound, because the gooey mixture wouldn't stay in place on the horse's flank, either sliding to the ground or remaining on his fingers. After several attempts, he decided it wasn't worth doing and threw away the rest of the so-called medicine. Shadow was glad to see him quit as well, turning his head toward his injured flank to investigate, then lying down on his side and rolling.

The young Ranger curled up again to rest for a few minutes before riding on. His trail coat and clothes were damp and the warmth of the new day felt good and caring. Even if the sky remained gray. But he didn't know about any of it for two hours. Once again, his dreams were a tortuous mixture of known and unknown people, familiar scenes and those known only in his imagination. Kayitah entered his nightmare to tell him to think, then rode off on a skeleton horse. Mallow himself followed, dragging a dead Dornan behind his own skeleton horse. Carlow awoke, sweating and fighting off the mental images.

He decided it was time to move on and began to repack his gear. Every move seemed slow, like he was watching himself from somewhere else. After readying his supplies, he saddled Shadow, explaining the need to move again, and rode out. He worked his way along a path most men would not have seen from only a few feet on either side even in daylight.

Few would have believed a horse and rider could pass through the trees, much less traverse the rocky incline. He chuckled to himself that a fellow could make some money just betting that it could be done. But the joke fell hollow as the realization that his tired horse had been forced to travel the incline twice consumed his mind. What bothered him more were fresh tracks at the base of the ridge. A rider *had* stopped at the ridge before backtracking. He remembered thinking so. It had to be Silver Mallow searching for him. A shiver strolled along his back.

"Yes, Thunder," he muttered. "I know that means someone is stepping on my grave. But not today, Uncle. Not today."

As Carlow approached the site of yesterday's ambush, he saw his second canteen resting in the middle of a split-apart bush a few feet from the trail. Only someone searching would have seen it easily. He dismounted slowly, reminding himself of the need to keep his head still so he wouldn't get dizzy again. Chance was fascinated by the fallen canteen and came close to inspect it before Carlow reached the bush.

"Still thirsty, boy? Here." Carlow removed his hat and poured in liquid from the retrieved canteen.

But Chance was interested only in a few licks. The young Ranger offered the remaining hatful to Shadow, who wouldn't drink at all. That was a good sign. At least the great horse was not hurting for water, Carlow decided. Drawing his hand-carbine, he remounted and rode around the hillside where Mallow had been. How innocent the land appeared now, softened by the rain. No one would view it as a place of potential death.

The outlaw's new tracks, created since the storm passed, were easy to read in the wet ground. Mallow was riding southeast and staying off the main trail. He rode without attempting to cover his tracks, or so it appeared. Carlow wondered if Mallow had decided it wasn't worth the effort, or if the outlaw thought Carlow was too badly hurt to follow. If Kileen were there, he would have reminded the young Ranger the only smart way to figure was that Mallow was leading him into another ambush.

Kayitah would have agreed and told him to watch for signs that Mallow's horse, too, was weary. It would mean the outlaw would have to stop and hole up, waiting for Carlow—or find a place to switch mounts. Carlow nodded his head in agreement with both imagined observations and rode with the hand-carbine resting across his saddle.

Mallow's cross-country trail provided ample opportunities for the outlaw to lie in wait for him. Gray rock formations jammed outward from the still green, grassy land like giant knives cutting into a carpet. Where the land was punched upward into a series of hills, the rock structures continued, looking like giant umbrellas. Big chunks of loose rock and silt covered his path, lined by rows of bedraggled bushes. At once both ugly and beautiful. In the distance was a river of cattle surrounded by swaying grass. Mallow's horse left a continuous string of hoofprints and whitish marks on the rocks. Definitely the story of a man pushing hard and not taking the time to cover his direction. Or was this exactly what Mallow wanted it to look like? Carlow's fierce pursuit had nearly cost him his life; he wouldn't make that mistake again.

With his gun cocked, Carlow studied each swale and crevice, every boulder and hillside, before moving forward. His head throbbed somewhat, but he was definitely feeling stronger and no longer dizzy. His shoulder cut was only a mere annoyance when he rolled it. Actually his stomach bothered him more than his wounds. Breakfast gurgled its discontent. Frustrated by the need to ride carefully, he found it difficult to stay focused on the countless places where Mallow might choose to hide.

Staying so alert was difficult with his head and stomach competing for attention. He eased the hammer of his cocked sawed-off rifle back down. It was safer in this rocky passage. A sudden jolt could bring an unwanted firing with possibly sad results. He shivered at the thought of accidentally shooting his horse and patted the animal's neck in a silent apology for the unintended danger. To himself, Carlow acknowledged his slow progress was also a way to give Shadow much-needed rest; he must forget about closing the distance between them for the moment. Either that or risk hurting his horse permanently. Shadow was game as ever but already stumbling over nothing and breathing hard.

At the last rock formation, he reholstered the weapon and dismounted to let his horse rest. Carlow shook his head, delivering pain to his wound. Chance came to his side and rubbed against his leg. The young Ranger filled his hat with water from his second canteen and gave it to the wolf-dog. This time Chance lapped it eagerly. When the wolf-dog was finished, Carlow refilled the hat for Shadow. Unlike earlier, the horse gulped the liquid and Carlow gave him more.

Carlow's mind drifted toward Silver Mallow. The outlaw's enjoyment of silver jewelry had led to his nickname. Paul Sedrick Mallow was the only son of a Methodist circuit preacher and was himself once a town sheriff in Ohio. When he wasn't in disguise, Mallow liked to wear a ring on each finger and a silver chain necklace with a solid silver cross. A look of opulence and greed.

In a strange bit of coincidence, Carlow also wore a silver chain with a Celtic cross under his shirt. It was the only physical thing remaining of his mother. On her deathbed, she told him his father had worn it. A bold and courageous Irish warrior, she had told him often, making a father's loss in the boy's life even greater, if that was possible. His father had died during the ocean-crossing to America. Time Carlow was born an American; his mother was very proud of that. She was a woman filled with the same romantic notions of other worlds and had named her only son "Time" because she thought the English word meant "eternal."

The physical similarities between Carlow and Mallow didn't stop with a chain necklace. Many thought Carlow and Mallow looked much alike, except the outlaw was at least ten years older and usually clean-shaven. Both were tanned, dark-haired, blue-eyed, and considered handsome by most women. They were nearly the same size and build, although Carlow was more heavily muscled. Carlow didn't see the resemblance and was annoyed whenever the comparison was mentioned. His uncle never brought it up, knowing his nephew's sensitivity about the subject.

In a more realistic mood, Carlow decided any likeness now would be further distorted by Mallow's swollen and bruised face, a terrible blackened eye, and two missing teeth, all courtesy of Kileen's whipping prior to his escape. But the idea of any physical similarity between Mallow and himself was difficult for Carlow to accept, regardless of the beating.

Especially since Paul Mallow—"Silver" as Texans knew him—was considered a half-mad killer. Satan incarnate, some said. A few excused his behavior, attributing it to either syphilis or a childhood head injury. Many thought his other fascination, music, was related to this imbalance. Others said it was a gift from

God. Supposedly he could play several instruments and enjoyed listening to everything from symphonic orchestration to sweet-fiddle waltzes to cowboy songs and popular music.

Carlow, Kileen, and the rest of the Special Ranger Force that had been formed to bring order to this part of Texas thought the former Ohio sheriff discovered he liked stealing and killing. Simple as that. In the end, what difference did it make? Silver Mallow was a cunning and evil menace. And Carlow's job was to bring him to justice. He and Kileen, with the help of some courageous Bennett townsmen, had already destroyed Mallow's gang.

Now there was only Silver Mallow himself, and he was running. It wasn't lost on the Ranger that Mallow was treacherous even to his own, leaving jailed friends behind to hang while he got away. He knew Mallow had realized a full jail break would have caused too much alarm in the town and would have jeopardized his own escape. So when the time came, Mallow turned his back on the very men who had pledged their allegiance to him.

Chance growled, and Carlow whipped his long coat back with his right hand as it headed toward his holstered hand-carbine.

Chapter Five

The young Ranger quickly realized the wolf-dog's anger was focused on a jackrabbit bounding across the hillside. Too far away for Chance to care to pursue.

"Next time, boy, next time."

Carlow remounted and rode on. The ground was uneven but not as cluttered with crumbled rock, shifting silt, and hardened brush. Horse, man, and wolf-dog finally cleared the hard, chewy terrain, and the flat prairie welcomed them with easier riding. His occasional glances at the sky kept confirming the threat of rain wasn't over, as clouds continued to gather their storm council. His long coat hadn't dried out yet from yesterday. Neither had his clothes, for that matter.

An hour later, he came upon a small, tidy ranch house, surrounded by a fence, half firmly in place and half defeated, lying on the ground. Mallow's trail led there as well. A stone cooling house for meat and milk, a silent bunkhouse, a sturdy-looking barn, and an unpainted shed were positioned around the house like old friends at a Sunday social. Near three tall cottonwoods was a wagon missing a wheel. Standing guard over the yard was a tall windmill, creaking to do its job for a stone well that looked older than the land.

Carlow drew his hand-carbine and held it across his saddle. A party of chickens wobbled across the bare earth, sharing the day's gossip with afternoon shadows, then hurrying somewhere important. As he passed the barn, an unseen milking cow bellowed, hoping the hens would come to visit. In the corral, twenty feet from the well, he saw a dozen horses milling and thought he might be able to buy one and let Shadow tag along behind for a while. It was the least he could do.

From the freshness of the tracks, Carlow thought Mallow had been there early that morning. It was impossible to tell if he remained or had ridden on. Certainly the place was quiet, but that was normal this time of year. Most hands would be out with their herds. He must assume Mallow was here. Hiding. Somewhere. Carlow's right fist tightened around the cut-down Winchester, and his fingers slid inside the trigger guard and circular lever. He thumbed back the hammer of the already cocked weapon

First, his eyes caught movement on the side of the house, and he realized almost instantly that it was just wet clothes trembling on a washday line. Through the front door burst a gray-haired lady holding a double-barreled shotgun. Her once-white apron carried something heavy in the right-hand pocket. A pistol, most likely. She paused on the unpainted porch like some alerted military sentry. Her stance was defiant, reinforced with a strong jaw and straight back. Hazelgreen eyes flickered with intensity. He reined up fifteen feet away.

Was Mallow inside, directing her? She didn't seem like a woman being forced to act or easily intimidated. Was anyone else on the place? Carlow wasn't certain but didn't think so. Even her husband would likely be with their herd.

Except for an apron, she was dressed for ranch work in a well-worn, faded blue shirt, leather cuffs, and a buckskin riding skirt fringed at the bottom. Her graying hair was pulled back under a wide-brimmed hat that obviously had seen much wear. Robust and thick-bodied, she was a woman for whom the perils of the land were respected but not feared. Of German descent, he guessed. A woman strong enough to handle some men in a fair fight. The shotgun in her hands looked comfortable there and no bluff.

"I'm Ranger Time Carlow," he announced loudly. "A dangerous outlaw, Silver Mallow, passed through—"

"*Ja*. A *reiter* stopped like yah *ist* now. Just before *der* sun to be rising, it vere," she interrupted, with German words and phrases slipping in and out of her speech with ease. "Sweet-talking, he vas. *Ja*. And handsome as a *neu tag*. At least, it seems so under *der* swelling. *Der* face vas full of beating, *Ich* think."

Carlow nodded his head in agreement as his eyes sought to determine if Mallow was inside the house, watching. But morning glare from the two small windows was not going to allow any discovery.

The German woman was eager to explain further. "He *reiten* in singing *der* song . . . ooch, vat is it? *Ja, Der* Roses of Yellow. That *ist der* song." Her gaze took in the gray hills behind Carlow. "A Southron gentleman. Not be seeing *viele* . . . Ooch, I forget *mein* words sometimes. Not seeing many of his kind around *hier*."

"He rode on?" Carlow turned his head slightly to try to avoid the reflection from the glass but still couldn't see any movement within the windows' darkness.

The possibility of Mallow watching—and aiming at

him—from there made him want to shoot the windows. Surely he wouldn't let this woman keep her weapons—or were they unloaded and designed to make him relax?

"After we to be trading hosses. That *ist sein*, ah, his bay, in *der* corral, it *ist*." She motioned toward the corral.

Carlow recognized the horse standing quietly at the far edge of the enclosure. A fine animal owned by a Bennett merchant, it had been stabled in the town livery. He took satisfaction in noting the white-sweat-dried animal was definitely trail-worn and couldn't have gone much farther. Out of the corner of his eye, he studied the windows and doorway for any signs of movement behind her; none were there. If Mallow were around, why wouldn't he shoot?

"Be a veek or so before *der* bay *ist* to work. Leastwise, that's vat Charlie, he be thinkin'. *Ja*, but *ist gut* hossflesh." She cradled the shotgun in her folded arms. "Do yah be a *bruder*? *Ich* see much of him . . . in your face."

Carlow's mouth twitched at the remark and his eyes flashed.

She realized the significance of what she had said, and her hand flew to her mouth. "*Verzeihung. Nein* offense. *Mein Gott, Ich* beg your pardon, *Herr* Ranger. Did yah be giving him *der* beating? He vere hurting in *der* shoulder, *ja*, he vere. Moving stifflike. Bad in *der* ribs, maybe so."

"No, ma'am, we aren't related," Carlow answered, irritation taking over for his concern about the outlaw hiding. "You're right, though, he was wounded and beaten by . . . another Ranger . . . when he was arrested. For murder and rustling. Did he ask for—"

"Vanted food," she interrupted again. "Charlie did

41

not to be liking his looks. Told him *Ich* had *nein* food to spare, so he to be riding on. *Ja,* and Charlie's Vinchester might be having to do with his going." She chuckled.

Charlie must be her husband, Carlow thought. He was probably covering him with a rifle right now. His eyes searched the windows again without discovery. No matter, these people didn't know how fortunate they had been; Mallow could have murdered them just for the fun of it. The young Ranger's mind released the worry about the outlaw's remaining on the ranch. If she was being held against her will, she was the best actress he'd ever seen.

"Yah sure *du ist nein* kin?" This time her eyes sparkled at her joke.

Not realizing she was teasing this time, the continued reference to their similar appearance brought a frown to his tanned forehead, but Carlow ignored the remark. "Ma'am, I'd like to buy a good horse if you've a mind to it," Carlow said, touching the brim of his hat. "Got gold to pay, not script. I'll ride on if you'd rather. My horse is a good one. He's just wind broke and—"

"Vere *ist* your badge?" Her question was like a blast from the gun she carried.

He smiled a lopsided grin and the last of his concerns vanished. "In my pocket. Here." He patted his vest with his left hand. "Don't wear it when I'm on the trail be—"

"Because yah do not vant it to be giving yourself away vit shining from *der sonne.*"

Carlow's smile broadened to his whole face. "Yeah, that's right. Would you like to see it?"

"Naw. *Ich* have *nein* need." She hesitated. "*Ich* to be Mrs. Beatrice Von Pearce, owner of *der* Cradle 6. *Mein* friends to call me Bea."

Owner? Carlow wanted to ask more but thought it would be impolite. Probably just a figure of speech. She and her husband would be the owners; Charlie must be his name, he guessed.

A wide smile warmed her next request. "Vould to be liking yah to be holstering *der* big gun. Not be seeing one like it, *Ich* think. *Ist* that to be a Vinchester?"

"Yes, ma'am. Cut down . . ."

"So yah can to be using it like *der* pistol."

"Yes, ma'am. Like the one in your apron." He eased the trigger down and holstered the weapon. He figured on carrying it again at the ready when he left.

She smiled and patted her apron. "Always there, it be. *Mein* husband . . . Herman . . . bless his soul . . . he said it should always be there. So it *ist* so." She patted the heavy shape in her apron pocket. "It *ist*, how yah say? Doubling *der achtung. Der* fine men, *Herr* Smith and *Herr* Wesserman, *Ich* believe, made *der* gun."

"Smith and Wesson." Carlow's thoughts went to the earlier name she had mentioned. If Herman was her husband, then who was this Charlie she talked about? He wanted to ask but thought that would be impolite.

"*Ja. Ich* clean *der Herr* Smith and *Herr* . . . Wesson . . . gun every day. It remind me of *mein* Herman." She turned her head away for an instant. "He *ist* . . . passed. It *ist* hard for me to say in English. *Mein* heart does not vant it said."

"I understand. I'm sorry." Her husband was dead so the reference to being the owner was no exaggeration. His impression of her late husband was that of a man who was thorough, but he was still curious about this Charlie, whoever he was.

"Go over to *der* corral. Put your saddle on *mein* buckskin. He vill run until yah be to catching *der* rainbow." She pointed at the corral with her shotgun, then

43

smiled broadly. "Vit der rain, yah just might do that. Catching *der* rainbow." She looked up into the sky. "More rain be coming tonight. *Ja*, it be."

"I think you're right. Sky looks kinda hard." His eyes caught her face. "How much for the buckskin?"

"If yah to be bringing him back, there ist *nein* cost. If yah vant to own him, twenty gold dollars."

"That would be pretty steep—but not as steep as trading for my black."

"*Ja*." Her smile was wide. "Now yah to come inside. Eat. A hot meal yah be needing. Make yah strong to catch bad man. Best sausages around *hier*, I make for yah." She studied him for a moment. "Yah *ist* need to clean *der* pants, too, *Ich* see. Yah *ist* been playin' in *der* mud."

A hard-faced woman with wrinkle maps around her eyes, yet warmth and laughter were just a smile away, he thought. Carlow's chuckle was the only answer needed. She returned it instantly with her own. Her eyes twinkled mischievously.

"Yeah, I look a mess, I know. Ate my own cookin' this morning, too—an' it's been workin' on me ever since." He grinned again. "But I better keep after him. I'm getting close. Sure is tempting, though."

"Looks like yah *haff* been too close already so," she said, cocking her head to the side, still smiling, and pointed at the side of Carlow's head, where redness had taken charge of the bullet crease.

"Yes, ma'am, that's true." His hand touched the wound, and he flinched. "I'll get him, though."

To stay and eat was something his mind thought was a grand idea. Spending time there seemed right. Maybe he should rest for the afternoon and night. Let the coming rain pass, instead of getting soaked again. After all, he had been able to pick up Mallow's trail after yesterday's rain. And the man was obviously headed for Presidio. His stomach readily agreed. Were hunger and weariness the reason, or was fear there, too? The only reason Mallow hadn't killed him yesterday was luck. Pure luck.

A thirteenth bullet. The thought hit him like another gunshot. Could that explain why Mallow's first shot barely missed? Kileen always preached avoiding the use of a thirteenth bullet because it would not fly true.

Carlow's mind rejected the superstition. Pure and simple, he had turned his head without realizing the significance of the movement at the time. His uncle would authoritatively advise the young Ranger that it was faeries who pushed him out of harm's way. Was that possible? Of course not.

He realized the German woman was watching as he reflected on his decision to stay. "Sorry, ma'am. I'm moving a bit slow today."

"*Ich* do *haff nein* doubt of such. *Mein Gott*, yah be lucky to be alive, *Ich* think. Be looking like he almost to get yah." Her expression was that of geniune worry. "*Der* little people must think high of yourself, *ja*."

Wishing she hadn't made reference to "little people," he touched the wound again. Gentler this time. He still winced.

She shook her head. "Vile yah be saddling *mein* buckskin, *Ich* vill fix yah food to take. Yah can eat on *der* ride. *Nein*?"

"That's mighty nice of you, ma'am, but you sure don't need to go to any trouble for me." His stomach wanted him to be more forceful in accepting her offer.

"*Ja*, yah must be eating to stay strong, *Herr* Ranger."

"Well, I wouldn't turn down good food. My stomach would disown me for sure. But I'd best keep moving."

"Do *nein* to giving vater to your black of yet. Let himself to be standing in *der* corral *und* rest. Vater now vill knot him fierce. Ooch, *schlecht*. Ah, bad."

"Yes, ma'am."

"You *ist* Irish, *nein?*"

"Yes, ma'am. Proud of it." Carlow's face stiffened. He knew what was coming next. In many homes, coloreds were more welcome than Irish. "If you wish, I will ride on."

"*Nein. Nein. Mein Gott, nein! Mein* Herman, he tell me *der* Irish are *gut*. Work hard. We *haff der* Irish to vork for us, *ja*. They be contrary some, but they be *gut*." Her smile was one of earnestness and concern. "There *ist* even Italians farming a half day of riding away. It *ist* changing around *hier*." She laid her shotgun against the porch railing and held her hands together as if to pray. "Yah *haff nein* Irish tongue." It was a question, presented as a statement.

"No, ma'am. My mother, bless her soul, made sure I didn't," Carlow said. "Never think about it much."

He eased himself from the saddle, aware that she continued to study him. He told Chance to stay where he was and be quiet. Surely the woman had noticed the wolf-dog before now, he thought.

"Now if my uncle was here, you'd have no doubt about him being a son of Erin. That's for sure."

"*Entschuldigung*, there *ist* something in vonderment about a young man vit all that gun—and a volf too." She cocked her head to the side as if part of an implied question.

Carlow stopped. "He will wait here, ma'am. Chance isn't all wolf . . ."

"*Ist* more volf than *ist* not, *Ich* to be thinking. Like his master. If he *nein* to scare *der* hosses or *der* chickens, *Ich* do *nein* care vhere he puts hisself." As an afterthought, the woman announced loudly, "Charlie's around back, fixing *der* tack he be. Charlie Two-Wolves."

Charlie Two-Wolves? What kind of a cowhand was an Indian?

"Vatch *der braun* mare. She be *der* boss of *der* corral—*und* she vill vant to make surely yah be *gut* to *der* others. Sadie vas *mein* Herman's favorite," Bea said, placing a hand to her forehead to help study the corral. "Sadie be old now, like me, but *var* strong, I be thinking."

Carlow knew it was normal for the oldest healthy mare to rule the herd. The pecking order in any herd of horses was determined by the horses themselves, with the youngest usually at the bottom.

"*Der* grulla, he *ist* to be liking to fight but never he bother *der* buckskin. *Nein*," she continued without looking away from the corral. "But *der* grulla vill carry *der* right man into var. That *ist* vhat *mein* Herman always to say. *Ja*. So vill *der* buckskin. He better fer yah, *Ich* think."

"Horses are always afraid," Carlow said. "That's what keeps them alive. Some run, some fight. But if they see you as their leader, they'll trust you."

Bea dropped her arm, looked at him, and smiled warmly. "Yah to be sounding like *mein* Herman."

"Thank you. Wish I had known him." Carlow nodded. "He must've been a very good man."

"*Ja*, he vas *gut* man." She glanced away.

His mental questions about her late husband were shoved aside as slight movement in the doorway's darkness caught his attention. His hand slipped under his long coat to his holstered sawed-off rifle.

Chapter Six

A small girl in a faded green dress and bare feet squeezed through the door and caught sight of Carlow and his wolf-dog. Her wide eyes matched those of Bea Pearce. The older woman put out her hand to stop the child but it was too late. She came toward Carlow, long blond braids bouncing across her back.

"Hi, I'm Hattie. I'm eight. Is that a wolf?" She stopped a few feet away.

Carlow knelt beside Shadow and quietly told Chance to sit. "No, but he's part that. His name is Chance."

"Can I pet him?"

Carlow glanced up at Bea Von Pearce. A long frown crossed her forehead. The young Ranger wasn't sure if the displeasure was because the girl was interested in an apparently wild animal or because she was standing directly in the line of fire of Bea's shotgun if she had to pick it up again quickly.

"It's all right, ma'am." Carlow told the girl to hold out her hand for Chance to smell before she tried to touch him, so he could check her out.

"I know," Hattie said. "We used to have a dog, but Luke was killed. By some bad men. A year back, it was. We buried him . . . over there." She pointed in the direction of a young oak tree twenty yards from the house. "Gramma thought the shade would be nice."

"I'm sorry. Hattie, right?"

"Well, actually it's Henrietta Anne. But my gramma calls me Hattie. I live with her."

Carlow patted her arm. "I'll bet you have fun together."

Hattie's large brown eyes studied him as she continued to pet Chance. The beast responded with a soft lick on her arm. "It was funner when Grampy was with us. He told me lots of fun stories. Do you know any stories?" She cocked her head to the side, and it reminded Carlow of the girl's grandmother. Not waiting for his answer, she asked another question. "Are you here to help us with all those bad men stealing our cows?"

"That to be enough, Hattie. Yah to be *helfen* me fix *der* supper. *Herr* Ranger needs to be saddling *der* buckskin."

"Are you taking Buck away?"

Before he could answer, a short, stocky Indian carrying a Winchester rounded the corner of the house. His dark eyes searched Carlow and showed no inclination toward friendliness. Something else was there, too. Fear? Sadness? Carlow couldn't read the emotion. The man was probably Comanche, Carlow guessed. He wasn't thick-featured as a Kiowa would be. Nor did he have the facial appearance of any Apache he knew. Certainly not like Kayitah or his family.

This must be the Charlie Two-Wolves that Bea had mentioned earlier. His age was impossible to guess; the Indian could have been twenty or forty or anywhere in between. A wide-brimmed hat kept a shadow across most of his face. Shiny black hair streamed to his shoulders. He wore a checkered shirt, breeches, worn mule-eared boots with aged and rusty Mexican spurs, and a large knife carried in a plain sheath on his belt. His stained necktie looked out of place on a cowhand, much less an Indian, giving him an oddly formal presence.

Carlow could imagine his Apache friend wearing such clothing if he were in the same situation. Except for Two-Wolves's stained white man's necktie at his buttoned collar. Like other Apaches, Kayitah would have shunned any showy attire and would not have worn paint or other decorations. He simply let his skills in tracking and warfare speak for him. Having a friend like Kayitah made Carlow appreciate the Indians' ways as his uncle did not. But it made him no less wary. Likely Two-Wolves was wild and dangerous, in spite of his dirty ranch clothes.

Why did this woman keep such a man around? Carlow wondered. Or did she not have a choice? Maybe he was holding both the old woman and the little girl captive. No, that didn't make any sense, not with her having a shotgun and a pistol. Carlow's gaze connected with the Comanche wrangler's eyes for a long moment. Two-Wolves's intensity was equal to Carlow's own.

Finally Two-Wolves looked away at the buckskin, but not before sunlight crossed his left cheek and Carlow saw heavy scarring. As if from a fire. The disfigurment covered most of the side of his face. The young Ranger tried not to stare, letting his attention follow toward the horse.

Bea Von Pearce spoke first, aware of the visual clash. "Charlie, this to be *Herr* Ranger Time Carlow. He *ist* after *der* man from this morn. *Mein Gott, der reiter* that ve traded with hosses, the one yah *nein* be trusting. *Herr* Ranger *ist* going to take *der* buckskin. He to be leaving *der* handsome black . . . to rest. Ve care for it. *Ich* go inside now and fix supper to take vit him."

Charlie Two-Wolves nodded. His eyes briefly showed a relief that Carlow didn't understand. Nothing else in the Indian's manner gave away feelings. A stray glance at Chance quickly returned to Carlow along with the hint of a question in the man's face. Without saying anything, he walked toward the back of the ranch where he had come from.

Carlow told Chance to stay where he was and hoped the wolf-dog wouldn't seek any of the chickens he had seen earlier. That was a lot to expect, but the young Ranger found himself telling two scurrying hens that Chance would not go after them anyway. He took a few steps, leading his horse, stopped, and looked back. Chance had eased into a full resting position.

"Good boy. You stay there, got it?" He continued walking toward the corral. He stopped Shadow outside the fence and flipped the reins around a middle pole.

The black horse stood quietly, barely noticing the other horses stomping and snorting inside the enclosure. After unsaddling and unbridling him, Carlow made a rope halter from his lariat and retied the animal to the same pole. Shadow's glistening back was wiped dry with his saddle blanket and handfuls of straw taken from a pile next to the corral. The big horse was breathing deeply. The young Ranger chastised himself for pushing the animal so hard. He agreed with Bea Von Pearce's observation about not letting the horse have any water yet.

He stood for a moment, apologizing to Shadow while he ran his hands along each leg to check for unseen problems. Shadow shivered when Carlow returned to the sore spots on the tendons in his forelegs.

Carlow touched them again, lightly this time. Shadow's reaction was slight but definite. Carlow sighed. He was lucky. A few days' rest should do it. The dense tissue was tender but not damaged. He was certain of that.

Finally satisfied there were no major injuries, he pulled the knife from his legging sheath as he took the right rear hoof in his left hand. He popped out a small stone from where it had lodged against the shoe. Further probing assured him the iron itself was firmly in place and needed no rehammering. The other three hooves were clean and the shoes, tight. He patted the black horse again, apologizing once more for working him too hard, and promised the powerful mount that he would now get to rest.

Grabbing a coiled lariat hanging over the gate pole, Carlow snaked out a large loop as he walked toward the milling horses in the corral and stopped with the rope at his side. Predictably, the brown mare took a position in front of the other milling horses. Whinnying, snorting, and stamping hooves filled the air. The fiery grulla reared and made frightening noises. The young Ranger didn't move. Gradually, the lead mare took a step toward him, ears alert, head up.

He made no attempt to move. "Good day, my lady. I came to borrow your buckskin friend. Would that be all right with you?"

His soft voice reassured her. The mare's head lowered and she stepped next to him, eager for his attention. He rubbed her nose and ears and patted her back. "You've seen some doin', lady. In your day, you were something, I'll bet."

After the exchange, the lead mare turned away to rejoin the rest. The animals seemed to relax—all but the fiery grulla, who continued to stamp and paw at the ground. With a smile, Carlow watched the horse. "Yeah, big fella, I know you're tough. But I'll bet you can go, too. Next time, maybe. I'm going with Bea's suggestion, all right?"

Carlow ignored him and walked toward the buckskin at the back of the corral. Horses parted like brown water hitting a rock. A quick flip of his wrist settled the hemp restraint over the buckskin's head, and the animal stood quietly. The horse accepted the saddle without moving but kept his mouth closed and shook his head up and down to avoid the bit.

"Come on now, Buck, that's no way to act," he admonished, and held the animal's head steady. Carlow's fingers pinched the horse's lips against his teeth and the buckskin opened wide to receive the metal bit. "That's better, my friend. We've got to get acquainted. You and me." He strapped on the head stall and walked the sturdy animal out of the corral. Outside he looped the reins over a corral pole ten feet from where Shadow stood. The buckskin looked every bit as good as Bea Von Pearce had indicated. Thick chest, long legs, and mile-eating frame.

To his black horse watching him, Carlow said, "No, he can't hold a candle to you, Shadow. I'll be back. You rest. I'll be back."

After filling his two canteens from the Von Pearce well, he returned to the black horse. Patting his proud neck, Carlow determined the animal had cooled down enough to drink, so he led Shadow to a large watering trough inside the corral. A large bay horse, standing apart from the others, studied Shadow, deciding whether or not the black horse would be an adversary for his position in the corral order. In the middle of the corral, the grulla's ears flattened and it turned toward Carlow and Shadow but didn't come closer. Watching from the far fence rail, the lead brown mare whinnied a welcome.

Carlow knew what would happen if he let Shadow loose now with the other horses. There would be a time of determining his horse's rightful place among the group. Leading or following, and if following, behind which horse. There was always a definite pecking order among horses. Like men, Carlow thought. Only horses dealt with it right up front.

"You could handle all of them, my friend. Together at the same time. But not today," Carlow muttered to himself.

After letting him drink, but not too much, the young Ranger led the black horse back outside the corral and retied Shadow to the corral post. His gaze took in the bullet graze on his flank; his fingers followed and assured him that the wound was healing. He would suggest to Mrs. Von Pearce that Shadow be left to himself for a couple of days until his strength fully returned. Off to his left, a sage hen scurried to a better hiding place and reminded him of the possibility that Mallow had doubled back and was watching the ranch right now.

As he patted the black's back, his eyes studied the land around him. Although it was mostly flat prairie, a knowing man could lie prone and be difficult to see. Kayitah had taught him that, disappearing in open land by seemingly becoming a part of it and not moving. Not moving at all. He took a deep breath and let the air slip back between clenched teeth. Nothing was there. Even the sage hen had disappeared. He looked again, forcing himself to concentrate. His head pounded, reminding him how close to death Mallow had just brought him.

He reviewed the land once more for shadows that shouldn't be there. Unless Mallow was a ghost, no one was within rifle-shooting distance. In spite of the tension crawling within him, he chuckled. If he'd heard

Carlow make such a comment about Mallow's not being a ghost, Kileen would have jumped and told him not to make fun of such things.

Of course, there was the possibility that Mallow assumed Carlow was too badly wounded to continue following him and rode on without worrying. He might. Presidio was only two hours away if he kept to the same trail. A man could lose himself there without too much trouble.

Or possibly the outlaw would select another place along the trail to wait.

If the young Ranger stayed to eat, Mallow might figure he was right about Carlow's wounds and let down his guard. Carlow acknowledged that his mind was trying to rationalize staying at the ranch. He must keep going. If it rained again, so what? He'd been wet before.

A stray question sashayed across his mind: If Hattie was living with Mrs. Von Pearce, did that mean the girl's parents were dead? Likely, he answered, and licked his parched lips. His head wound stung, and he rubbed the skin near it to ease the pain. Guilt about even thinking of stopping seeped into his thoughts, but his barking stomach made it retreat into the marshes of his mind. He didn't even try to tell himself that he could make up lost ground on a fresh horse. Silver Mallow already had a similarly fresh horse. And he was hours ahead. But the young Ranger knew he must keep after him. He must.

But yes, he finally admitted to himself, he was afraid of riding into another ambush. Only a fool didn't believe he could be killed. And only a fool was fearless. Carlow liked the exhilaration that came with fighting. Always had. But that was different from riding carelessly into another potentially deadly surprise. Kileen would be the first to agree, pointing to the grass or a bird or a rock or something that wasn't aligned properly—in his assessment—and insisting that a prudent man would wait for the warning to go away. More than once, his uncle had retreated upon hearing a wolf howl four times in succession. That was an old Comanche superstition, but it was good enough for Kileen. It was a warning that a warrior's medicine was not strong and he should turn back.

Such warnings weren't a part of Kayitah's life. Although he had his own beliefs about spirits and their role in this world. More importantly, though, he believed only in the story that every man made on the land, no matter how hard he tried to cover it. If a man could read that story, he would live. If he didn't, or misread it, he would die—and the spirits wouldn't help. Or couldn't.

Carlow decided it was Kileen's way of taking the time to plan instead of charging ahead. In a way, the same thing his Apache friend had tried to teach him. Some of his uncle's superstitions were onetime things that Kileen never brought up again. Carlow was certain these were created just for the moment. Carlow always would challenge him about such fresh observations. Like the time his uncle suddenly declared they couldn't ride any farther that day because he had just seen a bird flying from the west with a stick in its mouth. Carlow knew the man was just tired of riding. Not that it made any difference. The young Ranger had been too.

And once when they saw a gray cow lying against a tree, Kileen said it was a sure sign outlaws were close. The little people had asked the animal to do that to warn them. The Rangers didn't find any outlaws, but Kileen said the cow was working on old information, and the outlaws had ridden on. Or the outlaws themselves had recognized the little people's warning and left. There were no signs of that either.

And likely Kileen would say the invitation from Mrs.

Von Pearce was from the gods themselves, a warning that he needed to ease up on Mallow and let the outlaw make the mistake, not the Ranger. Carlow wasn't certain if his uncle's spiritual inclinations were more pagan than Catholic, but they definitely were Irish. All presented with a fascination with death and the devil. Sometimes it wasn't hard to understand why most of America didn't like the Irish. Wealthy families much preferred colored servants over their Irish brethren. It was a status thing. The Irish ways were definitely strange, more so when they were connected with whiskey.

Kayitah had admonished him about treating such superstitions casually and reminded his young white friend that the spirits upon the land could do just about anything they wanted. Once, he had showed Carlow a strange-looking hole hidden off a trail, which the Apache said was an entrance to the other world, the spirit world. He told Carlow he had seen the spirits come and go from there.

The young Ranger shook off the thoughts and called to Chance to come and stand near the two horses. The wolf-dog rose slowly and trotted toward him. Off to the right, Carlow saw a chicken dart around the barn and disappear inside. He shook his head.

"Chance, you stay right here. Leave those chickens alone. You hear me?" Carlow ordered. His voice was stern.

Looking up as if he had been falsely accused, Chance rubbed his head against Carlow's leg, and he patted the beast. "Yeah, you're a good fella. Just don't do anything . . . natural." He smiled. "Stay."

He went toward the house, ready to ride on; he told himself he would, food or not. His stomach growled, and he knew he would wait. Removing his hat, he stood at the door.

"Ma'am, I've saddled the buckskin. I do thank you—and I'll be back. For my black."

From somewhere in the house, Bea's commanding voice responded. "Please to come in and make yourself in comfort. Food vill be ready in *der* minutes."

Delicious smells of frying sausages greeted him as he stepped inside. Neither Bea nor her granddaughter was in sight, but he could hear joyful sounds from the kitchen just beyond the furniture-crowded living room.

Chapter Seven

A rush of warmth, a puzzling sensation of returning home, unexpectedly filled Ranger Carlow as he stepped inside. His mother was beside him with her arm around her small son, explaining their new home would be this tiny room above the saloon. A piano's tinkly sound from downstairs reached him, and he looked up at his mother with a question on his face.

He blinked away the recollection, knowing—without wanting to—what his mother had been forced to become. His uncle was gone; Carlow couldn't recall where. There was no money; that much he could remember. Hatred clanged inside his head, and he dragged that awful year back into its dark hole by studying the Von Pearces' main room.

The small, tidy area held a lifetime of furniture, memories, freshly cleaned parlor lamps, and knick-knacks. He smiled at the protective sheets lovingly covering the cushioned settee and two matching balloon-backed chairs. To keep them free of dust, he assumed. Ornate carvings edged the pieces of scrollwork of interlocking flowers and leaves. A hand-carved liquor cabinet stood proudly in the farthest corner. He was certain all of the furniture had come from Europe. Over the back of the closest chair and its protective sheet was an intricate quilt featuring a flower basket pattern. He walked over to examine it more closely. His fingers ran along the seams separating the different presentations of color and fabric. How many hours could that have taken?

The ticking of a clock caught his attention and he turned toward the sound. A wooden-framed timepiece was nestled on the second row of a three-shelved mahogany wall display. Surrounding the clock face were hand-carved insets of birds on tree branches. The shelves themselves held an array of yesterdays for this family. Most with their significance known only to them. A tiny glass shoe of dull purple and orange. A fat pinecone that held the secret of its significance. A pair of large-roweled Mexican spurs. A framed photograph of a young man in a Union uniform, his eyes stern with purpose and pride. Beside it was another picture in a gold-edged frame. A family greeted him from brownish eternity. He thought the small girl must be Hattie but wasn't certain.

Carlow was drawn to a small music box on the bottom shelf, boasting a ballerina with raised arms on its shiny walnut top. He wiped his hand on his coat and carefully raised the lid, and a German waltz invited him to dance. A metallic two-step gallop of notes in three-quarter time. Instead of daydreams of dancing with the widow Ellie Beckham from Bennett, Silver Mallow's face laughed at him from a dark corner of his thoughts. The outlaw leader's infatuation with music— any kind of music—would have compelled him to take the piece had he seen it. Carlow shut it quickly and looked toward the kitchen. Neither Bea nor Hattie had noticed, or were they too polite to say anything?

"Silver Mallow, where are you heading? Presidio? Mexico?" Carlow asked aloud, his fingers still touching the music box. "It doesn't matter where you go. Or if my badge makes any difference. I will find you, Silver. You killed Shannon." His fingers rose as if self-controlled and touched the small stones in his vest pocket. "On our blood stones, I promise."

A home was an idea he had almost forgotten. More than once he had fantasized about having a place like this, leaving behind his unwanted reputation as a man of the gun and going somewhere that didn't care who he was, only who he wanted to be. Could his uncle ever do that? Carlow wasn't certain. Kileen savored his time with his Mexican outlaw lady friend, Angel Balta, now and then, but that wasn't the same as becoming one and building something together. The young Ranger wondered if he would ever have anything like a real home, with a wife and family. Ellie Beckham whispered to him from a sweet place in his mind.

Carlow's gaze caught a hand-painted dressing screen, placed to separate the main room from the dining area. He blushed when he thought of what such screens were usually used for. He passed it uneasily and found, instead, a framed tintype resting on a rolltop desk alongside a parlor lamp. From another time and place, the young man and woman watched the room in youthful sternness, ever posed in typical wedding fashion, with him sitting and her standing behind him. He guessed it was Bea and her husband, although her face was much hidden by fewer years, fewer pounds, and no wrinkles. Still, he could see the same energy in her eyes.

A large fireplace, blackened from many days of good service, crackled with the laughter of a small fire. It felt good. He stood, holding his hat with both hands and looking at the fire's flickering ribbons of red, yellow, orange, and blue. On the mantel were three ornate candlesticks, each with a freshly lit candle.

He couldn't remember feeling so alone. Sadness sought to bring him back again to a yesterday he didn't want to remember. Then came another, more sinister sensation. Fear.

For the first time since he could remember, the touch of raw fear darted through his thoughts. The dark thought blossomed of how close this fine woman and her granddaughter had come to death. Silver Mallow. That was followed by how close he had come. Black images of the Mallow gang ambush that took his best friend's life, as well as the life of another young Ranger, and nearly his own, crept along the edges of his consciousness, seeking prominence in his thinking.

He shook his head to drive them back, and that triggered renewed pain in his forehead wound. His shoulder reminded him that it, too, had been hurt, and he rolled his arm to remove the annoying sting of the bullet's burn.

"I swear to you, Shannon, I will get Silver Mallow."

A single window was partially opened to invite autumn breezes to clean the house of stale air. He looked outside and saw Charlie Two-Wolves standing beside his black horse. His first instinct was to go and ask what he was doing, but he waited and saw the Indian cowhand run his hands over Shadow's legs as Carlow had done earlier. A short nod seemed to indicate he thought the animal was not harmed, only worn.

A low growl, not quite muffled by the window, meant Chance didn't like the Indian's being around Shadow.

Carlow hurried to the door and yelled from the porch, "Chance, no. It's all right, boy, he's a friend."

Charlie Two-Wolves immediately looked up. A brief smile flitted across his dark face, and he gave a quick wave.

"Nu tuhuya-ha tsaa-yu?" Carlow hoped he had asked, "Is my horse good?" in Comanche. He couldn't think of any other words to use to ask if Shadow was hurt or not. Two-Wolves's eyes lit up in appreciation. Carlow had guessed right; he was Comanche. Why wasn't he on the reservation? Weren't only a few wild bands not there yet?

Two-Wolves's response was a simple affirmative nod.

"Aho." Carlow thanked him but couldn't come up with the right Comanche words to say the rest, so he spoke in English. "I pushed him awful hard, Charlie Two-Wolves. Too hard."

The slight smile widened as the Comanche turned toward the horse, his black hair flailing against his back and his necktie flopping against his chest. The smile was gone when he looked back to Carlow. "Strong hoss. *Puhetu.* Fast. Legs *mucho* sore. *Sua soyuraperu.* Let rest. Two, maybe three day. All *gut. Ich* watch." His words were a flowing mixture of Comanche, English and German. An occasional Spanish phrase slipped in as well.

Carlow walked down the porch toward the Indian wrangler, his long coat flapping around his knees. *"Aho.* I appreciate that."

"Mark from *der* bullet. It *ist* so?"

"Yes. We had a close call." Carlow patted the side of his head gingerly.

"You are star warrior of *Tehannas.*"

"I am a Ranger, yes."

"Ich watch bullet wound on black horse. It will be *mucho* fine."

Carlow pulled the badge from his vest pocket and let

the sunlight pounce on the shiny metal. As he pulled it free, Kileen's gift acorn popped out and bounced on the ground. He leaned down, picked it up, and returned the nut to his vest pocket.

Two-Wolves nodded. *"Kuhtaaty puha. Grande. Ja."*

Carlow knew the words for strong medicine, mixed with the Spanish and German embellishments, and accepted the phrase as a compliment, although he wasn't certain if the Comanche wrangler was referring to his badge or the acorn. Could an Irish superstition be known by an Indian?

Repocketing the badge, he held out his hand, and Two-Wolves accepted it in a hard grip that showed more his discomfort with the white man's custom than any attempt to demonstrate strength. The young Ranger tried to avoid looking at the heavy scarring on the left side of the Comanche's face. However, his eyes kept returning to the slick, layered mass, in spite of his determination not to let them. Carlow told him about following Silver Mallow and what the outlaw leader had done. He complimented the Indian wrangler on making Mallow keep riding on.

Two-Wolves asked about Mallow's bruised face and stiff movements, indicating he assumed they were from a recent fight. The young Ranger told him about Kileen's giving him a beating, and the Widow Beckham's saving their lives by shooting and wounding him.

A thin smile crossed the Comanche's face when Carlow described Ellie's quick reaction, and he observed, "Such woman *mucho* welcome in warrior's lodge."

Embarrassed, Carlow nodded agreement and changed the subject by asking about the horse he was borrowing.

Together they walked over to the buckskin, and Two-Wolves lifted each hoof to check for cleanliness.

Carlow had done that earlier but said nothing. It was a typical reaction for a man who knew and respected horses. The Comanche grunted approval of each hoof as he let it down.

"Where you learn about talking to *der* hoss?" Two-Wolves asked unexpectedly, explaining he had watched Carlow in the corral.

Carlow smiled. "My uncle, mostly. Him and an Apache friend."

"You smart. You be lead mare."

"Something like that, I guess."

Finished with his inspection, Two-Wolves saw the Sharps carbine carried in the saddle sheath. When he rubbed his left hand along the stock, Carlow saw that it, too, was scarred.

"*Mucho* big gun. Shoot *der mucho* long way. Shoot today, kill tomorrow. Kill *numu kuhtsu?*"

"Yes, it could kill buffalo. I don't use it for that. Never have," Carlow said. "All Rangers carry them. Well, most do. Given to us—like our badges."

Two-Wolves nodded what passed for approval. "Buckskin hoss *mucho* runner. Long *hora*, no stop. Me like. *Ja.*"

"If you like him, I'm sure I will, too."

"Buckskin hoss *ist* like wild . . . ah, mustang. Wants go left. Remember this." Two-Wolves curled his left hand outward as if it were turning in that direction.

Carlow nodded. He knew wild horses naturally turned left. Such horses had to be trained to turn right. It was good to know about the buckskin. He wasn't certain how much English the Comanche wrangler could comprehend. Spanish phrases popped into his conversation, along with strings of Comanche and smatterings of German he assumed had been gleaned from being with the Von Pearces. Carlow tried to keep his descriptions simple as he told the Comanche ranch hand about Silver Mallow. The young Ranger knew some Comanche and used it where appropriate or where he knew the right words. Or thought he did.

Twice Two-Wolves grinned, and Carlow guessed he had used the wrong word. The Indian was a few inches shorter than Carlow but, like the young Ranger, definitely well-muscled in his chest and arms. Carlow knew he should be wary of the man but couldn't help liking him. Their eyes connected first as warrior to warrior, gradually as friend to friend.

In a verbal stew of broken multilanguage phrasing, Two-Wolves told Carlow about Mrs. Von Pearce and her ranch. Carlow had difficulty following the narration but tried not to interrupt, for fear the Comanche would simply stop talking.

Two-Wolves's concern was a man he called "Sachem Rem-eeng-ton Hold-den." According to him, this Holden was *pabo taiboo's puha tenahpy,* a white doctor, who wanted control of the region and was taking over ranches and farms with money or force. Mostly the latter. The Von Pearce land was his target now. Bea's husband had been murdered a year ago while out with their cattle. Two-Wolves was certain Dr. Holden's men had killed him. Only five hands remained, plus the Comanche wrangler. Her lands were being gradually stripped of cattle by Holden's men; especially now that most of her cowhands had been run off.

Carlow was puzzled by Two-Wolves's description of Remington Holden. "Charlie, I don't understand about this Holden. Are you saying he's a doctor but that he's crooked? Ah, *tutsu* . . . a bad man?"

Rubbing his hand along the back of his neck, Two-Wolves struggled to find the right English words. "Aiee, sachem. Doc-tor. *Tutsu.* Bad. Doc-tor Rem-eeng-ton Hold-den . . . he . . . doc-tor." He paused and frowned, wanting to express himself correctly. "He do *medicina* . . . mag-ic. Touch where hurt, hurt goes away. Or he bring hurt . . . in glass bottle. Or he cut off hand and say it must be. *Aiee*, he live Presidio. He rich." He smiled at his use of the word. "Own *mucho* white man's buildings. Own *mucho* cows. Say he own *mucho* Mother Earth—as white man do. His *hombres* all around. Like wind." Two-Wolves waved his arms to show that Holden's men were all over the land.

Carlow nodded but wasn't certain how he should respond. It sounded like the Indian wrangler had misunderstood the activities of a town doctor.

"No one sees real face of Doc-tor Rem-eeng-ton Hold-den. *Watsi habiitu tawohho*. His *hombres*. *Muerto*. Kill. Steal. No one knows. *Ich* know." Two-Wolves laid his open hand against this chest. "His wife *ist* like him. Aiee, devil woman. From the moon, she bring spirits. *Ja*. She like kill. *Muerto*. She call to spirits. They come." He looked away as if the woman he described might be hiding nearby.

Surely the Comanche horseman was mistaken, Carlow thought. If this Holden was truly a doctor of some kind, he wouldn't be directing a land grab. There must be another explanation. Maybe Two-Wolves had seen or heard something that he had interpreted incorrectly. The doctor's wife sounded like some kind of a witch— or worse.

Two-Wolves repeated his earlier assessment of the physician word for word to make certain it was understood and added, "Doc-tor Rem-eeng-ton Hold-den *mucho* bad *hombre*. Want to take land from *Frau* Von Pearce. *Und* her cows. No one help. *Nein*. Fear *medicina*. Mag-ic. *Kia*. *Ja*. May-be."

Carlow held back a smile at Two-Wolves's inclusion of German and Spanish words. Quite a mix of sounds, he mused to himself and realized the man thought his non-Comanche words were all from the same language. But Two-Wolves's face pinched in worry, and he explained that a week before, Holden's men had surrounded the Von Pearces' major pond and wouldn't let the Cradle 6 herd get to the water.

"*Ich* want go with cows. *Ja. Ich . . . haff* fear . . . Doc-tor Rem-eeng-ton Hold-den come when *Ich* not here." Two-Wolves finished his assessment.

The Comanche's eyes now showed frustration, then changed into the look of a warrior ready to stand and die in battle. A glimpse of his soul. But there was always a look of sadness there. Deep sadness, Carlow thought, even earlier, when he was happily talking about the buckskin.

Chapter Eight

Trying to understand more about this physician and his wife, Carlow asked what Two-Wolves meant by "cut off hand and say it must be." Most likely, this was a description of a surgery and the Indian wrangler had misunderstood its purpose.

His dark eyes glistening with anger, Two-Wolves rattled off a story of a cowboy, who had worked for the Von Pearces, being captured by Holden's men and that the doctor had cut off the cowboy's left hand as a warning to the others. His own branding iron was used to cauterize the wound. He said a big man with fiery hair had dragged the severed hand around on a rope while other gunmen with them laughed. Bea would not let Two-Wolves go after them. She cried when she saw the man without a hand. He did not die but left the ranch soon after.

Carlow was stunned. Had he heard correctly? Two-Wolves had carefully supported his explanation with sign language and Carlow knew it well from being with his Apache friend. Surely there had to be another reason for this action by the doctor. Surely the cowboy had injured his hand in a way that it had to be removed or gangrene would have set in. Surely.

Before Carlow could ask further, the Indian wrangler knelt and drew a circle in the dirt with his finger, adding marks that extended beyond it. Carlow knew this was a symbol of the moon and its strange power. Beside this crude design, he made a stick figure of a woman and expounded on the doctor's wife. He was certain her power came from the moon, which was also feminine in his view. With this lunar guidance, she could see things before they happened and could call on the spirits to join her.

The late Herman Von Pearce had told him that she had even killed two friends of his and Bea's. Carlow thought this had happened two years ago, if he understood the Indian correctly. The couple had owned a small ranch not far from here, but the doctor owned it now. Two-Wolves said an ear was cut off each body and the mark of the moon was made on their faces. In their own blood. He said they had come from the same place across the Great Waters that the Von Pearces had come from. Then he cautioned that he hadn't seen this himself; only heard about it from Bea's late husband, who was a friend of that family. With a shake of his head, he added that Comanches were blamed for the murders.

Carlow couldn't believe what he was hearing. He bit his lower lip and tried to make meaning of it all. His uncle would have readily agreed that the moon was a mysterious force to be reckoned with. Maybe the Indian wrangler had become unbalanced after the death of Herman Von Pearce, a man he obviously liked and trusted—certainly, such a mental state could occur. It had happened to him after his Ranger friend was murdered. Maybe he had misunderstood Herman's story. It wouldn't be the first time someone had heard words from another language and come away with the wrong impression.

As if he were no longer interested in the subject, Two-Wolves pointed at Carlow's wolf-dog, who was sitting quietly on his haunches. Carlow had forgotten about him and quickly glanced at the barn. No chickens were in sight.

"Where you get? *Tuhtseena?*"

"He's only part wolf. Chance, that's his name. Don't know what the other part is, though."

Trying to forget Two-Wolves's wild stories, the young Ranger explained the animal had come to him while he was on his way to avenge his best friend's death. He told about having just visited his friend's grave but didn't mention leaving his uncle there, pleading with him not to go and seek revenge. He thought the explanation might help the Indian express his feelings about his boss's being killed.

In his distinctive mixture of languages, Two-Wolves said authoritatively, "Wolf is strong *puha.* He is spirit of your *amigo. Ja,* it is so. Wolf is your *puhahante.* Spirit helper. Give you *mucho* wisdom. Courage. Guide you to spirit world. Strong *puha* against Doc-tor Rem-eeng-ton Hold-den *und* his wife. It *ist* so."

"Well, my uncle would agree with you," Carlow responded, rubbing the open palm of his right hand with his left fingers. "He's an Irishman, through and through, and believes that . . ." He stopped the thought, knowing its completion might offend the man, and changed subjects. "What about little Hattie? What happened to her parents?"

Two-Wolves wasn't ready to leave the subject of the wolf and its spiritual significance. His own name and his spirit medicine had come from a vision where a pair of wolves appeared and told of many things that would happen, including the fall of his people. He shut his eyes for a moment and added that he feared his spirit helpers had abandoned him, as the buffalo medicine had left the Comanche. Solemnly, he advised that Carlow's wolf medicine would go away if it was not cared for; the Comanche took the buffalo for granted, and it went to the spirit world.

Shaking his head for emphasis, the Indian wrangler said he had not mistreated his wolf helpers but thought they walked with their buffalo brothers to another land far away. He wasn't sure. Even Mother Earth had turned away from the Comanche now. All the buffalo were gone, and the Comanche were locked inside tiny lands no one wanted. Even Quannah Parker was in chains.

"Once, we ride like *mucho* storm. We are *Noomah*, 'The People.' Mother Earth happy to give us what we need. *Ja*. Live strong. *Mucho* pony herds. *Mucho* warriors. *Mucho* happy. All fear *Kwahadi*. Happy wives and children. Now we *ist* dust. *Huhkupy*," Two-Wolves said, looking down at his boots. He dragged the right one in front of the other. "*Mein* wife. *Mein* sons. They be burned to death by bluecoats. *Muerto*. *Ich* get this but *nein* save them. *Nein*." He touched the scarred side of his face.

"I'm very sorry."

Swallowing away the returning grief, his Comanche words came fast and blurred, but Carlow thought the man had tried to commit suicide after losing his family. Soldiers rounded up the remaining tribesmen and marched them all the way north to the Fort Sill reservation. Southern tribes were placed on a defined area of barren soil and told they must live there, learn to plow, and forget about the medicine of the buffalo, the wolf, and the eagle.

Carlow's eyes blinked with pain; soldiers had attacked Kayitah's small village on the pretense of gathering them for movement to the same reservation. His friend had died fighting for freedom. Freedom! How could the Ranger's countrymen do such things? He swallowed the bile of bitter memories.

Two-Wolves said something to Chance that the young Ranger didn't understand. The wolf-dog bounced upright and came over to the Comanche warrior. He grinned and rubbed the dog's face warmly and said again, "Strong *puha*. *Ja. Mucho*." He patted Chance firmly on the back. "Star warriors of *Tehannas* fight *mein* people. *Ich* believe you come for me. *Ich* believe we must fight." His reddened eyes sought Carlow's. "*Ich* know this *ist* not so. It *ist* well."

Chance licked the Indian wrangler's hand and triggered a faint smile on his bronzed face.

Watching in silence, Carlow knew isolated war parties of Comanche, Kiowa, and Southern Cheyenne rode through Texas and the Nations, cutting into civilization wherever and however they could, but their tribal strength was forever broken. He searched his mind for words that would comfort. Nothing came at first.

"Charlie Two-Wolves, you are a great warrior. I am proud to know you," Carlow finally said. "I am glad we did not meet in battle."

"*Kaaty* made it so. *Pabo taiboo*'s Jesus did agree."

Carlow nodded his acceptance of Two-Wolves's view that the Comanche God and the Christians' Jesus had guided their acquaintance.

The Comanche wrangler shrugged his shoulders. "After bluecoats leave, *Ich* bury *mein* wife and sons. All me *kamakuru . . . muerte*. Start them on spirit trail.

Ich ride *mucho* days. *Nein* care. *Nein* eat. *Kaaty* bring me here. *Ich* stay. *Ich* fight. *Ich* die here. So be it."

Carlow was moved by the man's simple declaration of courage. If what Two-Wolves said was true, it was obvious this ranch wasn't going to remain in Bea Von Pearce's hands long. How could it? She was outnumbered and outgunned. Before long she would have no more riders, then no cattle. Then it was only a matter of a few more days before this Dr. Holden, whoever he was, and his men came calling.

Surely, the Indian wrangler was wrong, for the scenario running through Carlow's mind was void of any optimism. The Comanche wrangler had to be mistaken. He had been through a lot and was probably seeing everything through that terrible agony. Seeing every action as evil, every situation as dire. Who wouldn't? Didn't he say that he first thought the young Ranger had come for him?

Two-Wolves began to speak, interrupting Carlow's musing. As if the question had just been asked, Two-Wolves explained that Hattie's parents had died of fever when she was an infant, and she had lived with Mrs. Von Pearce since she was three.

"Mrs. Von Pearce is lucky to have *haitsii* like you," Carlow said, pronouncing the Comanche word for "friend" carefully so he wouldn't misuse it.

Two-Wolves smiled at the compliment, then asked, "Why *pabo taiboo*'s Jesus listen to Doc-tor Rem-eeng-ton Hold-den *und* his wife who loves *der* moon *und* her spirits?"

"I don't know, my friend," Carlow said, watching Two-Wolves continue to whisper to Chance, and decided to tell him about the unfairness of both his friends, Kayitah and Dornan, dying young.

Before he could start, Two-Wolves motioned toward the knife held in Carlow's leggings. The Indian wrangler had studied the Ranger's gunbelt earlier without comment. "Comanche. Remembered fight?" It was a question of interest and not threatening.

"A gift from my friend. Kayitah. He was Mescalero. Said it came from a fight. In the mountains, I think."

"Apache. *Si. Mucho der* fights . . . Comanche and Apache." Two-Wolves grinned. "Comanche always win. Push Apache into mountain. There be remembered fight, *ja*?"

Carlow leaned down, withdrew the blade, and handed it, hilt-first, to the Indian wrangler.

As if to verify the friendship, Two-Wolves withdrew the large knife at his belt and handed it to Carlow in the same way.

Examining the sharp edge of Two-Wolves's knife, Carlow told him that Kayitah had been shot down by U.S. cavalry in an attack on his village. Carlow heard about it and had immediately sought his body for proper burial. With Kileen's support—and McNelly's—the army unofficially allowed him onto the site of the pitiful massacre. Carlow's best friend, Shannon Dornan, had joined him. They found Kayitah's favorite horse and took it with them to a cave where Kayitah's body was prepared and laid. It wasn't quite an Apache burial, but they feared reprisals by angry soldiers. They killed the horse so his friend would be mounted in the afterlife, as was Apache custom. Less than two years later, Carlow said Dornan died in an ambush by the Mallow gang. He didn't mention that he was badly wounded in the same battle.

"Kayitah lucky to have *haitsii* like you." Two-Wolves stood, repeated Carlow's earlier compliment about him, and returned his knife.

Handing back the Indian wrangler's knife, Carlow opened his mouth to answer, but Bea Von Pearce's clarion announcement from the porch stopped the conversation. "Ah, *Herr* Ranger Carlow, here *ist gut* food. Keep yah strong. Sausages *und* biscuits. Apples. Some for *der* sweet tooth being there, too. *Ja.*" She held a canvas sack with both hands.

Hattie peeked around the open door and giggled.

"Sounds good to me," Carlow said, and touched Two-Wolves's arm. "I'll see you again, *haitsii.*"

"*Kaaty* make it so. And *pabo taiboo's* Jesus, *haitsii. Ja.*"

Carlow told the wolf-dog to remain with the Indian wrangler. The beast's tail wagged and Two-Wolves rubbed his ears and head.

Walking toward her, Carlow frowned. "Ma'am, Charlie Two-Wolves tells me you are facing some tough times. I'd like to help you if I can."

Her reaction was not the one Carlow expected. Bea's expression rejected his question as if it were a slap in her face.

"*Herr* Ranger Carlow, Charlie should not be telling of such stories, *Ich* think. *Nein.* Fine are ve doing. That old Indian *ist* seeing *der* things. Or his speaking *nein* so *gut und* yah not hear true. Maybe he has found *mein* Herman's whiskey."

"What about this Remington Holden? The doctor? Sounds like he's trying to take your land." Carlow glanced back toward where Two-Wolves had been standing, but the Comanche wrangler was nowhere in sight. Almost as if he had been a figment of the young Ranger's imagination. Only Chance remained, sitting on his back legs.

Holding the sack against her bosom, she glanced back at Hattie before answering. "*Nein,* Dr. Holden *ist nein* doing so. *Mein Gott,* he to bring doctoring and medicine to all of us. *Ist* rich man, it *ist* so. He haff hotel in town *und* medicine store—*und* big ranch. *Ja,* much so *der* biggest for many *meiles.* His *mutter* and *vater* pass, him become rich. He *und* his beautiful *frau*." She shook her head to emphasize the woman's beauty. "Ven *mein* Herman be shot, Dr. Holden come to see if he could be of *helfen*. Too late, it vas. Comfort to me, he give." She hesitated and added, "He offer to buy ranch to *helfen* me." She swallowed to hold back the released anguish.

"What about the trouble at your watering hole? When Holden's men turned your cattle away?" Carlow pressed.

"There vas, how yah say, a mix-it-up at *mein* pond. Nothing, it vas. *Nein* to involve Dr. Holden, anyway. He vas *nein* there. At *mein* pond vas other neighbor's men."

"Charlie says you've only got five riders with your herd now, and this man is stealing . . ."

"Ooch, that Charlie. He to be teasing yah, *Herr* Ranger." She smiled. "Comanche joke, *Ich* am believing. Cradle 6 riders are *zehn*. Ah, ten. They be *gut* men, *mein* Herman hire them all."

"But your man getting his hand cut off? Didn't . . ."

Bea's frown stopped his question. "*Der* doctor to save his life, he did. *Der* gangrene was about him. Terrible. Dr. Holden *ist gut* man." Her expression didn't quite match her words, as if it didn't feel right to be saying them. Was that fear glistening in her eyes for a moment?

Carlow was puzzled by the contrast in descriptions. Bea pushed the food sack into his arms. "Now, off vit yah, *Herr* Ranger Carlow. Vorry no more of Charlie's words. He gets things in wrong places all *der* time. He *ist* Comanche, yah know, and they not be seeing our world so much."

Holding the food with care, Carlow continued to search Bea's face for the truth.

She smiled again and her eyes laid their warmth on the young Ranger. "Charlie come riding in *hier* one day, ask for job. *Mein* Herman hire him, and he tell me Charlie Two-Wolves *ist der* best man vit hosses he has ever been seeing. Charlie *ist gut* man also, besides . . . but does not to be knowing our ways. *Ich* forgive him." She crossed her arms in finale.

"I'm sorry to have bothered you about it," Carlow said.

"*Mein* buckskin vill carry yah far and fast. Your fine black horse vaiting it be vhen yah return." Her hand went to her mouth as she remembered something. "Oh, *Ich* write *der* bill of selling for *der* buckskin and place in *der* sack. If someone should be asking of it. And *Ich* hope yah can next time stay for *der* supper, *Herr* Ranger Carlow."

Hattie slipped past Bea and went immediately to Chance, presenting him with two small pieces of sausage. Kneeling, the little girl was preoccupied with petting the wolf-dog, who acted more like a puppy than a fierce wild animal. She leaned over and kissed his ear, looked up at Carlow, and asked, "Ranger Carlow, do you like to play make-believe?"

The young Ranger glanced at Bea and turned back to the blond-braided girl. "Well, Miss Hattie, I suppose I do."

"Oh, good! I like to play it, too. What do you like to pretend to be?"

He laughed. This wasn't a line of questioning he was used to hearing. "Now, that's a good question. What do *you* like to pretend to be?"

"I asked you first."

Carlow grinned. "Yes, you did. Let's see," he answered, "I . . . ah, I like to pretend I'm a mountain man. With a big grizzly bear coat."

"Oh, that is a good one. I like to pretend that I am a fine lady, and one day a handsome cowboy comes and wants to marry me."

"Well, that's a good one, too, Hattie," he said. "Such a beautiful—and smart—girl will have her pick of cowboys, I reckon, when the time comes."

"Will you come?"

His face reddened. The older woman knew he was coming back only for his black horse, and so did he. *What do you tell a little girl?*

"I'll sure do it if I can," he finally muttered, glancing at Bea.

"That's a promise, you know," Hattie added, her bright eyes seeking reasssurance in his expression.

Chapter Nine

Out of sight of the ranch, the young Ranger tested the buckskin's training by pressing and releasing his legs against the animal's belly. The horse reponded instantly with a trot. More pressure brought a lope. Laying the reins against the right side of the buckskin's neck turned it in that direction. A good sign, one of training. A spoken "whoa" brought it to an immediate stop without pulling on the reins. Carlow acknowledged to himself that Two-Wolves was, indeed, a good horse trainer. He pressed the horse's sides again with his legs and the smooth lope resumed.

At first, Carlow could see Silver Mallow grinning at him from behind every tree, every rock, and every swell in the land. Whenever his mind gave an alert, the Ranger's right fist tightened around the readied hand-carbine held across his lap. Gradually his mind assured him the outlaw leader was more likely to ride hard for Presidio, change horses, and head for the Rio Grande. That's what he would do if he were Mallow.

Of course, assuming an enemy was going to do something was an invitation to death. Still, it made good sense. He eased the hammer down but left his thumb poised on its lip, holding the gun in front of him. Bea's buckskin stretched out and began eating up the miles. Carlow let the strong horse run, preferring speed to the slower pace of tracking. Wind in his face relaxed him as the land flew by. He tried to concentrate, alternating his attention between looking for possible places for an ambush and watching the faint marks of Mallow's own fast-moving horse. The outlaw was also running hard, from the looks of the hoofprints.

On both sides of the trail, rich grama grass had invited cowmen and sheepmen to build good herds, and they were rapidly doing so. To the distant west, the green was stopped abruptly by the gold of hay fields and, next to it, a lighter shade of green from vegetables growing in long-cultivated soil. To the east, rolling sand-loamed plains controlled the world as far as he could see. Late afternoon was everywhere. The threat of more rain later in the day lay in a string of gray clouds waiting for reinforcements.

Above, a raven yelled at him for crossing its land. Running several yards behind the buckskin, Chance answered the challenge with a fierce bark, and the bird flew away, screaming obscenities. Carlow laughed, and the jolt shot a pain through his head. His forehead rolled into a frown to control the renewed ache. But it served to remind him of how close he had come to dying. Just the day before. And how lucky he had been. He rolled his shoulder out of habit, not pain—but its tightness served as a further indicator of what he might face again. Once more, he was vigilant.

Ahead was a slight rise, a narrow shelf of land created by belching within the earth that left a permanent scar on the prairie. Directly ahead, the incline was protected only by a stunted catclaw tree with its recurved thorns. Even the worst Texas sun couldn't limit its life, and today the sun was negotiating with the thunder. The catclaw tree belonged there. Likely the soil around the shelf was alkaline. Catclaw growth seemed to favor such an awful birthplace. It didn't matter that there was no water in sight, either.

A man could see a long way from this slightly elevated position. He reined up. Dismounting, he holstered his hand-carbine, leaving a bullet in the chamber but the hammer down, like a readied pistol. The buckskin could use a breather, and so could Chance. Carlow chuckled to himself; so could he. The head wound was continuing to remind him of its presence with an unrelenting tom-tom pounding. He stood and took a deep breath. It was difficult to reconcile what he knew of the region with what he saw. Everything looked peaceful.

Of course, the Red River War was over and the Comanche War Trail was becoming a dust-covered memory. But Mescalero Apaches were slipping away from the Fort Stanton reservation in the Sacramento Mountains of southern New Mexico and raiding settlements throughout this border region. He was happy not to have been assigned the task of finding them. That was the Army's job. It would have been too painful to go after friends of Kayitah's. Desperadoes from New Mexico also had sought Texas, but most had gone on to El Paso. Carlow knew the Rangers would be facing that wickedness soon, if the local law couldn't handle the situation. And he knew they couldn't. Or wouldn't.

He had heard thieves were even using the abandoned army post of Fort Hancock as a headquarters, some ninety miles from El Paso. Last year, one of the worst, Henry McCarty, becoming better known as "Billy the Kid Bonney," broke out an outlaw friend from the El Paso jail, and there was no telling where they were headed. None of those problems was his concern at the moment.

Silver Mallow was his problem, and his alone. Captain McNelly would decide what his concerns were. He accepted that. It was an honor to be given the assignment.

A striped whipsnake slipped from what slight shadow the tree-bush gave and slithered toward a boot-shaped rock several feet away. Bounding up the incline, Chance ran after the moving reptile.

"Hey, Chance, let the little fella alone."

With his tongue hanging out, Chance slid to a stop like a roping horse with a taut lariat pulling on a wild calf. Grinning, Carlow took off his hat and filled it with canteen water. The buckskin emptied it quickly, and he added more. Halfway through the refill, the horse quit drinking and turned away, satisfied. Carlow knelt, poured the hat crown full again, and held it for Chance to enjoy.

"It's not quite the same without Shadow, is it, boy?" He patted the wild animal. "He needed to rest. I was hard on him. You want some more?" He added water to the hat.

Chance finally stopped and licked his hand.

"Thanks, bud. Me, too."

After two long swigs from the canteen, Carlow returned it to his saddlehorn along with the other. He withdrew Bea's food sack from his saddlebags. It smelled as delicious as when he'd received it. Inside the sack, neatly wrapped in a cloth napkin, was a mound of fried sausages cut into eating wedges. He popped two into his mouth and let the savory juices take over. He tossed a morsel in the direction of Chance, who swallowed it whole.

"You're supposed to chew it first." Carlow laughed, tossed him another, and examined the sack further. Under the sausages was a thick layer of beef slices. He ate one and tossed another to Chance.

In addition to a half-dozen biscuits and two apples was a fat wedge of a fresh apple pie, delivering a tantalizing aroma of cinnamon and sugar. He took a large bite of the pie, smiled, and muttered, "Thank you, Bea."

A scorpion sauntered along the rock lip of the hillside. Carlow watched casually, more interested in the food. Certainly Mrs. Von Pearce's promise was no empty boast. After a few minutes of concentrated eating, he shared more meat with Chance, along with pieces of a biscuit, then cut up an apple for the buckskin. A cup of coffee would be nice, but he didn't want to take the time. He started to wipe his fingers on his long coat but thought better of it and rubbed them on his leggings instead. They were already streaked with the memories of many trails. He offered water again to both animals, drank a few swallows himself, and remounted.

Immediately his thoughts galloped back to the Von Pearce ranch as he nudged the buckskin forward. Was the Comanche wrangler just interpreting events and people incorrectly? That was possible, even likely. Charlie Two-Wolves had an Indian's limited understanding of the white man's world. He might have decided a friendly doctor was an evil white shaman. Certainly he had no reason to trust many white people. And the encounter at the Von Pearce pond may have been the simple misunderstanding Bea said it was, maybe even a courtesy granted, but seen by Two-Wolves as a warrior's stand.

Missing cattle may have been only the normal drifting that occurred with grazing, but the Comanche counted them as stolen. The cut-off hand was obviously necessary surgery to save a man's life. Stories of the physician's wife were nothing more than campfire gossip. Or someone pulling Two-Wolves's leg. The warrior may not have wanted to accept the fact that Comanches could, indeed, have killed some neighbors. There were still a few wild bands roaming the country.

Carlow granted himself all of those possibilities. But one of Two-Wolves's statements clung to his mind. He had said there were only five Cradle 6 cowhands with the Von Pearce herd. That number had been immediately refuted by Bea. How could Two-Wolves have misread ten cowboys as half that many? He seemed savvy enough to recognize riders would be working the hills and valleys for strays. Surely he hadn't just ridden out to the main herd, seen five men, and immediately assumed the others had left for good. Or had he? Why would he think a medical doctor, of all people, was involved? And his description of the man's wife left him imagining a snaggle-toothed woman in black, chanting at the moon.

If so, the young Ranger was back where he started: the Comanche warrior saw trouble where he didn't understand. Surely that was so. For a moment, Carlow saw Two-Wolves's eyes and remembered there was ever a sadness in them. How could there not be after all he had been through? Then it came to him: Two-Wolves was hiding. Of course he was.

Most of his fellow Comanches were forced onto the reservation. He didn't go. Nor had he joined any of the Comanche war parties frantically searching for a way to bring back the past. He had gone to the Von Pearce ranch to disappear. That's why he initially thought Carlow had come for him. No wonder the man saw trouble everywhere.

The buckskin loped easily as Carlow returned his attention to the widening trail ahead. Silver Mallow's horse tracks disappeared into layers of hoofprints and wagon tracks leading toward Presidio. The small settlement blossomed against the yellow horizon. As soon as he determined Mallow's move or found him, Carlow would seek out this Dr. Remington Holden and his wife to see for himself what kind of people they were. That would settle the matter. In his own mind, anyway.

Besides, he had no business worrying about such things as Bea Von Pearce's possible predicament. There were only a handful of hours left before darkness and rain took charge and finding Silver Mallow would become even more difficult.

His assignment was to find and capture Mallow. His only assignment. Kileen often warned him about straying from duty. Of course, the hulking Irish bear of a man was usually drunk when he told him. And that was against all Ranger rules. Superstitions and rules seem to slide around a bit with Kileen, changing and reshaping themselves to fit whatever point he wanted to make at the moment.

In spite of that, he was an enormously effective lawman and a fighter of considerable savvy, greater courage, and immense fighting skill. As a younger man, Ranger Aaron Kileen rarely passed up a chance to earn money prizefighting. He brought his sister and her small son from the New York docks to the Texas prairies on what he earned with his bare-knuckle fists. "Thunder," or "Old Thunder" as his fellow Rangers usually addressed him, had been a state policeman since the awful Davis administration. So had McNelly. In fact, Kileen's association with the Ranger captain went back to the War of Northern Aggression.

It was Kileen's insistence, years later, that led to Carlow's invitation to join the Rangers. There was certainly nothing holding him in the small town of

Bennett, Texas, where he grew up. Except the likelihood of his getting into trouble if he stayed there. His mother had died from the fevers, leaving her teenage son to find his way in a town that hated the Irish and all they stood for. A teenage son who would rather fight than eat—and usually did.

Something had happened in his uncle's past, something he wouldn't talk about. It had happened in New York not long after Carlow and his mother arrived from Ireland. Something so bad it had forced his uncle to change his name from Lucent to Kileen, the name of their village across the sea. He wouldn't say why, when his young nephew asked, only that it wasn't his business and that he should not tell anyone of his real name.

Carlow's hand went to the silver chain and Celtic cross worn under his shirt, which often happened when he was thinking of his mother. This small emblem was the only thing that remained of her, besides his memories. It was also his only tangible connection to his father. He took a deep breath, shook off the reminder that Mallow also wore a silver necklace, and relocked the sweet yesterdays into their place.

His mind returned him to the curiousness of this Dr. Holden, whoever he was. He had no illusions about the innate honesty of most physicians. They were only men, some misguided in their arrogance, some genuinely caring about others, and some who seemed to think cutting off a limb was the answer to everything. Most did other things besides doctoring. Barbering. Running a drugstore. Even being undertakers. Being a physician didn't pay too well, it seemed to Carlow. Dr. Holden might well be raising cattle on the side.

Actually, the best person he'd ever met for helping people get well was his uncle's sometime girlfriend, Angel Balta. She may have ridden the outlaw trail earlier in her life, but she certainly knew how to make a medicine that worked. At least with bullet holes. She had healed him after the Mallow ambush. She and Kileen. She had even called him *mi hijo*, her son. He remembered her fondly and hoped his uncle would return to the woman soon.

His shoulders rose and fell. He'd better pay attention, entering town. Presidio was no bigger than Bennett and nowhere near the size of towns like San Antonio, El Paso, or Houston, but it was big enough for a man to disappear. His attention was quickly drawn to two young women prancing along the planked sidewalks like queens of Texas. For an instant, he wished he had changed shirts as he glanced down at himself. At least his long coat had dried, as had his clothes.

Parasols matching oversized hats kept the late-afternoon sun from reaching the women's painted faces. They eyed him, and he touched the brim of his hat in passing. One woman winked. Both seemed disappointed when he rode on, but accelerated the motion of their backsides to erase the rejection by attracting other menfolk on the sidewalk.

Down the middle of main street, he rode past Harrison's Bank, the Grand Texas Hotel, Willard's Fancy Dry Goods store, a harness dealer, and a barbershop. Riding on, he saw a small warning sign in the watchmaker's store window: "No Irish. No Coloreds. No Mex." He tried to smile but couldn't.

The Holden Apothecary, promising every kind of sundry and patented medicine, appeared busy. Likely, this was the doctor that Two-Wolves had talked about. Carlow would visit the city marshal first to get information, then probably the saloons. But he would return to the drugstore if he didn't learn anything promising.

Chapter Ten

People scurried along the sidewalks and across the rutted street, intent on their day's business. A farmer's wagon rattled past him, and the farmer gave him a nod, which Carlow returned. A patrol of Union soldiers followed a few minutes later. From their saddle swaying and loud talking, it was apparent they had spent the better part of the day at the saloons on the other end of town.

One inebriated soldier spotted Chance trotting alongside Carlow's horse and jumped in his saddle. He shook his fuzzy head and said, "There's a wolf! A wolf!"

Halfheartedly aroused, the two Union troopers nearest to him looked around but saw nothing because Carlow had already gone by. He couldn't get either of them to look back at the horseman they'd just passed, and they laughed at his inability to hold his liquor. Mimicking him, the taller trooper yelled out, "Look, look! There's a green horse!" Most of the patrol joined in the whiskeyed chortle that followed.

Reining up, the young Ranger stopped at the hitching rack in front of the city marshal's office, squeezed between the Louis R. James Realty office and an alley.

"Stay, Chance. Beside Buck here. I'll be back in a minute." He pulled the badge from his pocket and pinned it to his vest, just inside his coat lapel. He gave the badge a quick shine with his cuff, tugged on the curled-up brim of his hat, and entered.

"Aftuh-noon, Range-uh, this hy-ar's a ree-al surprise. Thought yo-all boys was a'chasin' Mex rust-lurs down on thuh Ree-O." The heavily drawled greeting came from a large man with outsized ears, slicked-back hair, and a crumpled suit that only made his narrow shoulders appear even more so.

Marshal Laetner Dillingham made no attempt to get up from his chair behind a desk laden with papers. Or to extend his hand. Carlow could see the gunbelt at the man's ample waist. A walnut-handled Colt rested high in a fitted holster.

It was difficult not to focus on the man's ears—Carlow was certain they had wobbled when the sheriff spoke.

The young Ranger straightened his back. "Afternoon, sir. I'm Time Carlow of Captain McNelly's Rangers. I'm after the outlaw Silver Mallow. I believe he's in Presidio. Only a few hours ahead of me."

"Well, howdy, Range-uh Car-low, Marsh-hul Laetner Dillingham hyar. Thuh law in Pre-sid-eeo. But I reckon yo-all already knew that." He chuckled at his response, and his ears definitely wiggled.

Carlow tried to stare at the crowded desk. "Nice to meet you, Marshal Dillingham."

"Sil-vuh Mal-low, huh. Heard o' him. Nasty bastard, from what I been a'readin'. Yo-all leadin' a poss-ee after him, huh?" The marshal's excessive Southern drawl was delivered in a high, lilting voice that didn't fit his huge frame. Especially not his leaflike ears.

"No posse. Just me."

Marshal Dillingham stared at Carlow for a moment and shook his head, which made his ears wiggle more than usual. "Seems like thar should'a be a mite more o' yo-all."

Carlow wasn't interested in the man's opinion, only in any information he might have about Mallow's whereabouts. When he asked where the outlaw might try hiding, Marshal Dillingham rubbed his chin, causing his ears to bounce, and announced that it depended on what Mallow wanted. He might be in one of the saloons, the sporting house, the general store, or the livery.

"Could be, he's skee-daddlin' fer the Ree-O." Dillingham smiled and folded his arms.

"You want to help me find him? He shouldn't be hard to spot," Carlow said. "His face is swollen, black and blue, from fighting a Ranger before he was arrested. He's wounded too. Cracked ribs and a burn along his gun shoulder."

"Oooh, that'd be yurn busy-ness. Sil-vuh Mal-low ain't done nothin' wrong hy-ar. No o-ffense, Range-uh boy."

Carlow turned to leave, disappointed in the lawman's lack of interest. He would try the livery stable first; Mallow might have remounted and kept moving. At least the lawman had offered that possibility, one that hadn't occurred to him. A thought hit Carlow, and he turned back and asked about Dr. Holden and his wife.

Too quickly the city lawman assured him the doctor was a most generous man; the owner of a fine hotel, a comfortable saloon, a complete drugstore, and the region's largest ranch; and a gentle citizen who couldn't possibly be involved in any land grab—a respected leader of the community.

"May-be she's havin' a hard time o' it, ya know, an' is a'makin' excuses. Or may-be she's jes' a'seein' things. Ya know, ol' age an' all."

Carlow held back the words crouched on his tongue and turned again to leave.

"Yo-all think I should'a be a'warnin' the bank?"

Without looking back, Carlow answered, imitating the marshal, "Oooh, that'd be yurn busy-ness. No o-ffense, Mar-shal boy."

After checking the livery and assuring himself that Mallow hadn't gone there, he remounted and rode down the street with Chance at the buckskin's heels. Reflections from his badge announced his presence. Several people on the street paused to watch them pass, intrigued by the appearance of not only a Texas Ranger, but one riding with a wolf. He visited the general store and the hotel without success. Carlow assumed this was the hotel owned by Dr. Holden. It was the only one he saw.

The hotel clerk, a craggy-faced man with greasy hair, was especially talkative and shared that several strangers had checked in earlier that week. Drummers, he thought. The cooler air of autumn brought them; summer was too hot to make their calls here, he observed. But the only stranger checking in today was a very proper woman. Rigid and French, the hotel clerk thought. Carlow declined the invitation to go to the lady's room and see her.

The clerk was also eager to tell him that the hotel's owner, Dr. Remington Holden, might be able to help. He spurted out that the community leader owned this hotel, the drugstore, and the Rio Grande saloon, plus the region's biggest ranch, the Bar H. The chatty man was definitely awed by Dr. Holden's wealth and status.

"Thanks, I will talk with him," Carlow said without comment.

"Dr. Holden is our leading citizen, except for the mayor, of course."

"Surprised he's still doctoring—with all that other going on." Carlow backed toward the door.

"Oh, he believes in helping people. Yes sir, he does."

"I'm sure you're right."

"Oh, and his wife. My, is she a looker." The clerk pushed through his hair as if preparing for her entrance. "You won't want to miss seeing her. Makes a fella want to, ah, you know." His face reddened.

Carlow nodded and left with the clerk continuing his gushing description of the doctor's wife. It didn't sound to him like Mrs. Holden was anything like Two-Wolves had described. More like some kind of leading lady of the theater.

If Silver Mallow thought he was dead or badly hurt, the outlaw might hole up there for a few days and enjoy himself before going on. That meant music or women or both. Presidio had no regular theater or music hall, so Carlow rode to the far end of town, going first to the two-story sporting house at the end of the block. Assuming he didn't find Mallow, or information about him, there, Carlow planned to visit the string of saloons swelling the town.

Any one of them might be a good place to learn something. Or find Mallow enjoying himself. At the least, surely someone in Presidio had noticed a stranger, one with a battered face.

Reluctantly he entered the unpainted wood-framed house at the end of the street. No sign identified its function. A large card in the frilly curtained window said, "Cowboys welcome." Heavy lilac perfume visited his nostrils. Red-glowing lamps, Parisian wallpaper, and plush crimson velvet furniture filled his eyes. Tinkling piano notes slid into the entry parlor from the adjacent ballroom. It was the kind of place Silver Mallow would love, Carlow thought.

A thick-framed woman with square jowls, worldly eyes, and dark red hair piled high atop her head appeared from another room to greet him. The young Ranger thought she looked more like the socially proper wife of a governor than the madam of a whorehouse. A red satiny gown accented her bosom, tried to hide her skinny legs, and took on the glow of the surrounding lamps. Her dark-lined eyes examined Carlow professionally, then stopped at the badge.

"I am Rellena Kahn. How can I help you, Ranger?" Her smile was rehearsed but inviting. "Any of my girls can make your day a happy one. I would enjoy that myself. Two dollars in gold for a short visit, ten for all night. Got dancing in the other room. Whiskey and food too. I'm sure we could work something out—for a Texas constable."

Carlow felt redness snaking around his collar. "I'm looking for a man."

Her eyes sparkled. "Can't help you there, hon."

"Stranger. Dark-haired. Only been in town a few hours. He's a killer. Likes music. Wears lots of rings. Silver." He paused, hating what he was going to say next. "Some folks say he looks like me. But his face is all swollen and carrying a lot of bruises from a beating."

She shook her head appreciatively, then the smile dissolved from her face. "Can't say he's been here. Can't say he hasn't."

"Can't or won't?"

"Won't. But you're welcome to visit my bedrooms upstairs. All ten of them. We use clean linens, china spittoons—and all my girls are in their teens, except Black Bethinia, and no man seems to care how old she is."

Carlow thought for a moment. "Do you have a girl who sings?"

A teasing laugh came from deep in her throat. "No, honey, I don't. But I've got one who'll let you suck her toes. Will that do? Or how about a lovely Negress. Lots of men ask for her. That's Black Bethinia. And I've got a fourteen-year-old redhead who just joined us. She'll do anything you want but I've never heard her sing. Of course, I can hum a few bars of 'Dixie' while we do it, if you'd like." Rellena Kahn winked.

Gritting his teeth, Carlow asked to see the ballroom. She took his hand and led him graciously to the doorway of the small gray room. A piano player, a young woman who looked as if she couldn't have been older than twelve, was presenting a lively waltz. Eight men danced feverishly, holding women in frilly gowns. Only two men were making any attempt to move with the music. In the center, a crystal chandelier presented a cascade of yellow light down upon the dancers, streaking them with golden highlights.

With Rellena Kahn continuing to hold his hand, he studied the room and knew Mallow wasn't there. Satisfied, Carlow told her that he would now have to inspect each bedroom upstairs.

She winced visibly, squeezed his hand in reaction to the news, and released it.

He thought she was bluffing before.

"Oh, now, it wouldn't be good for business, you know, to have a lawman traipsing through." Her voice was soft, almost pleading. "If I told you there wasn't anybody here like the man you're after, would that be good enough?"

"Should it be?"

"Yes, it should." The smile returned to her square-jowled face, along with the same warm, rehearsed expression as earlier. "Let's go back in here." She grabbed his hand again.

As they returned to the parlor, Rellena Kahn spun into him, pushing her breasts against his chest. Her mouth was inches from his. Her eyes sought his attention, but he stepped back, holding her briefly at arm's length before letting go.

Folding her arms, she began to recite. A sly grin crept onto her mouth as she spoke. "The mayor's in the first bedroom, like always. Cowden Heckerson, a rancher south of here, is in the second. Three cowboys—regulars—have the next three. Black Bethinia is in the next one with a drummer. Don't know him, but he's bald and short and has a weakness for colored women." Coyly, she placed a finger to her mouth, then removed it slowly, letting it drag across her lower lip and chin. "In the next one is a German fella, owns a big farm. He comes in once a month and always asks for Gretchen. That isn't her real name, but she knows a little German. Says he likes to talk dirty to her. In German." Her eyes sought his for interest. "Let's see, in the next room is . . . oh yeah, the husband of the head of the church ladies' circle. He'll be in and out real quick, though. Always is. And the last two . . . are open, for the moment." The last phrase was an invitation.

Touching the brim of his hat, Carlow thanked her and left.

"Come back anytime, sweetheart, and I'll sing 'Dixie' to you" reached him as he closed the door.

Half amused, half frustrated, he went immediately to the saloon next door, glancing at Chance to assure himself that the animal was where he was supposed to be, beside his buckskin. An out-of-tune piano was delivering an unrecognizable song, played by a man who looked, to Carlow, as if he could have been the whorehouse piano player's father.

A narrow-faced cowboy with a choppy mustache caught a glimpse of the Ranger badge and quickly slipped out the back door. Carlow's arrival drew interest from the other patrons. It wasn't often a Texas Ranger came to Presidio. Several thanked him for coming to town.

A nervous townsman wanted to know if the animal with him was, indeed, a wolf. Another wanted help with a tenant who was late on his rent payment. Carlow didn't see Mallow, and no stranger had come in, according to the patrons, all eager to provide information. The hoarse faro dealer suggested the Remuda next door; he'd seen a man he didn't know walk in there at noon.

Carlow left and briskly passed a tiny dentist's office; the sign indicated the proprietor was also the town coroner and offered barber services and baths. Next to it was the Remuda. Only three patrons and a sleepy bartender. None remembered any man in the saloon all day, except themselves. A dreary place. Carlow couldn't imagine Mallow staying there for long.

The Rio Grande saloon, owned by Dr. Holden according to the hotel clerk, looked no different from the others he had visited so far. There was no sign of Silver Mallow. Two faro tables were busy, and a vigorous table stakes game was going on at the center table. An elderly gentleman in a crisp white shirt and fresh collar was at the piano in the corner, solemnly playing his own waltzlike version of "Turkey in the Straw." Carlow asked a few questions of the polite bartender and left. Only one stranger had been in all day: the baldheaded man in the poker game.

If Dr. Holden was to be judged by this saloon—and

the hotel—he was nothing to be afraid of, only a successful man, Carlow decided. Two-Wolves had to be wrong.

After checking all but one saloon, he had learned nothing except that there was a horse race scheduled for the next day and the betting was heavy. The remaining saloon, Charlie's Whiskey and Pool Hall, had music. But so had the last two. Sort of. Carlow was beginning to wonder if the outlaw ever came to town. And that meant the young Ranger had missed his turning off somewhere. He grimaced at the thought of the outlaw's fooling him again.

The jingling of Carlow's spurs preceded him as he stepped inside the last saloon. It looked like the others. Gray. Smoke laden. And filled with men from all walks of life.

One businessman at the long bar turned and saw the badge; then his gaze took in the sawed-off Winchester holstered at the weary young stranger's hip. Soon the rest of the bar checked out the newcomer, most trying to do so without drawing attention to themselves.

Chapter Eleven

In one corner of the dull barroom, an ex-Confederate soldier, still in a shabby uniform and sporting a full gray beard, played a banjo and sang songs, mostly from the war. Next to him, a grizzled fiddler, wearing a too-small kepi cap with a bill cracked down the center, tried to keep up. They stood in the open area twenty feet from the bar but were only part of the entertainment.

Two faro tables, a pool table, and a roulette wheel were the main attractions, plus a half dozen scantily dressed women serving drinks and smiles. On the wall behind the bar was a sign proclaiming all guns were to be handed over to the bartender while in the establishment. The order was signed by Marshal Dillingham. Curled at one corner, the sign was squeezed between two oil paintings of nude women in exaggerated poses.

Carlow hadn't recalled seeing such a notice in any of the other saloons, but this one seemed a notch above the rest. Definitely Mallow's kind of place, he told himself, but he saw no one resembling the outlaw. He walked past a pinched-faced businessman eating alone at a table near the door. Avoiding contact with the young Ranger's eyes, the man pretended to be engaged in cutting his steak.

However, the big-nosed bartender, with wild eyebrows that sought each other, watched him uneasily. Slowly he put down the glass he was wiping and let both hands disappear under the bar.

Without waiting for the request or the appearance of the hidden shotgun now at the bartender's fingertips, Carlow stepped to the bar, unbuckled his gunbelt, and handed it to him, complying with the sign. He wouldn't have to, but it seemed like the right thing to do.

The bartender's face was a sigh of relief as he reached for the guns. A faint snicker dawned at the corner of his mouth, thought better of it, and disappeared.

At the bar, most couldn't resist glancing at the emblazoned wood stock and well-oiled hammer, trigger, and lever guard of the cut-down rifle, accompanied by a short-barreled Colt in a tilted holster. A lean man in a black broadcoat suit whispered something to the man next to him. Carlow heard the words "Injun sign." After a quick wrap of the belt around the holsters, the weapons disappeared beneath the bar.

"I'm Ranger Time Carlow, and I'm trailing an outlaw, name of Silver Mallow. He's wanted for murder and rustling," Carlow told the bartender loudly enough for everyone to hear. "Any strangers in town today? He's got a badly bruised face."

"Lots of 'em, Ranger. People like comin' to Presidio—for the arts." The homely bartender motioned toward the singer in the corner.

His joke raised a chuckle that echoed along the bar.

As if he hadn't heard the remark, Carlow described Mallow.

"Sounds like Harry Beecher, don't ya think, Noah?" The bartender raised his aggressive eyebrows and looked down his potato nose at the bespectacled businessman in the middle of the bar.

"Now see here, Beecher ain't no stranger. He jes' strange. Ain't got no beat-up face, though. Hell, the one he's got is bad 'nuff." The response was riddled with supportive laughter. "Come to think on it, he's ugly 'nuff to kill somebody with jes' his face. That's fer sure."

An uproar of gaiety followed, with reinforcing comments.

"How come you ain't down in El Paso, after that Bonney fella?" roared another voice.

"Woher kommen Sie? Sind Sie bist du allein hier?" No one understood the German in a tight shirt and tighter suit standing with his shoulders stiff to the right of the bespectacled drinker. Carlow thought the man was asking where he had come from and if he was alone but wasn't certain.

"Try lookin' in Rellena Kahn's place, Ranger, if'n you kin handle all that sinnin'." The statement came from the far end of the bar before Carlow could respond to what he thought were the German immigrant's questions.

A seasoned drover in batwing chaps nodded his head at the remark and looked down for the spittoon. His thick brown spit hit its mark, and he grinned widely at his accuracy.

"Oh, he'd like to handle Black Bethinia, all right." The bartender slapped the top of the bar to reinforce his observation and snorted through his nose. It sounded like a horse whinnying.

Carlow's left hand shot toward the bartender's outstretched hand and held it. Instinctively the man tried to pull away but couldn't. Carlow's grip was prison steel. Raising his right leg, Carlow drew the knife from his leggings with his free hand and placed the blade against the wild-eyebrowed bartender's throat. Carlow's eyes drove their way into the man's soul.

As if it had been yanked offstage, the laughter jerked to a tense quiet and the saloon quit breathing. Even the old singing Rebel hesitated and stopped in the middle of "The Girl I Left Behind Me."

Carlow's intense gaze and the closeness of the sharp knife took away what little courage the bartender had as the young Ranger growled, "I didn't come this far to listen to some silly assholes jabber. The man I'm after killed my best friend. It sounds to me like you boys are trying to hide him. You wouldn't want me to think that, would you? Perhaps you'd like me to show you how Silver got that face."

"H-honest, m-mister . . . ah, R-Ranger, s-sir," the bartender said, his nose honking great anxiety. "I-I ain't seen nobody c-come in . . . l-like that. H-honest. R-right, boys?"

"He's right, Ranger. Nobody's come in that we didn't know. Except you." The spectacled man spoke with a controlled defiance that belied his meek appearance.

Carlow withdrew the knife and returned it to his legging. "I'm going to sit over here and have a beer. Maybe one of you assholes will remember something beyond the last time you had your pants unbuttoned."

He spun around and sought an empty table near the bar; all eyes along the bar followed. He pulled away the dark chair and plopped down into it. Dust from his long coat whispered around him for an instant.

As if a signal, the Rebel began singing again, right where he left off. "And to my heart in anguish press'd the girl I left behind me. Then to the East we bore away, to win a name in story . . ."

Pushing his hat off his head, Carlow let the tie-down leather thong hold it at his neck. His long black hair brushed along the edges of a dirty collarless shirt and his trail coat. Heavy spurs clanked against the wooden floor as he stomped his boots to free them and the protective leggings from the collection of trail dirt. He rubbed his eyes to clear away fatigue. His head ached from yesterday's bullet crease. At least Bea's food had settled his stomach. He rolled his shoulder to relieve the tension and that brought a stinging reminder of his other close call.

In the far corner, a five-handed poker game was into high stakes. A heavyset gambler with a well-groomed mustache and a tailored suit was winning. An immense belly appeared to have a life of its own, but his clothes, nevertheless, fit his corpulant frame without strain. Narrow slits for eyes were dwarfed by a large, oval face, reddened by too much weather and even more whiskey. Carlow glanced again at the card game, drawn to the sudden curse of a loser. The young Ranger caught the glimpse of a pearl-handled pistol under the black swallowtail coat of the fat card player. It made him feel undressed without his own guns.

"Hey, Jimmy, ya need whiskey?" yelled the bartender, concern in his uneven voice at the attempt to be intimate, casually calling the polished gambler by his first name.

The heavyset Southerner nodded his head affirmatively. "Bring a new deck. These are getting a bit worn, aren't they, Mr. Trevor?" He advised the big cattleman on his left to wait for the new cards, and the man did so without hesitation. "Bring a new glass for Mr. Decker, too. His has your fingerprint on it."

Carlow thought the gambler looked like a man who definitely enjoyed the pleasures of each day, whether it be poker, food, whiskey, women, or conversation. A man of breeding, at least compared with himself. All he owned was packed on the buckskin outside—plus his black horse back at the Cradle 6. It didn't matter. He was doing what he wanted to do; he was what he wanted to be. A Texas Ranger.

"Hi, honey, what'll you have?"

The tall waitress with tired eyes, a thin mouth painted red beyond her lips, and long brown hair stood beside him, smiling. Her perfume was syrupy. Her frilly green dress looked as if she had been in it for weeks, pushing up her bosom and accenting her long legs.

Before he could speak, she asked, "Would you like to go upstairs?"

"No thanks, ma'am. Just thirsty. I'd sure go for a beer. Maybe a cigar if one's to be had."

"Sure, sweetie," she responded with a bemused smile. "Don't mind Ben. The bartender. He's smart talkin' like that to everybody. But he's right. Every man that's come in here today I've known. Some of them real well." She winked.

Carlow's dark eyes, with thick eyelashes any woman would desire, were at the same time warm and distant. His responding smile was a magnet to the saloon whore. Quickly she returned with the beer and a cigar, stood close to his chair, and leaned over in front of him to place the filled glass on the table. Her right breast rubbed against the side of his face as she first positioned the beer, then laid the cigar beside the filled glass. She gazed coyly upward to make certain he had received an eyeful of her nearly exposed bosom.

"Now, honey, if there's anything else you want . . . you just ask," she said with her best smile. "My name is Lacy." He smiled again and thanked her. She touched his arm in response as she left, letting a veil of thick lilac perfume settle around him.

Ignoring the cigar for the moment, Carlow sipped the beer and examined the gray room. Letting himself relax in the chair, he rested his arms on the scratched oak table. He barely heard the Confederate, now into another sad song of lost love, trying to stay with the rhythm of the fiddler. It felt good just to sit on something besides a saddle, even if his time in Presidio had, so far, proved fruitless.

Maybe Mallow hadn't even stopped there. If so, he was nearing the Rio Grande by now. The ache in Carlow's forehead reminded him of the consequences of being surprised again by the outlaw. Where could he have gone, if not Presidio? And if he were in town, where? Was the outlaw just a step ahead? Why hadn't anyone seen him? Had he made the mistake of assuming this was Mallow's destination and missed a turnoff earlier?

His mind rerode the trail from the Von Pearce ranch and made up several possible places where the outlaw could have changed direction. A mind could do that, he reminded himself. See things that weren't really there. Like Charlie Two-Wolves imagined he saw. His thoughts slipped back to little Hattie and the promise he had made to her. Not quite a promise, he told himself. Not one anybody expected him to keep. That led his thoughts to Jeremiah, Ellie Beckham's boy. Hattie and Jeremiah had to be close to the same age.

Riding away from Ellie Beckham had been hard to do. Too hard. He tried to keep from thinking about her because it always made him want to race back to Bennett and into her arms. He had known the perky widow for only a short time. Just hours, actually. But their first kiss was always pushed up against his conscious mind, waiting to take over. Whenever he let her memory come, she was there. Even now, his body savored the feel of her warmth against him.

He chuckled when he recalled his uncle giving him advice about how to make her fall in love with him. All sorts of charms and chants. All of them involved and complicated. He could remember only one: he was to hold a mint sprig in his hand until it was moist and warm, then take Ellie's hand. She would follow him anywhere as long as their hands touched the mint. First, though, they couldn't speak at all for ten minutes. That gave the charm time to manufacture its spell. Maybe he should have tried it, instead of laughing. Of course, he didn't know where he could find any mint. Neither did Kileen.

With a sip of his beer, the thought occurred to him that he should visit the town physician. Mallow might have sought him out for medicine. It would give Carlow a chance to evaluate Dr. Holden for himself as well. Maybe he should go there under the pretense of getting something for his head wound.

"Hey, we don't want no one-armed beggars in here. Go away!" The big-nosed bartender waved a towel in the direction of a staggering man just entering the saloon. With him came narrow lances of gold from the sun nearing the horizon, after fighting a losing battle with the day's grayness.

The bartender's harsh command broke Carlow's daydreaming and he looked toward the saloon entrance. What a pitiful sight the beggar made in the doorway. His suitcoat was torn and awash in mud, straw, and worse. Carlow couldn't tell how much of the man's left arm was missing; his coat sleeve was simply empty at the cuff.

With heavy sideburns trailing from a filthy light brown flag of hair, the beggar stood weaving; his bloodshot eyes avoided meeting anyone's stare. Buck teeth forced their way past his upper lip and into the day. A floppy-brimmed hat covered most of his upper face, making his hawk nose appear even sharper, with a reddish tint from too much drinking. What passed for his shirt was a torn, once-red undershirt. Deep wrinkles in his Levi's looked like stretched-out coils, carrying months of constant wear.

The young Ranger couldn't tell how old he was, either, but guessed close to his own age. He tried not to stare at the forlorn-appearing man but was drawn to the deep sadness that oozed from his body. He assumed the beggar had once been a cowhand, by the looks of his bowlegged stance. Probably his hand was lost in a ranching accident; he appeared too young for the war, but one couldn't be certain.

Swaying slightly, like a sapling being tested by spring breezes, the drunken man looked around the room to discover whom the bartender was talking about, then resumed his stagger toward the bar. His glance caught Carlow's eyes and scurried away.

Chapter Twelve

"Hey! Dammit, I said get out. Your kind ain't welcome here," the bartender demanded again, slapping the towel against the bar.

The words angered Carlow. His eyes searched the room to see how others might react and caught those of the fat gambler across the open space. Shards of graying, yellow light passed Carlow's face on their way to the floor from the saloon's only window.

"That's all right, Ben. He's a friend of mine. Yo-all give him what he wants. Put it on my bill," the thick-bellied gambler yelled out, and returned to his cards.

Behind the bar, the bartender swallowed and his complexion lightened. "O-oh, I didn't know, Jimmy. I-I'm sorry. W-what can I help you with, sir?"

"Whiskey. Your good whiskey."

The bartender lifted a bottle from under the bar and waved it in syncopation with the Confederate's song. Like a cattle dog spotting a stray calf, the one-handed man hurried toward him. The combination of eager-

ness and drunkenness caused him to bump against the
pinched-faced clerk eating alone.

His contact came exactly at the moment when a
large bite of steak reached the clerk's open mouth. The
piece of meat bounced off his plate and wobbled across
the table. Watching it, the clerk tried to decide if he
should be angry or act as if nothing had happened.

"Oh, I-I didn't see you move. Sishsorry." The beggar
made a jerky bow, rubbed his buck teeth with his
tongue, and continued toward his objective.

With a look of relief in his eyes, the clerk mumbled
that it was nothing and stabbed the wayward morsel
with his fork. He glanced around to see if anyone was
watching before shoving it into his mouth.

The bartender filled the glass with whiskey and left
it on the bar for the advancing beggar. The spectacled
businessman and the German moved aside to allow the
man to reach the bar. Both noticeably distanced themselves four feet from him as he settled against the
countertop.

After downing the drink in two long swallows, he
waved at the bartender for another and yelled out to
the Rebel musicians, "H-heyish, c-can you s-sing 'The
R-Rose of Alabamy'?"

Someone at the bar groaned; another glanced
furtively at the well-dressed gambler. At his card table,
the fat man ignored the groan but his eyes wandered to
Carlow. The young Ranger nodded his appreciation.

His attention returning to the table, the gambler declared, "I'll play these." Without turning from the
table, he said a little more loudly, "And Ben . . . tell
that singer of yours to do that song. Ah, the 'Rose of
Alabamy' one. I'm in the mood . . . for that." He
glanced back at Carlow, and the young Ranger
grinned. The gambler's matching grin followed, taking

over most of his wide face as he drawled, "I'll see that an' raise you ten. Jenkins, don't play with your cards like that. It makes me nervous."

After lighting his cigar and taking a long, satisfying pull of smoke, Carlow heard Chance bark from outside. More of a threatening growl. Chance growled again, long and deep in his throat. Maybe someone was messing with his horse! Before he could move, the wolf-dog yelped. Somebody was trying to hurt him! Maybe someone thought a wolf had come to town.

As the young Ranger sprang from his chair with the cigar in his teeth, two men entered the saloon. Both wore belt guns. Carlow stopped next to the table. They were quickly followed by two more. Both cloaked in shadow. A shorter man with long blond hair. And a huge brute of a man.

One of the first two searchers, a slump-shouldered man with thick eye spectacles and an overgrown mustache cutting his face in two, spotted him. The man's eyebrows twitched nervously, then he hunched his shoulders to shake off the emotion. He said something to the darker man beside him.

The halfbreed grinned a mouthful of big teeth, bright against his skin, in response to the slump-shouldered gunman's comment. But the smile didn't reach the coldest eyes Carlow had ever seen. The halfbreed's eyebrows were plucked clean like a Cheyenne warrior's, giving him an even more sinister appearance.

The young Ranger had known the look before, and it loosened experiences that weren't helpful now. A shiver ran down Carlow's back.

Both men instinctively separated from each other with several side steps, allowing the two behind them to come forward.

Carlow watched the positioning without, at first, comprehending its significance. Then it hit him: they were there for him. But why? They were complete strangers. They couldn't be friends of Silver Mallow's—or could they? Could he have paid them to attack him?

From the shadows strode the blond man, only a few inches beyond five feet, with a jutting chin and prideful chest. Carlow sensed he was the leader of the group. Not the big man next to him. A leader used to having his way and liking it. Small men often made dramatic leaders, he knew. Grant himself wasn't very tall. Neither was "Little Phil" Sheridan, nor even the legendary Jeb Stuart. The small man wore a black suit and a black hat. The hat brim bequeathed darkness about the man's face, leaving only an angular shape to the pale skin and piercing light blue eyes. His blond hair was more white than yellow and fully covered his ears.

Many a woman would have yearned for locks so grand. Even in the room's consuming gray, the golden mane gave the appearance of a halo encircling part of his head. But it wasn't a color that came with aging; this man was fully in his prime.

This had to be Dr. Remington Holden. It had to be.

Carlow knew this wasn't a happenstance gathering, either. These were Dr. Holden's men. And they would kill. Anytime Dr. Holden said. The young Ranger had been in too many fights not to catch the signals.

At the bar, the drover's whispered conversation to the German beside him snapped through the forced stillness. "What's Doc doin' in hyar? Yah figger he's after some whiskey to put in his medicine bottles?" He chuckled and chewed vigorously on his tobacco. "Colonel Red Anklon's with him. Runs the doc's big spread east o' here, ya know. Wonder what's up?"

"*Ja*, an' that be Del Gato. *Schlecht. Schlecht.* He *ist var* bad man," the German immigrant observed, and quickly drank the rest of his whiskey.

"I heard tell Colonel Anklon kilt a cowboy—with his fists."

"*Ja.* That be so."

Drawing on the cigar, Carlow let the smoke drift across his face. It quieted his insides. He needed to think. He was cold inside. So cold. He was often this way before a fight. Kileen said it was a gift from the other side. Kayitah told him it was his spirit helpers joining him. Carlow felt unclothed without his guns. Why had he been so intent on observing a local ordinance that he didn't have to obey? How foolish it now seemed. "Bad luck," Kileen would mutter if he were there.

Dr. Holden was made even shorter by his closeness to the massive man beside him. Standing well over six feet and on the heavy side of two hundred pounds, Colonel Anklon wore a buckskin jacket highlighted with beadwork and a wide-brimmed hat with a matching beaded band. His forearms stretched the leather to its limit. A pistol, holstered at his waist, carried a silver star embedded in the walnut handle. He was an impressive-looking man and was well aware of it.

"They be wantin' that kid Ranger, I reckon." The drover finished his statement by launching another stream at the spittoon. He missed and looked around to see if anyone noticed.

"*Mein Gott!* I must be going home. *Ja*, I must." The German hurried toward the back door.

The drover watched him go, relieved the German's exclamation wasn't about his missing the spittoon, and spat again. Most of the stream hit its mark. Nodding approval, he ordered another drink.

The dark gunman called Del Gato smiled widely again and said something Carlow couldn't hear, speaking through clenched teeth. Dr. Holden nodded and stepped forward, waiting until all eyes were on him.

"Gentlemen, forgive this intrusion. While I personally do not find such places comforting, I do understand other men's needs—and weaknesses."

At the far end of the bar, a bald man asked the cowboy next to him what was meant by the statement. The wiry cowboy shrugged and muttered, "He's a'sayin' we're weak cuz we like drinkin', smokin', card playin', an' pokin'."

The bald man rubbed his chin. "Well, I reckon he's right."

Comfortable with attention focused on him, Dr. Holden took in the room with his gaze, reinforcing the moment. With his arms fully outstretched, he said in a loud, clear voice, "Please go on with . . . your pleasures. We will only be a minute with some unpleasant business. Colonel Anklon, if you please, sir."

Smiling wickedly, Anklon stepped up beside the doctor. "You there, are you riding that Cradle 6 buckskin?"

Carlow hadn't moved. He fought back the growing fear of facing four men unarmed except for the knife in his leggings. Surely they wouldn't attempt anything here, with so many witnesses. Their objective must be to scare him into leaving town. He took a deep breath to push away the nervousness. Would they think his long coat hid a gun?

"Afternoon, gentlemen. Obviously you have me mistaken for someone else," Carlow responded, "and I don't take well to questions like that from a stranger. I suggest you take your act somewhere else."

His words stung. They had expected him to be afraid, getting caught alone and unarmed. But showing fear wouldn't help him. Inside he was crawling with bugs. Bea's supper was not far down his gullet and inching up.

"You telling us that ain't a Cradle 6 hoss outside? The buckskin with the yappy wolf?" Anklon demanded, pulling himself up to his full height and further dwarfing the blond physician.

A sinister grin eased its way across Dr. Holden's face.

Maybe they thought he had stolen it or hurt the old woman. Carlow's answer was more emotional than he wished. "I'm Time Carlow. A Ranger with Captain McNelly's Special Force. I've got a bill of sale for the buckskin. Bought it from Mrs. Von Pearce just today. It's in my saddlebags."

Without saying another word, Anklon started walking confidently closer to the young Ranger, hands swinging easily at his sides. In midstride, he stopped as the significance of Carlow's words hit him. For the first time, he saw the badge pinned to Carlow's shirt. The two henchmen fanned out beside him as Dr. Holden disappeared purposely into the shadows.

Like a gunshot, Chance came charging inside and headed for the slump-shouldered man. The wolf-dog was bleeding behind his ear. Turning around at the sound of Chance's deep growl, the man swung his leg to kick the advancing animal.

"Don't touch my dog!" Carlow's command was instant and hot, followed by a demanding "Come here, boy."

Chance swerved to avoid the man's boot, then trotted proudly to the young Ranger's side, wagging his tail as if nothing had happened. Carlow's quick look told him the wound around the wolf-dog's ear was slight. He saw the slump-shouldered man's eyebrows twitch once more, followed by the hunching of his shoulders to remove the nervousness.

"Which one of you bastards hurt my dog?"

"Not Del Gato," answered the halfbreed through a toothy grin. "Only men I hurt. I eat dogs—and wolves."

"I did it. I'll kill him . . . later. Only good wolf is a dead one." The answer spewed from the slump-shouldered man. He glanced at Del Gato for approval, then pushed his glasses back up his nose. His eyebrows twitched, but this time he swung his shoulders from side to side and rolled the fingers of his right hand into a fist and opened them.

Carlow patted Chance and tried to think. Cigar smoke rolled across his tense face. Were these other people going to stand by and watch him get killed? What was he going to do without a gun? Could he get behind the bar before they fired? Should he rush into them with his knife—or his fists—and take his chances? Which one should he attack first? The slump-shouldered man was nervous, as if he wanted to prove something to the others. The halfbreed wouldn't do anything unless he was certain of victory; Carlow had seen his type before. The big rancher appeared confident and eager.

Would this doctor actually condone such an action—and watch it happen? Carlow swallowed his fear and patted Chance again. They had to try to make it look like self-defense somehow; maybe he shouldn't do anything. Yet. His mind whirled with conflicting thoughts. Maybe now that they knew he was a lawman, they would back off.

"I don't believe you're a Ranger, Mister. I believe you stole that hoss from an old lady. Lifted that piece o' tin from someone, too. As sure as I was a colonel in the Army of the Confederacy, we're gonna take it back to her—after I pound you into the ground." Anklon's announcement was followed by a savage smile and immediate advancement toward Carlow.

From somewhere in the saloon came a hurried warning. "Look out, boy! Run!"

From the fat gambler's table came his syrupy Southern command to "Keep a'playin', yo-all."

Carlow knew what was next and spat the cigar from his mouth but left his hands at his sides. It didn't surprise the big man that Carlow hadn't moved. His brute size had that effect on some men, causing them to freeze in terror. Three steps. Four steps. His upper body and arms were heavy with muscle. He was a powerfully built man and enjoyed its effect on others. But Carlow knew he would also be slow and overconfident. He had fought men like this before. Many times. He had walked away the victor all but once—and that was the first time.

Anklon paused a little more than two feet from Carlow, looked down at him, snorted, and cocked his massive right fist.

Carlow's well-placed boot was a terrible explosion into Anklon's groin. The big man's agony came from deep within his soul as the force rammed its way up into his stomach. Anklon's half-begun blow staggered in midair, and his fist hurried to the sickening pain, followed by his other hand. An instant behind came the smash of Carlow's left uppercut, snapping the big man's head backward as if it were on a hinge. Carlow's trail coat fluttered angrily with the powerful move. His right fist hooked hard to Anklon's cheek, loosing blood and a tooth. Anklon's groan rattled through the saloon and brought expressions of concern and wonder.

Anklon staggered backward, still holding his groin and the pain that wouldn't end. Carlow grabbed the big rancher's shirt and landed a left jab to his stomach. He released the shirt, stabbed Anklon again deep in his gut with his right, and followed that with a flurry of blows. The completion of the furious combination was an overhand right to Anklon's jaw. More blood flew across the big man's face and tattooed Carlow's cheeks.

Behind them came a syrupy threat. "Del Gato, tell your friend he's gonna get yo-all both killed. The Range-uh's a friend o' mine."

Strong but slow, Anklon had always depended on his sheer size to reduce enemies to frightful targets.

He'd never fought someone who knew how to fight. He'd never fought someone who wasn't afraid of him. He'd never fought someone like Time Carlow, who grew up fighting for Irish honor and anything else that he could think of.

Blind with pain, Anklon drove a right fist at Carlow's head, glancing against his cheek and ear. Staggering him for an instant, the impact made the young Ranger realize he must end this fight now, or the bigger man eventually would beat him with his superior strength. If Anklon ever knocked him down, Carlow would be finished. And dead. A broken neck or back would quickly follow. That fear was behind a blurry assault of swift, savage strikes, leaving the bigger man standing on memory alone. Then came Carlow's second uppercut. Anklon flew across the floor and thudded onto his back. Unknowing.

"Not in here." The tall waitress's throaty command came like a wind in the tense saloon.

She stood behind the bar, holding a shotgun. *Click-click*. Two heavy hammers being cocked seemed louder than her threat. The big-nosed bartender looked at her with fear controlling his face. At the poker table, Flanker looked over, surprise in his eyes that his earlier threat had apparently been ignored.

Chapter Thirteen

The slump-shouldered gunman's hand stopped its advance toward his holstered revolver, then looked at Lacy to evaluate the reality of her threat, then at the wolf-dog. With his back rolled into an attack position, Chance's white teeth snarled readiness. Lacy pressed the shotgun against her pale shoulder, with her right hand controlling both the balance and the triggers, freeing her left.

"Don't make me mess up the place with your head, honey." Lacy's smile was curled to the side.

With her left hand, she reached under the bar and grabbed Carlow's gunbelt. Swinging her arm back until it touched the counter behind the bar, she tossed the gunbelt toward him. Her attention never left the two gunmen, frozen in indecision.

Dr. Holden stood next to the wall of the saloon with his arms folded. A strange concern ate at his face. He hadn't expected any of this. No one had ever beaten Red Anklon before. Or even winded him. Who was this Ranger? Why was he here? Why was he riding a Cradle 6 horse?

Carlow's weapons sailed across the five-foot space, with the wrapped gunbelt holding them together. Carlow grabbed the tossed armament eagerly with both hands, now bloody and scraped. He yanked the sawed-off Winchester from its holster and cocked it in one continuous motion, letting the gunbelt and the holstered Colt fall at his feet.

Chance barked approval.

The slump-shouldered man's mouth was opened wide. His head turned slightly toward the waitress, disbelief in his eyes, then back at the young Ranger. This couldn't be happening. Dr. Holden said the man riding the Cradle 6 horse was likely someone the widow had just hired, and they would hang him under the pretense of stealing the animal.

Even Del Gato was caught off guard by the swiftness of his becoming armed. The halfbreed's face cracked for an instant into an ugly snarl, then disappeared behind a placid mask featuring that same unreadable smile. He was more surprised to see the young Ranger standing, after fighting Red Anklon. That's why Flanker's earlier threat hadn't bothered him. It was professional courtesy. But he wasn't about to be Carlow's second victim of the day. Or Flanker's first.

"Thank you, ma'am. I sure do appreciate your help. Reckon these boys would find daylight a mite more appealing," Carlow snapped. "Why don't you just mosey on out of here. Do it now. Leave your iron with the nice lady. You, too, Doc. I don't care much for your kind of medicine."

No one moved. Lacy's eyes sparkled with the stimulation of being in control. Her bosom rose and fell with the excitement within her. The bartender was as white as his apron. For one hard moment, Carlow thought the slump-shouldered man was going to draw anyway, but that thought passed from his spectacled eyes.

Del Gato held his sinister smile but didn't advance farther. A thrill of killing was behind the grin; that was easy to read. But the halfbreed was no braggard with a gun. Tomorrow would bring a sure thing. Or the next day.

Another shiver ran along Carlow's back and shoulder and into his head, reaching the wounds and immediately becoming pain. Energy was ebbing from his body as the intensity of the fight fled from him. The balance of the gun in his hand pushed back some of the ache. But his arms felt like they were tree limbs and he wouldn't be able to hold them away from his side. Air wouldn't return fast enough to his lungs and his hands were beginning to tell him that they, too, were bruised and cut.

"Hold on now, Ranger. You, too, miss." Dr. Holden cleared the shadows and held up his hands as if he were stopping a horse. His face was once again that of the kind physician. "Bless me if there hasn't been a great mistake here. These citizens came to me with the story that you were riding one of Widow Von Pearce's horses. We were naturally worried. She's had some trouble lately with rustlers. It is God's will that we help others."

The words rolled out of Dr. Holden's mouth with a smoothness that reminded Carlow of Tennessee sipping whiskey. He didn't know how anyone could talk and smile at the same time the way this man could. He half expected the blond-haired physician to break into a prayer or lead the saloon in a hymn. Dr. Holden's presence was riveting. And scary. Like some kind of white messiah. But Carlow knew he was looking at evil, and it wanted him dead.

At the bar, only the drunken beggar remained. He chuckled at Dr. Holden's remark, studied the amber liquid in the glass next to him, and then took it. A swift jerk to his mouth, and the whiskey disappeared with a gurgle. His tongue washed his buck teeth. The room was so quiet that the man's whining stomach could be heard by nearly everyone. He looked down, as if trying to determine from where the sound came. His curiosity satisfied, he resumed his new task of drinking the shots of whiskey hastily left behind when the fighting started. He grabbed each in succession with his good right hand and downed them in single, separate swallows. The purchasers had already found refuge under tables and behind chairs; three had managed to slip out the back door.

No one had moved from the poker table, where a faint "Let's get out of here" was followed by the soft, Southern "Wait, yo-all. I want to see this. Deal another hand. I'll cut. Well, all right. Just wait then. I want to watch this. Don't play with your money like that."

Tension clung to the skin of every man in the saloon. Around the nervous room came reactions to the fight. "Did you ever see anything like that?" "Red's never bin beat afore, has he?" "Is he daid?" "Look at all that blood. Did ya hear his jaw crack? That's what it were, you can bet on it." "Who is that feller?" "Them Rangers is flat-ass mean, I tell ya. You don't wanna mess with one o' them."

"He's alone," the slump-shouldered man said, his voice louder than it needed to be. "We've got to take him afore he rides back to that ol' bitch."

"Shut up, you fool," Dr. Holden snapped.

"But you . . ."

"I said . . . shut up," Dr. Holden commanded, glaring at the chastised man.

Carlow studied his adversaries and said, "Doesn't seem to me that such a fine lady as Mrs. Von Pearce would be wanting help from the likes of you." He waved the hand-carbine to take in the three gunmen. "What's it going to be? If it's a shooting you're after, I can oblige. Two of you won't leave here, though. The third will crawl."

"Oh my, son, let's not be hasty. I am a doctor of medicine. Not a gunman, for heaven's sakes." Dr. Holden cocked his head to the side.

"Bullets don't care much what you call yourself."

Chance growled low and bared his teeth again. Without looking down, the young Ranger told him to be quiet, and the wolf-dog obeyed.

Ignoring Carlow, Dr. Holden turned slowly to the others and said, "We've made a mistake, gentlemen. It's time to leave. Will someone help us carry the colonel here to my office? I believe he needs some medical attention."

The distraction was intended to make the young Ranger relax. As the doctor motioned grandly toward the unconscious Anklon on the floor, the slump-shouldered gunman reached for the Smith & Wesson .44 stuck in his belt.

Carlow's first shot drilled him low in the left shoulder, spinning the gunman sideways. Holding the sawed-off rifle with both hands, he levered a new cartridge into place and fired again. The empty shell flipped into the air. A second shot followed so quickly the two cracks sounded like one long explosion. It punched the gunman's chest and slammed him against the beggar at the bar. The collision splattered the one-handed beggar's drink across the bar, and he stared at the spreading whiskey, uncomprehending. A sad expression crowded his face.

The bespectacled gunman's pistol exploded harmlessly into the floor before slipping from his hand. Grabbing the beggar's leg, he tried to stand but couldn't. His groan was throaty and wild as he collapsed face-first to the ground. He curled himself into a ball and tried to hold his scarlet shoulder and chest. After three shallow gasps, the man lay unmoving, his eyes staring, unseeing, up at the sad-faced drunk.

As soon as Carlow fired, he levered the gun, spitting the second smoking shell into the air and aiming the weapon at Del Gato. The halfbreed hadn't moved, but Chance had already slipped from Carlow's side and stood in front of Del Gato, ready to pounce. Carlow was certain someone had warned the gunman not to draw. His mind told him the same voice had advised both gunmen only to watch when the fight started with Anklon. It had to have come from the Southern gambler playing cards. No one else in the room had that kind of guts.

Carlow glanced at him and nodded his appreciation, and the fat man grinned, touching the brim of his hat in response. Gunsmoke climbed across the gray air toward the ceiling, taking along the faint echo of the gunfire with its slow ascent. Trailing the white string came wisps of admiration and fright from onlookers.

"Better leave, honey." Lacy's voice was steady. "Do it now. But you come back, you hear? Lacy's gonna take real good care of you. Beer and cigar are on us, right, Ben? It was self-defense. Wasn't it, Dr. Holden?" From the poker table came the cold supporting words from the fat gambler, "Yo-all can assume I will testify to that . . . should the matter require further examination . . . by the authorities."

"Thanks, Jimmy." Lacy beamed, still holding the shotgun.

"Yes, thank you, sir," Carlow responded.

"That's Jimmy Ward Flanker, honey," Lacy blurted.

Carlow gulped. The name had been a part of trail stories as long as he could remember. However, the famed gunfighter didn't look a thing like Carlow had expected. Someone tall, lean, and hard was what he had envisioned.

"Our concern is not with you, Mr. Flanker." Dr. Holden didn't turn to face the known shootist. The doctor's voice had lost its pious lilt for the moment and sounded more like that of a hardened trail boss.

"Nor I with yo-all, Doc. But I do prefer a fair game. It's God's way, yo-all know. Please answer the lady."

Holden mumbled, "Ah, yes, I believe it was . . . self-defense."

"The lady—and the Range-uh—thank you, Doc," Flanker acknowledged, his devilish eyes catching Carlow's again for an instant. "As far as that big fool on the floor is concerned, Doc—the one without the bullet holes—I'd suggest you check first to see if his balls are in his mouth. Save you a lotta time. Nasty kick, that." He laughed, and his belly rolled up and down. "Whose deal is it?"

In spite of the animal-like viciousness of Del Gato facing him, Flanker's observation made Carlow want to laugh. His tongue pushed against his cheek, and he rubbed his chin with his left hand, holding the sawed-off carbine with his right. The smoking barrel continued to point its ugly nose at Del Gato's midsection. He called Chance to him, and the wolf-dog reluctantly obeyed, turning back to watch Del Gato as he did.

From outside, running footsteps closed in on the saloon door. Several shouts supported the movement. "Shots came from that saloon!" "Over here, Marshal!" "My husband's in there!" "Hurry, Marshal!"

Marshal Laetner Dillingham burst into the saloon. A

Winchester filled his hands. He had the look of a man aroused from a nap and not too happy about the interruption. His wide-brimmed hat appeared as if it had been placed on his head as an afterthought and his huge ears were wobbly flags.

In the back of Carlow's mind, a thought wiggled free. Had Dr. Holden told the marshal what was going to happen? With the lawman came a curious crowd pushing against the doorway but not caring to tread past it.

"Wha-at are yo-all a'doin' in hyar?" Marshal Dillingham demanded in his thick-syrup voice. He noticed immediately that the young Ranger's gun was now aimed at him.

As if on cue, Flanker responded first, without looking up from the cards in his hand. "Nothing really, Marshal. Nothing at all. The state constable here was forced to defend himself. According to our fair city's ordinances, he, of course, wasn't carrying a gun. The fine lady here provided that, shall we say, at the appropriate moment."

"Yo-all a' sayin' he weren't a'carryin'?" Marshal Dillingham asked sarcastically. "He were in my off-ice awhile back a'sportin' two guns, he be."

"Why, Marshal, yo-all know it's against the law to wear a weapon in town. I'm surprised at yo-all," Flanker said as he continued the card game. "Dealer takes two. 'Course he is a Range-uh—or hadn't you noticed—and the local ordinance doesn't apply to his noble status anyway. Surely, yo-all knew that. My goodness, of course, yo-all did."

Lacy spoke defiantly. "Red Anklon and his dogs came in here looking for trouble. Looks like they kinda dragged the good doctor along—without him realizing the truth of it. This fine young man would have been murdered." She pointed toward the underside of the bar. "If I hadn't thrown him his gun from here. Under the bar."

"Lacy, yo-all kin be a'puttin' that scatter-gun away now, ya hear? Is she a'talkin' straight, Doc-tuh Holden?" Marshal Dillingham's eyes darted from the bloody bodies on the floor to the doctor and back again, then to Del Gato with the evil smile, back to Lacy and her shotgun behind the bar. He avoided looking at Carlow and noticed Lacy had made no attempt to lower her gun.

Folding his arms, Dr. Holden spoke carefully. "A terrible misunderstanding, I'm afraid, Marshal. A sad one. My fine foreman, Colonel Anklon, told me he thought this young man had stolen a horse from Widow Von Pearce. She's been having some trouble that way, as you know. Things got out of hand. The colonel thought he was protecting the widow. And Mitchell, there, tried to take matters in his own hands. Poor fool, he thought he was doing right. Of course, we didn't realize this young man was a member of the state police when we first approached him. Our mistake."

"Who-ah dun shot first?" Marshal Dillingham asked tersely.

"Oh, there's no question this young man acted in self-defense." Flanker smiled as he spoke, looking directly at Carlow. "Of course, Presidio is not used to having such a shootist about. Mitchell was obviously no match for his professional skills."

"Thought yo-all was a'lookin' fer that Sil-vuh Mallow fella." The lawman tried to look fierce, but the expression was almost comical, with his ears wiggling with each word.

126

Chapter Fourteen

The young Ranger's hands were at his side, but the hand-carbine remained in his right fist. The throbbing in his forehead was reignited by this new challenge. When Carlow looked at Marshal Dillingham, the Ranger's face was hard. "I am. So far I haven't found him. Maybe Dr. Holden here can help me. It appears he knows just about everything that's going on around here. Mallow's hurt. He might need some tending—by such a notable physican."

"Looks like yo-all could be a'usin' some tendin' to yourself, Range-uh boy," Marshal Dillingham said with an appreciative grin. "Somebody's dun been messin' with yo'all's head, appears to me. Meant to ask yah be-fuh. That be Sil-vuh's work?"

Carlow responded only with his eyes, and Dillingham's smile was quickly swallowed.

A long inhalation and release preceded Dr. Holden's response. Rage glimmered in his eyes but wasn't allowed to find any other relief. "I don't care for your tone, sir. This is a small community that takes care of its own. You came riding in on one of our neighbor's horses. A well-armed stranger. I don't believe you were wearing a badge at that time, were you? You have badly injured one man and killed another. Haven't you inflicted enough pain on our town?"

Carlow's smile didn't match his words; his gaze bored into Dr. Holden's face. "That's an imaginative description of a lynching and attempted murder, Doc. Is that how you diagnose your patients' ills?"

At the bar, the buck-toothed beggar grabbed his hollow left sleeve with his right hand and muttered something no one heard. He studied the young Ranger with a strange gleam in his eyes, then shifted his gaze to Dr. Holden. The blond-haired doctor coughed and looked away from Carlow's glare, unaware of the beggar's concentration.

Continuing to stare in the direction of the big-nosed bartender, Dr. Holden skipped over Carlow's response. "I know of no such man you describe. Silver Mallow, is it? No stranger has come to my offices today. If he had, I would have informed our good marshal here. Law and order is the way of Presidio, sir."

Carlow chuckled. Chance's ears perked up, and the wolf-dog growled and started for the doorway. Carlow told him to stay. Chance held his place but continued to grumble.

"That's enough, Chance. I know what this was. No, we won't forget who tried to kill us—or why." He spoke to the animal in a conversational tone, loud enough for everyone to hear.

Marshal Dillingham asked if the young Ranger intended to ride on since he hadn't found Silver Mallow. It was clear he was hopeful that was Carlow's plan.

Carlow's reply was a knife into the taut room. "How

would you know, Dillingham? You don't seem to be able to tell the good guys from the bad. I'll leave when I'm ready."

In the far corner of the saloon, a man laughed. The drunken beggar glanced that way and burst into a forced guffaw; his extended front teeth gave him the appearance of a mule braying.

From the shadows of the saloon, a thin voice whispered, "I think that Ranger is a damn Mick."

"Damn, why would they let one o' them have a badge?" came an equally dismembered response.

"Who's gonna take it away from him? One o' you?" growled the tobacco-chewing drover standing next to them. He looked for a spittoon and finally swallowed the bitter juice, shaking his head as he did.

The drover's question brought another guffaw from the one-handed beggar, even louder this time, followed by a loud burp. He grinned and tried to do it again, but it came out a forced grunt. Flanker joined in the laughter, which brought an immediate nervous mirth from the rest of the room. Marshal Dillingham's neck blossomed crimson, his ears becoming red trumpets.

Allowing the saloon's resurging confidence to snuggle around him, the young Ranger reached down and retrieved the gunbelt at his feet. He slung it over his shoulder, letting the butt of the holstered Colt come to rest over his heart. Out of the corner of his eye, Carlow watched Del Gato for any sudden movement.

Frozen in place, the halfbreed's hands rested on a nearby table. His cold eyes indicated there would be no fight between them. Today.

"Thanks, Lacy. You saved my life." Carlow looked at her and smiled.

"Anytime, honey. Anytime." She winked.

* * *

Down the street, a black-haired man emerged from the whorehouse whistling. Immediately he stepped into the shadows lingering next to the building. The defensive move was a well-honed habit developed from being on the run. He massaged his right shoulder, trying to relieve the pain.

Sunset was attracted to the silver rings on his hands, shivering when it reached them. Erotic pleasure within the whorehouse had served only as a momentary diversion from the total soreness in his face and body. He cursed the big Ranger Kileen under his breath as he touched his swollen, bruised face and felt the empty spaces two teeth had once occupied. He ached everywhere, especially his cheekbones and ribs.

Trying to move his shoulder again, Silver Mallow expanded his cursing to include the young widow who shot him before he could kill the two Rangers. It never entered his mind that the bullet crease on his shoulder could have been much worse; he didn't hear Ellie Beckham tell Ranger Carlow later that she had been aiming for Mallow's chest.

Agitation returned to his dark eyes as they searched the town for any sign of the Texas Ranger following him. It surprised Mallow when Rellena Kahn announced the lawman was in town, searching for him; he was certain Time Carlow had been badly wounded. Or was dying. My God, he had shot him in the head! What kind of man was this young Ranger? Mallow's gang had shot him full of holes once before.

In spite of worn trail clothes, cracked ribs, a battered face, and a bullet-cut shoulder, Mallow carried himself with the air of an elegant Southern gentleman. A pearl-handled revolver was barely visible in his waistband, just above the gunbelt carrying a second holstered weapon. Still whistling, his hand slid from one weapon to the other for reassurance of their presence.

The madam's distinctive face watched him from the curtained window and smiled as he turned toward her. She held up a silver cross on a silver chain around her neck and blew him a kiss. He grinned and acted as if it had hit him in the chin, then returned to watching the street again. Although he felt undressed without it, the gift of the necklace was a small price for her help. The intensity of their lovemaking hadn't hurt, either. She had even brought a young whore into the room to sing while they enjoyed each other.

Continuing his own whistled song of "Dixie," he noticed a crowd building around the saloon. A white-shirted, skinny clerk hurried past, and Mallow stopped him with a question. "What's going on at Charlie's? I heard they had some music there."

The clerk wasn't eager to be retained, but something about the stranger's puffed face warned him to be polite. "Well, Lowry and Mickey are always there, if'n yah call that music. But there's a fight right now. Red Anklon and a Ranger."

"A Ranger? Are you sure?"

"Well, that's what I heard. There were a couple of gunshots, too. But I think it's over now." The clerk's hands waved in circles to reinforce his report. He found enough courage to add, "Goin' to see what happened. Wanna go along?"

"Thanks. You go on ahead. I'll join you in a minute."

"Say, looks like you've been in a fight, too. Are you all right?" the clerk asked curiously.

Mallow tried to smile, but it hurt when he spread his mouth. "Yeah. Jealous husband. You know how that is."

The clerk laughed, enjoying the fact he was considered worthy of having a similar encounter. He noticed Mallow's gun and commented innocently, "Ah, did you know there's . . . a law against carrying a gun in town?"

Mallow's smile was condescending but his words were controlled. "I'm leaving town."

"Oh. Sure. Say, you'd better hurry or the fight'll be over for sure. I heard the marshal's on his way," he said over his shoulder as he resumed his pilgrimage of curiosity.

Looking around to see if anyone was paying attention, the dark-haired stranger resumed his whistling and went back inside the whorehouse. A few minutes later, a man in a dirty trail coat came out and mounted a long-legged sorrel among the six horses tied to the hitching rack in front of the unmarked building. He yanked free the reins of the bay standing beside his horse and loped away, trailing the second. No one noticed the rider with a relief mount slip over the low ridges to the south of Presidio, pause beside an entangled mesquite treeline, and vanish behind them.

Back at Charlie's saloon, Chance slipped away from Carlow's side and headed for the door, uncomfortable with being inside. Carlow saw the fearful front row of the crowd and commanded the wolf-dog to return.

"Funny thing, Marshal, you asked about my guns but didn't seem to care about these men being armed." Carlow reached down to pet the obedient wolf-dog with his left hand. Chance returned the greeting with a lick of the outstretched hand. The young Ranger's right fist still held the hand-carbine; his thumb reassured him that it was cocked.

Dr. Holden's frown was brief, disappearing quickly into a practiced smile. "I believe the guns were quite justified under the circumstances, Marshal Dillingham. These men thought they were arresting a horse thief." He finished his statement by opening his coat with both hands to indicate that he wasn't carrying a gun. His eyes ordered Del Gato to disarm.

The halfbreed snorted, unbuckled his gunbelt, and let it drop at his feet.

"Kick it away, Del Gato," Carlow commanded.

A second snort preceded the halfbreed's ceremoniously pushing the holstered weapon with his boot in the direction of the bar.

"Now the gun in your boot." Carlow's challenge surprised even Del Gato. The gunman's gaze moved to Dr. Holden, but the physician broke the connection with a blink.

Del Gato hesitated, then leaned over, dropping his right hand alongside his boot.

"With your left hand," Carlow growled.

"I hardly think that's necessary. He's a law-abiding citizen." Dr. Holden crossed his arms.

Marshal Dillingham mouthed agreement.

"I'm sure he is. Just like you." Carlow raised the hand-carbine and motioned with it toward Del Gato. "Real slow. Fingers holding the butt and nothing else. Worry that no one else in the room moves—because I'll drop you first."

A snarl weaved its way across Del Gato's tightened mouth as he complied like a woman lifting a napkin with her thumb and forefinger. From the hidden holster inside his boot, a short-barreled Smith & Wesson revolver appeared. He tossed it casually next to his gunbelt.

"Nice to see what the law-abiding citizen of Presidio is wearing these days." Carlow lowered his hand-carbine.

Slapping his thigh with his only hand, the beggar roared. "*Hiccup*. That's a good one. 'Nice to see what the law-abiding citizen . . .'" He didn't finish, hiccuped, and turned back to the bar in search of more whiskey.

The big-nosed bartender gave him a look of disgust,

which the beggar either ignored or didn't see. A glance at the fat gambler preceded his refilling the one-handed cowboy's original glass. Peering intently at the two fingers of amber liquid, the beggar waved his sole arm vigorously at the bartender to continue. After it was three-fourths full, the bartender spun around and left.

The one-handed cowboy lifted the glass in appreciation. "To the Chisholm Trail. *Hiccup.*" He licked his front teeth with his tongue to savor any remaining whiskey.

Three gulps emptied it again. He set the glass down on the bar, stared as if waiting for it to fill magically once more. His bleary gaze at the bartender yielded no attention this time. Nor did his waving. His shoulders rose and fell, and he staggered around to watch Dr. Holden kneel beside the groaning Red Anklon. A low curse slipped from the beggar's lips, but no one heard it. His bleary stare went to Del Gato's weapons on the floor before recoiling to see if the bartender was going to bring more whiskey. His expression indicated the free drinking had ended.

Ignoring everyone, Del Gato sat down at the closest table and loudly told the bartender to bring him a bottle. The big-nosed man jumped as if he had been challenged to a gunfight and scurried to complete the request.

Watching the room warily, the young Ranger wondered why no one asked Flanker about his weapon, clearly visible beneath his coat. It felt as if this whole thing wasn't real and he was watching someone else, not himself. His eyes wandered toward the death-twisted face of the slump-shouldered gunman on the floor and recoiled from the sight. He had come to town seeking an outlaw. Not this. What was going on in this settlement? Was Silver Mallow somehow behind this?

No, that didn't make sense. He took a deep breath, reminding himself not to relax.

From the corner of his vision, he saw the beggar quietly squat beside Del Gato's gunbelt, start to take the short-barreled revolver, then lose his nerve and return to the bar. No one else noticed the attempted theft, except the halfbreed. Annoyed by the bartender's slowness, Del Gato appeared to be concentrating on the arrival of his bottle and glass. But his eyes slid toward the beggar, and his right hand slid from the table to his waist. A move so slow and easy that it didn't seem to exist at all. Carlow knew then he had miscalculated. Del Gato had a third gun. It must be in his waistband, under his vest.

His uncle would have told him the "little people" had arranged for the situation so that Carlow would see the third gun before it was too late. He would have reminded his young nephew that evil always comes in threes. This time Carlow found himself silently thanking the "little people" as his attention strayed to the one-handed cowboy. It seemed the miserable excuse for a man was even more shaky as he asked again for more whiskey. This time it was Lacy who responded favorably, mouthing it was on the house.

At the young Ranger's side, Chance remained quiet, but his powerful body was tensed and ready to attack. Carlow caught himself grinning. *You've got the right idea, my friend. We're not out of this yet,* he thought. Resting his hand-carbine on an empty table, he slid his gunbelt from his shoulder and under his long coat. He rebuckled it around his waist but kept the room's movement in his gaze. After returning the hammer to its safety position, he shoved new cartridges into the hand-carbine, hesitated, and holstered the reloaded weapon.

Would Del Gato try something?

Chapter Fifteen

Annoyed by the big man's ineffectiveness, Dr. Holden hovered over Red Anklon, wiping blood from his face with a white handkerchief and comforting him. Anklon's mental return to the saloon brought shock, pain, and fear to the beaten rancher's mind. He jerked back from the doctor's attention, his dazed eyes fighting to understand what had happened. Shamelessly, Anklon grabbed his groin with both hands and howled like an injured animal.

Dr. Holden cooed sympathy.

At the bar, the one-handed cowboy leaned over. "Sishsorry I am for your troubles, Anklon. S-screamin' like a little baby. D-did you pee in your pants? Or did the Ranger ram your pecker inside your belly? Peeing in your pants is a sad happenin' for a drinking man, I know. I wet all over myself just last week." He paused and added, "But you've still got both of your hands. Not like me. But I won't forget. Some day, Holden. Some day you'll get yours."

Dr. Holden stood. "Shut up" formed on his lips, but

the words didn't get any further. Instead, the short physician gave a measured proclamation: "I saved your life, you fool. Maybe you would have preferred to let the gangrene take all of you."

The disabled beggar squared off to face him, then lowered his chin and walked jerkily from the bar and out of the saloon. Dr. Holden watched the beggar leave with a strange smile on his face.

Pouring himself a full glass of whiskey, Del Gato was startled to sense someone standing close beside him. His first instinct was to reach for his remaining hidden gun. His second instinct was the one he relied on to survive: the uneasy feeling that he didn't have the edge.

"You can toss that third gun over with the others." Carlow was standing beside him, hands at his side. The message was little more than a whisper in a room blossoming with renewed conversation.

Del Gato's eyes charged at Carlow, but the rest of him was unreadable. The Ranger's coat covered his guns; could the lawman reach one as fast as he could reach his? It wasn't worth his life to find out.

"Or didn't you think I saw it?"

Del Gato's tongue ran along his lower lip as he pulled a Sharps four-barrel pocket pistol from its small holster held by a loop through his belt and nestled on the inside of his pants. He held the gun by the bird's-head grip with two fingers, hesitated, and laid the weapon on the table. With the back of his hand, Carlow slapped the pistol and sent it thumping across the floor toward Del Gato's other weapons.

A broad-shouldered businessman jumped at the noise, spilling his drink as he nervously turned toward Carlow and Del Gato. His deep sigh was an indication he was relieved that it was only the sound of a gun on the floor.

"You can go grab one, if you think you're good enough." Without saying more, Carlow walked on.

Across the room, Marshal Dillingham was gathering volunteers to help get the big rancher to the doctor's office. No one paid attention to the dead gunman or the darkening pond of blood surrounding him. Behind the bar, the bartender asked Lacy if she would get the undertaker. She told him to do it himself. His potato nose honked disbelief, but he untied his apron and headed for the back door.

Carlow strolled toward Flanker's table and extended his right hand. Wagging his tail in celebration, Chance followed at the Ranger's heels.

"Again, Mr. Flanker, I do thank you for taking my part."

"Why, anytime, anytime at all, my young friend. Call me Jimmy," Flanker responded warmly, shaking his hand. The man's ample belly wiggled with the exchange. "Range-uh Carlow, isn't it?"

"Make it Time . . . Jimmy. My friends call me Time." It seemed strange to be calling this infamous gunman by a boy's name.

Flanker's reputation was well known across Southwest Texas. Six known gunfights—and many other stories. All of his adversaries were facing him when they went down. As far as Carlow knew, there were no warrants for his arrest. Carlow was glad of that, for now.

"Why, thank you . . . Time." Laying down his hand showing three eights, Flanker added, "But I do believe you can take good care of yourself most anywhere. That's quite a weapon." He stared at the cards spread on the table and proudly announced, "Excuse me, Time. I believe the pot is mine, gentlemen."

"No problem. Maybe we'll cross trails again someday."

"Let us hope it is for a drink of friendship and that you remember my assistance this day." Flanker raked the coins, chips, and paper toward him, looked up at

Carlow, and smiled, then began placing the rewards into careful piles along with his other winnings.

"You can count on it."

"Good that it be so. Could I offer you a drink now, Time?"

"No, thanks, Jimmy. I've got a man to find."

"I almost pity that . . . Silver Mallow. I saw that, Leland. Shuffle those again. Let the ace go where it pleases." Flanker chuckled heartily as Carlow excused himself and walked to the saloon door.

After glancing back at Del Gato, who was sipping a drink, the young Ranger paused beside the marshal and the doctor, who had completed their tasks. Nearby, three men were helping a wobbly Anklon to his feet. The rancher told one of his helpers that his balls were cracked, and the man turned away, smiling. Dr. Holden's face was reddened, his mouth a thin line of disgust. Marshal Dillingham tried to appear in charge by pointing in the direction of the saloon door. No one was certain if he did it to show the men helping Anklon where they should head—or if he was hoping all the trouble would quickly leave.

"I am truly sorry for this mistake, Ranger," Dr. Holden said, his words rolling like salve on a wound. "We are all on edge due to the rustling problems."

"I hear that. Maybe you need a better marshal," Carlow said grimly, and resumed walking.

Marshal Dillingham's mouth dropped open and his arm followed, but Dr. Holden's eyes told him to remain silent.

The short physician brushed imaginary dust from his lapels and murmured in a warm, friendly voice, "Well, at least it's all over now, Ranger. You can go about your duties in peace."

Carlow couldn't agree more. Like Chance, he would be more comfortable outside. Especially away from this place. At the doorway, the curious backed up to let him pass, and many used his exit as a reason to return to their own lives.

Chance glanced backward to make certain his master wasn't being followed, then froze at the doorway. His warning growl followed.

Carlow stepped to the side of the entrance to determine what was waiting for him without revealing himself. People were moving purposely away from the saloon, dodging an occasional rider or rumbling wagon. He didn't see the one-armed beggar anywhere and shook his head in pity at the thought of the man.

Then his gaze settled on Chance's concern.

Across the street was a black man with heavily muscled ebony arms accented by a sleeveless shirt. He looked more like a pirate than a cowhand or a businessman, with a large gold earring dangling from his left ear and a red sash about his waist. His broad-brimmed hat was held in his left hand. His right hand wasn't visible behind the hat. Carlow guessed it held a gun, so the weapon wouldn't be evident to casual passersby. A second pistol was visible above the crimson band. Was he one of Dr. Holden's men? Why else would he be there? The saloon wouldn't have allowed black men inside.

Stepping back to avoid being seen, Carlow tried to find a remembered face in his mind but couldn't. Maybe the black man was an acquaintance of Flanker's; he was obviously a gunfighter. But this was not a moment to assume friendship. More likely he was the backup, assigned to stop Carlow if he managed to leave the saloon.

He turned toward the saloon and commanded, "Dr. Holden, I think you meant 'rest in peace.' There's a friend of yours—or Red's—waiting for me. Across the street."

Dr. Holden's face was pure hatred. The veins in his

forehead pounded against his skin in angry frustration. Adjusting his cravat, the blond physician spoke through clenched teeth. "I'm not sure to what you are referring, Ranger. This town is full of my friends."

"This one's black and holding a gun. Looks like a pirate. Big arms. Earring. Red sash."

From the poker table, Flanker's attention was immediate. "Well, well, that would be Viceroy. My goodness, Doc, you don't mess around, do you? He was in Houston the last time I saw him. Jamaican gentleman, I believe. Used to prize-fight. In New York and about." He nodded at Carlow and tossed his cards on the table. "I fold. Found out he could make more—killing." Glancing at Anklon, he added, "Viceroy will be sorry he missed your fight with Red there. He fancies himself quite the pugilist." He smiled mischievously. "Pugilist. That's a boxer, Marshal."

Tightly released chuckles rippled through the saloon suddenly on edge again.

"I know of no such man. Why would I?" Dr. Holden's manner had become that of the indignant citizen.

Marshal Dillingham didn't realize he had been shaking his head negatively the entire time, making his ears salute the air.

"I want you to step out first, Holden." Carlow drew his sawed-off Winchester. "Better have you come, too, Del Gato. If there's trouble, I want you in front of me. You look like a man who's fond of a man's back."

The halfbreed's plucked eyebrows rose in a snarled response to the young Ranger's insinuation.

Unexpectedly, Flanker announced with a flourish of his hand toward the bar. "Do as you wish, Time. But don't worry about our friend, Del Gato. If the boy tries anything, I personally will see that it is the last thing he does. Nice hand, William. Beats your two queens, doesn't it, Leland."

The halfbreed didn't even glance at Flanker. His grin reminded Carlow of a mountain cat's. Slowly, Del Gato downed his drink, and poured another.

"Thanks, Jimmy."

"Don't mention it. Time."

"Just you and me, Doc. I'm sure you won't mind going out first," Carlow said. "Be a nice opportunity for you to meet . . . a new friend."

"Say something, you fool," Dr. Holden snapped under his breath to Marshal Dillingham.

"Uh, yeah, uh, Range-uh, yah cain't do this." Marshal Dillingham continued shaking his head. "The doctuh, ah, he's . . . ah . . ."

"Well said." Carlow thumbed back the hammer of the hand-carbine. "You come along too, Marshal. You and the fine doctor here. We'll make it a threesome."

Excited, Lacy yelled fom behind the bar, "He's right, Marshal. It's your duty to see about this man outside." She beamed her confidence and winked at Carlow.

At the poker table, Flanker picked up his new hand, examined the cards, and tossed in a gold coin. "Price of poker just went up, gentlemen. Marshal, you'll like Viceroy. He talks real pretty." His attention stayed on the men at the table as he added, "Time . . . he can shoot with either hand."

There was no color in the lawman's face; his eyes pleaded for help but the only words from Dr. Holden were directed at Carlow. "You will regret this day, young man. I am not a citizen to be trifled with. I happen to know the governor quite well."

"Tell him howdy for me." Carlow's eyes matched the snarl in his voice. "After you."

"This is absurd." Dr. Holden grunted, shoving Marshal Dillingham out of the way as he strutted toward the doorway.

He passed Carlow without looking at him. A step before he reached the swinging doors, the physician pulled the handkerchief from his breast pocket and extended his arm so the dangling white cloth was outside before he was. Moving slowly through the entrance, he proclaimed in a loud voice, "I am Dr. Remington J. Holden—and I am an unarmed and peaceful man."

As soon as he reached the planked sidewalk, he wiped his face with the handkerchief and carefully replaced it in his coat breast pocket. A sense of relief settled on his face as the black gunfighter relaxed and nodded slightly.

Marshal Dillingham hesitated at the doorway, very uncomfortable with the rifle in his hands.

"Now you, Dillingham." Carlow's command was firm.

Chance growled a reinforcing threat.

From his back came a request from Flanker. "Oh, Marshal, tell Viceroy for me—he isn't good enough. The young Range-uh's quite superior. Tell him it's just a professional courtesy. All right?"

Marshal Dillingham bit his lower lip and looked down at the Winchester in his hands. It seemed heavy. Very heavy. He considered leaving it propped against the wall but realized he would be the brunt of jokes forever after. But that would be worth it if he could just get through this day. He shut his eyes, swallowed, and stepped out.

Chapter Sixteen

"Point your gun at his belly, Marshal." Carlow crouched slightly behind him to keep his appearance from the gunfighter. Chance was at his heels, focused on the dark shape across the street.

Slowly, Marshal Dillingham raised his rifle, holding it in both hands as if trying to tell the black man that he wasn't serious.

"Now, tell him to put on his hat," Carlow said. "Tell him it's a town ordinance, you have to wear a hat in public. Tell him anything you want—but I want to see the gun in his hand."

"But . . . ah . . ."

"Tell him."

Carlow could see through the narrow opening between the marshal's arm and body that the gunfighter's face had turned into a puzzle. The man called Viceroy twisted his head to the right and shrugged his shoulders, not understanding what the presence of the two men meant.

A slight nod of Dr. Holden's head was a signal to the gunfighter, but Carlow wasn't sure how to read it.

"You tell him, Doc," Carlow snapped.

"Me? Why me?"

Carlow's eyes flashed. "Take a guess."

Instead, Dr. Holden glared at the marshal. "Do your duty, Dillingham."

His ears wiggling compliance, the town lawman swallowed the intensity of the doctor's demand and turned back toward the imposing figure staring at them from twenty feet away.

"Ah, suh, I'd like ya to put . . . yo-ah hat on." Marshal Dillingham's voice cracked.

Carlow leaned around Marshal Dillingham so the black man could see him. The young Ranger touched the brim of his hat with the barrel of his gun as a greeting, then settled its steel nose at the black man's middle, mirroring the marshal's weapon.

A wide smile of white teeth stretched across the black gunfighter's face. He returned the hat to his head, spun the pistol in his hand, and shoved it into his sash. Laughing to himself, he turned and walked away. Carlow watched him disappear down the alley.

Marshal Dillingham grunted relief.

"I hope this satisfies you, Ranger, that I am an honorable citizen," Dr. Holden said in a conciliatory tone. "I made a mistake in listening to Red and his men—but I am no criminal. Only a humble doctor."

"You have a nice, humble way with a handkerchief, Doc."

"Well, I am not foolhardy either, sir. From the description I heard, one must always expect trouble."

"Good words to remember."

Behind them two Mexicans carried a limp body from the saloon; two other men helped Anklon stagger down the sidewalk. Dr. Holden excused himself and went over to the big rancher. The big-eared marshal looked at Carlow, then at the exiting physician, muttered something Carlow didn't understand, and walked away. Carlow tried to smile but couldn't.

He inhaled a long, jagged breath and let the anger slip into the cooling air. The town was settling into an early sunset that promised rain wouldn't be far behind. His hands throbbed from the fight, and he dared not look at them. He eased the hammer down on the hand-carbine and holstered it. The pounding sought his forehead and extended its ache to the crease there, then slid across to the bullet burn on his shoulder.

A clammy dusk clung to Carlow's nerves, and he spun toward a shadow emerging from the alley. He stood for a moment, watching and listening, letting his mind clear.

A cat.

No, Thunder, it's not a witch in disguise, he thought. *It's just a gray cat.* He shook his head. Ranger Kileen probably had some kind of belief about gray cats, too. It didn't matter. He looked again across the street. The black gunfighter was nowhere in sight. Instinctively, his gaze took in the windows. Nothing.

Growling, Chance took off after the small animal, down the alley where the cat had come from. Carlow's buckskin pawed the ground with its right front hoof and Chance skidded to a stop. Wagging his tail, he returned to check the spot where the horse was demonstrating its agitation. Carlow barely noticed the wolf-dog's activity. He wasn't yet convinced the black man had left so quickly, so innocently. A sideways glance at the doctor and marshal told him they were eager to leave the situation. The two Mexicans carrying the dead body laid it down in the street to rest a moment before continuing. Anklon was walking without assistance and the two men were dropping back.

Like the advancing threat of rain, the significance of the situation fully came to Carlow's mind. It wasn't about him at all. Not really. It was about Bea Von Pearce. They figured he was working for her; that's why they came. He wondered how many other Cradle 6 hands they had handled that way.

Of course! Why had he been so stupid? He didn't know how Red Anklon and Dr. Holden were connected, but they were. Del Gato and the other gunman were working for them. Like the slap of a glove across his face came the question: Was he going to leave Bea Von Pearce and little Hattie to the evil of Dr. Holden and Red Anklon and continue his pursuit of Silver Mallow?

That was his assignment: get Mallow. If he stayed to help Bea Von Pearce, the man responsible for killing his best friend would get away. Frustration dug into his mind, roughed up by indecision. He knew what he was supposed to do, but was it what he should do? Charlie Two-Wolves's story about a cowhand having his hand cut off by the doctor popped into his mind. Could the bucktoothed drunk in the saloon be that man? Possibly, but it didn't matter.

Chance rubbed against his leg, and Carlow bent down to recheck the powerful animal's head. The cut was dried and scabbing over. He glanced at his own hands and saw they were raw and cut. A little bloody but not much. He closed them tightly to ward off the stiffening that was sure to come.

Carlow scratched the wolf-dog's ears. "Well, boy, I don't like it either, but our job is to find Silver. Let's go back and check everything again. Hell, maybe he never came to Presidio."

Chance cocked his big head and looked at his master; Carlow figured the dog understood. He untied the reins and swung into the saddle.

Thinking about Hattie, the little girl at the Von Pearce ranch, and her not having parents had tugged out a memory locked away in his soul. It was something his Ranger uncle had said to him before a teenage Carlow rode away to help drive a herd of cattle to the railhead in Dodge City. He could see the man who cared for him as no other in this world. A huge bear of a man with a thick mustache to match barrel arms and a massive chest. "Old Thunder" Kileen had a bare-knuckle prizefighter's physical attributes: a six-foot-two, 220-pound frame; a broken nose; cauliflower ears; several missing teeth; and scarred fists the size of hams.

Standing beside sixteen-year-old Carlow mounted on a green-broke horse, the elder Texas Ranger's squinted eyes stared up—and deeply—into his young nephew's fresh face. A litany of superstitions followed, with Kileen reciting anything that might cause his young nephew a problem on the trail. Every time Carlow thought his uncle was finished, another superstitious concern would be expressed.

If Carlow came across a dead bird, he was to spit on it and keep riding. He was to watch out for a swarm of bees because this meant death was close. If the campfire turned blue, a spirit was near. A cat on the prairie was surely a witch. Of course, he should always count out his bullets and never use the thirteenth. And he should be careful never to lose a bucket; no water would be found until the bucket was secured.

If a weasel crossed his path, he was to drop a coin at that point so the evil would cling to it. But any horseshoe found would have ten times the power of any horseshoe acquired any other way. And there might come a moment when a steer would have to be sacrificed to the spirits to save the herd. However, spirits could not cross running water, so Carlow was to spit three times on the ground before crossing water at night to confuse them.

The young Ranger remembered biting the inside of his cheek so hard that it bled, to keep from laughing at all the shenanigans his uncle described. Kileen had even given Carlow the back tooth of a horse, which was very good luck, his uncle had claimed enthusiastically.

After that long-winded presentation, the hard-faced Ranger blinked twice. The young Carlow thought he was through and was glad none of the other trail riders were near to hear the goofy advice. But Kileen wasn't finished. He had one more thing to tell his beloved nephew.

Taking a deep breath, Kileen set his square jaw. "One day t'will be a stand ye be makin', me son. To your likin' it probably won't be, as to the where or when of it, laddie. But have it to do, ye will be knowin'. A man ye will be then, me son. An' wherever I be, Ol' Thunder knowin' of that stand, I'll be. An' proud as an Irishman on a fine morn in Dublin. Ride well, Time Carlow, me son. Ride well—and may the wee people ride with you."

That was before the Rangers, with Kileen's urging, offered badges to Carlow and his late best friend, Shannon Dornan.

"Maybe this is the time, Thunder. The time for me to make a stand," he murmured to himself, and wondered whatever had happened to that horse's tooth.

He patted his vest pocket where Kileen's gift of an acorn remained. The buckskin's ears twisted toward him, trying to understand the comment. He chuckled to himself at what his pockets would be like if he still had all of the things Kileen had given him over the years to keep him safe from harm.

Only last year, he discovered the crushed remains of a bumblebee in a pocket of an old pair of pants. Kileen had given him the dead insect several years before, announcing that it was the first bee of the spring and was, therefore, exceptionally lucky.

He glanced at Dr. Holden and his entourage, now a block away. Del Gato hadn't left the saloon. Standing there wasn't a good idea; the halfbreed could easily shoot from the doorway. This whole situation, with Dr. Holden and the Von Pearce ranch, wasn't his concern. Bea would have to deal with her problem as best she could. His job was to find and arrest Silver Mallow.

He was a Ranger, and Rangers followed orders.

Captain McNelly would never understand any other action. Would Kileen understand? Or was his statement years ago just the emotion of the moment? It didn't matter. He had a job to do. The captain was depending on him, had shown his confidence in him. He had sworn an oath to the memory of his best friend. With a sigh, Carlow decided to check again at the livery and the hotel, then the general store. If no sign of Silver Mallow surfaced, it meant the outlaw had fooled him and hadn't come to Presidio, and he must ride out and try to pick up his trail again.

The excited hotel clerk wanted to ask about the disturbance at the saloon, but something in Carlow's manner kept him from it. Instead, he responded to Carlow's question about any more strangers coming to the hotel. Eagerly the clerk explained two drummers had checked in since Carlow had been there.

Neither description came close to Mallow. Even in disguise. Both men were quite short, according to the clerk's hand-held measurement. The young Ranger declined an interest in going to their rooms. Nervously the clerk reminded him of the woman guest and said she had left the hotel, advising him that she was going to the millinery shop. That was an hour or so ago.

"Doesn't sound like Silver Mallow stopped at your place. Thanks anyway."

"Ah, sir, Ranger?" The clerk inhaled courage and slid a hand through his greasy hair as if to match the audacity of his next question.

"Yeah?"

"Were you . . . in that altercation at Charlie's?" The clerk continued. "Fortis Jones came in here talking all about a Ranger who beat up Red Anklon and shot Luke Mitchell. Was that . . . you?"

"No."

"Oh." The clerk was definitely disappointed. He was already thinking of the stories he would tell his friends. "Say, I've got a real nice room if you're staying over. Only a dollar. It's gonna rain, you know."

"No thanks. I'll be riding on. Doesn't look like the man I'm after came to town."

"But . . . you're wounded." The clerk motioned awkwardly toward Carlow's head. His hand barely paused before nervously retreating.

"Yeah. I am."

"A-and your hands . . . they're all cut. I'll get you some water."

"No thanks. I'm not thirsty."

The clerk's face jerked into a mechanical smile reserved for special guests and looked past Carlow. "Well, good day, Mr. Flanker. Didn't expect to see you so soon, sir."

Carlow turned to see the heavyset shootist standing in the doorway. He was more slump-shouldered than Carlow had realized. Flanker's ruddy, round face appeared like it was about to burst. His light brown eyebrows were nearly invisible over narrow, impish eyes that could turn hard and cruel faster than a bullet. He brushed at an imaginary fleck on his lapel.

"Thought I'd give the locals a bit of a break," Flanker grunted. "Besides, I haven't had any sleep since two days ago."

"Your regular room is ready, Mr. Flanker."

"I take it that means there are new pillows, new sheets, and a fresh bottle of whiskey as I requested." Flanker's expression remained unchanged. "Oh, and swept out good. There was a cobweb in the corner last time I was here."

"Oh yes, sir. Everything is just like you asked." The clerk looked like he was trying to remember about any cobwebs.

"Sounds acceptable," Flanker said, and nodded at Carlow. "Range-uh Carlow . . . Time . . . may I have a word with yo-all, suh?"

"Of course." Carlow saw no need to tell him that he was searching for Mallow; the gunfighter would know that.

Flanker's gaze took in the curious clerk who quickly found importance in his ledger.

Without looking to see if Carlow was following, the heavyset shootist walked toward the small adjoining restaurant. "Noticed yo-all's beer was interrupted back there. How about a try at somethin' to eat? This place has more than passable beef stew." His movements were steady but slow, as if an older man than he was.

Carlow liked the idea but it wasn't what he should be doing. "Another time, Jimmy. I need to find an outlaw."

Flanker nodded and stopped. "Of course. I should have known you'd be locked into duty. That's fine. I just didn't want anybody else to hear what I have to share. Then yo-all can be on yo-all's way again."

The message was free of sarcasm, simply a statement

of fact, or that's how Carlow read it. Or was it how he wanted to read it?

"I could use some coffee, how's that?"

"Excellent. Excellent."

Chapter Seventeen

Only three soldiers occupied the small hotel restaurant; they ate quietly at the farthest table. Flanker and Carlow sat at the first table in the room, and the thick-bellied gunfighter immediately waved at the waitress, calling her by name.

She brushed her hair with her hand and scurried over to them. Her soiled apron covered a dress that had long ago given up its shape. The stale brown cloth hung on her skinny frame.

"First, Wanda, honey, we need the table wiped off. See those crumbs? And that ring from somebody's coffee cup?" Flanker pointed.

"I'll get a rag, Mr. Flanker. Just take a minute."

"Of course, Wanda. I know it was an oversight." His smile cut his oval face in half. "Then, we'll take a pot of coffee. Fresh. Two cups, all right, honey?" Flanker winked. "Make sure they're nice an' clean."

"Oh yes, Mr. Flanker. Right away," she gushed, and fluttered her stubby eyelashes and timidly added, "We have a gooseberry pie. Just out of the oven. Smells real good." She glanced toward the kitchen. "Mr. Wilkinson said to tell you about it."

Flanker grinned. "Excellent. I'll take a big slice of that. Range-uh, suh, would yo-all's duty allow for that?"

"Sure. Sounds good."

"Two big slices then, Wanda. Make sure Wilkinson added a swipe of cream and sprinkled cinnamon on top, like I showed him last time."

She smiled her best smile and left. The expression reminded Carlow of a horse showing its teeth when annoyed.

As soon as she was out of earshot, Flanker declared in his soft Southern drawl, "Range-uh Carlow . . . Time . . . yo-all need to be watchin' your back. Yo-all really stirred up a hornet's nest by messin' in the good doctuh's business."

"Seems to me the hornets came after me."

"Yeah, they did at that." Flanker laughed, low and laced with old whiskey. "Yo-all handle yourself well, Time, if yo-all don't mind my sayin'."

The conversation ended as the waitress returned with a wet rag wrapped over her arm and carrying the coffeepot, cups, and pie. She set them down on the adjoining table and wiped off their table ceremoniously, going over the uneven surface twice, then presented the coffee and pie with her best flourish.

"Can I get you anything else?" It was an invitation delivered with the same horselike smile.

Flanker didn't respond, pouring coffee for both.

Carlow grinned politely. "We're fine. Thanks."

Her own smile seemed to say she couldn't decide what she should do next. The cook told her to ask if they wanted any supper. That was easy to suggest in the kitchen. Standing next to the two dominating men, it was a different issue. She had heard the story about the handsome young Ranger's victorious fight. He was courteous but distant, and the thick-bellied gunfighter was interested only in examining the pie to see if it met his standards. But what if they became angry at her? The decision was made. She curtsied awkwardly and left, not daring to ask anything.

Without looking up, Flanker asked, "How'd yo-all know Del Gato had a third gun?"

Carlow was surprised at the question. "Saw it . . . when he moved. Should've checked earlier. . . ."

"Not many carry three guns."

"Only takes one." Carlow tasted the coffee. It was definitely fresh. A cut above most restaurant brew.

"Yo-all carry two."

"So do you."

Flanker's thin eyebrows lifted in amused appreciation. "I do?"

"In your coat pocket, a small gun. A derringer, probably."

"Very observant, Range-uh Carlow. Very observant." Flanker looked up, his eyes flashing. "Good coffee, isn't it. Gave them the recipe myself. Has an egg in it. That's Swedish style, I believe."

"Real fine." Carlow took another sip. What did this notorious shootist want? His uncle would be angry that he was even talking with him. He could hear his Irish expletives now.

"Try the pie, Time. Just the right mix of crust and filling. Melt in your mouth, it will," Flanker advised. "Yo-all can't find a better pie maker in Texas. No suh."

Carlow was intrigued but growing impatient. He ate the pie quickly and washed it down with more coffee, hoping it would accelerate Flanker's getting to the point.

"Do you use the same cartridge in both the carbine

and the Colt?" Flanker asked. "May I see the Winchester? Here's my Merwin." He withdew the gun from his shoulder holster and held it toward Carlow, butt first. It was a pearl-handled Merwin, Ulbert and Company revolver, double-action. A beautifully made six-gun, Carlow thought from just his first glance.

"Ah, sure. Sure." Carlow took Flanker's gun in his left hand, pulled his sawed-off carbine from its holster rig, and presented it to the fat gunfigher with the gun sideways in the palm of his hand.

Carlow examined Flanker's Merwin revolver, liking its weight and feel. The gun had been quite popular throughout the West, even considered once by the U.S. military for its official sidearm, and was the pistol of choice for Union Pacific Railroad guards.

"It's got perfect balance; well, nearly so. A gunsmith in Houston worked on it—to my specifications," Flanker commented as he studied Carlow's weapon, raising the circular lever slightly, then easing it back into place. "Somebody good made this. An' yo-all handle it with the care it deserves. Did it take long to master? How much does it kick when you use it one-handed?"

"A little more jump than a Colt. Not much though." Carlow didn't like being quizzed like this. Was Flanker evaluating his chances against him?

Carlow handed the pistol back to the fat man, growing uncomfortable with the situation. Was this a ruse? Had Mallow engaged Flanker to keep him under watch? Or delay him? It didn't seem likely, still . . .

"I've got to get going, Jimmy. I've got to find Mallow, that's my assignment. My first . . . alone," Carlow said as Flanker returned the hand-carbine.

"Oh, of course. Of course. How rude of me," Flanker replied. "I just wanted to share something I thought yo-all should know."

With that, Flanker tilted his head to the side, crossed his arms in front of his massive belly, and proceeded to tell Carlow about Dr. Holden. Carlow holstered his gun and leaned forward to listen. Flanker's presentation was as measured as his earlier requests from the waitress. The doctor's father had built the hotel, the Rio Grande saloon, and the original Bar H. Both were immensely successful ventures. But his son never had any interest in lodging or cattle, only in the wealth they brought. Not long after Dr. Holden returned from New Orleans with his new wife, his parents died. Flanker's face indicated neither were natural deaths.

"Ol' man Holden was tough but fair, so I've heard. Young Holden only got as far as the tough part," Flanker declared and picked up the coffeepot, offering to pour more for Carlow.

The young Ranger muttered, "No thanks," and the fat man filled his own cup.

After sipping the added brew, Flanker continued, saying that the loss of his parents made Dr. Holden a wealthy man overnight. That was five years ago. Dr. Holden had gradually expanded his cattle operation by taking over three smaller ranches. His current target was the Cradle 6. With it, he would own all of the significant year-round water and the best pastureland for a hundred miles. Red Anklon was Mrs. Holden's brother; a cruel, sadistic rancher who ran the Bar H like a military post.

Flanker thought the Bar H riders were mostly solid cowhands left over from the elder Holden's days, with a small group of outlaws brought in to help expand Holden's hold on the region. Del Gato and Mitchell were the best known of the group. Viceroy, the black gunfighter, had evidently just been hired; Flanker hadn't seen him before today. He surprised Carlow most by telling him that the physician had secretly underwritten Kahn's pleasure house and took good profits from it, as well as enjoyment, especially with Black Bethinia. He didn't think anyone of significance in town was aware of either fact.

Questions shot from Carlow. "How do you know all this? Didn't you just get into town? Why are you telling me?"

Chuckling, the fat man pushed his fork against some remaining crumbs on his plate and placed them in his mouth. "Hmmm, mighty good." Without hurrying to respond, he sipped his coffee, put down the cup, and leaned forward. His slitted eyes caught Carlow's and held them. "Old habit, listenin'. Ran into the big colonel, Red Anklon, two days ago—at Kahn's. Just after I got here. Being with a woman loosens up a man, yah know. Makes him talkative. That and some whiskey at that excellent bar of theirs. He told me pretty much everything."

"That's one answer." Carlow made no attempt to look away. If this was the beginning of a fight, so be it.

Flanker threw his head back and guffawed so loudly the troopers at the far table looked up and the waitress hurried from the kitchen. She stopped as she cleared its door.

"Yo-all are a man to stand with, Time Carlow," Flanker said, shaking his massive head. "I'll bet it never entered your mind that Red might whip yo-all, did it?"

Carlow wasn't certain how to respond. Of course he had been afraid. That's what drove a man sometimes. The fear of losing. Only a fool didn't know fear. "It entered my mind. Just didn't see much use in the idea."

Flanker pursed his lips and the smile returned. This time it was curled higher on his right side. "I like yo-all, Range-uh Carlow. Like the way yo-all handled things in the saloon. I guess that's why I wanted to make sure yo-all knew what was goin' on. Had a feelin' yo-all would care—about the widow."

"Thanks. I believe you, Jimmy." It still felt strange to call this imposing figure of a man by a boy's name, but it was beginning to feel more natural. "But I'm only interested in Silver Mallow." He let the words settle in his mind but they didn't want to. "If he's not in Presidio, I've got to find him. The problems around here aren't my business." He swallowed, not liking his own statement.

"I haven't seen this Silver Mallow fellow. Yo-all been after him a long time?"

Carlow explained his history with the outlaw, including the murder of his best friend.

"Well, don't count on ol' Big Ears, the marshal. I figure Holden's got him paid off—or just buffaloed," Flanker said, studying the young Ranger.

"I read it the same way." Carlow reached into his vest pocket and retrieved two coins.

"Let me get this, Time." Flanker held out his hand to stop Carlow's movement. "Least I can do. I won a hundred on the fight, bettin' on yo-all."

Carlow stood, letting the coins hit the table. "Next one, Jimmy."

"Watch your back, my young friend."

"I always do." Carlow held out his hand.

Flanker shook it vigorously. "I hope we meet again—as friends."

"So do I, Jimmy."

"It wouldn't be a fight either of us would walk away from, yo-all know."

Carlow nodded, not caring for the comment but acknowledging to himself that the gunfighter was probably right.

As Carlow left, Flanker reverted to an earlier subject,

Bea Von Pearce. "Time, I understand duty. I really do. No disrespect, but I believe yo-all do be carin' about that widow. She won't be able to hold on long. Yo-all know that as well as I. Heard she's down to five hands—plus some crazy Indian who lives at the ranch."

Carlow's mouth tightened but no words came as he continued his exit. He heard Flanker calling to the waitress for a large bowl of stew. "Make sure it's hot. Lots of vegetables. No pepper. Got any fresh bread? Bring a bottle of your best, too."

The young Ranger smiled and the clerk said something that Carlow nodded a response to, without caring what was said, and studied the far side of the street before stepping onto the sidewalk. Where could Mallow be? Finding him now—if he was in town—would mean Carlow could ride back to help the old widow, assuming Marshal Dillingham could be trusted to hold the outlaw in his jail. Carlow's threat if something happened might be enough to make it so.

Outside he stepped quickly into a deep shadow and studied the buildings across the street, then around him, to assure himself Del Gato wasn't waiting. Or the black gunfighter.

At the livery, a pimple-faced stableboy of fourteen or younger told him only the mayor had rented a horse so far today. He stared at Chance, gulped, and whispered, "That a wolf, mister?"

Carlow smiled. "Sometimes."

The boy stared back at the young Ranger and frowned, but his eyebrows lifted as he recalled something. "Say, a stranger done left his hoss hyar. A while after ya was by."

"Well, good. Let's take a look, son."

"Yessir. It's a brown. Sort of."

They walked to the stall, passing horses eager for attention or oats. Probably the latter, Carlow thought.

When they reached the stall of the stranger's horse, the boy turned to the young Ranger and said, "Hyar 'tis. Not much fer lookin', I suppose. The feller who brought 'er said he was gonna sell 'er. She was limpin' a mite when I led 'er back hyar. Jes' a lost shoe, though."

Carlow wasn't certain whether he was happy or sad. The horse was definitely not one of Von Pearce's mounts. The sway-backed mare looked as if it couldn't run if the whole world were on fire. His mind was working on a rationalization about why it was all right to let the outlaw get away for the time being—and return to help Bea Von Pearce. After all, his duty was to all Texans. Not just a few. Bea was a Texan who needed help. And she needed it now. Even if she didn't want it. He pushed away the rationalization. No. His assignment was to get Silver Mallow.

"You think the owner's coming back?" Carlow asked, running his hand over the mare's nose.

"Ah . . . prob'ly not. Only paid me twenty cents." The stable boy noticed the red cuts across Carlow's knuckles and knew what had happened.

"Here." Carlow reached into his pocket and retrieved several coins. "This should pay for at least three, four months. Right?"

"Oh, yes, sir! Yes, sir."

"I'll be coming back—an' I want to see that mare well taken care of when I do."

"Yes, sir. I'll even get iron fer her back foot. No extry charge. You'll see."

"I'm counting on it."

"Ah, you need some water . . . ah, to put your hands in? Looks like ya done hit something."

"Yeah, I did. Accident. It's all right, though. Thanks."

Outside Chance greeted him eagerly. Carlow's gaze took in the Holden Apothecary across the street. There was no sign of the halfbreed killer, but that would be Del Gato's style. An examination of the windows in the lone second-story building directly across the street yielded nothing ominous. Would the black man who looked like a pirate be waiting somewhere? Viceroy? Wasn't that his name? Jimmy Ward Flanker knew him. He glanced back at the buckskin, and his attention slid to the dark brand on its pale flank. If Dr. Holden and Red Anklon came after him because he was riding a Cradle 6 horse, why didn't they go after Silver Mallow when he came in earlier? Or did they? The only ones who could answer that were Dr. Holden and Red Anklon.

By now the yellow-haired physician should be back in his office, tending to his beaten brother-in-law. Maybe they would tell him the truth, if he made it clear his only interest was to find out if there was an earlier stranger on a Cradle 6 horse. Why not ask?

Chapter Eighteen

Anger stutter-stepped at the back of his mind as Carlow told himself it would do no good to put them on notice that he knew they were after the widow's ranch. It would only accelerate their plans, and he wouldn't be around to help her. Accepting the awkwardness of his task, he left the buckskin tied where it was, ordered Chance to stay with the horse, and walked across the street.

An older man greeted him as he reached the raised sidewalk. Carlow returned the salutation and stepped inside the store. Three couples looked up with mild curiosity before resuming their shopping. Everywhere he looked were shelves lined with rows of colorful apothecary containers, cod-liver-oil bottles, patent-medicine packages, pressed soaps, and glass jars containing touted combinations of herbs. Scattered among them were other displays of bolted cloth, pots for cooking, cigars, tobacco sacks and plugs, men's hats, and shoes for both men and women. Glass showcases throughout the store displayed a wide variety of merchandise, from perfume and fine linens to jewelry and eyeglasses. Gas lamps on the walls gave the store a mysterious glow.

Dr. Holden wasn't in sight. There was a door in the back. That must be his office, Carlow thought. He could barge in but preferred a less aggressive approach. It made more sense for what he needed from them. A woman, blocked by several customers, was handling the cash register. She was currently helping an older couple. Yellow light from an overhanging gas lamp on the far wall desired only to touch her amber hair. But some of the glow dared to reach beyond, to the counter, where it highlighted a stone mortar and pestle, a large pill press, and a brass balance scale.

Carlow paused to read a label on a medicine bottle, then another, waiting for customers to clear so he could ask the lady clerk about the doctor. All of the labels and boxes were adorned with gushing guarantees to cure everything from indigestion to consumption, from liver and bladder ailments to "female diseases" to childhood disorders. Hall's Catarrh Cure even offered a "One hundred dollar reward for any case of catarrh that can't be cured with Hall's Catarrh Cure."

There was Hood's Sarsaparilla, Quinine Sulfur, Ayer's Cherry Pectoral and Ayer's Cathartic Pills, Dr. Pierce's Favorite Prescription, Hostetter's Celebrated Stomach Bitters, Dr. Kilmer's Swamproot Kidney Liver Bladder Cure, Cuticura Antipain Plasters, Microbe Killer, Kickapoo Indian Sagwa, Dr. John Bull's Worm Destroyer, Warner's Safe Kidney Liver Cure, Lydia E. Pinkham's Vegetable Compound, Hamlin's Wizard Oil and Balm of Childhood.

He noticed an old remedy from his childhood, Tuscarora Rice, and read the bottle: "the said Corn so refined is also an Excellent Medicine in Consumptions & Other Distempers." He smiled. "I guess ground-up corn couldn't hurt you," he mumbled to himself.

Many medicines proudly proclaimed they contained cocaine or opium or both. Mrs. Weenlow's Soothing Syrup for infants made certain everyone knew it contained the newest miracle cure, morphine. Next to it were six different toothache powders, plus an elongated bottle of toothache drops with cocaine. Below them was an entire row of catarrh medicines for relieving head and chest congestion. Another cluster of bottles held cocaine-containing medicinal wines.

Reminded by the plethora of medicines, he ran his fingers along the scabbed line on the side of his forehead. It was tender and full of heat but had ceased to throb. At least for the moment. However, his knuckles were in more than enough pain, and he rubbed his hands together to ease the soreness. His shoulder wound had become a mere annoyance.

Two customers left, but six more crowded around the woman. He could see only the top of her head and an occasional glimpse of her sleeved arms moving briskly. Her voice sounded pleasant and friendly, calling the customers by name and adding warm greetings or questions about each one's family. "Good afternoon, Mr. and Mrs. Hildingham. You are both looking well. Oh, really? Well, that should help. Yes, Dr. Holden prescribes it often for that. How is Matilda? Oh, that's so good to hear. Please greet her for me."

Trying to act busy, Carlow picked up a bottle of Lydia E. Pinkham's Vegetable Compound. He had heard about the stuff. Some said it contained 15 to 20 percent alcohol. However, its label proclaimed a much different story: "A sure cure for PROLAPSUS UTERI, or falling of the womb and all FEMALE WEAKNESSES including leucorrhoea, irregular and painful menstruation, inflammation and ulceration of the womb, flooding . . . for all weaknesses of the generative organs of either sex, it is second to no remedy that has ever been before the public, and for all diseases of the kidneys it is the GREATEST REMEDY IN THE WORLD."

"I don't think that's going to be much help for that head wound. You need Dr. Holden's own special salve. It's over there."

Carlow looked up and was stunned. Standing near him was the most beautiful woman he'd ever seen. Shadows raced to embrace the stunningly attractive store clerk now a few feet away. His earlier glimpses of her reddish brown hair had not prepared him for such a sight.

She ruled the room with her regal presence and engaging charm. Cradled in her arms was a gray cat. Carlow thought it looked like the stray from the alley by Charlie's saloon. He wasn't certain, though; his attention had been on other concerns. This animal had a solitary darker gray stripe down its chest; he couldn't remember if the alley cat did or not.

A rose glow touched the clerk's rich cheeks, but it was from working, not powder. Her eyes were turquoise, accented by thick lashes that blinked charm, and burned with a secret only she knew. Any man would be greatly blessed to see one such woman in his lifetime. She smelled of lavender—and of woman. Her appearance rattled his mind and sent a tingle to his loins.

Although her hair was pulled back in a bun, rich amber ringlets lined her forehead; several had broken free, cascading down onto her shoulders. A white apron covered her blouse and skirt but couldn't hide her ample bosom, and she knew it, keeping her shoulders back and straight.

The magnetic clerk seemed oblivious to her effect on

men, or was she simply no longer surprised by her lustful appeal? Perhaps she was immune to a man's advances, for there was something about her that Carlow couldn't quite figure. A hint of coldness in those blue-green eyes. A wall of arrogance. Or superiority. Or was it a hint of madness?

Carlow sensed no man could ever reach her heart. She reminded him of a perfect pink rose frozen in an unexpected spring snow he'd seen a few years ago. Unable to change or grow, pale petals were held in place by the frigid cold. It was outside a small family's homestead near the Red River. Other flowers were similarly trapped in a small garden beside their house, but only the pink rose continued to lurk in the back of his mind. Something about it connected with his soul. Was it to be the same with this woman, a frozen pink rose of femininity?

Carlow closed his open mouth and swallowed his awe. "Actually, I was hoping to see Dr. Holden himself for a minute."

Her indifferent gaze changed almost imperceptibly to a wary one. "Aren't you the Ranger from the fight at Charlie's?"

"Yes, ma'am, I am."

"I saw what you did to my brother. You should be ashamed. Red's a fine gentleman." Her voice was cold, almost demanding.

"Afraid he gave me no choice, ma'am. He wanted to tear my head off. Is the doctor's office through that door?" Carlow's mind caught up with the fact she called Anklon her brother. Was this Dr. Holden's wife?

"Did you kill Mr. Mitchell?" The clerk's turquoise eyes snapped with accusation.

Carlow's irritation was growing. "If he was slump-shouldered, wore eyeglasses, and pointed a gun at me,

I did. He didn't introduce himself before he tried to kill me."

Her unexpected response was a cozily warm smile that dissolved his frustration. But the sweet glow didn't come from her eyes, which remained aloof and vacuous.

She said softly, "I'm sure he didn't. Remmy told me all about it. He was quite sorry to be pulled into the affair. He was told you had stolen one of Mrs. Von Pearce's horses." Her eyes began to probe Carlow's for more than attention, but he couldn't read her intentions. "Of course, Presidio is not used to having someone riding into town as well armed as you. A stranger on a neighbor's horse. Surely you understand."

"It doesn't matter what I understand."

"Did one of them do that?"

For an instant, he didn't realize she was referring to the bullet burn on his forehead. His attention was focused on the realization that she had referred to Dr. Holden in a way that suggested a close relationship. This had to be the doctor's wife.

"Remmy said he couldn't stop them from—"

"No, this came from an outlaw I'm trailing," he interrupted, touching his forehead as he responded. "Your husband is Dr. Holden, I presume."

"Well, yes, of course. I'm Jessica Anne Holden." Her eyes stalked his face, hunting for lost secrets.

The intensity of her gaze made him uncomfortable. Yet the close attention of such a beautiful woman played with his emotions, sending shafts of red up the back of his neck.

"It's nice to know you, Mrs. Holden. . . ."

"My friends call me Jessie."

Carlow grinned. "Well, I sure would like to be your friend . . . Jessie. I'm Time Carlow."

"Time. Oh, what an interesting name." Her hand

touched his arm. He sensed it was calculated, not spontaneous. As if she knew well the effect it would have. The same effect her touch had on all other men. "Your mother must've had a strong vision to have such a name come to her. She wants to tell me about it, I can tell."

"My mother is dead."

"I know. She has talked to me about you."

From a black place in his mind roared a revelation. This had to be the wicked woman Charlie Two-Wolves had talked about. The devil woman from the moon. A murderer. Could that be? The recognition punched into his consciousness so hard that he almost blurted out the words. Kileen told him the spirits talked with humans all the time but rarely did people listen. A person's sudden insight, or an uncanny sense of what was to be, came from the spirits talking, his uncle would solemnly advise. He would have proclaimed her to be a witch and warned his nephew to not look her in the eyes because she could easily put him under a spell. Two-Wolves would have said the same. Or worse.

Crossing his arms, Carlow took a deep breath to rid himself of the urge to tell her what he thought, and said, "I'd like to ask your husband if he—or your brother—saw another man ride in on a Cradle 6 horse. This morning. Before I came. I'm after that man. He's a murderer, among other things."

"A murderer? Did he kill poor Mrs. Von Pearce?" Jessie's voice was heavy with concern, but her eyes wished for an affirmative answer.

"No. He killed my best friend and another Ranger. He and his gang."

Briefly, Carlow told her about trailing Silver Mallow after his breakout from the Bennett jail and about the outlaw's getting a fresh horse from the Von Pearce ranch this morning. He explained about Mallow's attempted ambush and losing his trail close to Presidio.

She listened intently, as if he were the only man in the world, and she, the only woman. Part of his recitation was pulled by her magnetism, but part of it was also the sense that if she believed he didn't intend to pursue her husband, she would let him advance. At least that's what he told himself.

Warnings from Carlow's subconscious hammered at him as her manner changed to one of subtle seduction. He wasn't sure if her sensual attention was to see if she could make him another conquest or just an extension of her uncommon beauty. It was difficult to concentrate with her gaze caressing his face, for a tiny message kept assuring him that she was actually attracted to him. Worse, it was a message he wanted to believe. Yet, he knew it wasn't true.

His mind battled to stay clear of the lust that sought to consume all of his reasoning. He told himself again that she was an evil woman and had no interest whatsoever in him. Nor should she. Jessie Holden was a married woman! To himself, he recited what Two-Wolves had said about her. *Devil woman from the moon. Devil woman from the moon. Devil woman from the moon.* According to him, she had killed a German couple, cut off their ears, and marked their faces in their own blood. Once he almost spoke the words out loud to strengthen his resolve as she took another step closer.

"Looks like you're a very lucky man, Time Carlow. The spirits care about you, don't they? Yes, they do. I can see why. Your hands, oh, they are hurting, aren't they?" Her fingers lightly touched his head wound, then slid down his face, passing over the edge of his lips, and the sensation raced to his groin. She took his hands gently in her fingers and examined the results of the fight.

He was afraid to look down at his pants, certain that a bulge would be there.

Chapter Nineteen

"Remmy should have a look at your head—and your hands. You should be in bed, instead of running around." Her smile followed the word "bed," and her eyes lowered to his groin, then back to his face. Her eyes glittered with victory, and the crimson flickers at his neck swooped onto his face. She returned her hand to the cat in her arms and slowly stroked its arching back.

Behind them, a heavyset woman with eyeglasses and a bonnet resting off-kilter on her head urgently asked where the lavender soap was located. Carlow noted that the woman smelled faintly of freshly cut hay and manure.

Fixing a caring smile on her face, Jessie pointed in the direction of a long shelf displaying soaps of different sizes, colors, and wrappings. She added, "That's my favorite, too. Doesn't it smell wonderful? You know, the men like it too."

The woman bit her lower lip and exclaimed agreement, joyous to be included in Jessie Holden's assessment.

After watching to see that the woman went to the right place, Jessie turned back to Carlow and said, "Remmy's with my brother now, but I'll go ask him—or do you want to wait and talk with him yourself?"

Coldness laced her question, as if she had discovered Carlow could be hers and the experiment was now over. Carlow rubbed his chin to buy a moment to consider how he should answer. If he let her take the message to Dr. Holden, it might carry the innocence he needed for an honest response. He reminded himself that his job was to find Mallow, not interfere in a possible local land situation. Dr. Holden was not his responsibility. Neither was his wife. Ellie Beckham skipped into his mind, and he silently told her to wait for him and not to worry about his momentary attraction to this spellbinding woman.

"Oh, I know he's busy. If you wouldn't mind asking him—and Red—that would be great." Carlow added, "Jessie, I know they were given the wrong information about me. But I was glad to see citizens caring about an old woman. I've seen many towns that wouldn't."

Her smile was again a devastating combination of sweetness and mystery. Come-hither yet cold at the same instant. She leaned over and released the cat to the floor. The animal purred and wrapped itself around her high-buttoned shoes. After straightening herself, Jessie touched his arm again. The tingling of her fingers on his skin followed her burning eyes toward the silver chain barely visible around his neck.

Seeking permission with a faint smile, she pulled the Celtic cross from beneath his shirt. Her eyelids closed. Both hands held it tightly for a tantalizing moment. She opened her eyes. Her gaze was fixed on some other place, some other time. Carlow was puzzled by the performance but said nothing.

"This . . . was your father's. He was . . . a great warrior." Her voice was an unsteady whisper, as if forced through eternity. "His spirit stands close. So does your mother's. The fullness of the moon brings them so. She worries about you. Another Irish warrior of this world . . . rides with . . ."

Jessie stopped in midsentence and blinked. Her eyes were huge; a glaze covered them like the veil of a just-cast-off deep sleep. She released the cross, her fingers pausing against his exposed chest hair. Carlow took a half step back to avoid the words reaching his mind. But they did anyway. *Who is she? How does she know about my father? My mother? Thunder?*

A wistful smile dawned on her face. Beads of perspiration followed on her upper lip. Acting as if nothing had happened, she said blandly, "I'll be right back."

Carlow watched her disappear into the office, with the gray cat happily trailing behind her. He fought to regain his composure. Had she actually gone into a trance? He was sweating, but he was chilled, and his head wound was pounding again. The hammering was enough to force him to balance himself with an outstretched hand against a display of bowls and containers.

Although he had never seen one, he knew about spiritualists, so-called mystics and mesmerists. It seemed like spiritualism had sprung upon the land sometime before the war and had even been embraced, in some cases, by serious ministers and zealous churchgoers. Some champions of women's rights had been drawn to spiritualism as well, or so he had heard.

Perhaps Jessie Holden was such a leader; she seemed quite suited for it, he thought. Before Carlow joined the Rangers, his uncle had arrested a "professor of Egyptology" over in San Antonio; the man was bilking older people out of their money to reach dead loved ones.

Most of the "high arts of the ancients" were actually well-practiced magic shows, parlor ghost tricks, and clever charades. Some of these spiritualists were quite gifted at reading people for clues or even getting them to talk about something personal without realizing it. A light trance, some said. Hypnotism, he thought it was called. Had she hypnotized him and he hadn't even known it?

He was breathing hard. The thought of reaching his dead parents, or of their spirits being close, had never occurred to him. The idea sounded more like something a Comanche believed. Like Two-Wolves. Or his late Apache friend, Kayitah. Or someone superstitious like his uncle. What was this woman up to? Had she just guessed correctly? Was there someone in town who knew him? Silver Mallow? Mallow could've heard about his past from Kileen while the outlaw was in the Bennett jail. He pushed out his jaw and shook his head. This was silly. He was letting her get inside his mind.

A wall of memories rushed into his consciousness, like water bursting through a broken dam. Gleaming spray revealed glimpses of yesterday. One shard of memory might have been his father, but that couldn't be. His father died on shipboard headed for America, leaving a pregnant young wife with no money or hope. The young Ranger was depressed and elated at the same time. His mother put her arms around him.

He shook his head and tried to concentrate on something else. He must. Something earthly. Something real. It did no good to analyze what had just happened. Dr. Holden's wife's beauty masked evil, he told himself. Her husband was a bad man; why should he expect anything different from his wife? He was answered by a voice within his mind. Or was it? The voice said she was close to the spirit world. He shook his head again and his head wound rattled with pain.

With great deliberation, he made himself walk over to the display of cigars lined up carefully in a large box. He remembered tossing his cigar at the saloon and decided to buy several for the trail. It gave him something to do while he waited. He lifted three from the container and saw her reenter the store from the unseen office. As she walked briskly toward him, her eyes sought to embrace his, and Carlow felt like his mind was being pulled from his head. Her cat bounded along, playing a game with her moving feet.

"Remmy said that you were the only one who's come to town on a Cradle 6 horse in weeks. That's what made them suspicious. He told me to apologize to you again—and to give you this." She held up her hand and opened it to reveal a small jar of salve. Her voice and manner were normal and casual. "He said to put this on your head wound and your knuckles. There is no charge. He said it was the least he could do."

Carlow accepted the jar and thanked her.

"Of course, I think little of man's medicine myself," she said. "There is an unseen world of spirits that can do so much more. All one has to do is ask them to come. They are all around us, especially in the glorious resurrection of the moon's power that comes with a full moon. Do you believe in spirits, Ranger Time Carlow?"

She stepped closer to him, her gaze never leaving his face, not waiting for his response. There was an urgency in her manner; a strange gleam returned to her eyes. A triumphant sparkle. Her back straightened, and her bosom reached out to him. "The stones in your pocket. They are a connection to your friend. Your dead friend. He wants me to tell you he is happy that you are going after his killer." She was staring. But not at him. She was focused on the ceiling. For a moment, she ruled him completely.

Licking his lips, Carlow said with a forced grin, "Did he like what I had for lunch?"

He might as well have hit her in the stomach with his

fist. Her eyes flew at him with a wild rage beyond reason. He thought she was going to slap him. But her hand stopped as it started to rise from her side, as if by an unseen force. A polished mask quickly slipped over her anger.

Her cat discovered the fringe on his Kiowa leggings and began batting it enthusiastically. He didn't notice, concentrating on his own words. His natural combative nature was taking charge, overcoming her powerful enchantment.

Carlow spoke through gritted teeth, determined not to fall under her spell again. "Maybe my father's spirit can give me a few pointers on how to catch Silver Mallow. Or, better yet, how to help a fine widow lady keep her ranch." He deliberately avoided including Dr. Holden in his assertions. "Or tell me where Del Gato or that black shooter—the one who looks like he just came off a ship—will be waiting for me."

Her smile would have felled most men. It was a long, deep kiss promised. The hint of a delicious night together. Her hand started moving upward again, sliding and slowly crossing over her right breast, until it finally found a strand of hair that had dropped across her cheek and flipped it away.

"Your Irish uncle would call me a witch," Jessie whispered. "And you? What do you think?" Her gaze invited him closer. She knew she was irresistible. Spellbinding. "The man you seek looks much like you, isn't that so? That bothers you, doesn't it?" She expected him to gasp at the observation.

Instead, Carlow forced himself to laugh. "Only that I haven't caught him yet. How much for the cigars?"

This time she joined his mirth. "They are yours at no cost. Remmy would insist. If you can wait a few minutes, he said he'd be out and would enjoy talking with you." She caught the wave of a young woman at the counter and waved back. "Oh, I need to help a customer."

The woman, in her late teens and wearing an azure bonnet that accented her brown curls and matched her eyes, continued to gaze at them. Her smile was directed at Carlow. He touched his hat brim with his hand in a greeting. Her smile widened.

"I see you have an admirer, Ranger Carlow," Jessie said. "Are all women drawn to you . . . as I am?"

The young Ranger's face reddened. He didn't know what to say. He glanced at the young woman at the counter still watching him for more response, then back to Jessie, whose eyes were seeking further conquest.

"Sure, I'll wait. Thanks for your help, Jessie," Carlow finally said, "and for the cigars . . . and the ghost stories." He wanted to say the young woman didn't compare to her but that would be foolish talk. It took all of his determination to do so as he shoved the medicine jar and cigars in the pocket of his trail coat.

Jessie glanced at the waiting woman, then back to the young Ranger, as if dismissing her from competition. "Time Carlow, are you staying in town? I hope so. We can talk about spirits and spiritualism . . . seances . . . and the mysteries of ancient Egypt. It's so far beyond anything you'll hear around here or most places, I fear. You might find me most interesting. Some men do, you know." Her smile was laced with arousal.

"I reckon most would find you quite hard to walk away from." He looked over at the cash register, then down at his boots, where her cat continued to play. He forced himself to close and open his fists. "But you'd better go take care of your customers. They might have some ghosts getting riled up, too."

Her eyes studied him again and he felt like she was trying to climb inside his head.

To break the connection, he leaned down and picked up the cat. "Hey, you, I've got a big dog outside who'd like to meet you." The cat meowed softly, squirming in his hands as he scratched behind its ears. He handed the animal to her.

"They say he is a wolf. From somewhere else," she murmured. "That his spirit comes from beyond the grave. It is so."

"Who's they?"

Her forced smile turned into one of lopsided annoyance. "I don't think you would believe me."

"Probably not. Because he isn't."

She cradled the cat in her arms. "Marianne likes you. She usually doesn't take to men." Like a queen before her subjects, she slowly raised her eyes and stared at him. "Do you want that woman at the counter? Esther McCollough . . . she is a virgin."

He was pulled toward Jessie and, for a moment, wanted to be in her arms.

"Or maybe we can talk with your father and your mother some night. I feel their spirits are close, don't you?"

His attempt at smiling was a wistful curling of his mouth at the right corner. His attention was returned to her and she knew it. Her eyes sparkled with victory.

"I was born under a Witch Tree, you know. Just outside of New Orleans. My real mother is the moon. She watches over me—and those I care about." Jessie's beautiful face twisted into a smile that wasn't quite a smile; her eyes glowed with an animal look that saw nothing and everything.

Before he could respond, the store's front door swung open, and Marshal Dillingham came charging into the quiet. His ears wiggled as he stomped inside. He squinted to adjust his eyesight to the grayness, spotted the young Ranger, and hurried to him.

"Range-uh, a hoss has dun been a'stole. Ex-cuse me, Mrs. Hol-den, down by Ree-llena's, ah, place. A fella soundin' a lot like your Sil-vuh Mal-low skee-daddled outta town. South. Headin' for Mexico, don-cha reckon?"

Carlow cocked his head to the side. "How long ago?"

"Accordin' to Clemens—the cowboy who dun had his hoss stole—he be . . . ah, inside . . .'bout a hour back—or so." Dillingham waved his arms to support his estimate of time, forcing his huge ears to flap.

Touching Carlow's arm again, Jessie Holden interrupted. "Pardon me, gentlemen, but I have customers. You come back, Ranger, and we'll talk." Her face was again a mask of indifference as she walked away, carrying the cat. "Oh, what shall I tell Miss McCollough?"

Out of the corner of his eye, he could see the woman was pouting and had put her hands on her hips in a demonstration of impatience. However, her shoulders were thrown back to accent her bosom.

"Ask her if she likes ghosts." Carlow pulled his gaze away from Jessie's retreat and studied the lawman. It helped him to concentrate. "You say the stolen horse was taken from in front of the Kahn house?" He was glad Jessie wasn't near; her eyes would have glistened with satisfaction that he knew about it. He remembered Flanker saying the doctor secretly owned the whorehouse.

Chapter Twenty

Carlow knew he should have been smarter than to trust Rellena Kahn. Mallow was there when he searched her place, and the madam was trying to get Carlow into a room so Mallow could kill him. Kileen told him often not to believe what a woman with fancied-up eyes had to say; if she didn't want you to see her real eyes, she wouldn't be telling you the truth, either. He wasn't sure what his uncle would say about a beauty like Jessica Anne Holden. Probably what she had said herself.

A witch.

Dillingham glanced over at her as she greeted the young woman, who seemed to fade before Jessie's beauty. He nodded an appreciation for Jessie's appearance and continued his report. "Yeah. Clemens dun came to my office, a'hollerin' an' a'bellerin' somethin' fee-erce. Be a fine lookin' red hoss. Front white stockin's."

Carlow headed toward the door without another word.

"Whar ya a'goin'?"

"After Silver Mallow."

"It'll be dark afore long, Range-uh. Rain's a'comin'."

"You're right."

"Shall I tell Clemens that ya be gittin' his hoss fer hee-um?" Dillingham grinned as he asked.

Carlow hesitated at the doorway. "Finding town horses is your job, Marshal—or did you forget?"

Jessie's words trailed him. Soft. Polite. Yet poetic and pleasuring. A forbidden invitation at their edges. "Please be careful, Ranger Time Carlow. Come back now, so we can . . . talk. The ones we spoke of are asking for you." She patted the young woman's hand; her whisper wore a definite condescending tone. "All men are alike, aren't they, dear? Someday, maybe, you'll know that, too."

Esther McCollough was pretending to examine the label of a medicine bottle before her; her upward gaze was an attempt at indifference.

Jessie's cat jumped down from the counter and scurried in pursuit of Carlow, as if to reinforce its mistress's cryptic message, but arrived as the door closed behind him.

Carlow was riding in minutes, with the buckskin eager to be on the move again. So was Chance. And he was, too. There was a sense of freedom that came with leaving Jessie Holden's animal magnetism and mystical ways behind him. He saw Del Gato standing in the doorway of the saloon as he rode past and gave him a nonchalant wave. The halfbreed's right hand jerked to respond; then he snorted and was still. Carlow chuckled.

Someone recoiled from an upper window on the opposite side of the street. Carlow sensed the movement more than saw it. It could have been anyone. But he was reminded of the black gunfighter from the alley earlier. The thought was enough to make him draw the hand-carbine as he rode and to kick the buckskin into a gallop. His long coat fluttered around his leggings as the horse raced toward the end of town.

Chance barked and bounced alongside the horse's legs as they quickly cleared the last buildings of Presidio and headed toward the Rio Grande. The young Ranger saw the hoofprints immediately. Fresh among a trail of tired marks in the land, heightened by the long fingers of dusk.

Two horses. One being ridden, the other trailed.

He didn't like what the advantage meant and cursed himself for not stopping at the livery to get a second horse. Worse, ahead of him, blackness was rising at the edge of the world. Fat and angry clouds eyed the land ravenously. More rain was less than an hour away. Hard rain. At least as heavy as last night. Nightfall would come with it.

Around Carlow, the prairie held its breath, bracing for the coming storm. How far was it to the Rio Grande? Would Mallow cross before the rain came? What about Fort Leaton? Would he go there instead? It was right on the way. The huge adobe home overlooking the Rio Grande wasn't really a fortress, but in the past, it had provided protection from Indian attacks for the Leaton family and others. Even been an occasional base of operations for Army and Ranger units. The forty-room enclosure had been owned by John Burgess since before the War.

No Rangers were there now, Carlow was fairly certain. Unless they just happened to stop over for the night. Still, he imagined Mallow would avoid the place and head straight for Mexico.

Carlow passed a worn-out stream bed. Brown ghosts of dead willows lined a natural stone wall forming a long crease in the land, breathing from a spring whose life lay deep within the earth. Mallow had waited there to see if he was followed. The young Ranger could see where the outlaw's knee had pushed into the embankment for leverage. His wolf-dog charged into the tired land crease to examine its hidden stories firsthand. Resuming hoofmarks headed directly toward the Rio Grande, disappearing into the graying horizon.

What were the chances of catching up with Mallow before the storm wiped out all traces of his escape? Carlow tried to decide if he should seek shelter or keep riding. If Mallow reached Mexico, Carlow had no right to cross after him. That was the stuff of international incidents. Not even Captain McNelly and the rest of the Rangers would be allowed to cross the great river after the Mexican rustlers ravaging the corners of Texas. At least not with permission from Washington, D.C. But McNelly would do anything if he thought it was right. That was good enough for Carlow.

He glanced down at the Ranger badge on his shirt and pulled it off. He would follow Mallow as an ordinary citizen. Shoving the badge into his vest pocket was a reinforcement of his decision. His mind didn't quite agree. Returning to help Bea Von Pearce tugged at his determination to follow Mallow. He tried not to think of what would happen to her. Or Hattie. Or Charlie Two-Wolves. Or his great horse, Shadow. He bit his lower lip as he pictured Dr. Holden riding the fine horse into town.

No, that was not enough reason to stay. If that happened, he would simply seek the return of the animal when he came back through, with Mallow in tow. What kind of a man was he, anyway, to feel worse about something happening to his horse than to good people? The question rammed into his mind and made him uncomfortable.

"Silver Mallow, I will find you. You will pay for Shannon's death," he screamed into the graying air to reinforce his commitment to himself.

The shout echoed through his sore forehead, across his burned shoulder, and down through his pummeled hands. Only the buckskin and his wolf-dog heard the promise, and a stunted oak tree with most of its roots outside the earth, struggling toward water that no longer lived in the streambed. Shrugging his shoulders, he wanted to pull the words back. He was weary from the fight with Red Anklon. It had taken all his strength to prevail.

Or was the weak feeling from his strange encounter with Jessie Holden? That made him think of the medicine jar and cigars. He shoved his hand into his coat pocket, past the cigars, and withdrew the jar. He glanced at it momentarily and heaved it away.

How could he let Bea Von Pearce and little Hattie down? How could he ride away from them? What chance did Bea have against men like this? How long would it be before they eliminated the rest of her riders and took the remaining herd? How long before the fearless Charlie Two-Wolves was cut down? What would happen to Bea? To Hattie?

A feeling of being followed tugged at him. He ducked his head and glanced back. A rider. Barely a shape against the darkening sky. Probably one of Dr. Holden's men. Maybe Del Gato himself. Or that black shootist. Or did Flanker have something more to say? Carlow dismounted and led the buckskin into the creek bed. After a quick wrap of the reins around the haunting stub of a tree, he pulled his hand-carbine and lay against the bank.

Chance came beside him, and he told the beast to lie quiet. From a distance, the oncoming rider wouldn't be able to see anything out of place. Carlow considered using his Sharps but decided against it.

Only a single rider. He was certain of that now.

Surely Del Gato wouldn't come after him on his own. The man killed only for money—and only if he had an edge. Had Mallow somehow doubled back on him? Carlow acknowledged to himself that the outlaw had already outfoxed him twice. This could be a third time. If so, it would be the last. After opening and closing his fists to relieve some of the stiffness, he cocked the hammer of the hand-carbine, reassured by its hard *click-click* in the unmoving air.

Minutes passed like shadows across the prairie. Carlow wiped a bead of sweat from his forehead. His wound was pounding again, as if to remind him of the last time he was this close to Mallow. He wiped his right palm on his pants to dry it and resumed his grip on the gun. There was still time to get the Sharps from his saddle, but the rider would likely see him.

Whoever it was made no attempt to hide or to zigzag into a more difficult target. Something about the shape was familiar to Carlow. He squeezed his eyes into narrow slits to add details to the advancing threat. It didn't appear that the rider was holding a gun.

The one-handed beggar from Charlie's saloon!

What in the hell is that bucktoothed buffoon doing out here? Is he trailing me? For what earthly reason? Carlow started to stand but decided, instead, to fire a warning shot. His gun crashed into the air and the man stopped his horse, wrapped the reins around the saddle horn, and waved with his sole right arm; his left arm rose with it, revealing a scarred stump as his ragged suitcoat sleeve slid away.

"Ranger, it's me! Nichols . . . from Charlie's saloon. I came to find you. Don't shoot. Don't shoot." The man's arms extended in surrender; his front teeth slid below his upper lip and stayed there.

Angry, Carlow stood at the edge of the creek bed, his hand-carbine at his side. Chance rose beside him, tensed and ready. "Nichols, is it? What brings you after me?" He wanted to ask if the man was following to beg for drinking money but resisted the cruel question.

Nichols's face puckered with both disgrace and determination. "It's something that needed sayin'. To you. Alone. Then I'll ride on. Been a'feelin' it since you took on that bunch like you did. Kinda like the wind it is."

Carlow studied the horizon to assure himself this wasn't some kind of diversion to make him vulnerable to an attack. But he saw nothing on the edge of the land as Nichols continued. Questions lingered, though. Who sent this man? Why?

"You know, you can't see the wind—only what it does to trees an' such. You started that wind in me." Nichols made no attempt to lower his arm or move his horse closer. It didn't look like he was feeling the effects of his earlier whiskey. He appeared calm—and sober. Even his exposed teeth gave him a look of concentration.

"Who sent you after me? Holden? Dillingham? Flanker?"

"Nobody sent me. I'm tellin' you why I came. With . . . with the Cradle 6, I once rode. Proud of it, too. Until this hateful day." Nichols pointed with his right hand at the empty left sleeve. A sob followed, a long-held cry that rang down along the flat prairie, out toward the coming storm.

"You used to work for the Von Pearces?"

"Yes, sir—an' as good a cow man as there was around here. Ask anyone about Will Nichols." His eyes glistened with lost pride. "Until Anklon and the fine doctor and Del Gato—and Mitchell, and some others . . . they caught me alone. A year and three months back, it was. A year, three months, and six days."

Carlow was immediately more interested.

Sobbing, Nichols pushed the sleeve back to reveal a scarred-over stump that ended inches below his left elbow. "They held me down and the good doctor cut off my hand. He used my own brandin' iron . . . to burn the bleedin' to a stop. A warning, he said. Leave the Von Pearces or lose the other. A favor he done me, he says—by not cuttin' away my good right arm." He choked back old terror and continued, "Or lettin' me bleed to death. Red and his men were laughin'. Laughin'. An' watchin'. Watchin' an' laughin'. I can still see them laughin' an' watchin'—when I sleep."

Carlow eased the hammer back in place and holstered his hand-carbine. It gave him something to think about instead of the cowboy's awful story. He saw his own reddened hands and thought how quickly Nichols would trade places.

Nichols's entire face was frozen as he continued his recounting of the loss of his hand, explaining how Red Anklon had dragged his severed hand away on a rope behind his horse. He stopped and swallowed away another sob, straightened his back, and described the widow's reaction when he returned. She was crying and wailing, but she had kept Charlie Two-Wolves from going after them. He would never forget that the Indian wrangler had been ready to die to avenge him.

Carlow's shoulders rose and fell. He had judged the young man wrongly. Whatever else he might be, Will Nichols had seen more than most at his age.

Nichols's lone hand went to his face to hide the anguish bursting from his body. "I didn't stay. I couldn't. Wouldn't let her touch me, either. Or Charlie. I was afraid of my shadow. Thought everybody was comin' for my right arm. Hid in a barn. Outside of town. Almost died, I reckon. A Russian fella found me and took pity. Nursed me back to walkin'. Yeah, he did that. A saint, he was. Been drinkin' ever since, though—to make me forget how I ran. An' they kept laughin'. Until today."

Carlow didn't know what to say. A soft "I'm sorry" stumbled from his mouth.

"Don't say that, Ranger. You made me know what I must do. Back to the Cradle 6 I'm goin'. You gave me the belly for it. I swear by my sweet mother's grave, I will die beside Widow Von Pearce and the red man. Yeah, I will stand." He held up his shortened left arm along with his clenched right fist. This time it was a reinforcement of his commitment.

Carlow thought the man in front of him looked years younger. His face glowed with determination; guilt and shame were gone as if peeled like the shell from a cracked nut. Without being asked, Nichols proceeded to tell Carlow of the situation. It was similar to what Flanker had already told him. Only different. This was personal—and more horrifying.

Nichols thought it was only a matter of days before Holden took over the widow's ranch, too. They would drive off or kill the remaining handful of Cradle 6 riders, then Charlie Two-Wolves. Next he expected the town to hear that Mrs. Von Pearce was quite ill and Dr. Holden was going out to treat her. The doctor wouldn't be able to save her and would express his great regret. Of course, he would poison her. Probably little Hattie too.

"Why are you telling me this, Nichols?" Carlow asked, and swallowed. "I have orders to catch a murderer. He was in town. At the whorehouse. I shouldn't have trusted that woman who owns it to tell me the truth. I must keep after him. I can't help Bea. Wish I could, but I can't. Surely you understand. Can't Marshal Dillingham help?" He knew the answer before the words took shape.

Will Nichols stared at the young Ranger for what seemed like minutes to Carlow. "Dillingham? He's about as useful as tits on a boar. More afraid than I was." He took a deep breath and exhaled slowly. "I didn't expect you to do anything. Really. Guess you being a brave man an' all, I just wanted you to know. About me. Didn't expect you to stop bein' a Ranger." He glanced at his right arm still held high. "I'm sorry to bother you. I'll be ridin' back now."

Chapter Twenty-one

"Why didn't you talk to me in town?"

"Well, I was gonna, but you went into Holden's store," Nichols explained, looking away. "I was afraid of his wife seeing me. Then you rode out."

"I see." Carlow started to ask why he didn't come to him when he was in the hotel but didn't. It didn't matter. The man had been through a lot—and fighting himself was the worst of it. He knew that feeling. "What do you know about Mrs. Holden?"

Nichols's face brightened for the first time. He lifted his chin and shook his head. "A grand sight, she is, that's for sure. Makes a man want to do it himself, just thinkin' about her." His chin lowered as he licked his front teeth and stared at Carlow. "But wicked as the night is long or my name isn't William Frederick Nichols. She's every bit as mean as he is. Full of spirits and witchcraft, she is. Her brother's Red Anklon, the man you whipped. Next to her, he's a puppy dog. Hear tell she's especially wild when the moon's full. Like it will be tonight." He looked up as if expecting to see the moon in the darkening sky. A shiver that worked through his frame followed.

With his eyes upward, he continued with his recounting. Jessie Holden was with the physician and his henchmen when Nichols's hand was severed. She had wanted to kill him as a sacrifice to the moon and was quite upset when her husband wouldn't let her. The bucktoothed cowboy shivered again at the recounting and returned his gaze to the young Ranger.

Another terrifying story of her violent nature was connected to one of Holden's ranch conquests. Nichols told about her conducting a seance two years ago for a German couple who owned the farm adjoining the Cradle 6. They had a pond almost as big as the Von Pearce watering hole. The couple lost a son they loved dearly and wanted desperately to believe she could reach him. She had been telling them that for a long time, and they finally agreed to do it. During this spiritual encounter, they were murdered; Jessie Holden claimed it was Comanches. An ear from each was cut off and never found. On their still faces were some strange symbols made from their blood. She said the Indians thought she was holy and left her alone. The land was now part of the Bar H.

Impatience was growing within Carlow as the one-handed cowboy continued. The young Ranger already knew about Dr. Holden's treachery and that he wanted Bea's ranch, but he couldn't resist asking, "How do you know this? Were you there?"

" 'Course not," Nichols snapped. "Herman Von Pearce himself told me. He and the missus were friends with those folks, being German an' all."

"How did Herman know?"

For the first time, Nichols eyed the young Ranger with suspicion. "Their sons came for him. Told what happened."

"What happened to . . . them?"

Chance moved to Carlow's side, nuzzled his leg, and left to examine Nichols, who was intent on completing his assessment. "Hanged. For rustlin'." He explained a bill of sale for the family's ranch showed up and the sons were arrested and hanged for attempting to steal what were now Dr. Holden's cattle. "Nobody really cared, I guess—'cept Herman. An' they got him." Nichols concluded, "I don't know anything about the other ranches the doctor took."

"Sounds like Herman Von Pearce knew his land—if Holden wants it so bad." Carlow glanced upward at the darkening sky; only his observation was about rain. Mallow's trail would soon be washed out; he would have to assume the outlaw was headed for Mexico and resume his search in the closest border town—as a civilian. For the moment, he rationalized that it was important to know more about the Holdens. When he returned from Mexico with Mallow, he would check into the situation with the Cradle 6 ranch.

"He sure did. He was a studier, he was. Tough too. But a good man to work for. Tough but damn fair, he was." Nichols folded his arms to hide the missing hand. As if anticipating the question, Nichols said, "The good doctor likes to do things so they look right. In case any real law comes around."

Carlow's mouth twitched; he was "real law."

"That's why he's taking his time with the Cradle 6. Don't want anybody talking. Keepin' his crazy wife under control on this one. Nothing will point to him doing anything wrong. Just a doctor takin' care of others." He swallowed the bile rising in his throat. "He even had a story in the newspaper about how he bought the Germans' place to give their remaining son a chance to start over, instead of struggling on alone. Said he saved my life by taking off my hand. Gangrene." He bit his lower lip and continued, "By the time you get back, Widow Von Pearce will have sold out to him. Or it'll look that way. Nobody will be left to argue about it. We'll all be dead." He raised his chin and the protrusion of his upper teeth settled over his lower lip once more. "Who knows? Maybe we'll get lucky. But it don't matter. I ain't runnin' no more."

Eagerly he told about Jessie Holden's having a seance the past summer for the mayor and his wife and two other couples. This time she only scared them by bringing the ghost of the mayor's first wife to talk with them. Nichols chuckled and explained that the mayor ordered Marshal Dillingham to tell Jessie not to do any more seances, but the lawman was afraid of what she might do to him and didn't tell her. He had heard that story in a saloon; he didn't remember which one, though.

Nichols's face curled into a frown. "Might be her that the doctor sends to see the fine widow. To speak of things nice and soft. But it will be poison she brings. Or a sharp knife. Mark my words, Ranger. But they'll do it over my dead body—an' Charlie's."

"I think you're right about her being evil. A real shame, isn't it? So much beauty wrapped around so much bad." Carlow shook his head.

"Yeah. Makes ya wonder about what the Devil himself looks like."

Carlow was surprised at the difference in the man. He looked tired, almost spent, but he appeared cold sober and bursting with determination.

Nichols leaned forward in the saddle, unwrapping the reins as he did. "I feel sorry for the fella you're chasin'. Silver Mallow, isn't it? Never did see any man fight like you did. Damn, no man ever laid out Red Anklon before this day, I can tell you that. But you'd better know Mrs. Holden, his sis, will want you to pay dearly for it. Good thing you're ridin' on, I reckon."

"I got lucky, Will—an' Silver Mallow's already come close." Carlow touched the crusted-over wound on his forehead. "I have to find him. Those are my orders. But I'd be after him anyway. He murdered my best friend."

Nichols nodded. "Never had a friend like you . . . Carlow, isn't it?"

"Carlow it is. Time Carlow." The young Ranger studied the beggar with growing appreciation.

"Time? That your pappy's name?"

Carlow chuckled. "No. My mother thought it meant something else. She was . . ."

"Irish."

"Careful how you say that."

Nichols sat up straight in the saddle; his right hand retreated to his heart. "Hey, I didn't mean nothin'. My best ridin' pard on the Cradle 6 was a Mi . . . Irish. Before they shot him. O'Brien. Jamie O'Brien."

Chance yipped for attention, rubbing his huge head against the Ranger's leg affectionately.

"Damn, you know ridin' with a wolf makes you one scary *hombre*. Don't think I've ever seen anything like that." Nichols moved his right hand from over his heart and pointed toward Chance

Carlow looked down and scratched the wolf-dog between its ears. "Scary, huh? How about that, Chance?" He glanced up at Nichols. "He's only part wolf."

"Part's enough. I ain't scary, but I'm better than I look," Nichols said, staring down at himself. "They'll have an extra gun at the ranch. If not, I'll take what I need from one of Holden's men."

"Like you almost did in the saloon?"

Nichols shook his head, and a smile came out of the motion. "Saw that, did you? I was gonna shoot the doc—right then an' there—but I lost my nerve."

"I'd say you were playing it smart. You would have died before you took three steps."

"You would've shot me?" Nichols's face was rigid. His Adam's apple skirted up and down his throat searching for a place to hide.

"Del Gato would have."

"B-but you took his guns."

Carlow's smile was mostly chagrin. "He had a third. Didn't see it until he sat down. A Sharps short gun."

Nichols looked away for a moment, then turned back.

A question struck Carlow. "Say, where'd you get that horse?" As the words found life, he wished he hadn't asked. It was like telling Nichols that he knew he didn't have any money.

But the query brought only a laugh. "I stole it. That four-eyed fella you killed. It was his. Figured he wasn't going to need it anymore. I saw it tied outside of Holden's saloon. Slipped loose the reins, pretty as you please, an' rode out. I figure they owe me at least a horse. A horse for a hand. Not many would make that trade."

Carlow nodded.

"If you don't mind, I'm going to call you Ty. Had me a good friend growing up by that name. *Time*'s a bit much for me. That all right?"

Carlow smiled. He probably wouldn't see this man again. "Sure. Ty's fine. Hey, you'll find a good-looking black horse in the Von Pearce's corral." Carlow folded his arms and squeezed them against his chest to reduce the ache that was building. An ache that had nothing to do with his hands or his forehead. It was in his soul. "He's mine. The widow lent me this buckskin. I nearly wore down my black chasing after Silver. Good horse. Take care of him until I get back, will you?"

"Sure. As long as I'm breathin'," Nichols said, glancing over at the tied buckskin and letting his eyes rest on the Cradle 6 brand.

"Will?"

"Yeah?"

"You are a good friend yourself. Bea is fortunate to have someone like you on her side. I'm proud to know you."

Nichols grinned widely. "Well, it's likely the last time I'll be seein' you on this fine earth, Ranger. Ride strong, Ty."

"You, too, Will. You've got a hard ride ahead. It'll be dark pretty quick now. Rain's coming, too."

Nichols stared up at the sky again as if it held significant answers for him. "There's an overhang an hour back." He grinned self-consciously. "I-I used to go there when I couldn't get into the livery to sleep. I'll wait out the night an' ride to the ranch in the mornin'." He pulled on the reins to swing his horse around.

"Wait a minute, Will," Carlow said, and went to his saddlebags. He returned with the double-action Smith & Wesson revolver he carried as a backup, and handed it to Will. "You might be needing this before you have a chance to get another. It's fresh loaded. Five in the wheel."

"Well, thank you, Ty." Nichols's face was bright with determination. He laid the reins across his saddle and took the handgun in his right fist, staring at the weapon.

Carlow cocked his head and swallowed the angst swirling in his throat. He felt like a traitor. "Godspeed, Will Nichols. May the good Lord keep you in his hand and never close his fist too tight." It was one of his uncle's favorite blessings, one of the few recitations that wasn't a toast.

"Thank you for that, Ranger. We'll be needin' it." Shoving the gun into his waistband, he retrieved the reins, swung the horse around in one motion, and kicked it into a run.

The young Ranger watched the one-handed Nichols gallop away. He was silent. Until his soul began to talk. Words crawled their way into the darkening air. "Shannon, you've got to understand, my friend. I won't let Silver Mallow get away. I won't. I'll find him if it takes the rest of my life. But if I don't help these folks now . . . If you were here, Shannon, you'd be telling me that we have to help them. I know you would. I know you would." He touched the blood stones in his vest pocket and wished Jessie Holden were there and could actually make the spirits speak to him.

Once again, the memory reached him of Kileen advising him, a teenager, before Time left to help drive cattle to Dodge City. "One day t'will be a stand ye be makin', me son."

"I doubt you'll be knowin', Thunder, until it's too late—but this is the time. I will stand," he muttered to himself, bent down, and scratched his wolf-dog's ears. "Chance, you want to see that little girl again? Or do you have better things to do?" He pushed aside the concern of having to explain to Captain McNelly why he hadn't recaptured the infamous outlaw or trying to rationalize catching up with him later. His soul jumped happily as the decision turned into action.

Yanking free the reins, he sprang onto the buckskin, and they cleared the creek bed in three bounds, with Chance leading the way. The Celtic cross flipped up into Carlow's face as the horse landed on the level ground. With his left hand, he grabbed the chain and the ancient symbol. A quick shove returned them to the inside of his shirt. His gaze locked onto the silhouette becoming larger in front of him. Was the cross coming free an indication that his father approved of his decision? Or was it a warning? Or was it the fact that his top shirt button had broken off? His fingers assured him it was the latter as he spurred the buckskin into a full gallop, passing the barking Chance. His long coat flapped out behind him like a ghost in the wind.

Nichols turned in the saddle, hearing the thundering hooves behind him. The look on his face was that of a small boy unwrapping an unexpected birthday present. Carlow nearly ran past him in his eagerness to catch up. Chance skidded to a stop a few yards away from the one-handed cowboy and barked enthusiastically.

"What brings you here this fine evenin', Ranger Carlow?" Nichols yelled with a lilt in his voice. "You an' your growlin' friend here."

Carlow grinned and blurted, "I didn't think you'd know how to care for my horse. Thought I'd better come along."

Nichols rocked in the saddle with laughter. "Mercy upon Red Anklon, the fine doctor—and his witch wife. The wrath o' God is comin' for the bastards—an' they don't know it." He frowned. "But what about that Silver fella?"

"He'll just have to wait to hang." Carlow grinned. "Can we get to that overhang before it rains?"

"It'll be close. Follow this ol' cowhand."

Carlow remembered the cigars from Holden's store and offered one to Nichols. It took three matches to get the cowboy's lit, but he savored the tobacco, almost forgetting they had riding to do.

Looking over his shoulder, Carlow said, "We'd better get moving. That rain is coming fast."

Nichols blew a white circle and watched it proudly. "Let's go."

Barely aware of the storm charging at their rear, Nichols led them on a little-used trail west of Presidio. They were soon drenched but kept riding, both too enthusiastic to stop or find shelter. Carlow tossed aside his cigar, unable to keep it lit in the downpour. But

Nichols continued to hold his soaked cigar in his teeth. Carlow couldn't remember feeling so good. His forehead didn't ache; neither did his hands. The strange gnarling in his stomach had vanished.

His mind was swirling with ideas about what they must do to stop Dr. Holden from getting the Von Pearce ranch. Jessie Holden kept appearing within the ideas to suggest a seance. He glanced at the angry sky but couldn't see a moon. What would Kileen say that meant? Carlow wondered how many Cradle 6 riders would still be there and if any could, or would, fight. Was the Comanche wrangler's statement of only five riders correct? Or Bea's ten? He was certain now Two-Wolves had stated the situation accurately.

Assuming her cowhands wouldn't help or couldn't, Charlie Two-Wolves, Will Nichols, and himself would make three against how many? Red Anklon would be more leery when they met again, more likely to shoot than to fight. He glanced down at his partially swollen hands when the thought reached him. They had to find a way to take the battle to Dr. Holden, instead of waiting to be attacked. He had learned that lesson the hard way in Bennett. The only advantage the three men had would be surprise. It would have to be enough.

Darkness and the rain had managed to shove them back into a weary reality. Even Chance seemed beaten down by the storm, a water-logged ball of fur trailing the two riders with his tail almost dragging on the saturated ground. Carlow glanced back to make certain Chance was close. The wolf-dog was soaked and running hard; his growl told the Ranger that he didn't like either.

"Come on, boy, you've been wet before," Carlow yelled cheerily.

Nichols pointed with his stump. "It's not far now, Ty."

Minutes later, they rounded a hillside littered with boulders that looked like sitting men, swung their horses to the left, and galloped along a narrow spoon of land between hills. Soon they were under the protection of a wide rock shelf that had shoved its way out of the adjoining hillside. Both were sopping wet, but attempts to start a fire proved fruitless. Carlow had used up the kindling in his fire-starter sack the night before.

They unsaddled their horses without talking; Nichols refused help, using the stump of his left arm for leverage and support. Carlow suggested tying their horses to a sprawled bush, and they did. Chance sought a corner of the shelf where it seemed dry and lay down to watch. After caring for the horses, the young Ranger took the extra shirt from his saddlebags, the only thing he had that was still dry. He wiped off the wolf-dog as best he could and checked his paws for any cuts.

"Thanks, my friend. I know you believe we're doing the right thing." Carlow boxed the wolf-dog's head with the shirt. The young Ranger inhaled his emotion. "Thank you, too, Shannon."

Chance responded with a low purr and licked Carlow's hand.

Nichols asked if he had any more cigars. Carlow felt for the remaining smoke and withdrew a damp tobacco roll. Nichols took it anyway and laid the cigar carefully beside his bedroll to dry out. They shared what remained of Bea's food. Carlow handed most of his share of the meat to Chance, who gobbled it eagerly.

Both were soon asleep, with a very wet Chance curled beside Carlow.

Chapter Twenty-two

In Presidio, the night rain pounded against an imposing two-story white house that intimidated the neighboring homes with its sheer size. Occasional lightning made it clear that a line of well-groomed bushes along the front of the house had surrendered to the storm and lay against the soaked earth.

Inside, darkness ruled, except for a lone lamp in the den. Rain splattered relentlessly against glass windows displaying fine silk drapes. Dr. Remington Holden sat in an evergreen overstuffed chair, sipping on a glass of Tennessee sour mash whiskey. Shards of yellow light sliced across his pale face, making him appear angry. But he wasn't. Not anymore. He was pleased with himself.

Quite pleased, in fact.

His men would drive off the Cradle 6 herd tonight, after taking care of the rest of the Von Pearce riders. The rain would provide perfect cover, leaving no trace. His men didn't like the idea of going out in the rain, especially Del Gato, but they would go. Even Del Gato.

Anklon had asked to lead them like always. The former Confederate officer needed to regain some lost ego, the physician had surmised, and so he had agreed, although he warned his brother-in-law to ride with some padding on the saddle.

Earlier in the evening, Jessie had declared she wanted to ride with her brother. Holden was a little leery of the idea, but she had insisted and he had reluctantly approved. She would have gone anyway. So far, though, she hadn't left the house. Chuckling, he doubted she would go, even if it stopped raining this instant; she didn't like rain any more than Del Gato did.

He was certain she remained upstairs, doing whatever it was she did when the moon was full. Some kind of mumbo jumbo. He had never understood any of it. Of course, he was never certain what she might do either. He had his suspicions there were others before they met. She had murdered three people that he knew of since they had been married. The murder of the German couple who owned the Double-R had, at least, been turned into a positive: he owned the Double-R now. But he never did understand why she had killed that stranger who came to town last year. A Frenchman, he thought, and he had a feeling the man had been an old lover from New Orleans. She had never explained. Murder was bad enough, but cutting off ears and drawing on the victims with their own blood was nauseating.

However, she had promised to end that kind of behavior. Today, though, she had become highly agitated over her brother's beating by the Ranger. She had always been protective of Red Anklon. He shook his head; how could a man the size of Anklon need the protection of a woman? Maybe Jessie knew something about Red that he didn't.

He took another sip and let the whiskey excite his throat. If she wanted to go on the raid, that would be fine. Even if she went into one of her fits and wanted to cut off an ear of one of the Cradle 6 riders. It was too late for her to mess this up.

Two of the widow's cowhands had already been bought. They would make it easy to get close. The herd would be held in an out-of-the-way valley until he had purchased the Von Pearce ranch. That would be tomorrow when Bea Von Pearce was alone. After Viceroy killed her fool Indian wrangler. That reminded him of Jessie's silly comment about that Indian's having magical powers. *We'll see how magical he is filled with bullets.* His own shrill laugh bounced around the room.

Tomorrow.

Today had not gone well, he admitted to himself. He didn't like events—or people—out of his control. The young Ranger's showing up was unexpected; his whipping of Red Anklon was an even bigger surprise. Dr. Holden shook his head and giggled. After the agonizing pain subsided, the big man wanted to find the Ranger and shoot him. Dr. Holden had told him the Ranger was on his way to Mexico. Anklon's injuries, other than to his ego, were relatively minor. His groin, stomach, and face would be sore and bruised for weeks, but his jaw wasn't broken and only one rib was cracked.

There was nothing to do for the busted tooth, except laudanum. At least it wasn't a front tooth. Jessie's brother had been effective in the physician's careful land grab; there was no reason to doubt him now.

The young Ranger had proved to be a tough man to get rid of. The best idea was to get him out of town. Way out of town. And make it his own decision. Mexico had a nice ring to it. That was Holden's idea—with help from Kahn and the outlaw Silver Mallow himself.

He took another sip of his whiskey and stared at the window.

He liked Mallow; the outlaw could be useful, perhaps, sometime. The man owed him. Big time. Even though the attempted ambush in the whorehouse had failed. The young Ranger would definitely had cornered Mallow if the doctor hadn't decided to intervene.

It was a spur of the moment decision; Anklon had agreed. Del Gato didn't like the idea—but he hadn't liked hiring Viceroy either. Holden figured it was an insult to the halfbreed's reputation, but he didn't care. Having a killer to direct was the ultimate weapon; he could always see that the man was arrested and destroyed, leaving Holden free of the situation.

Lightning flashed and declared the rain was letting up. Definitely letting up. Anklon and his men should be on their way by now.

In the five years since his parents had died, he had done well. A lot better than his stern father had. "The son of a bitch deserved to die," he muttered. His father had never suspected the poison in his food. Neither had his mother. He felt a twinge of guilt about her death; she had been the one who supported his becoming a doctor. But his mother's continued presence would have only complicated things. Jessie had been steadfast on that point.

"Besides, she always sided with the old man, except about my becoming a doctor," he muttered again, and poured himself more whiskey.

At least his father had been right about a physician's never becoming wealthy. Too many of them got paid in eggs, chickens, and baked goods. *My fool of a mother thought it was a noble profession, regardless.* He raised his glass in tribute to her memory.

He remembered clearly the day Jessie told him they

should return to Presidio and use medicine to gain immense power, initially over his parents, and then over the region. Power over the region. The fire of that idea fed him daily. Most in town thought he was simply a caring doctor who had inherited his parents' wealth but had continued serving the people's needs. The charade had kept him close to town news, provided a wonderful way to remove an occasional obstacle, and given him the appearance of respectability.

That would be important later. When he ran for governor. Governor Holden. What a wonderful sound.

The underwriting of Kahn's pleasure house had been his first investment after his parents were gone. Something neither would ever have done—or come close to understanding. The investment had yielded significant profits as well as enjoyable diversions—and, once in a while, important information. It had been kept silent; Rellena Kahn was a woman who knew how to keep secrets. She had also been helpful with the Silver Mallow situation and getting the young Ranger out of town without further trouble.

Holden's taste for black women had been ignited at medical school in New Orleans and had been fully flamed by his dalliances with Black Bethinia. His loins responded favorably with the thought. Bedtime with his beautiful wife had become colder as her interest in moon magic and seances grew and took her warmth from him.

Yet, she had been an effective partner in his scheming. An enthusiastic partner.

They had met in New Orleans and he had been engulfed in lust for her immediately. At the time, her interests in witchcraft and the like were minor annoyances in his enjoyment of her body. Now she was becoming a liability—to a growing degree—to his image of respectability. He knew she wouldn't be able to quit her obsessions, no matter the goal. At least he was able to cover up the killing of the German couple by presenting it as an Indian raid—and managed to explain the death of the Frenchman as a random hotel robbery gone bad.

But some in town feared her. To some degree, he did, too.

When the time was right, she would come down with some incurable illness that was beyond his skills and prayers. He had even practiced his mournful presentation to the town. Might even help his campaign for governor; people liked to vote for a man dealing with grief.

But using poison disguised as medicine was effective only if it was applied rarely. And it always had to look like the person was nearing death before the doctor was involved or appeared to be. Otherwise, it would be self-defeating. That's where Red Anklon, Del Gato, and their small band of outlaws came in. Anklon's men had proved effective in changing brands and blending stolen cattle with the Bar H herd. Of course, no one ever thought the kind doctor was being anything but helpful by buying out a beleaguered rancher.

A knock on the dark walnut front door interrupted his thoughts. More pounding followed, then the testing of the locked brass knob.

Who in the world would be coming here tonight? In this rain?

It couldn't be Viceroy; Holden was going to meet him tomorrow morning. He shivered when he recalled their parting. The physician had proudly proclaimed, "Tomorrow is a big day for me. I take over the Cradle 6." Viceroy had responded without emotion, "Tomorrow I kill a widow, an Indian—and a little girl." The words were as smooth as the doctor's whiskey.

Dr. Holden had halfway expected the black gunman

to chase after the Ranger when he left town. Viceroy wasn't like Del Gato; he would want to face the fierce young man. Just for the thrill of it. Then again, Viceroy was also interested in the black whore at Kahn's place. Knowing Rellena, she would let him in the back way. The physician chuckled to himself. Given the choice, he would choose being with Bethinia too. Any day. She was something special in bed. He shivered with delightful memory and decided he would enjoy her again after this was all over. And that would be soon. The Ranger wasn't a threat anymore. By the time he returned, if he ever did, the valley would be Holden's and all signs of illegal activity would be gone. Forever.

Viceroy didn't know it, but he would be blamed for the deaths of the widow and the others. Eyewitnesses would tell the marshal—and the newspaper—about seeing a black man in a red sash ride away from the Von Pearce ranch house. The witnesses would be Anklon and some of his men. If Jessie did decide to ride along with the rustling raid and killed one of the Cradle 6 riders—because the moon was full or whatever crazy reason she always gave—Vicerory would be blamed for that, too.

Oh, it was perfect. Perfect. He took a long swallow, choking on the volume.

Another knock. Even louder this time.

"I'm coming. I'm coming." Dr. Holden took another drink, a smaller one, rose and headed for the door.

Straightening his cravat, he picked up the gas lamp and strolled toward the entryway hall, umindful that the person at the door was exposed to the rain. He passed a large golden dragon statue that guarded the hallway's end. To his right was a winding staircase. Family portraits followed up the steps. An examination of the gold-framed photograph of himself was disrupted by more pounding at the door.

Smiling, he resumed his walk to the door, past red walls lined with great scrolls, ornate tapestry, and tall, slender Egyptian vases. A long red runner with gold accents covered the wooden floor. All were purchases made by his wife. He didn't care for any of it, except that it showed wealth.

He shook his head, chuckling, and gripped the doorknob.

Opening the door brought a sprinkle of dying rain. Marshal Dillingham stood there with his wide-brimmed hat sagging and his long coat following the contours of his narrow shoulders and thick midsection. His hat was pulled down so far that his large ears curled out where the brim pushed against them.

"Good evening, Laetner. What brings you here of all nights?" Dr. Holden made no attempt to apologize for his slowness in getting to the door. "Come in. Come in."

Marshal Dillingham stepped inside, his wet boots bringing more water to the floor. He was unsure of what to do next; he knew only that he needed some answers. He wouldn't be able to sleep until he got them. As an afterthought, he took off his hat. Damp hair flopped around his ears.

"I-uh wanted to ask yo-all some questions . . .'bout today, Doc."

"Well, sure. Come into my study for a little whiskey to warm you—and we can talk." Dr. Holden's manner was that of a physician caring for a patient. "You can put your coat and hat there." He pointed at the golden coat rack against the wall.

"Yeah, sure, that-ud be real fine."

Without another word, the small doctor spun and headed back to the study, holding the lamp in front of him.

Marshal Dillingham took off his soaked coat and rain-beaten hat, placed them on the rack, and hurried behind the physician like a puppy chasing someone's feet. His large ears flapped with each step and a trail of water traced his path. The lawman's gaze took in a particularly large carving mounted on the wall. The centerpiece was a tree; behind it was a full moon. All kinds of animals and birds hovered around the tree. Worshipping the tree, he thought, and decided it was a nice idea. Next was an image of a nude female torso with the wings and tail of a bird, holding a crescent moon in one hand. Her other arm was raised in a blessing. He didn't know what to think of it.

Inside the den, Dr. Holden motioned for him to sit in the companion sofa and poured whiskey for both. He had a good idea of what this was all about: the young Ranger. Marshal Dillingham was no fool, even though he often acted like it.

The marshal sat and studied the room with its spare, but elegant, furnishings. One wall was completely taken up by shelves filled with books. He could remember seeing so many only once before, and that was when he visited a school friend, now a college professor, in Austin. He wasn't certain why a man needed more than one book at a time anyway. The other walls were wood-paneled, with framed paintings highlighting them. One painting he liked; it was of a bunch of horses in a pasture. He didn't understand another but thought it was a lake. Or maybe it was a closeup of a woman's face. It didn't matter; that wasn't why he was there.

"What's on your mind, Laetner?" Dr. Holden handed him a glass half filled with whiskey.

"Bin a-chewin' on the day, Doc—an' I cain't figger what-uh dun went on." Marshal Dillingham made a loud slurping sound as he tested his drink.

Settling into his chair, the physician smiled, sipped his own refreshed whiskey, and said that it had been a trying day for everyone. Then he recited the story of how Red Anklon and his men had thought the young Ranger was a horse thief and finished with the resulting saloon fight. He didn't mention the black gunfighter.

"Yo-all surprised the Ranger boy dun whipped the colonel?"

"Well, I'm not much of a student of violence, Laetner," Dr. Holden replied, laying his left hand on the arm of the chair and trying to appear relaxed. "But it looked to me that the young man was lucky, caught the colonel by surprise."

"Not-uh the way I heard it."

"As I said, I'm not a student of violence."

"Yo-all think that Range-uh came to town aftuh that outlaw, like he claimed?" Marshal Dillingham slurped more of his whiskey and Dr. Holden tried not to show his annoyance at the sounds.

"What do you mean?"

"I mean, do yah think he dun came in to check on what's goin' on around hyar?" Marshal Dillingham ran his left hand over his hair in an attempt to bring it back under control. The motion failed to return most of the wet strands to their former position. Only his ears responded to the movement.

"I'm afraid I don't know what's going on, Marshal." Dr. Holden's tone was suddenly harsher, more formal.

Swallowing to regain the confidence he had found walking over, the stout lawman recited the rustling problems at area ranches, the killing of the Germans, two other ranchers leaving abruptly, the killing of Herman Von Pearce and a stranger in the hotel—and the removal of Nichols's hand. Dr. Holden's countenance showed no signs of being surprised at the directness of the discussion or the depth of the lawman's knowledge. The short physician took another sip of his drink and decided to wait on his response. He was glad he did.

"Ya know, I-uh could be a he'p to yo-all, Remington."

A smile leaped across Dr. Holden's mind but didn't reach his face. So that was it. Dillingham wanted in. Of course. Why didn't he figure that before?

"Ya know, it were me that-uh helped get the Range-uh outta hyar. He's probably holed up somewhars, a-waitin' out the storm," Marshal Dillingham observed, and downed the rest of his whiskey. "Or-uh did somebody go after him?"

Dr. Holden stood and went back to the crystal bottle holding the liquor. Without speaking, he walked over to Marshal Dillingham and refilled his glass. The physician's face was void of expression, as if he were examining a patient.

"An' who-uh is this Viceroy fella? Biggest damn Negra I-uh ever saw." Marshal Dillingham watched the whiskey rise in his glass. "Haven't seen him since . . . ah, the hat thang. He go after the kid Range-uh?"

"You ask a lot of questions, Laetner."

"That-uh is my job."

"No, your job is keeping the peace," Dr. Holden said, and smiled. "And I intend to see that you are well compensated for that."

Marshal Dillingham licked his lips, and his ears wiggled. "That-uh is what I dun come fer."

"How much do you think keeping the peace is worth?"

Pressing his tongue against the side of his mouth, the lawman blinked and swallowed some of his whiskey, then more. "How-uh 'bout, ah, a hundred . . . a month?"

"A hundred . . . dollars . . . a month?"

Marshal Dillingham scooted forward in his chair

and waved his arm for emphasis. The motion brought drops of whiskey to his pant leg and more wobbling of his ears. He explained that he could do a great deal for the physician, but he was careful not to be specific. But he wondered if he should have said fifty dollars.

"You know, Laetner. There's no telling how far a savvy lawman like yourself could go." Dr. Holden nodded. "Why, with the right backing, you could become mayor. Ever think about that?"

Marshal Dillingham's face lit up with pleasure. He hadn't. But why not? He was well liked in town, and a powerful man like the doctor could make it happen. He and his wife.

That made him think about Jessie Holden.

As he was arriving, a flash of lightning showed her in the second-story window. She was naked. He knew the stories about her. More than most. First, there was the strange story about Comanches raiding the German ranch when she was there, killing the rancher and his wife but leaving Jessie unharmed.

Then there was that dead Frenchman staying in their hotel two years ago. One of the man's ears was gone. Just like the German couple's. Holden had explained quietly to him that it was a robbery and murder; the culprit had escaped in the night. Of course, that didn't explain the blood drawing on the Frenchman's face. Holden said the killer may have been a halfbreed; he had seen a stranger in town that day. The explanation had been followed with a hundred dollars in gold to cover the lawman's expenses in the investigation.

It was difficult to imagine someone as beautiful as Jessie Holden being so evil. His mind examined her nude body from its brief presentation in the window and pictured her being nice to him in return for his help.

"I think a hundred a month ... for keeping the peace ... can be arranged, my friend." Dr. Holden's pronouncement broke Marshal Dillingham away from his sensuous thoughts.

Upstairs in the darkness, Jessie prayed to the goddess Diana as she always did during the full moon, the most powerful time of the month. She stood next to her window, letting the rain splatter against the glass as if it were trying to reach her naked body. She watched the soft rays of the pale moon caress her breasts, making her tingle with excitement. It had angered her that the rain dared to fall at this time, but she had waited for it to pass and allow the moon's majesty to take its rightful throne in the sky.

Finally, a glorious sight of rebirth and complete resurrection.

Her late mother had thrilled her with stories of the moon goddess Diana. The full moon was a symbol of Diana's domain, and she could control the fates of men and women. The dark spaces of the moon were the forests where she hunted. Some called her the "Goddess of the Hunt." As a small child, she especially liked the story about the moon's being Diana's spinning wheel, where she spun the fate of the lives of men and women on Earth. Another favorite was that the moon was actually a jewel on Diana's necklace, and the stars were decorations on her dress.

Over the years, she had added ideas of her own, from reading Greek mysteries and forbidden dark books, mixed with her personal assessments of the power of moon magic. However, it was her own decision to become a huntress and to kill with a ceremonial knife, then cut off the victim's ear as a trophy to commemorate her fate. Drawing symols of the moon and arrows on her victims was a tribute to the moon. Also her own idea. It was her destiny to become Diana on earth. Her own mother had told her so in a dream.

On the window ledge, in front of her, was a clay bowl filled with water, eight seashells, and a small clear piece of stone. The water was from the Gulf of Mexico, gathered on a trip there years before. Under her bed were a dozen bottles filled with similar liquid. Water was the common element in her moon rituals, learned mostly from her mother. The moon's phases affected the tides of water, and since man had water in him, too, man was also affected by these changes. She had been aware of them since childhood and knew she was extraordinarily powerful during the full moon.

Around the bowl was a leather thong holding eight dried ears. One from each of her chosen victims. Five had been hunted before she met her husband. She had decided not to include his mother and father as her trophies. Partly because she hadn't been the actual executioner, and partly because she didn't think he would let her cut off their ears.

Next to the bowl was her ceremonial knife. Although the bowl had been her mother's, the knife had been crafted herself from one of her husband's scalpels and a bone she had secured.

Breathing deeply and slowly to absorb the energy of the ritual, she recited an incantation of her own as she passed the palm of her right hand over the bowl. Eight times. Then she repeated the ritual with her left hand. Eight more times. She could feel the moon's energy gather within her and her knife. Most of her chants were her own. She preferred them over her mother's gentle requests for health and happiness. Jessie's sought power over specific people. Her demands were always met. By the moon.

Of course, she was Diana, goddess of the moon, goddess of the hunt. But when her husband finally took control of the region, she would truly become a goddess. There would be wealth beyond her imagination.

And power. She and her husband were brilliant, far too smart for the fools around Presidio. Their plan to control the region's cattle ranching was nothing short of masterful. She fully expected him to become governor in a few years. One of her chants asked for that.

Her magic was at its best during the full moon. So were her seance techniques. She had been good at such presentations since she was a teenager. Once in a while, she would recall her early attempts to talk with the spirits and would laugh at her clumsy skills. But she had learned how to get the information—without appearing to do so—to make her spirits come alive. She had learned the craft from a mesmerist in New Orleans. The man had gladly showed her all of his secrets in exchange for her body. He was also her first victim. Her first ear. The moon had asked her to prove her worth as a huntress.

And like the goddess Diana, no man could ever watch her bathe. That's why the town clerk, William Reisler, would have to die; he had seen her bathing in the creek last week. That's why he had to be sacrificed to the moon. She wasn't certain if the marshal had seen her nakedness tonight or not. She would seek answers from the moon water. If he had, then he must be sacrificed as well.

Her words and movements were faster now. She must dress and ride to catch up with her brother when he and his men moved the Cradle 6 herd. A final prayer to the moon to protect him was necessary, though. He must not have to endure such a terrible beating again. He was a proud man and no one had the right to take that away from him.

That's why Ranger Time Carlow must die. He had done this, then had the audacity to challenge her connection to the moon, to the spirits. Her earlier conversation with Silver Mallow had provided the insight she needed to cast a spell over him, but she was uncertain of its extent. Oh, he wanted her body all right. Any fool could see that. She smiled. Too bad, that might have been most enjoyable. Maybe she could do both. Lure him to her bed, then kill him. Her tongue walked across her lower lip. Oh yes, that would be nice.

Her incantation began to focus on his death. "Water to water, moonlight to moonlight, a witch's spell, hear me, oh Goddess . . ."

Chapter Twenty-three

Neither Carlow nor Nichols heard the rain retreat during the night. Sometime before false dawn, Nichols screamed out, and the young Ranger jerked awake, his hand-carbine in his hand. Chance was at attention, with his back knotted in fierce anticipation, white teeth bared and ready. The young Ranger couldn't remember where he was or why. He looked over at the sleeping Nichols, and recognition returned. A quick word to Chance relaxed the beast into a resting position.

With a deep sigh, Carlow slowly stood, letting his saddle blanket, draped over his body, fall to the wet ground. His damp long coat clung to him like it had always been there. He couldn't remember when it hadn't. Riding now might put them at the Cradle 6 by breakfast. His stomach liked the idea a lot. He looked out at a rain-sodden world and nudged Nichols's leg with the toe of his boot.

Curious, Chance went over to investigate the sleeping cowhand.

"Y-yeah, yeah, I didn't hurt your damn straw any. I'll

be . . ." Nichols stopped in midsentence. "Hey, I'm wet an' I'm . . . I'm sober. My head's pounding somethin' awful. You're not the regular stable guy. Who are you?"

"I'm Ranger Time Carlow. We're headed for the Cradle 6, remember?"

Nichols squeezed his eyes shut and shook his head. "Oh . . . yeah. I knew there was something I was supposed to do." Nichols patted the ground. "Let me sleep on it."

"No. Get up. Bea'll have breakfast on, if we hurry."

"I'm not hungry. You got any whiskey?"

"No—and you don't need any. Get up. Now. We're riding." Carlow leaned over and retrieved his saddle blanket. It was as wet as his coat and pants. Quickly, he rolled and tied the blanket with the loose rawhide strings and headed for his saddle. He had decided to stuff his extra shirt back into the saddlebags even though it was damp, too.

Chance barked his support of moving on.

"Oh, all right. You don't have to shout." Nichols remembered the cigar and examined it. His frown indicated it was too wet to smoke. Carefully, he pushed it into his shirt pocket.

They were saddled and riding in minutes. Nichols was definitely showing signs of a vicious hangover and stopped three times to vomit.

Carlow wondered if the man would make it through the day without returning to the bottle. After each retching, though, Nichols would utter a recommitment and spur his horse. Carlow told Chance to stay away from the pungent mess.

Into the misty dawn, they rode without talking, both lost in memories of better days. A drenched sun was trying hard to clear the horizon as the two rode up to the small ranch house.

Carlow remembered the half-beaten fence, the broken wagon, the outbuildings, the aging cottonwoods, the well and the tall windmill. Nothing had changed. Nothing had been damaged. It was reassuring to see Shadow where he had left his black horse, standing quietly outside the corral. Within the rail confinement, wet horses milled nervously. Only one chicken scouted the open yard; it looked like a ball of water with soaked feathers. The house itself was dark.

Were they too late?

A bear of a man stepped through the door and onto the porch. Carlow knew who it was immediately.

His uncle. Texas Ranger Aaron "Thunder" Kileen.

Damp shadows made the former bare-knuckle prize-fighter look even bigger than he was. Streaks of dawn lay across his battle-marked face. At his side was a Winchester, looking more like a stick in his huge fist.

He was dressed, as usual, in a worn tweed suit showing signs of trail and battle. So far the fabric had not given way to the strain of resisting his powerful arms and thick chest, but it wouldn't be long. A high-crowned black hat extended his appearance in the uneven light; the upper crease was decorated with an old bullet hole. Over his wrinkled suit was a heavy bullet belt carrying a holstered pistol and a sheathed Bowie knife.

"Mornin' to ye lads. An' would the handsome Ranger be lookin' for a fine black horse an' a wee bit o' breakfast?" Kileen's voice boomed across the open yard. His smile was a jack-o-lantern's display of missing teeth.

Nichols looked over at Carlow and grinned. "Hope you know this mountain talkin' to us."

"That's my uncle. Not sure why he's here—but he's a mighty good sight."

"If he fights like he looks, he's sure welcome."

"Oh, he does that—and then some."

"Get yourselves down and come on in, me lads."
Kileen's welcome boomed again. "Meself just rode in
this morn. Captain McNelly hisself sent me to find the
gallant Ranger Carlow. We be taking three herds back
to their fine owners—but the Mexicans be findin' the
great river too fast."

"You did better than I did, then. Silver got away."

"Aye, I not be thinkin' the lad at your side be Silver.
His masqueradin' not be so good as that."

A small shadow squeezed past him, studied the riders
for a moment, and ran toward them.

"You came back! You came back!" Hattie yelled. "I
knew you would."

"I think the lass is talking about you, Ty," Nichols
said with a wry smile. "Alas, I've never had much luck
with the ladies. At any age."

Dismounting quickly, Carlow knelt with his arms
outstretched to receive the excited Hattie. She ran into
his chest and held him tightly around the neck. Carlow's hat spun to the ground.

Chance barked happily, with his tail snapping briskly
in spite of its wetness. A lick on Hattie's arm followed.

Carlow laughed and hugged her back. "How are
you, Hattie?" He patted her head, then motioned toward Nichols as he swung down from his horse.
"Here's another friend of yours. Remember Will
Nichols? He came back to help with the ranch."

She looked over at Nichols, who was adjusting his
saddle cinch with his good hand, more to have something to do than because of a real need. Hattie's eyes
widened. "Has your hand grown back?"

Carlow winced.

Nichols only smiled, patted the cinch, and flipped
the stirrup back into place. "No, it hasn't, little lady,
but my backbone has."

Her eyes were a question. Carlow whispered in her

ear and stood. The girl glanced at him for reassurance, then walked over to Nichols. "I'm glad you came, Mr. Nichols. Can you teach me another song? I sing the other one all the time. Do you want to hear it?"

Nichols beamed; crimson crawled from his torn undershirt up the back of his neck as he tugged on the brim of his forlorn-looking hat in response. "Well, sure, I'll like that a lot."

With that, Hattie began singing "The Rose of Alabamy" in her clear little voice: "Away from Mississippi's vale, with my ol' hat there for a sail, I crossed upon a cotton bale to Rose of Alabamy. Oh brown Rosie, Rose of Alabamy! A sweet tobacco posey is my Rose of Alabamy, a sweet tobacco posey is my Rose of Alabamy."

Redness completed its tour of Nichols's face, and he looked at Carlow and mouthed, "It's the only song I know."

Carlow turned away to hide his smile while Nichols told Hattie quietly that it was a special song she shouldn't sing around her grandmother. Hattie said her grandmother liked it and asked again if he would teach her another. Nichols promised he would when he had the time, glancing at Carlow as if to secure his help in the matter. Satisfied, she skipped over to the wolf-dog to return the beast's friendly greeting with a hug and began singing the verses to Chance.

A large paw of a hand was laid on Carlow's shoulder, and he looked up into Kileen's craggy face.

"Aye, 'tis a shame ye be losin' Silver's trail an' have to come back here." Kileen's eyes studied his nephew. The huge brawler's concern for the striking young man he loved like a son was easy to read. "An' praise the good Lord, where did ye be gettin' the fine cut on your head, me lad? An' your hands have been in a round of fisticuffs. A button ye be losin', too."

"I almost rode into one, Thunder. Silver was waiting for me. I got lucky." Carlow grinned mischievously at this use of the word "lucky" to his uncle. He also told him about the fight in town.

Kileen had seen that look often. It was a smile that indicated everything was under control, or would be. It was a smile of great confidence and courage. It was the smile of the young man he thought of as his son. "Glad that Silver be not knowin' enough to count his bullets."

"Probably so."

"Aye, but we'll get the blackguard," Kileen said. "Have ye wired the fine captain hisself about this?"

"No. Haven't had time. Silver's in Mexico by now."

"Aye. We'll be wirin' Captain McNelly when we get to town."

"Sure. When we get to town. I doubt he'll be sending me on any assignments by myself for a long spell. I failed." Carlow turned toward the waiting Nichols. "Will, come and meet the mountain, my uncle, Ranger Aaron Kileen. Call him Thunder."

"My pleasure, Ty," Nichols announced, and walked over to the two Rangers. "Glad to meet you, sir . . . ah, Thunder."

The bedraggled-looking cowboy saw Kileen's eyes review him and catch his missing hand. Embarrassed, Nichols tugged on his empty sleeve and said, "I know I don't look like much, but I can hold my own. I came to fight. No one's going to take Mrs. Von Pearce's ranch."

Kileen's voice lowered to his idea of a whisper. He told them the Cradle 6 had lost its remaining herd during the night's rain—and the last of its riders. Two men were found dead by Charlie Two-Wolves; he assumed the other three had ridden away. A full moon was partly to blame, Kileen thought; it was an omen of death. His heavy eyes widened as he described the condition of the dead riders; each was missing an ear and their faces were painted with moon and arrow signs in their own blood.

With a hitch of his shoulders, Kileen said he had asked Two-Wolves if it was the work of renegade Indians. Without any outward emotion, the Comanche wrangler assured him it was not; he said it was the work of the "devil woman from the moon"—Dr. Holden's wife. Kileen shrugged his shoulders again, and Carlow nodded his understanding.

Stretching out his neck, Nichols asked, "Who's dead?"

Kileen pursed his lips. "It t'were hard for me to understand the brave Two-Wolves. But the fine widow be tellin' me the names of the blessed dead were Keller and Winnard."

"Addison Keller . . . an' Emmett Winnard. Damn. They were friends of mine. I'll kill those—"

"Widow Von Pearce be havin' only a wee day or two before she be forced to leave," Kileen interrupted. He didn't mention the other obvious option: or die. Without saying so, it was clear Kileen understood Carlow had returned to aid the widow.

With an enormous frown, the thick-shouldered Ranger added that he had heard a whippoorwill calling for the souls of the dead as he rode in an hour earlier. Kileen said he had come to the ranch shortly after the Comanche wrangler returned from the valley. Two-Wolves had heard shooting the night before and went out to determine the cause, even though it was raining. Kileen figured Two-Wolves had heard cattle mooing, and at night, that meant death for certain.

Carlow looked over at Nichols.

The one-handed cowboy's expression indicated disbelief. He saw Carlow's grin and smiled back through his grief at hearing about the loss of his two riding companions.

Kileen caught the exchange, and his mouth spread again into a wide, awkward grin, something he didn't do often because it showed his missing teeth. The look was the result of a combination of fighting and a drunk Mexican dentist. Of course, the big Ranger had been equally drunk. If he ever explained his loss of teeth, which was rare, Kileen would attribute it to a dream about rattlesnakes the night before the dentist worked on him. He never explained the relationship between the dream and the tooth pulling, however.

But it wasn't like him to explain much of anything about himself. Carlow recalled the occasion, as a boy, when he'd asked his uncle why he had a different last name than his mother's maiden name, if they were brother and sister. Her maiden name was Lucent, the young Ranger's middle name. Kileen had said he was surprised his nephew hadn't thought of that before. Then the big Ranger had told him in one sentence that something had happened in New York, not long after they arrived in America, that caused him to become Kileen. He wouldn't elaborate. Carlow had quit asking years ago.

Now Nichols found the nerve to challenge Kileen's superstition about cows mooing, saying that he had heard cattle mooing many an evening riding nighthawk and nothing bad happened.

"Aye, 'tis much going on that is beyond your be- lievin' I know," Kileen said. "But such is the way of things. How do you know there were no deaths on those nights."

"Well, there weren't."

"Ye mean ye know of none. Close by."

Nichols changed the subject, not wishing to argue with the huge man. "We have to bury Addison an' Em- mett. We have to."

Kileen took a deep breath. "Laddie, I know how ye be feelin'. We all have lost friends. Aye, too many, it be." He folded his arms and his body sagged slightly. "Ye understand we must find the widow's herd first."

"Where's Charlie now?" Carlow knew his uncle didn't like having his beliefs challenged—and he didn't want to think about the dead men being torn apart by animals.

A glance at Nichols told the young Ranger that the latter was on the one-handed cowboy's mind.

Chapter Twenty-four

Kileen was animated as he described the Comanche wrangler's objective. "Aye, he left once more, he did. Told me hisself would track the herd and come back for me. The wolves told hisself to follow." His hands waved to help describe Two-Wolves's attire when leaving. "And painted for war he be. Naked except for a breechcloth, a necklace of wolf teeth, and a pouch at his waist. Wolf medicine, he be sayin'."

Carlow and Nichols listened intently; both glad to be away from the big Irishman's insistence that cows mooing at night indicated death.

Kileen motioned with his head toward the house, where Bea Von Pearce was working in the kitchen. "I be thinkin' 'tis a good thing for meself to be waitin' here."

"Yeah, she makes great sausages." Carlow smiled.

"Aye, that she does, me son," Kileen said. "But, alas, I be no tracker—and this was a doin' for one man. One can be goin' where two would be seen." He paused as if deciding whether to say something or not.

"What's the matter, Thunder?"

"Oh, 'tis nothing. When the noble red man rode away, he be tellin' me that he saw ye coming back here—in his dream. He be sayin' to tell ye that his spirit helpers came back. Said ye would be understandin'. Do ye?"

"Should we wait for him here?" Carlow asked, ignoring any comment about the dream or the question.

"Aye. When he comes, we ride." Kileen twisted his mouth. "Ye didn't answer me question about the spirit helpers hisself said."

"Nothing much to tell, Thunder. He just felt his way of life had disappeared. I guess it has for the most part."

"Does he believe the spirits be mad at hisself?"

Carlow's eyes twinkled, knowing this would be his uncle's highest concern. "I think it was more feeling sorry that his life had changed. Comanches don't control the Staked Plains like they used to."

"Aye. *Llano Estacado*. The great Comancheria. Kings of all they once be." Kileen waved his arms to complete a circle and went on to describe the vast land controlled by the nomadic warriors—north to the Red River, but not across it since the Five Civilized Tribes held the land there; south into the northern Mexico settlements and all the way west to villages in New Mexico; and east to the Cross Timbers. He shook his head at the description, using his hands to indicate the tremendous range of their influence.

Carlow wasn't interested in the geography lesson. "Maybe we should ride out that way now. Why wait?"

"I agree. Been running . . . from myself," Nichols added, his eyes hard. "All the way to the bottle. I'd like to keep after 'em." He thrust out his jaw. "An' I still think we should bury my friends . . . first. I ain't gonna let wolves an' such tear 'em up."

Kileen put his hand on Nichols's shoulder. "A brave soldjur ye be, lad. Proud to have ya with us. A memorable fight 'twill be. A memorable fight. But we wait. Here. We wait, lads."

Carlow told Kileen about Dr. Holden, Red Anklon, and the attempt to control the region's cattle business. He didn't mention the doctor's wife but told Kileen that Dr. Holden had cut off Nichols's hand. He left out the cowhand's personal nightmare of whiskey and fear but told about his coming to get Carlow and returning to fight. Nichols looked embarrassed with the telling and kept glancing down at where his hand had been. Carlow made no mention either of Del Gato or the black gunfighter. Or the heavyset shootist, Jimmy Ward Flanker, who had helped him.

All of that could come later. None of it mattered right now. They were outnumbered and should expect an attack of some kind soon. Everything in him wanted to attack first, but he trusted his uncle in matters of battle. There was always a reason for Kileen's actions, a reason beyond some expressed superstition.

Bea Von Pearce appeared in the doorway and cupped a hand to her forehead to see better. Her smile indicated recognition. She waved and shouted, "*Mein Gott*, it's yah, *Herr* Nichols. *Oooch, Ich* thought yah had passed." Her hand dropped to her eyes to wipe away the sudden teary rush.

And in a mixture of nervous German and English, she ran to Carlow and gave him a warm hug, then the same greeting to an even more embarrassed Nichols. She held his face in her hands, but no words would come through the tears that shredded her stout cheeks. Finally she gathered her emotions enough to say, "*Herr* Ranger Carlow, yah vere *nein* to *kommen* back until yah vere catching *der* evil man. Silver, he be."

"Yes, Bea, that was my plan. It just didn't happen

that way. He got away. For now. I'll get him though."
He raised his chin. "But right now, I have no more important thing to do than to help you, Bea. I assure you."

She looked at him in disbelief, wiping the dampness from her cheeks. "*Ja*, but *Ich* be *sehr* happy yah *ist hier*. Your uncle tells me *sehr* much." She looked at Kileen and smiled warmly. She drew in a long, hesitant breath and continued, "They *haff* taken *mein* Herman from me—and *der* brave *reiters* of *der* Cradle 6. Now they have *mein* cows. They do not know of *mein* feelings. *Ich* vill not leave *mein* land. *Ich* vill die *hier*."

Carlow looked at Kileen and Nichols before responding. "Bea, nobody's going to take the Cradle 6 from you. I promise."

She tried to smile. "Vhat *ist* about Charlie? To me he vould not listen . . . this time." She glanced at Carlow, adding that the Comanche wrangler was right when he'd told about her troubles. She just didn't want to bother the Ranger with them.

"Charlie's doing what he does best. He'll find the herd—and then we'll go get it," Carlow said, believing the statement. "We're going to make them hurt for a change. We're going to end this. You've suffered too much. So have others around here. Rangers are supposed to help Texas. That's what we're going to do."

Her smile wobbled, and a fat tear escaped from the emotion still building in her eyes. She insisted they stay for breakfast before riding on; Carlow acknowledged it sounded wonderful, but they shouldn't take the time. He agreed with Nichols that they should ride out to meet the Comanche wrangler instead of just waiting. Two-Wolves might try to take back the herd himself, instead of returning. Carlow thought his one-handed companion hadn't given up on the thought of taking care of the dead riders first either.

Kileen noted to himself that waiting was not a preferred way for his nephew even after his teaching and that of his nephew's Apache friend. For once, he decided not to dissuade him. His primary reason for waiting had been to protect the ranch house from attack. It would have been easy for someone to watch their movements and to strike the home after Kileen and Two-Wolves rode off. His reasoning hadn't included the wonderful smells of breakfast cooking or Bea's attractiveness to him. They weren't factors, he told himself. Not at all.

Encouraged by Carlow's support, Nichols suggested they switch to fresh horses after he searched the bunkhouse to see if any guns had been left behind.

Pushing his tongue against his cheek, the big Ranger looked up into the reddening sky. "Aye, an' three times 'round the ranch as the clock be movin', we will ride—before leaving for the red man, and the findin' of the herd." He smiled at Bea with his mouth closed. "That will keep the wee people close to watch over this fine house."

"I'll get horses saddled, Will. You look for guns," Carlow said, and led their horses toward the corral.

From his tied position at the outside corral post, Carlow's black horse greeted him with a loud and nervous whinny. Stomping hooves demonstrated eager readiness. Immediately the young Ranger looped the reins over the closest rail and went over to Shadow. The powerful horse whinnied softly this time and lowered his head.

After rubbing his dark face and ears, Carlow checked Shadow's legs and was pleased to see the animal was recovering fast. But he explained to the horse that he was not ready to run again. "Not yet, my friend. You must rest here first," Carlow whispered. "I know. I know. I will have to take a lesser horse, but soon we will travel together again. I promise. You stay here—and get well."

Chance strutted next to them but was quickly distracted by a courageous rooster that challenged the wolf-dog with a loud *cock-a-doodle-do*. The bird's outstretched neck and cocked head signalled defiance at this strange beast stalking his domain.

"No, Chance. No. Stay with me, boy." Carlow looked up from talking with his horse.

The wolf-dog growled his response. Tentatively the rooster backed away to a safer stand and crowed once more.

Coming up behind him, Nichols laughed and said, "That's one stupid rooster."

"Yeah. It's one thing to yell a challenge. Something else to make it stick," Carlow said casually. He leaned over to talk with his wolf-dog and waved at the rooster, telling it to use this moment to leave.

Nichols thought about Carlow's comment and headed for the bunkhouse, shooing the farm bird as he passed. With one last crowed declaration, the rooster trotted out of sight behind the barn.

"See, Chance. He's gone. You can relax. Those are Bea's and you can't have them." Carlow rubbed his fingers along the bullet graze on Shadow's flank, noting Charlie Two-Wolves had drawn a circle of red paint around it.

Mysterious marks danced within the shape and a yellow salve of some kind had been placed along the entire cut. He smelled it and decided the medicine was mostly beeswax mixed with vinegar and herbs. Out of the corner of his eye, he saw his uncle discussing something with Bea. He was holding Hattie's hand. Carlow scratched his chin and returned to his examination of Shadow's wound.

Kileen's heavy stride could be felt as well as heard. The young Ranger looked up and smiled. Bea and Hattie were nowhere in sight. He assumed they had gone back inside.

"When I see your fine mount be carryin' a bullet line and be worn from much ridin', me heart worried." Kileen ran his thick finger along the horse's creased flank.

"Yeah, I rode Shadow too damn hard. It was dumb."

"Duty did the riding, me son. But proud I am that ye come back to help the widow."

"I couldn't ride on, Thunder."

"I know, me son. I know."

It was decided Kileen would remain behind in case Dr. Holden's men made an unexpected move on the ranch. It was the big Ranger's idea. Recalling Bea's engaging looks at his uncle, Carlow grinned to think there was more to the tactic than simple smart defense, but he didn't comment. He also guessed that was what Kileen was sharing with the woman earlier.

The strategy made sense for the same reason Kileen had stayed behind when Two-Wolves left. They had to assume the ranch was being watched. Carlow suddenly raised his arm and waved at the hillside.

"What ye be doin' that for, laddie?" Kileen asked.

"Well, if they are watching, it'll make them think we know it."

Kileen laughed deeply and his belly rolled with emotion. Then, he raised his arm and joined in the salutation, laughing and shaking his head.

"That should make them wonder what we're up to," Carlow said, and returned to his buckskin and Nichols's horse.

"Aye, or be thinkin' we're a wee bit touched in the head." There was something else Kileen wanted to say.

Carlow could sense it as he pulled the saddles from their horses. He expected Kileen to blurt out what was on his mind as Carlow walked the horses into the corral, removed their bridles, and let them loose. Neither horse was inclined to do anything but observe the others. The same brown lead mare watched them with laid-back ears and a definite inclination to make sure they understood who was in control. The fiery grulla stomped and snorted. Carlow wondered why Bea and Two-Wolves hadn't suggested he take that horse instead of the buckskin.

But his mind wasn't really on selecting horses. It was on his uncle. Sometimes he thought Kileen acted more like a mother sending her child off to school than a Ranger giving orders to another lawman. He knew the big man wanted to tell him something. He wished he would just say it so they could get on with their plan.

After rubbing his unshaved chin, Kileen pulled a small buckskin pouch from his coat pocket and held it out toward Carlow. "This be from the red man hisself. Before he rode away, he told me that ye be comin' and to be givin' ye this fine gift." He looked down at the discolored bag closed tightly at the open end with a wrapped thong. " 'Tis wolf medicine, he be sayin'." He licked his lower lip. "Strong she be, I'm thinkin'. Don't know what be in the bag—for sure, ye know. Likely there's a wee bit of spirit grass, a wild herb or two. Aye, an' a bird's claw, I be thinkin'." He paused, as if trying to imagine what else was in the pouch, and continued, "Probably a small stone. There would surely be a wee bit of ground-up white powder from a wolf's tooth, sure as the Isle be green. And ye know, one of those little hard balls from the great buffalo's own belly. Aye, but I not be knowing for sure. Just guessin', ye know."

Chapter Twenty-five

A wide smile popped across Carlow's face. He couldn't help it as he leaned over and placed the small pouch in his saddlebags resting on the ground. Of course his uncle had examined the contents carefully, touching each thing and adding an Irish blessing. There would have been no way the big Ranger could have resisted, unless Two-Wolves specifically told him it was unlucky to do so.

But he quickly pulled in the smile; he didn't want to embarrass his uncle. He knew Kileen had studied the ways of the Comanche, the Kiowa, and the Apache. Unlike most of his fellow Rangers, Kileen had never seen them as universal adversaries. Rather, he connected them to the early Irish warriors driven from their homeland. Carlow figured his uncle was also drawn to their rituals and beliefs, with many quite close to Kileen's own. He had always approved of Carlow's friendship with Kayitah—and had been greatly angered by his death and the way it occurred.

The younger Ranger had always suspected it was his

uncle who beat up four troopers in a saloon shortly after Kayitah's death. None of the soldiers would press charges and professed not to know their adversaries. Carlow guessed they had been bragging about the massacre and his uncle overheard them. He surmised they were embarrassed to admit one man had beaten the four of them. If the truth were known, they were lucky to have survived Kileen's wrath—and his massive right fist. Carlow knew of at least one outlaw who hadn't.

Carlow loosened a lariat from his gear, lifted Nichols's saddle over his shoulder with his left hand, and entered the corral. After watching the milling horses and letting the lead mare approve him, Carlow focused on a sturdily built bay. He laid the saddle beside him, shook out a loop in his right hand, and walked toward the animal. The horse's head came up as the lariat settled around its neck and tightened. For a moment the bay tensed, then relaxed as Carlow walked toward the animal, recoiling the rope and talking comfort.

As Carlow gathered the horse, Kileen explained what everything meant in the pouch. Protection from the spirits came from the sweet grass, healing from the herbs, courage from the bird's claw; long life from the stone since it was the most ancient of beings, strength and victory in battle from the smooth ball from the stomach of a buffalo, and wisdom and night vision from the wolf powder.

After a few strokes along the horse's back to reassure himself of its soundness, Carlow led the bay to the far corral fence and began saddling it for Nichols. Kileen followed, pursing his lips and noting that Two-Wolves had sung a special song over the pouch before giving it to him. The Comanche wrangler had said there was also the howl of a wolf, the scream of an eagle, and the roar of thunder placed in there. He had said it quite seriously, as if recounting a recipe.

Carlow finished saddling the bay and flipped the reins twice around the top rail. After removing his rope, he returned to his own saddle gear to repeat the switchover. Kileen was still talking, but it was difficult to catch many of his words over the restlessness of the horses in the enclosure.

With his right fist holding the lariat, Carlow swung both saddle and head tack over his shoulder with his free left hand and returned to the corral.

To make certain he was heard over the noise, Kileen yelled, " 'Tis not for seein', the wolf howl an' the eagle scream' an' the thunder. Only a Comanche can see them."

"That was nice of him." Carlow studied his uncle. Would the wily old Ranger ever give him advice about how to succeed against Dr. Holden's men? That would be helpful. The rest was just silly superstitious talk and he didn't have time for it now. He tossed his noose over the neck of the grulla and tightened it. The horse straightened its neck and snorted; its front legs dug into the ground and its rear dropped to provide strength against the restraint.

Carlow assured the animal everything was all right. "Come on, big fella. I know you're the best in here. You don't have to prove it to me."

The horse's ears cocked toward the man walking toward it, soothed by the comfort in his voice.

"Takin' the piebald, ye should. 'Tis a horse full o' good luck," Kileen said, pointing toward a speckled white horse in the middle of the huddle.

"Not half the horse this grulla is. Have you watched him at all? He's a fighter."

"Aye, but struttin' is for roosters an' such."

"He wasn't strutting, Thunder, he was making a stand. Reminds me some of Shadow."

The grulla's head cocked to the side, understanding

what was next. Carlow walked toward it, talking softly. He liked the animal's attitude already.

"Just one wee hair from a piebald will be curin' the whooping cough." Kileen's further observation interrupted Carlow's study of the horse.

"I don't have whooping cough."

"Don't be lookin' at his tail, though, me lad. 'Tis the only way ye get bad luck from a piebald."

"How about a brown tail? Or a grulla's? Is that all right to look at?" Carlow's voice couldn't hide the sarcasm. Surely his uncle had some observations about recovering the herd and dealing with Dr. Holden's men. *Enough of this superstition nonsense for one day,* he fumed to himself. At least Will Nichols wasn't superstitious.

He tied the horse next to the first, laid his saddle blanket over the tall animal's back, and smoothed it. He was surprised to see Kileen enter the corral. *What now?* he thought, and swung the saddle into place.

Without glancing at his nephew, Kileen strode directly to the piebald, waving his arms to get the other horses out of the way. The speckled horse whinnied and lowered its head as Kileen stopped a few feet away. The other horses sought the railings, and a gray wandered over to Carlow and his two horses.

After spitting on the fingers of both hands, the big Ranger bent down and touched the toes of his boots. He took several steps closer, crossed his fingers, spit over his left shoulder, and touched the piebald on the right shoulder with both hands, his first and second fingers crossed.

Loudly he proclaimed, "Shakespeare come true."

Stepping back, he stood quietly, then spun around and went to his nephew.

As if nothing had occurred, Kileen immediately gave his nephew some advice. "If ye be hearin' four wolf cries close together, ye be turnin' back. Charlie's wolves be tellin' ye that your medicine is not strong this morn." Kileen's giant forehead was a series of furrows.

"Four. I got it," Carlow replied, tightening the cinch. "Say, what was that Shakespeare crap all about?"

Kileen explained it was part of the piebald ritual he'd learned from an Irish witch.

"Oh. Well, you didn't let out all those noises when you opened the pouch, did you? You know the thunder, howling, and all."

"What are ye askin'?"

"Never mind."

Satisfied, Kileen spoke again, "An' ye be lookin' for nine."

"Nine? Nine what?" Carlow stopped after checking the thongs holding the sheath of his saddle gun in place.

Disappointment took shape on Kileen's craggy face. "Nine o' anything, me lad. That is the sign the wee faeries be close at hand. Very lucky indeed. Three times three, it be. Three times as lucky."

"Nine it is, then," Carlow snapped back, easing the bit into the horse's mouth and curling the leather head stall over its ears. "Here comes Will. Looks like he found a Winchester."

" 'No heat like that of shame.' " Kleen whispered an Irish saying.

"He'll stand, Thunder."

"Maybe," Kileen responded, "but ye do not be expectin' hisself to be at your back. Do ye hear your fine uncle? The drink be ownin' him still."

"Yes, and you're wrong." Carlow frowned and waved at Nichols.

"He'll be lookin' first for a reason to go bury the dead."

"What's wrong with caring about friends?"

Kileen sighed. "Friends be the great feast of life, me son. But there be livin' friends an' dead friends. Which do ye think should get attention first?"

"That's not a fair question."

"Aye—an' this life not be fair either . . . Ranger Carlow."

Shrugging his massive shoulders, Kileen finally turned his attention to the challenge facing them. He was certain Two-Wolves would locate the stolen Cradle 6 herd even though the rain had washed away their tracks. It hadn't rained since the Comanche wrangler left, so his own tracks should be easy to follow, if he decided to make them.

Surprise would be their best weapon, the old Ranger advised; when they found the herd, they should spread out, use the land to get close, and start shooting. Don't worry about the cattle stampeding. No first announcement of being a Ranger. He told Carlow to capture one of Dr. Holden's men alive, if possible, so they would have a witness to the physician's involvement.

At last his uncle was making sense, Carlow thought, then teased him to be careful around the widow.

"She carries a pistol in her apron. All the time. Something her late husband told her to do," Carlow said.

"Aye, I be seein' that. I be partial to women with fight in their bosoms."

"Well, that's a fact." Carlow grinned and slapped his uncle on the back. "Angel's got enough fight in her for three men."

Kileen's smile showed his vacated teeth.

Twenty minutes later, Carlow and Nichols rode away. Nichols had found a gunbelt with a short-barreled revolver to go along with the rifle. He thought both had belonged to a rider named Harrison, who was killed months ago. Carlow told him to keep the extra handgun he'd given Nichols tucked in his waistband as well.

Bea came out with two steaming cups of coffee, which Carlow and Nichols gratefully downed. Nichols winked at the young Ranger and said it would taste even better with a bit of whiskey. Hattie brought three sacks of food for the two of them—and Charlie Two-Wolves, when they had the opportunity to give it to him. At Kileen's insistence, all three men rode around the house three times before the two young men left.

After watching his nephew and the one-handed cowboy disappear toward the east, Kileen turned his own horse out in the corral and went to the front porch. As a courtesy to the German widow, he removed his long trail coat and pistol belt and laid them a few feet from the doorway. His saddle rifle was propped against the house next to a basin of fresh water on a sturdy washstand, presumably moved outside for his use. A fresh towel lay on the stand as well.

This was no rawhide outfit, he thought as he soaped his hands and face. A lot of hard work had gone into building this ranch. A bit run-down at the corners, perhaps, but definitely built to last. Nothing like the one-room hacienda of his longtime girlfriend, the outlaw Angel Balta. His return visit to her run-down place was brief after Silver Mallow and his men were arrested. Their orders were to rejoin Captain McNelly's main force immediately. However, it had been long enough to apologize for the way he had acted upon learning she had once ridden with the outlaw leader. As usual, Angel had accepted the apology warmly—and lustily.

The cool liquid felt like fingers were touching him, and he repeated the soothing treatment. It also helped to dissolve the lust rebuilding from the memory of that last visit to Angel's. She would have to wait. Kileen brushed down his hair with wet hands. Another woman was worthy of his attention. Angel would understand, he was certain.

Happy with his refreshed appearance, he picked up his gunbelt with one hand and his rifle with the other. Pausing at the doorway, he tapped the doorframe three times with the barrel of the Winchester as he entered. Quietly, he propped the gun against the wall beside the front door and laid the pistol belt next to it. The courtesy would impress Bea, he thought, showing his polite side. But the weapons would be handy if any trouble came while they ate. He didn't expect any.

He took a step, stopped, and returned to his guns. Withdrawing the Colt from its holster, he shoved it into his waistband and covered the handle with his vest. That felt better. Something about being unarmed didn't seem right. For the first time, he noticed the vest was discolored in places. He rubbed on the spots vigorously but soon gave up on the idea. Trail dirt had long ago taken up residence in the fibers. He would just have to rely on his charm and headed for the breakfast table.

Bea Von Pearce and Hattie were already seated at the heavy planked table. The dining area was set off from the main room by hand-painted dressing screens. He removed his hat and laid it on a chair, drinking in the coziness of the room and the memories lingering there, before coming to the table. He couldn't help noticing three heavy candlesticks on the mantel. All three candles were lit. *That's good luck, it 'tis,* he told himself, but worried that the middle candle seemed to be spitting flame.

He shrugged his shoulders and went on, reciting a silent chant to counteract the potential bad news if that candle went out unexpectedly.

On the wall behind Bea was a heavy gold-framed

painting of a rich-looking countryside. It wasn't land Kileen could recall seeing. Perhaps it was Germany. Or, maybe, the Texas hill country around Fredericksburg. He knew many German families had settled there.

"*Ja, Herr* Ranger Kileen, it *ist der Vader Land. Mein* dear Herman brought it over."

"Looks mighty fine, mum."

"Please to call me Bea."

Kileen gave his best closed-mouth smile. "Aye, Bea it shall be. An' all blessin's on ye."

"Sit down *hier, Herr* Ranger Kileen." She motioned toward the empty chair to her right.

" 'Tis Thunder friends be callin' me. Please . . . Bea."

"Thunder. You *ist* full of *der* power, like Thor." Her eyes sparkled and sought his.

He blinked, shrugged, and sat down.

Bristow china and heavy iron utensils awaited them at each setting. In the center of the table was a dark red glass vase proudly presenting a fistful of flowers plucked from the garden out back. The table was laden with bowls of steaming potatoes and sausages, one plate piled with hot biscuits, and another with fried eggs. A gravy bowl was nearly overflowing with heavy gravy. A smaller dish held yellow butter. On an adjoining narrow table sat a large blackened pot of coffee.

Kileen couldn't help thinking how unreal it was. The woman was nearly ruined, her last cattle run off, and here was a breakfast fit for royalty.

Bea's cheeks were rosy from the heat of cooking and she looked at the big man with her best coquettish smile. "Ve are *sehr* happy to *haff* you join us. Few Rangers come *hier* . . . or any strangers to come, for this matter. It *ist* good to *haff* a man in *der haus* once more." The gun in her apron pocket clanked against the table as she sat.

Kileen was amused and wondered to himself if she went to bed with that apron on. His wondering slid further, picturing the robust woman welcoming him to the same bed. He returned her warmth with a fetching grin of his own but remembered to keep his mouth closed.

"This sure be lookin' mighty fine as a fresh Irish morn, mum," he said in his most gallant manner. "Mighty fine. Me stomach be thankin' ye already. 'Tis too bad the lads had to go without such a celebration, carryin' only a little sup they be."

She nodded, and her eyes lowered toward the folded hands in her lap. The move surprised the big Ranger, who was about to grab his fork. But he lowered his hands to his lap and watched her in silence.

Quietly Bea asked, "Hattie, vill you please to read to *der* table. *Ja.* Be thankin' *Gott* ve be for *der* breakin' our fast."

Hattie glanced at Kileen self-consciously as he tried to appear accustomed to such a procedure. "Dear God, thank you for this food and for this day and for all the blessings you have given us." She peeked at Kileen through half-closed eyes. "An' thank you for Ranger Kileen and Ranger Carlow. An' Mr. Nichols. Amen."

"Amen," Bea added. "*Danke,* Hattie, that *ist* done vell."

"Amen it be, me lass." Kileen nodded. "I be likin' that, too."

"Please to help yourself, *Herr* Ran . . . Thunder. There *ist* plenty."

"Thank you, Bea. I not be seein' food this good in a long time."

The compliment spread across Bea Von Pearce's face as a wide smile. "Oh, it *ist* naught. *Ich* am to fear *der* biscuits *ist* not so *gut.* They be not vat *Ich* to vish for."

His mouth half-full of a bite of biscuits and butter, Kileen hurried to swallow the morsel so he could refute her statement. "Mum, this be tastin' like it be made by the sweet angels themselves. By me blessed mither's grave, none better have I had."

Bea's cheeks glowed. "Yah to make a woman proud, *Herr* Thunder."

Chapter Twenty-six

After serving Kileen and Hattie, Bea filled a plate for herself. Kileen asked her if she sang while making her biscuits. Wide-eyed, she responded negatively, and he was clearly relieved but didn't explain further. Soon they were busy with their food, eating in silence as was the habit of most Western people.

It was Hattie who first severed the mealtime quiet. "Ranger Kileen, do you like these flowers? I picked them today, just for you. They're from our garden." As an afterthought, she added, "An' for Ranger Carlow an' Grandma an' Charlie, too. Mr. Nichols, too."

Wiping his mouth with the cloth napkin, Kileen said, "Oh, they be very pretty, me lass. Thank ye for the kindness. It gladdens me heart." He was glad to see the flowers weren't red and white, for that was an omen of death. Purple, pink, and blue blooms were just fine, he assured himself.

Outside, a noise trying not to be heard caught his attention and he froze. " 'Tis the sound of company, me thinks."

Before Bea could respond, Kileen was at the front window looking outside, grabbing his rifle as he passed. A buggy pulled by two marching gray horses crossed the open yard and pulled up in front of the house. Morning sunlight danced off blond hair under the driver's bowler hat.

"It *ist* Dr. Holden." Bea was standing next to him. She smelled of biscuits and woman and a light scent of something sweet.

"Aye, the blackguard hisself. I shall be greeting him meself." He strode to the door and whipped it open with his left hand, holding the gun in his right. He stood framed in the doorway, levering the gun into readiness.

"Be of care, *mein* Thunder, he *ist der* devil," Bea said as she turned to see where Hattie was.

Dr. Holden's surprise came immediately to his eyes and just as quickly disappeared into a polite stare. "You have me at a disadvantage, sir. I am Dr. Holden. I came to call on Mrs. Von Pearce and see how she is doing." He stepped from the buggy and wrapped the reins around the hitching rack. "I brought along something to make her feel better. A tonic of considerable performance."

"Aye, the only tonic the fine lady be needin' is the re-turnin' of her herd," Kileen growled. "The herd your men be takin' last night."

"I beg your pardon? My men did no such thing. You must be mistaken, sir."

From behind Kileen, Bea declared, "*Ist* no mistake, *Herr* Dr. Holden."

Kileen cocked his head to the side. "An' that witch o' a wife of yours killed two innocent men an' be takin' their ears an' paintin' their faces—with their own blood." His face was dark and his eyes narrowed. "Ye both will hang."

The second part of Kileen's statement hit the doctor like a bullet. His face whipped itself into a rage, then fell back again into placid gentleness so fast Kileen wasn't certain he had seen it.

"Sir, I am a humble practitioner of medicine. Not some bandit. My wife is at our home—in town." Dr. Holden straightened his shoulders and reached back into the buggy for his bag. "Now, if you don't mind, I would like to see Mrs. Von Pearce and make sure that she is well."

" 'Tis a good idea that you stay," Kileen said, pointing his rifle at Dr. Holden's stomach. "Until me nephew and his friends be returning with the lady's fine herd."

"Who are you, anyway?" Dr. Holden's question was a hot poker.

" 'Tis a question for the ages, me doctor. Who do we be?"

"Your name, I meant, sir."

"Oh, of course. How rude I be," Kileen said. "I be Texas Ranger Aaron Kileen. Me friends call me Thunder. Ye can call me Mr. Ranger."

"Drop the gun, Lucent. Or I will kill the little girl." The hard, crisp voice was behind Kileen. From inside the house. It was strangely familiar, even though he hadn't been called by his real last name, Lucent, in years.

The big Ranger eased slowly around to face the voice that demanded his surrender. Bea had already turned and was frozen in place.

An ebony-skinned man with a gleaming face and tiny eyes glared at him. He held Hattie with his left hand as if she were a toy. His sleeveless shirt revealed powerful arms. Under his flat-brimmed hat glistened a gold earring dangling from his left ear. A red sash held a black-handled pistol matching the one in his fist.

Kileen knew the man as soon as he faced him. Selar Viceroy. They had fist-fought in New York. On the docks. For money. Everyone wanted to see the two hated races, Irish and Negro, go at it. Viceroy had won in a long, bloody contest that left both men battered. That was years ago. But it wasn't seeing an old adversary from those bare-knuckle days—or even the gun in Viceroy's hand—that bothered Kileen. It was the black man's manner: he had become a killer. Kileen had seen that look before in John Wesley Hardin, Clay Allison, Silver Mallow, and a few nameless others. The war had done it for some—or been the excuse.

Viceroy would break Hattie's neck and not think about it. Ever again. He would do it as Kileen fired. If he did.

"Put down the gun, or I will kill the girl. She would not be the first child I have killed, I assure you." The black man's voice was clipped, almost musical, and his English precise. "It is good to see you again, Aaron. What a nice surprise. I have thought often about beating you again. Your name was Lucent then. I heard about what happened, and I am not surprised that you have changed it." His white teeth glistened as a sneer took over his face. "You should be ashamed of yourself, robbing a bank and putting a policeman in the hospital. My, my. But I can see why you weren't making enough money fighting. You weren't good enough, were you?"

Kileen's shoulders rose and fell as his gaze took in Hattie's terrified eyes. He tried to concentrate on the moment instead of yesterdays. Behind him Dr. Holden's footsteps onto the porch were hurried, shuffling to a stop and rushing on again. The physician strutted inside, brushing past Bea to examine Kileen haughtily. He grabbed the Winchester from Kileen's hands.

"Well, well, big man, looks like things have changed a bit." Dr. Holden's voice clicked into a condescending whine as if prescribing treatment to a patient. "I'd like you to meet Viceroy. He's Jamaican, or something like that." He licked his lower lip. "He gets paid to kill. I pay him well. I want you to do exactly what Viceroy here says, or have you ever seen a child's neck snapped? It's quite an interesting sight, medically speaking."

Everything in Kileen wanted to attack, and the black man guessed it. "Don't try it. She will die before you strike him. I won't wait for orders, Aaron. This is about money. Nothing personal. That will come later— after the girl and the woman are dead." His white teeth returned in a leering smile. "I want you to remove that pistol now, too. Use your left hand."

Kileen's angry glare frightened the doctor so much that he stepped back three steps to keep the big Ranger's intensity from reaching him. He tried to point the rifle but couldn't find the courage to do it.

"I said drop the gun." Viceroy moved his left forearm against Hattie's neck. Her eyes pleaded with Kileen. A tiny tear escaped from the corner of her right eye and trickled down her cheek.

Kileen's pistol thudded against the floor, and the big Ranger stood with his hands at his sides. "Don't ye hurt the wee lass, or . . ."

"Or what?" Dr. Holden couldn't hold back a snicker. He gradually aimed the Winchester at Kileen but kept the same distance.

"Or ye will not be havin' enough bullets to stop me from snappin' your black neck." Kileen's challenge sought Viceroy's eyes, then went back to Dr. Holden. "An' your puny one."

The black man's dark eyes sparkled in response, and

he, too, looked at the physician for approval to complete his task.

Moving slowly toward the black outlaw, Bea began to sob loudly, holding her hands to her face. After three small steps, she dabbed her eyes with her left hand; her right hand slid into her apron pocket.

Kileen knew well what was hidden there. What would she do? Threatening Viceroy and Dr. Holden with a gun would only result in a surrender of her weapon or Hattie's death. Or both. He frowned and started to tell her not to try it.

"*Lassen* . . . p-please . . . not to hurt her, *Herr* Viceroy. Take me instead." Bea's face was painted with tears.

Viceroy watched her and looked again at Dr. Holden for direction.

The physician smiled. A long, thin smirk full of satisfaction settled on his pale face.

Kileen's fists tightened, but he didn't move. Should he risk grabbing Dr. Holden? Could he reach him before the doctor ordered Viceroy to kill and force a trade? Or would the black man not wait, like he said? Maybe he should rush the black man when Bea neared. Could he be swift enough? Kileen's mind was a murky fog, fighting through regurgitating memories of New York, awful things he had long ago locked away. No one out here knew what he had done back there to give his sister and her young son a place to live and food to eat.

He had already decided to die trying to save Bea and Hattie. The only question was how to accomplish the saving.

"Not a bad idea, Viceroy. Let them trade. An old woman's neck is just as interesting to break. We'll make it look like an accident," Dr. Holden declared, and winked.

Viceroy nodded and reached out to grab Bea's left

arm, releasing Hattie at the same time. The widow's right hand stayed in the apron pocket as he yanked her to him. He pulled the German widow close and locked his left arm under her chin. It was too swift for Kileen to move.

The black man's eyes found Kileen's to acknowledge he had anticipated the big Ranger's trying something. "Don't try it, Lucent. You aren't that good."

Kileen's gaze went gratefully to the little girl scurrying toward him.

Bam! Bam! Bam! Bam!

Kileen flinched as a bullet thudded into the wall a foot from his right arm. Dr. Holden dived for the floor. The rifle he held clanked against the wood. His hat spun away and raced toward the doorway. Hattie stopped in midstride. The black man's eyes bulged as blood streamed down his throat and swamped his shirt. Smoke from Bea's previously hidden pistol encircled his face.

As soon as the black man had pulled her to him, Bea had drawn her gun from the apron, jammed it under his chin, and fired three times as fast as the double-action could work with her finger squeezed against the trigger. Her bullets drove directly up through his chin and into his brain, taking away all but reflex. The fourth shot was from Viceroy's gun. It was his bullet that flew past Kileen.

Another bullet from Bea's gun tore into Viceroy's heart as she reached across her body, pushed the gun against his heaving chest, and fired. His left arm tightened momentarily against her throat, but the death wounds in his brain and heart caught up with the instinct and his arm flopped downward. His pistol slid from his limp right hand and found the floor. She shoved the dying gunman away and pointed her gun at the cowering Dr. Holden.

Staggering from the destruction to his being, Viceroy opened his mouth but only a rush of blood came out. He took a half step forward, wobbled, and tried again. A river of blood preceeded a crackling declaration. "L-Lucent, I . . . I was so l-looking forward to b-beating you to d—" He slammed headfirst into the floor.

From his crouching position, Dr. Holden stuttered, "M-my G-God, you . . . you k-killed him."

Kileen moved more swiftly than anyone would expect a big man could. Putting his boot on the rifle to keep it in place, he yanked Dr. Holden to his feet. He grabbed the doctor's hat and jammed it on the frightened man's head. Half dragging and half carrying him, Kileen took the protesting doctor out of the house and into the ranch yard. Dr. Holden struggled against the big Ranger's powerful grip, his feet barely touching the earth.

"See here, sir. I am a phys—"

Kileen's huge right fist smashed into Dr. Holden's face. Blood and teeth popped like corn over a fire. Kileen's second punch tore into the man's stomach, jackknifing his body and taking away his air.

With a childlike whimper, the doctor collapsed, but Kileen held him upright, with his right hand grasping Dr. Holden's bloody shirt.

"Ye miserable excuse for a man, talkin' of a little girl's neck, were ye?" Kileen's backhanded slap snapped Dr. Holden's cheek sideways, tearing his lower lip and turning his teeth crimson. "Hopin' to take the fine lady's ranch, were ye?" A second slap rammed the physician's head in the other direction.

Kileen pulled back his left fist, holding the doctor upright with his right, for a final blow.

"*Kommen, Herr* Ranger Kileen. Be *der* dear *fruend*—and please to *helfen* me to get the dead

254

African from *mein haus*, vill you?" Bea stood on the porch with Hattie clinging to her leg. Her pistol was nowhere in sight. Her face sparkled with dampness, and her usual glow was deeper.

"Aye, me lady. Just one wee moment longer."

"*Ach der lieber, der* doctor *ist nein* a problem. *Meine haus ist.*" Her voice was insistent.

Shrugging, Kileen released the unconscious doctor and let him slump to the ground as if a bundle of laundry. The big Ranger walked straight to Bea and stopped a foot away. He grinned without opening his mouth. He had just realized she had not been crying in the house, at least not from fear; she had been setting up Dr. Holden and Viceroy so they would allow her to get close. Then she had acted without hesitation. *I'd best be rememberin' the Widow Von Pearce be dangerous when angry,* he told himself, and wondered if she would be as aggressive in bed.

"I be likin' a lady who be takin' the care o' herself."

Bea's smile was a mixture of pleasure and the sickening realization she had killed a man. "*Ich* did *nein haff* choice."

"No, you didn't." Kileen put his hand on her shoulder, as gently as he ever did anything. "Why don't ye an' the sweet lass be checkin' on Ranger Carlow's fine black hoss. Be needin' a wee bite o' grain—or just a nice pat or two."

He turned toward Hattie, whose face was drained of color. "After, if ye be willin', I'll tell ye about the faeries an' where they be livin'. 'Tis a fine bunch they be. All happy an' singin' an' dancin'." He shuffled his feet awkwardly to support the idea of dancing. "They be livin', ye know, down under a pond. Or inside a hill. Aye, that's where they be. I've seen them meself, I have." He cocked his head, hoping for a response, but none came.

Only a strange look from Bea.

Undeterred, he continued, "Ye know, lass, they can make a wee hoss from a bit of straw. Aye, they can. An' ride upon the land like kings and queens." He swallowed and kept trying. "An' 'tis milk and honey they love. Why, they even sip the sweet right from the flowers." He smiled his best closed-mouth smile and ignored the stare from Bea.

Hattie nodded, but her lower lip trembled and gave way to a wail. Bea knelt beside her and held the little girl close. "*Mein* little love, it *ist* all over now. *Nein* can hurt you," Bea said, stroking Hattie's hair and trying not to cry herself.

Kileen stood watching, unsure of what to say or do.

Bea looked up at him, her eyes reassuring. "*Vielen dank, mein freund.* Hattie vould to hear such . . . fun stories. A little later, ah, perhaps." Her smile was faint but she was trying. "An' if yah vould like to be telling me of New York . . . if it vould get something off your great chest, Aaron . . . Lucent . . . *Ich* vould be listening. If *nein, Ich* vill *nein* ask again. All men *haff der* secrets, you know." Her smile had become warm and understanding.

"Aye, later." Kileen nodded and looked away. "I'll be takin' the doctor—an' his killin' man—to town now. The jail be the doctor's home until we be gettin' him in front o' a judge. A nice Irish judge 'twould be to my likin'."

Bea stroked Hattie's hair. "Vill you to be *kommen* back *hier,* Thunder?"

"Aye, that I will," he said, "if'n ye be wantin' to see an ol' prizefighter a wee more. A saint I not be."

Her smile was an invitation.

"Back in the old days, I be doin' bad—to get money for my sweet sister, God bless her soul, and her wee lad . . . me nephew, Time." His concerned gaze studied her face. "I had to change me last name . . . an' hide. I robbed a bankin' house. Aye, that I did." His great shoulders rose and fell, then fire reentered his eyes. "Them that owned it were to be payin' me for a fight . . . an' they decided not. After it were done. A constable who be one o' theirs be tryin' to arrest me after the robbin'. I be hurtin' hisself with me fists."

She leaned over and kissed him on the cheek. "Does *nein* matter, *mein* Thunder. You *kommen* back, yah?"

He beamed, touched his hand to his cheek, and marched into the house, tapping the doorframe three times with his knuckles as he entered.

After watching him disappear, Bea knelt beside Hattie, kissed her on the cheek as well, and whispered in her ear. Hattie's smile was feeble as her small hand reached out to Bea's.

From the window, Kileen watched them walk hand in hand toward the corral. Bea was pointing and talking excitedly. Turning away, he glanced at the candlesticks resting on the mantel. The middle candle was out. Just as he suspected. He shivered, knowing the candle's going out by itself was, indeed, a warning of a death in the house. It had foretold the black man's demise. He was glad he hadn't seen the death candle earlier.

He propped the rifle against the wall again, in almost the same place as before. As he picked up his dropped pistol and gunbelt, a part of him wondered if he could have handled the muscular Viceroy in a fistfight. His memory told him the black man had won in thirty rounds when they met. Kileen had fought with a broken right arm for ten of them. He blinked away the rest of New York when he had become a wanted man. The banking house wasn't the only place he had robbed. Or the policeman the only crooked lawman he had beaten.

Or worse. He would not let the rest of that awful time reenter his mind, or the horrible things he had been forced to do.

Holstering the gun, he buckled the gunbelt into place and walked over to the dead Viceroy. A scarlet pool under his head and chest matched his sash. Bloodstains were not easy to remove, he noted to himself.

"Selar, ye should've stayed in New York. A fine champion ye could have been. Look at ye now."

He shifted the dead man's weight on his shoulder, holding the body in place with his left hand, and he walked back to the door and picked up the Winchester with his right. Tapping the doorway three times with his rifle, he proclaimed, "Here's to ye, Herman Von Pearce, for teachin' your fine lady to shoot." As he headed for the buggy, he muttered, "Aaron Lucent is dead. God bless his black-hearted soul. Ranger Thunder Kileen is alive."

He laid Viceroy in the buggy, struggling with the dead man's weight. Lines of blood decorated the side of the vehicle. Next came the unconscious Dr. Holden. Kileen plopped his smaller frame on top of the black gunfighter, then pulled the reins from the rack.

A few seconds later, the loaded buggy eased toward the front gate. From the corral, Bea watched and waved. Hattie looked up from feeding Shadow. Kileen's big hand reached out of the buggy and returned Bea's greeting. He didn't see her fingers go to her mouth and stay there.

Chapter Twenty-seven

Will Nichols saw the Comanche wrangler first. Charlie Two-Wolves was little more than a suggestion among a line of trees.

"There, Ty. Charlie's down there." Nichols held the reins in place against the saddle horn with his left forearm and waved his good hand.

Carlow wished he would have waited until the young Ranger verified who it was, but the responding wave assured him Nichols was right. They kicked their horses into a gallop and headed toward Two-Wolves, spraying wet grass and mud as they rode. Chance was between them, his tail wagging fiercely as some of the earthen bursts splattered on his body.

"*Ich* find *der* herd. We get *der* herd, *amigos*." Two-Wolves's first remarks were brief and to the point, even if they were a mixture of languages, as usual. He completed his statement with a long Comanche phrase about his spirit helpers returning to help him find the Cradle 6 cattle. Nichols looked at Carlow, who nodded his understanding.

Two-Wolves's hat was gone and his old necktie had been tied around his head like a headband, letting long black hair stream down around his neck. Kileen had described him well. A necklace of wolf teeth set off a broad chest, naked except for the thin strap holding a quiver of arrows and a bow. A breechcloth was his only clothing. A pouch similar to the one he had left for Carlow hung from the waist-bound leather thong holding up his breechcloth. A sheathed knife was held there as well.

His feet were bare, and his legs were soaking wet to his knees. The young Ranger thought the man's scarring on his left cheek was darker than he remembered. And thicker. Across the bridge of the wrangler's nose and both cheeks were two parallel lines of red paint. At the ends of both lines were series of dots, representing a wolf's paw, Carlow decided. The thick scars had turned the lines and dots into a maze of jagged marks on that side of his face. For the first time, the young Ranger noticed a small white circle of paint surrounding a scar on his chest. Probably a "remembered fight" from his warrior days, Carlow guessed to himself.

Two-Wolves studied Nichols for a moment; his hard eyes strayed to the missing hand, then back to the young cowboy's face. "Will Nick-holds. You warrior. *Mucho tekwuniwapi.*"

Carlow thought *tekwuniwapi* meant being brave and told Nichols of the compliment. There was something about Two-Wolves that seemed different to Carlow, and it wasn't his appearance. Not entirely. The Comanche wrangler was much more than an Indian who was good with horses. He was a leader. A war leader. It radiated from him. Carlow would ask Two-Wolves more about himself when they had time. If they did.

Smiling, Nichols extended his right hand. "It is good to see you, Charlie."

The Comanche grasped it awkwardly but understood the gesture. Two-Wolves's eyes blinked away a memory. He turned toward Carlow and brought his right fist to his heart in tribute. "I know you *kommen*. See Star Warrior in *mucho* dream. *Ja*. You *haff* wolf medicine from big Star Warrior . . . *ara* . . . uncle?" He repeated "wolf medicine" in Comanche and made sign for it with great reverence and added a phrase in Spanish that Carlow thought meant "victory or death."

"Yes, I do. Thank you." Carlow patted his saddlebags.

Two-Wolves nodded and explained, mostly in Comanche, that the wolf medicine was secured during a full moon, and that the wolf would forever be Carlow's spirit helper if he would let it be so. Proudly the Comanche explained his own spirit helpers, a pair of prairie wolves, had returned to him during the night as he trailed the herd. He said Carlow's wolf-dog was, indeed, a present from the spririts. That statement reminded Carlow of Kileen's observation that the animal was the spirit of Carlow's late best friend, Shannon Dornan, mainly because the young Ranger had found the wolf-dog shortly after leaving Dornan's grave.

Carlow grimaced slightly, not wanting his thoughts to go there, and asked, "How far is the herd?" He supported his question with sign, not knowing the right words in Comanche.

In a string of English, German, Spanish, and Comanche words and phrases, Two-Wolves explained the herd had been taken onto a pasture that nestled behind a long ridge; it was Bar H land but used to belong to the River S. The land was flat and grassy, with a stream along the southern edge. It wasn't far, just beyond the second rise. Six riders were watching the herd; Red Anklon and Del Gato were there. So was Jessie Holden, dressed as a man. But not Dr. Holden himself. The Comanche wrangler had gotten close enough to notice Anklon's face was bruised and swollen.

Nichols told him about the fight in town, and Two-Wolves nodded as if he expected Carlow to be victorious against the bigger man. Then Nichols asked about the two dead riders and if they could bury them first. Carlow looked away; it was what Kileen said would happen.

Before the young Ranger could respond, Two-Wolves told them that he had moved the bodies to a shallow cave cut into a hillside not far from where they died. He had closed off the entrance with rocks so they wouldn't be bothered by animals until they could be buried. His explanation indicated he understood the white man's way of placing the dead back into Mother Earth for eternity. He finished by saying he had told his own spirit helpers, the wolves, to tell their brothers to leave the brave men alone.

Tears welled in Nichols's eyes as he thanked him. Carlow quickly asked if a black man was with the rustlers and described him as wearing a red sash and gold earring. Two-Wolves appeared puzzled and asked in sign for Carlow to repeat his description. Upon hearing it again, he shook his head negatively.

At Carlow's urging, the Comanche wrangler agreed they could get to the cattle without being seen. As Two-Wolves had done earlier, they could sneak close by using the streambed that meandered around the hillside and cut along where the herd was grazing.

"So that's how you got so wet," Carlow said, pointing at Two-Wolves's legs.

"*Si*, that *ist* so. Get *mucho* close. No one see Two-Wolves. Spirits make no see."

"You got any more of that invisible stuff?" Nichols asked with a grin.

Two-Wolves shrugged his shoulders, not understanding.

In his best Comanche, Carlow said, "Your spirit helpers have done well. I hope they help me, too." He supported his words with sign language.

Two-Wolves smiled, and the cheek scars looked as if they were sliding forward toward the corner of his mouth. "Wolf medicine keep bullet away. *Nein* kill a wolf with gun, only bow and arrow. I give to Will Nick-holds."

He shoved his hand into his pouch and withdrew fingers covered with white dust. He reached over to Nichols's face and put four dots of white on his cheek.

"Still like the idea of that invisible stuff," Nichols said. "Either that or a bottle of Kentucky's best."

"That only makes you think you're invisible." Carlow cocked his head to the side and grinned.

"Oh, I think a lot of people used to see right through me like I wasn't there."

"They won't anymore, Will."

Nichols drew in his stomach, rubbed his tongue across his front teeth, and looked away.

Carlow noticed a slight tremor in Nichols's hand. Was it a sign of withdrawal—or fear? *Can he be counted on?* It was Carlow's turn to glance away.

Little more than an hour later, their horses were left tied to a lone live oak tree at the base of a widely girthed hill. Two-Wolves said the narrow tree hadn't paid attention to its elders and lost its way from the rest of the trees. He mused that the tree must be related to the Comanche, then insisted Carlow carry the wolf medicine pouch with him.

With a simple "yes," the young Ranger pulled the pouch from his saddlebag and pushed it down inside his shirt, letting it rest against his stomach. At the last moment, Carlow also grabbed a set of army binoculars kept in his saddlebags. He ran his hand over his tied long coat. It wasn't any drier than when they had left the overhang. He shrugged. He had gone this far without it. Besides, the whitish color would make him easier to spot.

Turning away from his horse, he told Chance to remain with the horses, but Two-Wolves objected to the idea.

"*Puha natsuwitu*. He . . . come." Two-Wolves's forehead was laced with frown lines as he pointed at Carlow's shirt where the pouch was held.

Carlow recognized the Comanche words for "strong medicine" and scratched the wolf-dog between the ears. "I was worried about him barking."

"He no bark."

With that, the young Ranger told Chance to come with them. The wolf-dog's tail indicated pleasure at the notification and a thin grin replaced Two-Wolves's frown.

After giving Two-Wolves his sack of food, the three gobbled cold sausages and biscuits as they moved toward an elbow in the stream that anchored the south end of the former River S pasture. Chance received his share from both Carlow and Two-Wolves. The Comanche wrangler reminded him that the land had once belonged to friends of the Von Pearces, the ones from across the great waters.

Two-Wolves remained barefoot, while Nichols and Carlow only removed their spurs. Soon the three men were sloshing their way along the cold stream; Nichols carrying his rifle, Two-Wolves holding his bow, and Carlow with his cut-down Winchester. Water was halfway up Carlow's pants, nearly reaching the top of his Kiowa leggings. The bone handle of his knife bobbed above the waterline as they moved swiftly. Chance bounded through the stream behind him, sometimes swimming. No one could see them unless one of Dr. Holden's men happened to ride close to the creek; the three men would be easy targets if that happened.

A proud sun beat down on them as they rounded the hillside and headed toward the open prairie, moving within the meandering high-banked creek. Only Two-Wolves seemed at ease. Carlow was breathing through his teeth, as if it would help keep any sound from escaping. Behind him, Nichols's breath was coming in short nervous bursts, and Carlow worried the noise would be heard if any Holden riders were close. Several times the cowhand gagged, and Carlow's concern about him increased with each cough.

At Two-Wolves's silent command, they stopped and raised their heads enough to see over the creek bank. A thick line of cattle was only yards away, but all carried the Bar H brand. Carlow was surprised. Had Two-Wolves been mistaken? At least no riders were close; the nearest was twenty yards from the stream and to their left, staring toward the far treeline.

Several cows raised their heads in surprise and Carlow worried their interest might alert the guards. Instinctively he turned to the waiting wolf-dog and told him not to bark. After a few minutes, the animals returned to grazing. Carlow could see only four men on horseback.

Two-Wolves guessed his concerns. "*Suchen. Reindfleisch* . . . ah, cows of Doc-tuh Rem-eng-ton Hold-den all 'round cows of Cradle 6." He made a circular motion. "*Ja, seis hombres. Kohtoopy*, ah, fire . . . under trees." He held up six fingers to support his statement. "Beeg *hombre* with hair of fire there. One you beat. No see devil woman—or *muerto* 'breed, Del Gato. *Mucho* coffee. *Mucho* whiskey, maybe. *Ja.*"

"Sounds good to me. I could use a swig right about

now," Nichols said. He put the palm of his hand above his eyes and squinted. "There's five . . . no, six. Yeah, six by the fire, Ty."

Taking off his hat, Carlow raised his head to study the herd and saw they were right. Cradle 6 cattle had been placed in the center of the grazing Bar H herd to hide their appearance from any casual observation. He held the binoculars to his eyes and studied the far end of the pasture.

Nichols's eyesight was sharp, as was Two-Wolves's. There were, indeed, six men standing or sitting around the fire. He knew one man, and only one. Red Anklon. Dressed in his beaded buckskin jacket and hat with its matching beaded hatband, he was easy to identify. Other than his facial bruising and puffiness, he looked no worse for their fight.

Carlow thought it must really grind against the tall man's ego to have to take orders from the short Dr. Holden, even if he was his brother-in-law. A grin sneaked across his face. He studied the rest of the relaxing men. Where was Del Gato? Surely he was there with Anklon. Somewhere. And where was that Negro gunfighter? The one who looked like a buccaneer. Viceroy, the fat shootist had called him. Three shadowed men were moving around the horse string. Likely one was Del Gato, or perhaps the black man, but he couldn't make out any of their features.

Then his mind clicked to another concern. Where was Jessie? Two-Wolves said she had done the killing of the two Cradle 6 men. Where was she? Two-Wolves hadn't seen either Del Gato or Jessie now, but said they were both there earlier. According to the Comanche wrangler, she had been dressed as a man. He studied the six men at the fire again. He was certain none was her.

His binoculars picked up four rifles stacked against the closest of two cottonwood trees ten or twelve feet behind the campfire. That made him restudy men around the fire; this time to see if they were holding rifles. It didn't appear so.

As Carlow watched, Anklon reached for a coffeepot settled among the coals, refilled his cup, and said something to the man next to him that both thought was very funny. Spread out on the middle log, a thick-jawed cowboy with a thick, curly beard was in control of the whiskey bottle. He pushed away the younger man next to him, grabbing at the drink.

Carlow replayed to himself his uncle's advice about getting close and opening up on the rustlers without warning. He wasn't against the idea in any moral sense; these men were trying to destroy Bea Von Pearce. Rather, he was concerned about the execution of that approach. They might get the four riders watching the herd. Might. But they wouldn't get the men at the fire. Anklon would have them dug in the minute any firing started. He didn't like the idea of not knowing where Del Gato and Viceroy were either. Jessie wouldn't be a long-range threat—or would she?

He handed the binoculars to Two-Wolves and, with his own eyes, returned his attention to the riders in charge of the cattle. The closest remained twenty-some yards away to their left. A second was fifty yards to their right but only fifteen yards from where the creek bent to the north. The third rider was on the far side of the grazing animals, and for the moment, Carlow had lost track of the fourth rider. Where was he?

There. A head surfaced above the herd on the far side. He was moving toward the other rider. The boredom of watching cattle, mixed with a long night, had dulled the alertness of the herdsmen, Carlow hoped. Steamy sunshine returning after two days of rain would also help take away their tension. Ducking down again behind the embankment, he outlined what he thought would work if they were careful. And lucky. It would start with eliminating the closest rider. He explained his idea in whispers to the other two.

Two-Wolves's response was to make the sign of a slash across his throat, creep up the bank, and slide into the long grass. An instant later, he was little more than a ripple of green. Carlow glanced at Nichols and shook his head. The one-handed cowboy nodded his own agreement to Carlow's plan, as if it made any difference.

As they watched, Two-Wolves reappeared, leapt onto the back of the rider's horse, and held his other hand over the surprised man's mouth as he cut his neck. Moving forward into the saddle itself, the Comanche wrangler let the bleeding body slide toward the ground, grabbing the man's hat as it passed. He placed the hat on his head and resumed a position similar to the rider's own. Unless someone was watching closely at that moment, no change would be readily evident.

Carlow held his breath, waiting for a reaction from the campfire or the other herdsmen. None came.

Two-Wolves motioned for Carlow to come forward and the young Ranger eased himself over the bank and moved in a crouch toward him. Chance hesitated and followed, only after Carlow indicated he should. The wolf-dog moved as if he were tracking something, keeping pace with Carlow's advance. Carlow shook his head in wonderment; maybe Two-Wolves was right. He didn't let his mind seek out Kileen's opinion about the animal's true spirit.

"Take shirt, *amigo*. Vest. *Ich* give hat," Two-Wolves ordered.

Quickly Carlow replaced his shirt with the rider's more distinctive checkered one and added the man's black leather vest. Blood covered the shirt collar, but he didn't think it would matter. Two-Wolves swung down and handed the rider's hat to Carlow, and he gave the

Comanche his own Stetson with the pushed-up brim. The young Ranger sprang smoothly into the saddle. With a pat on Carlow's leg, the Comanche wrangler returned silently to the creek with Carlow's hat in his hand. Chance went with him at Carlow's command and Two-Wolves's hushed encouragement.

Carlow yanked the brim of the hat lower to cover his face and turned the horse toward the second rider. He wished he had heard the first rider speak so he could imitate his voice. A hand signal would have to do. As he rode toward the other man, he made motions that he needed a cigarette. The other man welcomed him over and reached into his shirt pocket for makin's.

"This sure is one long damn day, Thresher. Wonder when Doc's gonna get rid of that German widow. Hey, you're not—"

A gurgle ended his words as Two-Wolves was suddenly behind him on the saddle; his knife flashing in the sun.

Holding the dead rider in place with his left arm, Two-Wolves motioned for Nichols to leave the creek bank and take his place on the second man's horse. As Nichols came toward them, Two-Wolves let the dead man slump to the ground.

Chapter Twenty-eight

Carlow pointed at the man's hat. Nichols replaced his own miserable excuse for one with the herdsman's new-looking white Stetson, with its fancy woven-leather tie-down and a hawk feather stuck in the band.

"Should I take his shirt, too?" Nichols whispered, his front teeth grasping his lower lip.

"Just his vest. Hurry," Carlow ordered, then realized the poor condition of Nichols's clothes. "Yeah, you'd better take it. Someone might notice. Where's Chance?" Carlow asked after a quick look around.

"I told him to stay in the creek," Nichols said with a smile, unbuttoning his filthy shirt. "He likes me."

"Of course."

Initially Nichols fumbled nervously with the buttons on the rider's shirt, but soon he steadied himself, freed the garment, and put it on, then the vest. He stood for a moment, examining something in his old shirt.

"What's the matter, Will?"

"Your cigar. I forgot about it," Will said without looking up. "It's all broken."

"I'll get you some more when we go to town."

Nichols grinned and finished dressing.

Two-Wolves slid from the horse, and Nichols mounted.

"Good luck, Ty," Nichols said, and nudged the horse a few steps toward the remaining two riders nearer the front of the herd.

"Same to you, Will." He noted that the one-handed cowboy was pale and shivering. Maybe he should have offered him a drink from the small flask in his saddlebags.

Two-Wolves patted both men on the leg with his medicine pouch and disappeared into the grass.

"What are we gonna do now, Ty?" Nichols said as they rode toward the other two.

"Ride toward them. Easy like. Start talking to me."

"What about?"

"Anything. Horses. Women."

"Whiskey?" Nichols's tongue swabbed his front teeth.

"Sure."

Nichols began to jabber about the delicious wonders of Kentucky bourbon, its color, its taste, how he liked to hold his glass up to the light before drinking it. Carlow nodded and made several comments that made no sense to Nichols, except for the Ranger's telling him to keep his left hand down to his side.

They were only ten feet away from the two Bar H riders, who were alternately talking and glancing at Nichols and Carlow as they casually approached. The riders showed no sign of alarm, only an interest in breaking the monotony of watching the herd.

From the corner of his eye, Carlow noted that a stretch of long grass near the riders was waving in the opposite direction of the wind. Two-Wolves was there and ready.

"Close enough. I'm getting down now." Carlow jumped from his horse and bent over, holding his stomach. His groan was painful to hear.

Nichols reined in his mount and swung down. He hurried toward Carlow and said, "My God, Ty! What's the matter? Are you sick? They're gettin' close. Come on. Get up!"

The two Bar H riders looked at each other and kicked their horses into a lope toward the two downed men. Reining hard a few feet away, the taller rider, with an elongated face and eyes set too wide apart, said, "What's the matter with Thr—"

"Don't move. Don't say a word if you want to see the rest of this day," Carlow said, his hand-carbine appearing from under his bent-over frame.

Neither rider was any more surprised than Nichols, who jumped and blurted, "Well, I'll be."

The second rider's right hand moved to the holstered Colt at his waist. Carlow's hand-carbine swung to meet the threat. Before he could fire, an arrow tip burst through the man's chest. His cry was a cut-off gurgle. The rider straightened before slumping over onto the neck of his horse. The rest of the arrow stood shivering from his back.

The frightened horse stutterstepped, trying to decide if it should run.

Quickly Carlow stared at the camp but saw no reaction. "Grab your friend's horse, mister." Carlow motioned toward the remaining rider. "Ride toward us. Nice an' slow. Unless you want the same. Two-Wolves has lots of arrows."

"N-not me, mister. I—I didn't do nothin'. Honest, I didn't." The tall man started to raise his arms, with the dead man's reins in his right fist.

"Leave your hands down," Carlow snapped, and

glanced in the direction of the camp. "Will, anything happening at the camp?"

"Nobody's moved. I'm watching."

"Good," Carlow said. "If anybody stands and looks this way, take off your hat and wave at them."

Will wanted to ask why but didn't. He studied the campfire as he asked, "Why didn't you tell me what you were gonna do?"

"Didn't know how good an actor you were."

"Oh."

As the man rode slowly forward, Two-Wolves pulled the dead body from the other horse, yanked the arrow free as if it were little more than a flower in the earth. He sprang into the saddle and took the reins from the remaining, terrified rider. The Comanche wrangler studied the camp, too, but saw no suspicious movement, so he signalled for advance to something in the long grass.

Chance bounded forward. Carlow shook his head in surprise at the wolf-dog's obeying Two-Wolves's command. A silent command, no less.

"Now we're going to ride together to the rest of your friends," Carlow said. "You're going to go first. If you do this right, you might just stay away from a hanging rope."

"I—I ain't nothin' b-but a c-cowhand, m-mister. I just do w-what I'm told. Them others is the rustlers. H-honest. Red's got a bunch of 'em."

"Did Dr. Holden tell you and the others to steal the Cradle 6 herd?" Carlow's eyes searched the man's narrow face and stretched-apart eyes for the truth.

"W-we got our orders from Red—an' Mrs. Holden." The man's eyes moved from Carlow to Two-Wolves to Chance.

"His wife?" Carlow wanted to hear the response; he

looked at Two-Wolves and a slight smile flashed across the Comanche's face.

"Yeah, I was surprised to see her. Rain an' all." He licked his parched lips. "It wasn't rainin', though, when she caught up with us. Red was glad to see her. They're brother an' sister, ya know."

Carlow nodded.

"H-hey, sh-she's a scary w-woman. Likes cutting off the ears of dead folks . . . an' paintin' their faces . . . with their own blood." He swallowed twice to keep down his revulsion. "She killed them Germans a while back. Two years, maybe." The rider's face sagged. He told about her killing two of the widow's cowhands last night. She had Red and Del Gato hold them while she did it. The rider gagged with the telling and said he threw up when he saw what she had done.

"She's a crazy woman." He shook his head. "I hear tell she's cut up some others, too. Keeps their ears on a string. Damn."

Carlow tried to imagine the beautiful young woman doing something like that, but his mind wouldn't draw the picture.

"An' she can bring ghosts on you. Del Gato calls her 'Ghost Queen.'"

Carlow's eyes studied the frightened man. "Is Del Gato . . . over there now?"

"Not now. He never stays around long. Doesn't want to do this kind of work. An' nobody's gonna make him. He rode back to town with Mrs. Holden. Hour or so ago, I reckon." He tried to smile. "Ya know, she were wearin' man's clothes, ridin' with us. But you could tell she was a woman anyhow. Hard to hide all that."

"How about that black fella, the one with the ear-ring?"

274

"Oh, you mean Viceroy. He's from one of those countries way down south. Lower'n Mexico, even. Speaks real pretty. Haven't seen him. He's scarier than the halfbreed." Pulling in air to calm himself, the rider asked, "A-are you the Ranger that wh-whipped Red?"

A shaking Will Nichols answered for Carlow. "He sure is, and he cut down that son-of-a-bitch Mitchell, too, when he tried to shoot him."

As the one-handed cowboy eagerly expanded on the saloon fight, Carlow holstered his gun, rode beside the rustler, and stopped. Nichols droned on, but the man wasn't listening; he was trying to determine what was going to happen to him. The Bar H rider watched Carlow reach over and draw the frightened man's handgun from his gunbelt. For an instant, he considered grabbing the long-barreled Colt himself, but his mind ruled out the idea almost as fast as it settled there.

Carlow flipped open the loading latch and emptied the gun of cartridges. As he returned the unloaded Colt to its holster, he looked up at the rustler. "Nice-looking gun. That's some real fancy carving on the handles."

"Ah, th-thanks. I—I ain't very good with it."

"I see. Not many cowhands carry a gun like that."

"Uh, it was my brother's."

"How about that Winchester? Any good with that? Or is that your brother's, too?" Carlow slid the man's rifle free from its saddle sheath.

"Ah, snakes an' varmints, that's all. Not sure it's even carryin' fresh lead."

After relieving the bullets, Carlow replaced the gun and told the rider that the three of them were going to ride to the camp. Carlow would feign being sick but would have his gun aimed at the rider's midsection. The rustler couldn't help but glance at the holstered hand-carbine, then at the Colt, at Carlow's waist. Turning to

Nichols, the young Ranger told him to veer toward the horse string when they got close, as if he sought a fresh mount. That position would put him nearly behind the men at the campfire and also would give Nichols a clear look at the men near the string itself.

"Keep your head down like you're sleepy," Carlow added. "That whole bunch looks pretty damn relaxed. Let's don't give them a reason to change."

"I'll keep my left arm crossed over the saddle."

Carlow studied the young cowboy. "Can you hold a Winchester there with your left . . . arm?"

Nichols answered by yanking the gun free and balancing it in front of him. His expression was determined but fearful. "I'd give a lot for a little whiskey right now."

"It *would* be a lot. Your life," Carlow said. "You need to be sharp, but don't worry. They're going to see what they expect to see."

"What if they don't? There's a lot more o' them than us. I've got the shakes real bad, Ty."

"They'll go away. Shoot low and often, if it comes to that. Get off your horse, if there's time."

"You really believe I can do this, don't you?"

"Of course."

As if to emphasize his confidence in Nichols, Carlow turned to the Bar H rider and told him what he was to say when they got close, and reminded him that if anything went wrong, he would be the first to die. Gulping his understanding, the rider's attention moved to Two-Wolves and Chance. His eyes spoke of fear and bewilderment at the combination. A question was at the edge of his mouth, but he didn't have the courage to give it sound.

Studying the camp to make sure there weren't signs of alarm, Carlow rode over to the Comanche wrangler and told him what they were going to do next. After touching Carlow's leg with the side of his knife blade as a tribute, Two-Wolves disappeared again into the grass, Chance alongside him. Carlow admitted to himself that it felt odd to see his animal companion so comfortable with another man.

Carlow rode back to the waiting Nichols and the Bar H rider. He stared at the wide-eyed rustler and said, "Yeah, it's a wolf. Mostly he likes to chew on men who steal cattle from a nice lady."

Nichols chuckled.

"You're gonna keep him an' that wild Injun away from me, aren't ya?"

"If you do like you're told," Carlow growled. "Let's ride."

In minutes they approached the camp, riding three abreast. Slowly. At a walk. The scared rider was on the left. Carlow was in the middle, bending over and groaning. Hidden by the masquerade was the Colt in his right hand. He preferred the cut-down Winchester, but it would have been difficult to conceal. Nichols was on his far right.

From under the brim of his hat, Carlow assessed the men sitting around the campfire on close-drawn logs or squatting on the ground. Six. All armed with belt guns. But they were a band of self-satisfied, overconfident men more interested in a nap or another swig of whiskey than in examining the three incoming riders. Red Anklon was there, sitting with his men. Had Del Gato really gone back to town with Jessie—or was that a lie to make him relax?

Two shadows now moved near the string of horses. Each held a saddle. Likely some relief for the current herdsmen. He couldn't tell if they were armed but figured they would be. These were rustlers, not drovers.

They would be Nichols's responsibility. Where was the third? Had the shadows played tricks on his eyes? Maybe that was Del Gato. Or Jessie. He glanced at the group around the fire. Still six.

One rustler, sitting at the far right side of the camp-fire, glanced curiously in their direction, then said something to the man beside him.

"Now," Carlow whispered. "Tell them Thresher has a bad stomachache. Must be something he ate." Turning his head slightly, he said to Nichols. "Will, swing wide and head for the string."

"Here's to strong wolf medicine," Nichols mumbled, and rubbed his teeth with his tongue.

"Yeah."

The Bar H rider's too-far-apart eyes glistened. Loudly, he proclaimed, "Ah, Thresher's got a bad bellyache. Ah, must be somethin' he . . . ate." He glanced at Carlow for approval.

Guffaws from the men around the campfire followed, then a snickering response from the man on the right side: "Probably too much whiskey."

Other sarcasms quickly followed from the rest of the group. "Yeah, that's it." "Nice going, Thresher." "You wanna see your maw, Thresher?" "Does it take all o' ya to take care o' Thresher's belly?" The laughter swelled, urged on by the release of whiskey and the longness of the day. "Where's Lucas, is he sleepin'?" "Naw, he's got a bellyache, too." Another round of guffaws followed. "Who's watching the beeves?" "Who cares? They ain't going nowhere."

Good. Keep laughing, boys. Keep laughing, Carlow thought, and liked the comfort of the Colt resting against his stomach.

Chapter Twenty-nine

After the initial surprise of the three returning riders, the group returned its attentions to the whiskey and interrupted conversation.

"Hey, pass the bottle, you silly bastard," Anklon growled. "You've been holdin' it for an hour."

"Hell, I brought it."

"An' I pay your wages. Pass it over here."

Anklon stood. "Just a minute." He was a dominating figure and knew it. His gaze went to Nichols. Did he recognize Will? Carlow's fingers tightened around his Colt.

"Hey, are you comin' in or switchin' hosses?" Anklon demanded of Nichols.

Carlow was proud of the way Nichols patted his horse's head with his right hand holding the reins, said nothing, and kept going.

"Good. Jamison, Matthews," Anklon continued, waving his arm in the direction of the men nearest the horses. "Hurry up an' throw your leather on and get out there." He turned back to his sitting men. "Where's that bottle?"

"Here, boss." The bearded man with the bottle jumped up.

So far, so good, Carlow thought. *Just a little longer.* No one was paying any attention as Nichols neared the string. Was Del Gato really gone? Or was the third man he had seen earlier next to the horses? Only two were visible now and Anklon had said only two names.

About twenty feet beyond the left side of camp was a gathering of rocks under the protection of the two aging cottonwoods commanding the area. Was it large enough for a man to hide behind if he lay down? Carlow couldn't tell. Shadows, born from the trees, hovered there, making it impossible to determine anything. If Del Gato was in the camp, that would be the place he would hide; Nichols could see the rest of the back side of the camp, but there was only grass anyway. Then he remembered how easily Two-Wolves had disappeared within the flat grazing land. His chest rose and fell in a nervous response but his attention didn't stray from the rocks.

Carlow and the outlaw herd watcher drew nearer the gathered rustlers. *Another ten feet, that's all I need*, Carlow told himself. He groaned again, leaning over farther, nearly lying on his horse's neck.

A short, spectacled man on the left side of the rustler with the bottle was studying Carlow but attempting to hide his interest by rubbing his face and playing with his glasses. A walnut-handled revolver was carried in a shoulder holster under his left arm. No one else was watching them at all, the young Ranger was certain. So far Anklon hadn't paid any further attention to the incoming group. It was beneath him to worry about a rider's stomach.

The young Ranger kept his eye on the curious rustler as Carlow and the herd watcher reined their mounts eight feet from the fire. Casually the short man stood, pushed his glasses back on his nose, and turned away to head for the horses. He took two steps and spun around, the walnut-handled gun in his right fist.

The roar of Carlow's Colt jolted the land. Anklon dropped the just-received whiskey bottle, and the liquid exploded on the already wet ground and splattered across his boots. Carlow's horse reared at the loud noise. The short man's back arched, and Carlow's gun snarled again, this time firing from the side of the horse as it balanced on its rear legs.

"Anybody else want to die this morning?" Nichols's voice was clear and eager, his Winchester pointed at the two men near the horses, then at the rest around the fire. The barrel rested on his left forearm. "Give me a reason, boys. Any one at all. Especially you, Red."

Anklon's hand stopped halfway to the star-handled pistol holstered at his waist. He had already forgotten about the whiskey. His cheeks flushed in rage. Who did these fools think they were messing with? Did these three idiots think they could steal the cattle? He hadn't yet recognized either Nichols or Carlow.

Both rustlers nearest Nichols raised their hands quickly. He tried not to pay attention to the frightened horses pulling against their tie ropes, whinnying and kicking. Some were upset by the gunfire; others were simply agitated by the responses of neighboring horses. A long-legged bay reared, snapping loose its tie rope. Aware of this new freedom, the animal wheeled and ran toward the horizon with the lariat's end skipping along the ground.

In the pasture, the seven closest cattle raised their heads to assess the situation. When nothing further disturbed them, all but one returned to grazing; the remaining cow continued its examination. Finally satisfied, the animal bellowed its dislike and turned to find its calf.

At the campfire, a balding cowboy with a long reddish birthmark below his right ear glanced in the direction of Nichols, and his face showed the shock of recognition. He whispered to the taller man next to him.

Carlow's horse returned to the ground, stomping its forefeet and snorting. It wanted to run from this awful noise, but the thing on its back pulled on the reins and told it to be still. Carlow slid his boots back into the stirrups after removing them in case he needed to jump free if the animal reared again.

"I'm Ranger Time Carlow, and you're under arrest for rustling and murder," Carlow said, trying to decide whether it would be better to dismount or stay in the saddle. He held the Colt with his right hand, reining the horse with his left. The horse hadn't settled yet, but dismounting now could give the rustlers a momentary edge.

Red Anklon's face dawned with crimson rage as realization reached his mind. This wasn't some goofy hold-up attempt. No. This was that damn Ranger again! How could this be happening a second time?

Everything in the big rancher wanted another opportunity to fight the young, confident Ranger who had embarrassed him in front of everyone. His forearms flexed against the leather coat sleeves. But a flicker of doubt caught the corner of his mind. Involuntarily he looked down at the dried blood spots decorating the front of his jacket. His face and body ached from Carlow's blows. No. This man couldn't beat him again. The saloon was a fluke. He hadn't expected a kick in the groin. If the Ranger tried it again, his leg would be snapped in two.

Dr. Holden told him the Ranger had outgunned

Mitchell after he had drawn on the young lawman and then stared down Del Gato into disarming. The half-breed said he wouldn't face Carlow for any amount of money, only backshoot him. The tall foreman had the realization that this was a man to walk around. But why was he there? Now? He was supposed to be chasing an outlaw into Mexico. That was the strategy. He hadn't liked it when Dr. Holden told him, wanting permission to kill the cocky Ranger. The physician thought it was smarter to get him out of town; killing a Ranger would only bring more Rangers.

This disruption in their plans angered him as much as seeing Carlow again. This was supposed to be easy. No one would care what happened to the widow or her ranch. Anklon and his men were to take the Cradle 6 herd, and the physician and Viceroy would finish off the widow and that fool Indian who worked for her. Dr. Holden would produce a deed to show she had sold the ranch to him. She would sign it eagerly to protect her granddaughter from harm. After the signing, all would be killed anyway. Only Anklon knew Viceroy would be blamed for the murders. He was to pick one of his men to serve as an additional witness to attest to seeing the black man flee from the Von Pearce home.

Anklon's coiled defiance was obvious to Carlow; Dr. Holden's men were in varying stages of surrender and surprise. The bearded cowboy who had handed the whiskey bottle to Anklon stood beside him now, examining the ground as if trying to figure out how to retrieve the lost fluid from the broken glass and wet earth.

Watching the rustlers for any wrong movement, Carlow ordered the herdsman at his left to dismount and stand with the others. The rustler's long face was a single stretched-out grimace as he swung down. He mouthed, "They made me do it," as he walked toward Anklon, leading his horse. Swallowing his fear, he stood next to the tall rancher, but not too close. His wide-apart eyes blinked and sought the ground, the fire, anything but Anklon.

Nichols pointed at three riders sitting together on logs around the fire. "That's Baldy Demetrie an' Wallace Hutton an' that third one with the stovepipe chaps, he's Morgan Lewis," Nichols said. "Sorry to see you boys ridin' for the wrong brand. What did Mrs. Von Pearce ever do to you, except give you a steady job an' good food?"

"What the hell does a one-handed drunk know?" Baldy Demetrie waved his arms defiantly.

"I know the difference between workin' and stealin'."

"Big deal." Demetrie spat, glancing at his two Cradle 6 friends for support. Both nodded slightly.

"Big enough to hang for," Carlow said, his eyes holding the bald man apart from the other two.

With his hands outstretched and away from his holstered gun, Anklon slowly rose. He acted as if the herdsman now standing beside him didn't exist. He was at least two inches taller than any of his men and proud of his stature, equating it to authority. His gravelly voice was laden with contempt.

"I'm getting real tired of you, Ranger boy. I don't know what you've been eatin', but we're just cowhands here. Hard-workin' cowhands."

"Sounds like you've still got a problem with truth, Red."

"What'd you say, you scrawny son of a bitch?"

Carlow's Colt was pointed directly at Anklon's head. "I said you're a liar and a thief who just stole his last cow. Unbuckle the gunbelt."

At the horse string, Nichols snickered and glanced at his own left arm.

"Come on, Ranger boy. Just you an' me," Anklon sputtered.

Carlow's face took on a savage smile that matched

his eyes. "The problem with you, Red, is that you actually believe being big makes you good. I saw what you could do in the saloon. It wasn't much." He waved the pistol at the rest of the outlaws. "They know it, too. Right now the only thing I want from you is to tell me where Del Gato is. An' Jessie Holden."

"They ain't here."

Carlow's attention remained on the shadows dancing around the rocks at the far edge of camp. Could Del Gato have seen them coming and hidden? Why would he do that? Or is he already back there and just dropped down, just in case? Carlow wished he could remember if he saw a man standing near the rocks earlier. *If he was, I would be a perfect target now. The only thing saving me is that Nichols would get him if he shot me. And Del Gato doesn't like those kinds of odds.* His mind had discarded the idea of Jessie's being there, but he reminded himself that she was as dangerous as Del Gato.

With that thought, Carlow decided to dismount and swung off to the right quickly, instead of the normal left, letting his horse shield him. The sudden movement caught Anklon off guard. His hand had only decided to move when Carlow's gun reappeared from under the horse's neck. The young Ranger's body and head remained mostly hidden.

Nichols should be able to see if anyone was hiding near the remuda, Carlow thought. Only grass was there. No rocks. No mounds. No trees. Carlow wanted to yell to him about searching the high grass but didn't.

"Red, I can take off your gunbelt after you're dead, if that's how you want it." He continued to point his Colt at the tall rancher.

Anklon's hands went to his belt buckle, then hesitated. "How you figure on stopping all of us? That one-armed drunk ain't gonna be much help."

"Well, you won't be around to know what happens. I'll shoot you first," Carlow said. "But I figure there might be two or three of your boys standing when it's over." He paused. "Will, put your first shot into this tall piece of crap, too. All right?"

"I can't wait. I've heard his laugh for too damn long."

Anklon's eyes widened. His gaze took in Carlow's holstered hand-carbine for the first time, then Nichols's readied Winchester.

"Now, come over here and stand. In front of me." Carlow motioned with his gun to indicate where he wanted Anklon.

"Why?"

"In case you're lying again. Del Gato will have you to aim at."

With a sarcastic snort, Anklon ambled to the spot Carlow had indicated. It unnerved him when he realized Carlow had switched the Colt to his left hand and now held the cut-down Winchester in his right—and he hadn't seen the transfer. Carlow's horse stood, ground-tied, beside him; Carlow's left boot held the reins against the earth, just in case.

As ordered, Anklon stopped three feet from the young Ranger and stood directly in front of him. He wanted to take two steps closer, to get Carlow within range of his fists, but his legs wouldn't cooperate. He stopped where he was told, facing Carlow. A curling smile tried to hide the lack of courage, as if daring Carlow to order him to turn around. It was safer than challenging the young Ranger to let him step closer.

"Can you shoot a man when he's looking at you, Ranger boy?"

"You'd be a long way from the first, Anklon—and you're starting to annoy me."

The big man's Adam's apple jerked up and down. In

a blur, Carlow moved forward, jammed the nose of his hand-carbine into the man's stomach and stepped to his left, pointing with the Colt.

"You—with the beard," Carlow said, his revolver singling out the curly-bearded rustler who had been standing next to Anklon and was the owner of the broken whiskey bottle. "Let's see if you know how to tell the truth. Where's Del Gato?"

The outlaw's chest rose and fell. "Del Gato rode off—to town an hour ago. Maybe longer."

"You're sure of that?"

"Well, I'm sure he rode off then—and that's where he said he was going. Him and Mrs. Holden," the man said, his eyes averted. "But I don't know for sure. I ain't his secretary."

Chapter Thirty

Guarded chuckles followed the bearded rustler's remark, but a faint gurgle stopped them. It came from the grass ten feet from the horse string and was immediately cut off by the sounds of shuffling feet. Carlow's Colt shifted toward the noise, as did Nichols's rifle. Carlow's hand-carbine punched farther into Anklon's stomach. He advised Anklon that if he even flinched, he was gut-shot.

Anklon grunted his understanding.

A rifle shot exploded from the middle of the undisturbed grass. The bullet sailed ten feet over Carlow's head but he ducked instinctively.

From where the gunshot came, a lanky outlaw staggered to his feet, his just-fired rifle sliding from his twitching hands. Around his neck was a bright crimson ring. Nichols's gun rose to respond, but he didn't shoot. Behind him another horse broke free of the remuda and galloped away, then another.

The hidden gunman held out a shivering hand, hesitated, and gurgled something that sounded like "Rose

Marie." Then he collapsed headfirst onto the wet earth.

Nichols was stunned.

Carlow's eyes immediately sought the rocks where he thought Del Gato's attack would come from, if it did. *How could I have been so wrong? Maybe he isn't here. Like they said. Him and Jessie.* His gaze returned to the grass where the hidden gunman had been as Two-Wolves stood with a bloody knife at his side.

At that instant, Anklon grabbed for Carlow's hand-carbine with both hands, shoving it away from his stomach. The gun went off, spitting dirt toward the fire and the closest rustlers as Carlow's left-fisted Colt came down on the side of Anklon's head with enormous force.

Anklon's eyes rolled skyward, and he collapsed at Carlow's feet.

A growl behind the sitting men came like an extension of the young Ranger's blow. Snarling savagely, Chance ran toward the remaining seated rustlers. Two jumped up to get away. The third, Baldy Demetrie, jerked his right hand from under his vest and tried to join their escape. His hidden gun popped from his hand and thudded against the log before sliding to the ground. The wolf-dog sprang toward him and sharp teeth sank into the man's lower arm.

Shouting his pain, he stumbled and fell with Chance's jaws clamped firmly around his forearm.

"That's enough, Chance. Let him go. Let him go. Good boy, Chance," Carlow said. An unexpected shiver down his back reminded him of how close he had come to being killed twice in a matter of moments. *I wasn't even looking in the right place either time*, he told himself.

"Ty!" Nichols's voice was filled with sudden fear. "Stampede!"

Behind Carlow was a thunder that made sparks jump from the fire as the earth began to tremble. The additional gunshots had sent tremors through the herd. Every steer, every cow, an entire wall of beef was running. Half of them toward the camp.

Dropping his Colt, he grabbed for the reins of his horse with his boot holding them in place. He held the leather as the animal's head came up and half jumped, half swung into the saddle, with the horse already running. Neither boot was in a stirrup. Off balance, he grabbed for the pommel with his left hand and fought to stay upright, waving the hand-carbine in his right for balance. For a breath, he thought the cinch would snap with his off-balance weight pulling against the saddle. His left arm strained to hold him in place; his legs squeezed the flying horse. In seconds he was upright. His right boot slipped into the iron stirrup, then his left.

Rustlers screamed and ran, some for the horse string, others for the trees. Crazed steers slammed mindlessly through the campfire, trampling the already downed men and running over the slow.

Baldy Demetrie grabbed his fallen revolver and aimed it at Carlow as he rode toward him. The first shot missed. Carlow swung his hand-carbine, and the barrel smashed into the outlaw's head. Blood splattered onto Carlow's hand and face. Demetrie's pistol blasted once more, aimlessly, inches from Carlow's ear, deafening him momentarily before the former Cradle 6 cowboy collapsed.

Struggling to retain his balance after the impact to his ear, he saw Nichols down, his horse bolting. Carlow urged his wild-eyed horse toward the winded Nichols as steers flew past him on either side.

He turned his horse toward his staggering friend.

Powerful rear legs of the fearful horse slammed into the prairie dirt as he fought to bring it to an unwanted halt beside Nichols. The horse shook its head, snorted, and pawed the ground, wanting to be a long way away from the advancing madness.

"Go on, T-Ty. Go on," Nichols said, his left leg covered in blood. "I can't make it."

"Grab my arm. You're going with me. Come on."

Nichols's strength was leaving him fast. Shock was eating into his grit. Carlow was proud of his rustler's horse, blowing and sweating and wanting to run but standing in place, as if understanding the need to get the wounded man on its back fast.

Carlow helped the wobbly cowboy get his boot into the right stirrup, then took Nichols's right hand in his left and lifted. Nichols's leg quivered but held as he swung his wounded leg up. Carlow's strength took on Nichols's full weight to keep him from falling when he stalled halfway onto the horse. Reaching his left arm backward to grab Nichols's belt, he pulled the one-handed cowboy's limp leg over with his right hand.

Carlow whistled the animal into action. It responded as if the double weight were nothing. Ground-eating strides took them away from the army of cattle that had once been the camp. Carlow turned in the saddle and fired once, twice, then a third time with his hand-carbine, into a gray shape shooting at them from a low tree limb. A groan from the outlaw was swallowed by the ground shaking all around them.

Behind him came a scream. A scream that rammed itself into Carlow's mind. Where was Two-Wolves? Where was Chance? Impulsively, he glanced backward but saw nothing but a brown sea. He turned back, and a scrub oak slapped him viciously in the face. A grunt, and his outlaw hat was gone. On they ran, clearing a low ravine in a thunderous bound and skirting a limestone ridge that ran ten feet high for a half mile into the prairie. The rustler camp was almost that far behind them. He began to slow his blowing horse. He was certain they were safe.

Running wasn't natural for cattle. He figured they would soon play themselves out. Behind them, cattle were agreeing with his thought, slowing themselves gradually into a walk. Some were already grazing again. He held the reins of his own horse tightly as a precaution as a few steers lumbered past them on the way to something only they understood. Fear was fierce in the horse's nostrils, and the animal yanked on the reins, prancing and snorting, resenting the curtailing of its escape.

Carlow's gritty voice was low and calming. "Easy, boy. Easy now. We've got to be smart. Easy now." Gradually the horse stood without jerking its head, blowing, or stomping. He patted its wet neck in appreciation.

For the first time, he realized they were beside the ridge. He couldn't remember seeing it before. A stray brown-and-white steer wandered through, mooing for brethren. Three loose horses from the outlaws' remuda burst past with heads held high and nostrils flaring. Carlow's horse tensed and wanted to bolt. His restraint eliminated the possibility.

Nichols was no longer holding on; Carlow thought he might have passed out from loss of blood.

A sound above him!

He spun his hand-carbine toward the new threat.

"It *ist* I, Two-Wolves. *Nein* shoot, Star Warrior of *Tehannas*." The Comanche wrangler appeared on top of the ridge, his bare feet just inches above Carlow. He was bleeding from his right arm. From the looks of it, a steer's horn had caught him.

Charlie Two-Wolves! Carlow's mind said. *Where is Chance?*

An eager bark answered the question. In an instant, a familiar shape stood beside the Comanche wrangler, barking happily to see Carlow.

Carlow realized Nichols was leaning against his back. "Will, we made it. Will . . . Will?"

There was no response.

Carlow holstered his gun and turned around in the saddle, fearing the worst.

Nichols was gulping for air. "I . . . I had the . . . breath . . . knocked outta me." He inhaled and exhaled as fast as he could to bring in precious air. "Wh-when we . . . cleared . . . that damn hole . . . back there. You ever hear of goin' around things?"

Smiling, Carlow jumped down and offered a hand to Nichols. Both looked up. Standing next to them were Two-Wolves and Chance. The wolf-dog ran to the young Ranger, who greeted him with equal enthusiasm. In Two-Wolves's right hand was Carlow's hat; in his left, a bow.

"*Ich* bring hat. *Bueno* medicine. *Ja.*" The Comanche wrangler held out the hat and Carlow smiled and pushed it onto his head.

An examination of Nichols's leg showed the cut was shallow; his weakness had come from being thrown, and not the wound. The three men decided to return and assess the situation with the herd and the outlaws. On the way back, an occasional steer watched them with mild curiosity. The camp itself was barely recognizable as a place where men had been. The fire was flattened ashes with tiny sparks breathing their last. Only one sitting log remained in place; the others were strewn about the area as if picked up and tossed. The only thing remaining of the remuda was a broken rope.

Saddles were scattered everywhere like large brown toadstools. Surprisingly, the rifles remained exactly as they had been stacked, propped against the tree. Except for one. It lay near a body hanging in the crook of the tree.

The next dead man they saw was Red Anklon. The side of his face was bloody from Carlow's blow. His legs were twisted awkwardly from being trampled, and his leather shirt and pants were tattooed with hoofprints.

Morgan Lewis, one of the turncoat Cradle 6 riders, sat on a log not far from the line of rocks where Carlow had thought Del Gato might be hidden. He was staring into the sky, the left side of his stovepipe chaps nearly ripped off. Beside him was the third Cradle 6 traitor. Unmoving.

Gradually they found the others, except for two. Nichols guessed they might have been the men closest to the remuda and thus able to grab horses and get away. Three more had been trampled. Demetrie appeared mildly dazed and was walking around, holding his bitten arm and talking to himself. Another outlaw was trying to find coffee for the pot, as if nothing had happened.

The hidden gunman's body was gone. Two-Wolves didn't seem alarmed by its absence, indicating he thought they would find it, assuring Carlow that the man was dead.

"Dr. Holden is through," Carlow said, staring at Anklon's body. "I've got the evidence we'll need."

"What about these boys, the ones still walkin'?" Nichols motioned in the direction of Demetrie. "How about they help us round up the Cradle 6 beef?"

"Good idea. I've got paper and a pencil in my saddlebags," Carlow said. "I want a signed confession about the Holdens from each man. Anybody who saw Jessie Holden kill your friends, I want that in there, too."

"What if they can't write?" Nichols didn't look at him.

"Write it for them an' have them sign it," Carlow said. "You can write, can't you?"

"Better'n most. I can count to a hundred, too." Nichols looked up, defiant. "Then what?"

Quietly, he asked Nichols and Two-Wolves to handle this detail while he headed for town. Carlow told Nichols to let any man go if Nichols knew he was just a cowhand and not an outlaw, but only after he wrote down what he knew. The rest should be tied and held until they could be moved to a proper jail. That would have to come later; he didn't want to wait and take a chance on the Holdens getting away.

Two-Wolves glanced up from searching the trampled grass south of the remuda. "Doc-tor Rem-eeng-ton Hold-den . . . he buys . . . white man law."

"Not my law." Carlow's response came through clenched teeth. "Not Texas Ranger law." He didn't mention expecting to find Del Gato and the black gunfighter there as well.

Crossing his arms, Two-Wolves glanced down at Chance. "*Ich* go with. *Si.*"

"Me, too, Ty," Nichols said, still breathing deeply and acting like his leg wasn't bothering him.

Carlow felt tired and weak. His head was pounding again from Mallow's bullet graze. "No, there's unfinished business here. We'll need those confessions and Bea's cattle need returnin'. I'll be fine. I don't want the Holdens to get away."

Two-Wolves's face was unreadable.

"If I'm not back before you finish, go to the ranch. Tell Thunder . . . ah, Ranger Kileen."

"You take wolf. Medicine good. *Mucho gut.*"

Chapter Thirty-one

Cocky shadows were strolling across the main street of town as Carlow rode in. Nightfall was flirting with the horizon. Chance trotted at the heels of the young Ranger's grulla. Neither Will Nichols nor Charlie Two-Wolves liked the idea of staying behind. Both were worried that Carlow would ride into trouble alone. The young Ranger assured them that he would be all right. That came with his usual confident smile, one that belied his own concerns about what waited for him in Presidio.

This was Ranger business; this was what he was paid to do.

He would stop first at the marshal's office and notify him of his intention to arrest Dr. Holden and his wife for murder and attempted rustling.

Whether the syrupy-talking lawman went with him or not wasn't important. The announcement was just a courtesy. There would be a threat attached. The Holdens would be held until a circuit judge could be brought in. No local justice. And no excuses if they escaped.

Presidio was looking forward to the evening; saloons were getting louder, and the stores were closed or closing. People scurried about, hoping to complete their tasks before the evening took them inside. Most seemed happy that the rain of the past two days was over. An occasional puddle reminded the town of the recent weather. The streets themselves were nearly empty, except for riders headed for the saloons and an occasional wagon headed home.

Outside Holden's hotel, a hooded priest watched from the porch as Carlow passed. The priest held his hands behind him as if contemplating the wonders of another day. Carlow wondered if the cleric had any idea of how fragile the town's peace was. Especially tonight. The young Ranger decided to stop and ask if he had seen either Del Gato or the black gunfighter. But when Carlow swung his horse toward the porch, the priest turned and went inside. Just as well, thought Carlow, it would have taken more explanation than he wanted to give.

But the two gunmen were around somewhere. Waiting.

The realization that neither would announce himself in advance made him glance at his hand-carbine, held across the saddle as he passed the general store. He read the sign in the window without interest: "Manufacturers' agents for Ladd's Celebrated Sheep Dip. The Only certain Cure for scab and its prevention. It destroys vermin and increases the Growth of Wool. The cheapest, most safe and effective remedy known. Orders Promptly Filled." His gaze jumped to the watchmaker's familiar, hateful sign: "No Irish. No Coloreds. No Mex." He tried to concentrate. This wasn't the occasion to deal with a prejudiced store owner, and he breathed away the desire to confront the man.

The Holden Apothecary looked as if it, too, was

closed. Gray inside and no sign of movement. He would return there anyway; the Holdens might be in the store, closing up.

A freight wagon rumbled past him on its way north. The driver spat and nodded his head as a greeting; his eyes slid toward Chance. He shook his head as if disbelieving what he saw. Carlow returned the greeting with a nod and rode on. He stopped at the hitching rack in front of the marshal's office. Swinging down, he told Chance to remain with the horse and walked inside with his cocked hand-carbine at his side. He didn't like the marshal and wasn't certain whether he was just inept or owned by Dr. Holden as Flanker and Nichols suggested.

"Wal, wal, this hyar's quite the day for our litt-ul town. Two Range-uhs." Marshal Laetner Dillingham's large ears wiggled as he greeted Carlow. He was seated behind his desk, sipping from a porcelain coffee mug.

Carlow was surprised. "Two Rangers?"

"Yas suh, two o' yo-all. A big fella. Biggest thang I dun ever seed came in hyar. Hour back, it were, I reckon. No, more'n that. Hour an' a half. Yah, hour an' a half." Marshal Dillingham took a swig of his coffee. From his expression, it either wasn't hot or wasn't very good. "Yo-all git that Silvah Mal-low feller, huh?"

Carlow waited, but his impatience with the man was shoving against his judgment. "No, I haven't. Not yet. Right now, I'm after justice for Bea Von Pearce and her late husband—and others around here."

"Uh, I see that."

"Good. Now tell me what happened here."

Gradually the slow-talking lawman explained Kileen had come to town and deposited the beaten Dr. Holden. It took minutes that seemed like hours before Marshal Dillingham finally said the doctor was in a jail cell.

Carlow's eyes widened, and he walked to the dark cell area. The closest cell contained a man sleeping on a cot, probably a drunk. The next cell was empty. The last space was occupied by a bloody Dr. Holden, who also appeared to be sleeping. The young Ranger guessed Kileen had worked him over, and that meant the physician had gone to the Von Pearce ranch when he and the others were after the Cradle 6 cattle. Just as Kileen had suspected someone might.

But would the physician have come alone to Bea's place? Was he watching and waiting until they rode out? Carlow wondered. Dr. Holden didn't seem like the kind of man who did anything without hired men to back him up. Or did he plan to pay a doctor's visit to give Bea something for her "health"? Will Nichols had warned of such a move. So had Charlie Two-Wolves.

"He dun tolt me to hold Doc for ah-tempted mur-dah—and for stealin' the widow's beeves. Yas suh, that's want he said," Dillingham hollered. "Said Doc fell down a'gettin' outta his buggy. That's how he dun come to hurt himself, ya know." Marshal Dillingham waited for a response from Carlow. When there wasn't one, he continued, "Didn't say what ev-uh-dence he dun be havin'. Gotta be a miss-take. Doc Hold-un bein' a fine up-standin' citi-zun an' all, ya know."

Carlow realized the lawman was talking loud enough for the physician to hear.

Finally fed up, Carlow spun and returned to the desk. "Well, you're wrong again, Dillingham. We have plenty of evidence—and witnesses." Carlow's eyes went after the floppy-eared man. "Holden's nothing but a murderer and a thief. So's his wife." He crossed his arms. "I hope you're not involved."

"What do yo-all mean, 'in-volved'?"

"You guess." Carlow's glare forced Dillingham's eyes downward.

"Wal, I reckon we'll be a'knowin' the strai-ught o' it when Doc comes a-round." Dillingham lifted his cup to take a deliberate sip.

Carlow reached across the desk and took the lawman's arm, stopping his effort halfway to his mouth. "Holden better be here when I return. I'm going after his wife. She murdered two men last night." Carlow released Dillingham's arm.

Marshal Dillingham's fearful expression turned into a knowing smile. His silly grin vanishing as quickly as it rose, he said, "All I meant was that Doc might-ah . . . confess, ya know."

"And all I meant was Holden better be here." Carlow rubbed his chin. "Damn, I remember the time when a local lawman let a prisoner of Ranger Kileen's go." He paused again. "It was a nice funeral, though."

Dillingham put down the cup, staring at it as if the liquid were poison.

"By the way, Red Anklon is dead. And Holden's gang of rustlers has been arrested. We're holding them outside of town. They've all signed confessions about your friend in there. And his lady."

Marshal Dillingham couldn't hide the surprise on his face.

"Red got run over by the cattle he stole," Carlow added. "I'd say that's justice."

Dillingham wanted to ask if Del Gato was dead or captured but decided he shouldn't. He was trying to keep his lower lip from trembling.

"Where is Ranger Kileen now?" Carlow asked, regaining his patience. Somewhat.

Eager to change the subject, Dillingham pronounced, "He had a body to get rid of. Nig-gra fella— ah, the one ya met . . . yest-tuh-day."

The corner of Carlow's mouth twitched in response to the use of the word. He didn't like it, especially coming from Marshal Dillingham. He asked if the dead man was the gunfighter named Viceroy. Dillingham's ears wiggled as he assured him it was. Kileen had his body in the doctor's buggy. The young Ranger told him Viceroy was on Dr. Holden's payroll. Dillingham's ears wiggled as he expressed surprise. Too much surprise.

"So where is the coroner?"

"Now that is a goo-ud quest-shun. Yas suh, a goo-ud quest-shun. This time o' the day, he could be 'most any-whur."

Carlow was fuming again but he waited.

Marshal Dillingham's explanation was long and hard to follow. But essentially the coroner was also the town dentist and barber. His office was next to the Remuda saloon. Carlow vaguely recalled it.

"If'n I had to be a'guessin', I'd say the big fella would be in a sa-loon by now, a'washin' away havin' to touch a dead nig-gra."

Carlow's anger reached his eyes. "Have you seen Del Gato?"

"'Course I-uh have," Dillingham answered. "Not too-day though. Not too-day." His voice was loud.

Carlow stepped toward the door. "It isn't necessary to yell, Dillingham. You can tell Holden what you said when I leave."

Marshal Dillingham's ears flapped in silent response as he shook his head to negate what the young Ranger implied.

"When we come back, Holden better still be here." Carlow grabbed the door handle.

"Are yo-all a-sayin' I would be lettin' him go?" Marshal Dillingham leaned forward in his chair, resting the coffee cup on a short stack of papers.

"No, I'm saying if he's gone, we'll hang you for conspiracy. No matter whose fault it is." Carlow turned and left.

Dillingham glanced at the far cell and reached into the bottom drawer of his desk to retrieve a whiskey flask.

Outside, Carlow's mind was pulling him toward finding Thunder and going after Jessie Holden together. *Or should I let Thunder enjoy a drink or two? He's earned it, bringing in Dr. Holden and that black killer,* he told himself as he holstered his gun and swung into the saddle. *I don't want to take the chance on her getting away, either—and I don't know where Thunder is. There are a lot of saloons in town.* He recalled his search for Silver Mallow.

Obviously there had been a fight at the ranch, and Kileen had won. Carlow thought of his first meeting with Bea Von Pearce, her shotgun and pistol in her apron. He smiled. Most likely she had been right beside his uncle when the fighting began. Bea and Hattie must be unhurt or he would have brought them to town. Or would he? The only doctor was in jail. No, they were all right or his uncle would not have come in.

He nudged his horse into a walk toward the main string of saloons. His thoughts returned to finding Jessie Holden.

Ghost Queen. Carlow mulled the phrase over in his mind. That's what the outlaw said Del Gato called her. Ghost Queen. She had told him about his own mother and father. How did she know that? How did she know about Thunder? *Maybe I said something without realizing it. Could she have hypnotized me, right then and there?* That seemed far-fetched to him. It had to be Silver Mallow.

Into Carlow's mind seeped the recollection that several childhood friends had been a part of Mallow's gang. Why didn't he think of that before? They would have known about his parents—and his uncle. Between them and what he overheard while in the Bennett jail, Mallow could have have easily known the details she came forth with.

He straightened in the saddle. If he talked with her before escaping, that meant he most likely talked with Dr. Holden and Red Anklon. It meant they lied about not seeing Mallow. Of course. They had to be in on his escape from the whorehouse.

He returned to his encounter with Jessie at the drugstore.

"This . . . was your father's. He was a great warrior. His spirit stands close. So does your mother's. She worries about you. Another Irish warrior of this world . . . rides to . . ."

Her smile would have felled most men. A long kiss promised. The hint of a delicious night together. That's what made her presentation so mesmerizing. He shook his head to clear away the rest of her and decided to wait on looking for Kileen. His priority should be on finding her. He told himself once more that this was his duty and that he wasn't interested in seeing her again for any other reason. *Ghost Queen*, he repeated to himself. *Ghost Queen*. He reined the horse to the right and urged it forward. She might still be in the store.

In front of the Holden Apothecary, he swung down and flipped the reins twice over the rack. There were no signs of anyone in the store. He walked over to the window and peered inside. Nothing. She definitely wasn't in the front. Perhaps she was in the back storeroom.

Chance followed him after his admonishment to be quiet, and they walked around to the rear of the quiet building in a long alley. About thirty feet away from the back door was the darkened shape of an outhouse.

Carlow glanced in its direction to assure himself that no one was hiding there. The drugstore door itself was fettered with a shiny long-nosed padlock, and there were no windows.

He drew his gun, placed its nose against the lock, and fired. For a moment the shot controlled the evening stillness; the lock shivered and sprang apart. He yanked it off and stepped inside. This wasn't the time for subtlety. If she were here, she probably knew he was coming. He assured himself that her awareness would have come from seeing him through the window—and not from some vision or hearing about it from a ghost.

A neat storeroom greeted him. His spurs danced on the floor as he moved between neatly arranged lines of boxes. Satisfied, he entered the store area itself. Nothing. His eyes were now accustomed to the darkness, and he studied the shadows carefully. Certainly she could have seen him coming and hidden. His mind was unclear on his own motives, and he frowned to rid it of haunting thoughts of her beauty.

Shelves of jars, containers, and bottles were menacing shapes of gray and black. Displays of cloth and pots and shoes were crouching enemies. Glass showcases teased with softly reflected light that could be a gun. He took a deep breath and continued his search.

His mind reminded him that Del Gato could be with her. "Find them, Chance."

The wolf-dog sprang from his side and disappeared inside the store. Only the soft padding of his feet on the floor indicated where he might be. Carlow waited. He started to draw his hand-carbine, then decided not to.

A few minutes later, Chance reappeared in the aisle, wagging his tail. Still nothing.

Dr. Holden's private office for patients was behind Carlow and to his left. The office door was slightly ajar and opened with a defiant screech as he pulled it toward him. This time the nose of his hand-carbine led the way into an even darker room. He had convinced himself that she was fully capable of killing him—and Del Gato, if he were with her, definitely was.

He studied the silent space. A long table for surgery dominated the space. The only other pieces of furniture were a rolltop desk and chair and a counter with a well-ordered display of instruments. He recognized an amputation kit filled with various-sized knives, scalpels, pinchers, and picks. That made him think of the horror Will Nichols had been through. A half-empty bottle of Hostetter's Stomach Bitters rested next to the assembly.

Where could she be? he asked himself. The immediate answer was their house in town. Would she already know her husband had been arrested? He would have to assume she did and would be expecting the Rangers to come for her. Probably with Del Gato at her side. If she wasn't there, he would check the livery. After that, he had no idea. *Maybe get Thunder.*

"Come on, Chance." He retreated from the office and headed for the back door, holstering his gun.

The dog hesitated and broke away toward the counter.

Carlow waited. Could they have missed her? Or the halfbreed?

A gray cat sprang from the darkness, screaming its hatred at the wolf-dog. Carlow jumped at the sudden appearance of Jessie's pet. He stopped his right hand from continuing to pull his weapon. Why would she leave the animal behind? Mice? Carlow knew his uncle would say the cat was actually Jessie in disguise.

"Chance, that's enough, boy. Let it go."

Tail wagging, Chance appeared. The cat was nowhere

305

in sight as they went to the door and Carlow opened it. Moving beside him, Chance suddenly stiffened and growled.

"What is it now, boy? We haven't got time for that cat."

Chapter Thirty-two

Three gunshots rattled in the alley. The young Ranger slammed the door but didn't think the bullets were directed at him. Drawing his hand-carbine, he cracked the door enough to see out.

In the gloomy alleyway was Jimmy Ward Flanker, a few feet from the outhouse. At his feet was a body. Unmoving. Carlow squinted to examine the dead man.

Del Gato.

"Yo-all don't need to be worryin' about Del Gato at your back no more, Range-uh Carlow." Flanker slipped new cartridges into his shiny revolver.

"I can see that." Carlow responded without opening the door further. Was this a trap?

"Come to think of it, the back-shooter went out with bullets in his back. Fittin', I'd say," Flanker pronounced, and added, "A first for me." He returned his reloaded gun to its shoulder holster.

Without moving closer, the heavyset man explained he had seen a big Ranger bring Dr. Holden to the jail, along with the body of Viceroy. Del Gato had slipped into the jail shortly after the Ranger left, and Flanker guessed he was after him when he saw Carlow ride in.

"I don't want yo-all a'thinkin' Jimmy Flanker thought yo-all needed help now," Flanker concluded, and stepped over the body. "Just tired of that back-shooter givin' us professionals a bad name." He chuckled and his stomach rippled.

"Thanks, Jimmy, I owe you one. Or is it two?" Carlow cleared the door with Chance at his side. He holstered his hand-carbine, easing the trigger down as he did. He walked toward the fat shootist with his right hand extended.

Chance eased toward the dead body and sniffed, then returned to Carlow's side.

"Someday I'll collect." Flanker shook his hand. "Had a feelin' you'd stand an' help the widow. I take it yo-all's Silver man got away."

"For now, anyway."

"Yo-all will get him. Of that, I'd take odds. Yo-all an' that wild-lookin' creature with ya." He shook his head.

Brushing imaginary dust from his coat, Flanker added that he was headed to Charlie's Whiskey and Pool Hall, where a game waited. He asked and Carlow said he was going to Dr. Holden's house to arrest his wife if she was there.

"Be careful, young Time," Flanker cautioned. "Roses have thorns."

"Especially frozen pink ones."

The shootist's face was a question, but Carlow didn't elaborate on his comment. "Say, is that mountain of a Range-uh who I think it is?"

"It is—if you think it's Thunder Kileen."

"Ah yes, Thunder Kileen. His name does ring a bell." Flanker smiled. "Don't think I've had the pleasure though."

"He's my uncle."

"Well, I'll be." Flanker nodded. "That explains a lot."

It was Carlow's turn to wonder what the fat man meant.

Flanker turned away, headed back toward the outhouse. He stopped in midstride; his immense belly shook with the change. "Now, Range-uh Carlow, don't yo-all go 'round sayin' Jimmy Flanker dun he'ped yo-all. Wouldn't be good for business."

Carlow waved, smiled thinly, and replaced the broken lock in its hinge and left it hanging. He would buy a new one in the morning. Even Chance seemed eager to leave this place.

After remounting, he looked around the street for someone he might ask for directions to Dr. Holden's home. A well-dressed couple were strolling down the board sidewalk, and he rode over to them. Both were startled by his sudden presence.

"Sorry to bother you, folks, but I need to find Dr. Holden's house. Got a friend in need of some doctoring."

The woman, wearing a silk scarf tied over her head, returned his smile and politely gave him directions. Her dress was quite proper, covering her ankles when she walked. It matched her evergreen scarf. Her husband felt it important to add that the doctor didn't like visitors after hours. His suit was obviously tailored, showing gentle wear. A fresh celluloid collar was quite stiff and uncomfortable-looking. His short-brimmed hat was curled and trimmed with silk. Carlow guessed he was a banker.

The young Ranger acknowledged both statements and started to ride away. Her question stopped him. "Is that a wolf?"

"No, ma'am, he just looks that way. Real gentle soul."

Authoritatively the man added, "Well, he surely looks like a wolf. I believe there is a town ordinance against such."

"A lot of things look like what they're not." Carlow touched the brim of his hat and loped on.

The couple watched him for a moment.

"I'm not at all certain Dr. Holden will treat an Irishman," the man said.

She agreed. "Yes, he's a good man, but good has its limits. We did right giving him directions, though. Him being a Ranger."

"It was our duty, Mary. We've always known our duty."

They walked on, seeing Carlow turn left at the corner they had indicated.

Their directions were accurate, and Carlow soon found himself nearing an imposing two-story white house with well-groomed bushes lining its front and a welcoming presentation of poplar and oak trees throughout the property. There seemed to be a garden in the back; Carlow could see a rocked edge and a few plantings.

The house was dark inside. No invitation of light anywhere on either floor. Maybe she wasn't home after all. Maybe she had left for their ranch. Maybe she hadn't come to town at all. Or maybe she went directly to the stage. He hadn't thought of that before. Was there one today? Possibly. If so, he could wire the authorities at the various stops with instructions to arrest and hold her. He chuckled about the phrase to himself. What man wouldn't like to hold her?

Carlow dismounted and led his horse to the ornate hitching rack outside the Holden house. He scratched Chance's head and told him to stay.

A turn of the heavy brass knob told him it was locked. His knock on the dark walnut door sounded loud in the stillness. It seemed a bit silly to be so cordial when he was going to arrest her, but he knocked again anyway. Giving up that approach, he walked over to the window and started to draw his hand-carbine to break the glass.

Her voice floated through the door. "Come in, Time Carlow. I've been waiting for you."

Carlow hurried back and grabbed the doorknob. This time it turned easily in his hand. He stepped inside, entering an intimidating hallway. She wasn't there. No one was. He removed his hat by instinct.

A world unknown to him gave birth as he walked along. It was as if he had been transported to some strange land. Red walls were lined with great scrolls, ornate tapestry, and tall, slender Egyptian vases. A long red runner with gold accents covered the wooden floor. *Should I take off my spurs? What is that smell? Incense?* His eyes were attracted to a large carving mounted on the wall; the centerpiece was a tree with many animals and birds hovering around it. He decided it was a nice idea. Next was an image of a human female torso with the wings and tail of a bird. An arm was raised in blessing. He shook his head. Maybe Charlie Two-Wolves would understand it. Or his uncle.

In the dark shadows, he almost stumbled into a large golden dragon statue that guarded the end of the hallway. To his right was a winding staircase. Family portraits followed up the steps. He took a deep breath. At least they looked normal. In the uneven light, he saw Dr. Holden's portrait among them.

"Come in, Time. Please. No one will harm you, I promise." Her voice came from the room straight ahead.

The nearly black room was cold. Colder than outside, he thought. Tiny shreds of timid light slid through the dark-curtained windows but could give only hints of the room—and of the beautiful woman sitting by herself at a small table in the middle of the empty floor. He would have sworn the walls moved closer as he walked toward her.

Chinese devil masks studied him from every wall. He thought the rest of the room's furniture had been shoved against the edges of the room but wasn't certain. Barely more than shadows. The air in the room was heavy. To his left, on the wall, was a huge moon. A painting, he thought. It was filled with gods, demons, spirits, animals, and men. Below it on a waist-high display was a statue of a man with eight arms and ten ever-smaller heads ascending from the main one. One hand held a crescent moon. Just inside the door to his right was a box inlaid with gold and an oddly shaped statue of a bull stag, a wolf, and a hound, with a stag-antlered man sitting among them.

His gaze returned to his task. She sat with her golden hair unbound and glorious. As far as he could tell, she was alone. He didn't see a knife, either, but that didn't mean she didn't have one—or a gun—in her lap.

"There is no one here but me—and the spirits of your mother and father." Her voice sounded as if it were coming from a cave. "They told me you were badly wounded last winter and were healed by your uncle and a Mexican bandit woman. Does her name have something to do with the Heavens?"

Carlow shivered, even though he was certain now her information had come from Mallow.

A long, tapered candle snapped to life at her table. Its glow caressed her hair and slid along her cheeks. She appeared to be without a body. Only a luminous head.

Gradually the light revealed the rest of her. She was as beautiful as he remembered. Her golden hair was down around her shoulders. Dressed in a crimson silk gown with gold patterns around the neck and wrists, she looked like one of the displays. The bite of incense was embracing the hint of her perfume. Both were flirting with his nostrils. Here, indeed, was the Ghost Queen, he thought.

"I came to arrest you for murder and rustling," he heard himself say. "Looks like you've changed from your earlier outfit." It was hard for him to envision her looking like a man.

Her turquoise eyes glowed and sought his. "I know, but I thought you might first like to hear from your parents. I promised." Her outstretched arms beckoned him forward. "Please, come and sit with me. I will go with you afterward. I am not dangerous." Her smile was inviting. "Or are you afraid of me?" Her hands returned to her gown, slid slowly over her breasts, and came to rest on the table. "Or of what the spirits will say?"

He didn't respond.

"You know, the hardest part of dressing like a man is hiding these." She smiled and cupped her breasts with both hands. "Wrapping them is so hard. I like them better like this, don't you?"

"You're a beautiful woman, Jessie. That's for sure."

"I was afraid you hadn't noticed." She let her hands slide to her side.

For the first time, Carlow realized the candle was placed in a small, strangely shaped bowl in the center of the mahogany table. It was made of brass and appeared quite old. He had never seen anything quite like it. Dragons chasing a moon going through its phases were carved into its curved sides. Inside the bowl, holding the candle upright, was a layer of fine sand. Lying on top of the sand was a large piece of crystal, a small red stone, and a larger black one.

Around the bowl was a leather string holding brown ears. Two of them were fresh.

"In here is the moon, anew and vibrant. In here is the river of—"

"Looks like sand and three rocks to me."

She frowned. Her eyes sought his soul and undressed it. He had never felt such penetration. His body was chilled.

"In here is the river of light. Dancing. In here is the heart of the earth. Breathing."

The words rattled uncomfortably in his head as she continued with her rhythmic incantation.

"All hearts sing with the spirit in this world and the one beside it, drawn together by the lust of moonlight," she recited huskily, drawing a triangle with her finger around the candle and stones. "The red stone is you. The black stone is for your mother and father, waiting to hear and be heard. I am but a singer to the spirits."

Her hands moved smoothly across her face and down over her bosom as she explained. "The crystal is a living being. It is the moon. It is not truly solid. It is song. The song of creation. The song of the wheel of life. With it we can reach out to the spirits who live beyond us. Waiting. Waiting. It is our friend." Her hands repeated the same rhythmic motion, around her face and down, but never touching herself.

He glanced at the bowl. "Hard to believe there's so much there." He cocked his head. "But I've seen some sand down around the Panhandle that sure looked like spirits had been working it over." He chuckled to himself.

"Please, Time. Your mother and father have waited a long time to talk with you. They came at my request, the moon's strength, and the crystal's song—but they cannot stay long."

Carlow laid his hat on the floor and pulled the empty chair back. His spurs caught the lowest rung as he sat.

Again she repeated the circular motion with her

hands about her face and body, each time her hands came closer and closer to her eyes. Smoothly and slowly like ripples on a pond. Barely making the flame of the candle sway. Finally her fingers encircled only her turquoise eyes. They seemed wild. Unblinking. Unworldly.

Lavender sought his nose and loins. Watching her hands made Carlow's head ache. A pounding in rhythm with her movements. She had taken possession of the room. If he closed his eyes, he knew he would sink into the crystal.

"Take my hands in yours." She held out her hands and he did as she asked. The soft touch of her skin was cold. So cold. "Close your eyes and empty your mind of the day. Close your eyes and do not let disbelief enter your soul. Nay, not now. Spirits are sensitive and will not stay where there is disbelief. They trust me. You must trust me. Close your eyes."

Carlow closed his eyes.

Her chin rose and she began to chant. It wasn't like anything Carlow had ever heard before. Strange-sounding words. He had no idea to what language they belonged. Long, almost tearful phrases that ended wistfully. Soon she began to talk in a calibrated, thin voice that seemed to be coming from somewhere else and not from within her body. A glaze covered her eyes like the veil of a just-cast-off deep sleep. Her grip tightened around his hands.

"Yes, I know. He is here. He is waiting. He believes. Please come. He would like to hear from you." Her entire body trembled. "Yes, she comes . . . yes, she comes, the Irish one, fair as the day. She is with us now, the Irish one, fair as the day. She has been waiting . . . waiting so long." Her body jerked spasmodically, and her hands were iron around Carlow's. "Yes, he is with her.

Yes, he is with her. It is now. Speak to us . . . through the sacred stone that is the moon. Speak to us."

Silently a shadow spread from the far corner of the room. A shrouded image took shape from behind a heavy couch shoved against the wall.

Chapter Thirty-three

Five gunshots tore through the room, then a hesitation, and a sixth ripped the air.

The shrouded figure stepped sideways as if to clear the couch, weaved to one side, then righted himself. He tried to recock his silver-plated revolver but the hammer was too heavy to pull back. Something was terribly wrong with the gun. No longer would it stay in his hand. The weapon thudded to the dark floor. The would-be assassin tottered and fell. Face-first. And was still.

A thin string of smoke sought relief from Carlow's Colt. He was on his back on the floor, still sitting in the overturned chair. The instant he sensed movement, the young Ranger had ripped his hands away from Jessie's and shoved himself backward in the chair, drawing his Colt as he fell. Not expecting Carlow's reaction, the assassin had delivered his bullet where the Ranger had been a moment before. Carlow's four shots found his heart. The assassin's second shot thudded into the floor.

Wild-eyed, Jessie screamed and stood, shoving the table in Carlow's direction. The crystal and two rocks flew into the air and disappeared into the darkness with a rain of sand following. The candle rattled on the floor near his head, spitting its last spark. The table toppled onto its side, shivered, and decided to remain there. As did the necklace of ears.

"My God, what have you done!" she cried out. A large knife was in her raised right hand.

"Shot a ghost," Carlow said, lying on his back in the downed chair. His cocked revolver was pointed at the prone figure. "Actually it looks a lot like a priest. A priest with a gun." He swung the Colt toward her. "Drop the knife, Jessie. This man's ears are going to stay where they are."

She threw the blade at him, and it clanked off the corner of his overturned chair. Screaming madly, she ran and knelt beside the shrouded figure. It was the priest from the hotel porch. Her outfit didn't appear to leave room for hiding a gun, but he knew that was a dangerous assumption.

Before she pulled the priest's black hood free of his face, Carlow knew it was Silver Mallow. Still, Carlow's mouth tightened with the confirmation. The priest on the hotel porch. He should have guessed. Then.

The outlaw leader stared unseeing at her. Unseeing. Jessie leaned over and spat. Her spittle crawled across his still face. "You fool," she roared. "You complete fool. Remmy should never have believed you. I told you both that the Ranger was good. All you could do was talk—a-an' play the fiddle—an' wear a stupid d-disguise."

"I think you're going to have to reach him through one of your seances, Jessie. He's dead." Carlow pushed away from the chair with his left hand and stood. He couldn't help wondering if Mallow had held a gun behind his back when watching him from the hotel porch and hadn't liked his chances.

She looked up, tears of anger masking her face. She looked crazy. "Y-you were the one who was to die. T-the spirits deemed it. The m-moon agreed. I—I am Diana. You are m-my next—"

"Maybe they got confused. We look a lot alike," Carlow said, shoving new loads into his Colt. "Sorry I had to break up your little song and dance. I knew you had somebody hiding, but I couldn't tell where. Had to wait for him to make an appearance."

"H-how did you know it was...this musical clown?"

"When you said something about me being wounded, I remembered seeing a priest outside your hotel when I rode in." Carlow spun the bullet cylinder to check its capacity, then closed the loading hinge with his thumb. "That had to be Mallow. I should've known you and your husband had set up his fake escape to get me out of town." He cocked his head to the side. "Unless you really did talk to my mother and father."

She spat at Mallow's face again, and her hand slid toward the gun just beside his right leg.

"Don't do that, Jessie. The spirits wouldn't like it. Neither would I."

"You would shoot a woman?"

Carlow cocked his head to the side. "A woman trying to kill me, yes."

"You are despicable."

"I thought I was the red rock."

Commotion at the front door caught his attention. Carlow slipped the Colt to his left hand and drew his hand-carbine. "Looks like you've got some friends coming to join the party."

Her drawn face was unreadable. She sat cross-legged next to Mallow's body, her arms folded defiantly. He thought she was quite likely insane. He glanced down at the turned-over table. It would be as good as any to fight from, and he eased toward it.

A bark broke through the stillness. Chance!

"In here, boy," Carlow yelled. If he was going to die, at least his wolf-dog would be with him. He cocked the Colt and spun the hand-carbine in his right hand by the lever, readying it.

The shadow at the doorway was familiar and immediately raced for Carlow, almost knocking him over. Chance's tail wagged vigorously, and he licked at Carlow's hand. The young Ranger laid down his Colt for a moment to return the greeting, then picked it up again.

"Stay behind here, boy."

The next shadow was Kileen's, filling the door.

"What be goin' on in this damn cave?" His voice boomed in the darkness. "Don't the doctor be ownin' a candle?"

"Yeah, they had one, but it went out."

"I missed ye at the marshal's office. Went back to make certain the fellow be understandin' his charge," Kileen explained, trying to see in the darkened room. "He told me ye had been in. Gave him a few instructions ye did." The big Ranger's laugh was comforting.

"That's Silver Mallow . . . there."

Kileen stopping laughing, squinted, and walked over to the body. Squatting next to the dead man, Jessie Holden glared up at him. Ignoring her completely, he proceeded to tell Carlow that he had awakened Dr. Holden after talking to the marshal. With some "wee encouragement," the frightened doctor had confessed to confronting Mallow when he first rode into town. Holden's men had stopped him as they had Carlow later, thinking he was riding for the Cradle 6. After Mallow explained his situation to Red Anklon and Del Gato, they told him to hide in the brothel.

They set up the ruse about Mallow's escaping to get rid of Carlow. A Holden rider, pretending to be the outlaw leader, was to ride hard for the border and not stop. Although assured that he wouldn't have to face Carlow, the man hadn't yet returned. They hadn't expected the young Ranger to ride back to the Von Pearce ranch, and thought he also had gone into Mexico.

In return, Mallow was expected to help them if any repercussions arose after taking control of the Cradle 6; the outlaw said he could handle Viceroy if necessary. Holden said Mallow had moved to his hotel this morning. He thought it was funny that the outlaw decided to disguise himself as a priest.

"Meself went to the hotel to see if the priest be ready to do some confessin' hisself." Kileen chuckled at his joke. "The fine hotel clerk be tellin' me that the sweet lass herself came and left with him. Sounded like it was shortly after meself be enterin' town with the fine doctor." He patted her head and she hissed a curse. "Oh, melady, that be not a fittin' sound from ye." He grinned and patted her head again as she continued cursing.

Carlow couldn't resist his own smile.

"When I told Holden that Will Nichols be leadin' ye to Widow Bea's," Kileen concluded, "well, the fine doctor, he almost choked, he did. I had to slap hisself a bit to straighten out his constitution. Always glad to help a fellow man, I be." Kileen looked down at the distraught Jessie. "Well, me lass, it be lookin' like your husband hisself an' ye did not be hirin' too well. Your black man is with us no more, either. God bless his black soul."

Her eyes spit at him. "Del Gato will kill you both."

"Aye, 'tis a thought. 'Tis a thought," Kileen said. "But a fine citizen, Mr. Ward, he be showin' me where Del Gato be lyin'. Facedown, Mrs. Holden. Facedown. Behind your store, he be." He nodded toward Carlow. "Ye didn't plan so well, me darlin'."

"Don't let me forget to replace the lock," Carlow said. "Whoever the new owners are will want that, I'm sure." He didn't intend to explain how Del Gato was killed.

For the first time, Carlow noticed there was a second wide shadow. Behind his uncle. The shape in the doorway was too distinctive to be anyone but Jimmy Ward Flanker.

Flanker! What is he doing here?

The fat shootist stepped closer to let the gray light salute him. His wink told Carlow to keep his charade as "Mr. Ward."

"Thank you . . . Mr. Ward. Citizens doing their duty are most appreciated," Carlow said.

"Ah, any citizen would have done the same," Flanker grinned. "I found the good Ranger here, finishing his tribute to a hard day's work, and told him of what I had seen."

"An' where I was going?"

"Ah, that too. That too." Flanker licked his lower lip and wiped his lapels of something only he could see.

An expression of having a great secret took over Kileen and he turned toward Carlow. The young Ranger thought he was going to blurt out Flanker's real identity. Instead, it was about superstitions again—and Charlie Two-Wolves.

"Did ye know Charlie Two-Wolves be a war chief?" Kileen's face was beaming. "Aye, he be tellin' me. He got away from the bloody reservation. Bea's late husband, God bless his soul, hired him on." He crossed himself and continued, "We be sharin' a bit about spirits an' war medicine . . . an' Chance."

Carlow knew what was coming next.

"He be knowin' who Chance be, me son. Just as I said he be."

Jessie stared at them. The look was murderous yet puzzled by the discussion between the two Rangers. Flanker looked amused. Kileen reached down and yanked her to her feet.

"Let me go! I'll have the marshal on you." She slapped at his arm and hand.

Kileen ignored the attack and moved her toward the door. He paused and looked back. "Ye be joinin' us, me son? Or be this place to your likin'?"

"Go ahead, I'll be right behind you. Gotta pick up some stuff."

Kileen nodded and continued walking, forcing Jessie Holden to walk with him. His firm grip on her arm gave her no choice. He tapped on the doorway three times. " 'Tis a wise thing this be to do, lass. Ye must get the attention of the wee spirits who live there. In the wood, they be. They need remindin' to honor your wish."

"I don't believe in stuff like that," she snarled.

"Aye, an' they don't believe in ye, Mrs. Holden. Will ye be joinin' us, Mr. Ward?"

"Certainly. Certainly." Flanker patted the big Ranger on the back and followed.

Carlow went first to Mallow's body. It was almost like seeing himself dead. Chance followed, sniffing at death, then pulling away. The young Ranger studied Mallow's hooded cloak. "I should have guessed it was you . . . at the hotel, Silver. I'll bet you liked this idea, didn't you? Getting to wear a costume to kill me." He picked up the outlaw leader's gun and shoved it into his waistband. "You should've tried at the porch. I wouldn't have expected it."

Staring at the outlaw's face, he decided Silver Mallow didn't really look like him after all. It was only the dark hair and the silver he was wearing. Carlow's glance took in Mallow's right hand, with a silver ring on each finger. His left hand was folded under his body.

"No wonder you kept your hands behind you at the hotel," Carlow muttered. "You really enjoyed all her mumbo jumbo, too, I know," Carlow continued. "Did you expect I'd think you were my mother or my father? Or that she could hypnotize me? You didn't rate me very high, did you, Silver?"

Carlow touched the cross necklace under his shirt. He didn't see one around Mallow's neck. The outlaw had worn one in the Bennett jail before he escaped. What had happened to it? It didn't matter. Not anymore.

One question was seeping into his mind: *Was Marshal Dillingham involved in this? He was the one who told me about the stolen horse. He knew where I was.*

He turned away and saw the large circle display on the wall. This time it just seemed gaudy. The devil masks glared at him, and he was glad to be leaving. It had been a risk to enter the room, but he couldn't see how he could have done it any other way. If he had tried to take Jessie right away, Mallow would have shot him in the back. He'd had to let them play out their game, but he admitted to himself that he hadn't expected her accomplice to be Mallow. What if the outlaw had fired at him from the hotel? Carlow muttered, "Just lucky," and looked up, glad that Kileen hadn't heard the phrase.

He felt his shirt for the pouch of wolf medicine. Two-Wolves would appreciate hearing it had helped him. Without thinking, he fingered his vest pockets. Next to the old watch were the acorn and the two blood stones. *I'll have to ask Thunder which one helped me,* he mused. *He'll have an opinion, that's for sure.* He tried to laugh but couldn't.

Touching the stones made him think of Jessie's rocks and piece of crystal. Funny how much importance some people put on rocks, he thought. Looking back at the turned-over table, he decided to get the crystal. Kileen would like having the clear rock. He walked over and picked it up, holding the piece in his open palm. Was she right about this thing not really being solid? That sound could go right through? Chance followed, sniffing first at the crystal, then heading over to explore the two other rocks.

Carlow's mind wandered back to a yesterday when he and his mother were living alone above a saloon. He wanted to tell Jessie that his mother's presence was never far from him—and that it didn't take all kinds of ceremony to have her there. He couldn't say the same about his father, having never known the man. Yet there was always something within him that he couldn't quite explain. It was like a tiny fire burned deep within his heart. A sensation that seemed to steer him when he needed it most. Maybe this was just his conscience, well planted by his mother. It didn't come from his uncle, that's for sure. Kileen had no qualms about cutting corners when and where he thought necessary.

Tossing the crystal in his hand, he left the room with the wolf-dog at his heels. Chance growled at the big dragon at the entrance. Carlow chuckled. "You could take him." They continued down the strange hallway and went outside.

Kileen had placed Jessie on his horse and was standing beside it, holding the reins and waiting. Her head was down. She was singing softly to herself. Carlow thought it sounded like a cradle song, one a mother sang to her child.

"Where's Mr. Ward?" Carlow asked.

"Oh, he needed to get back to his family."

"Well, that was certainly good of him to help us."

"Aye, me son. It 'twas."

He handed Kileen the piece of crystal, and the superstitious Ranger accepted it reverently. Staring at the rock in his fat hand, Kileen mumbled something Carlow couldn't quite make out. Celtic, he thought.

Carefully the big Ranger shoved it into his coat pocket. "A sacred stone, it 'tis, me son. Givin' itself to the wise. Singin' songs to the pure. Whisperin' secrets to the knowin'."

Carlow thought Kileen's description was close to Jessie's explanation and shook his head. He told Kileen about how the young woman had ordered the rustling of the Cradle 6 herd and murdered two of Bea's cowhands by herself. He included the ear cutting and face painting, and her murder of a German rancher and his wife. He told about her necklace of ears.

Kileen eyed the woman on his horse. "Did ye check her for a knife, laddie?"

"She threw it at me."

Changing the subject, he told his uncle of his concern about Marshal Dillingham's possibly being involved. Kileen's lack of response surprised him. Instead, the big Ranger asked if he knew where Red Anklon was since the fight. Carlow explained, for the first time, about finding the cattle and how the stampede had trampled Anklon and the other outlaws. He told about Nichols and Two-Wolves using the few remaining rustlers to round up Bea's herd. He said the Comanche warrior had killed a hidden outlaw and that the gunman would have shot Carlow if Two-Wolves hadn't done so. He told how Chance saved his life by attacking a rustler with an unseen gun. Silently, he repeated to himself that he was "just lucky."

Kileen started to tell his nephew about Bea's shooting the black gunfighter, whom he had known in New York. He stopped in midsentence and observed that the Indian's wolf medicine must have been strong, then chided his nephew for going after Jessie alone and not coming for him first.

"Yeah, I should've. Didn't expect such a welcome, I guess," Carlow said, and swung into his saddle.

"Ye didn't be expectin' Silver Mallow, either, me son. How dare he dress hisself as a priest?" Kileen crossed himself.

Carlow nodded but didn't respond.

"How did ye get behind Del Gato, me son?"

The question surprised Carlow. "I, ah, I saw him—an' sneaked around the front of the drugstore."

"Did ye be givin' him a notice of arrest—before ye be sendin' him to the gates o' hell?" Kileen cocked his head to the side and sought his nephew's eyes with his own.

Carlow looked away. He had never lied to his uncle. At least not about something like this.

"Or did Mr. Ward be havin' somethin' to do with it?" Kileen's mouth became a jack-o-lantern smile again.

"I promised not to tell, Thunder."

"I can be seein' why. 'Twill not be in our report to the fine captain. No, indeed." He shook his head and chuckled.

"Jimmy Ward Flanker is a friend, Thunder. He helped me. Twice."

"Such be talk for another day, me son. Another day."

Kileen was the only one who talked as they headed back to the jail. Walking beside his horse, the big Ranger told Jessie that Chance had sensed the spirit leaving Mallow's body before they entered the house; that was why he had barked. Dogs had that ability, he said.

She stared straight ahead, her expression sour and annoyed. Kileen either didn't notice or didn't care, and asked her if she was careful when she called to the spirits. He had heard that a ghost-seer who didn't do all of the proper preliminaries or told a mystery in front of someone who didn't believe would be punished. Only her slight grimace followed his observation.

Carlow watched her and tried to hide his smile. *She'll be glad to get to the jail*, he thought.

"Why don't you just shut up?" she finally blurted.

Kileen looked at her, an amused expression on his face. "Why, Mrs. Holden, whatever do ye mean? I thought ye was a woman full of sweetness and light."

"Go to hell, you old fool."

"An old fool, is it?" Kileen asked, then told her that he had heard there was only one hour in the day when a ghost-seer could see spirits. The rest of the time no one had that ability. Unfortunately, no one ever knew when that hour would be. It was a mystery.

"I guess ye not be knowin' the hour either, me lass."

She spat down at him.

The spittle rolled down his chin as he brought the horse to a stop. He stood for a moment. Without warning he reached up and dragged her off the horse. "Ye can be walkin' the rest o' the way, me darlin'. No one be spittin' on a Ranger an' stay mounted. No one." He gave her a shove, then another, and she began walking. He placed his boot in the stirrup and pulled himself into the saddle.

After a few steps, she paused and turned to Carlow. The innocence of a little girl filled her face. "Where is my brother?"

Carlow's response produced a scream from her that linked itself to a curse about the moon and her being Diana. Both Rangers watched her ranting for a few moments, then Kileen told her to walk or he would drag her to the jail on a rope. She began walking again, spewing chants and strange phrases.

As they approached the marshal's office, Kileen whispered something to Carlow, and the young Ranger kicked his horse into a lope toward the closest alley and disappeared into it. Chance raced along, three strides behind.

Slowly Kileen swung down from his horse, and Jessie took advantage of his momentary distraction and began to run. The big Ranger watched her, a strange smile on his craggy face. Shadows quickly wrapped themselves around the fleeing woman.

"Ye will be the first lass I have shot. Well, the first in the back. But ye shouldn't be countin' that," Kileen said almost casually. "Mary Shagnon, bless her soul, she be dead of me bullets for sure."

He had never even shot at a woman, much less killed one, and didn't want to start now. If she kept running, he would have to holler out to Carlow to come back and go after her. Running wasn't anything he was interested in doing, either.

But his bluff was enough. In the middle of the street, Jessie halted; her shoulders drooped. She stood, looking like some forgotten waif.

"Now would ye be so kind as to be walkin' back to the constable's office?" Kileen's voice changed into a cutting growl. "Or do ye want to be dragged in? 'Tis your own choosin'—but be makin' it. I be tired o' this nonsense with ye an' your husband."

Her shoulders rose and fell, but she didn't move. Kileen thought she might run again. The shuffle of his

Cotton Smith

boots on the hard street was enough, though, to spur her into a quick return to the hitching rack.

"That be a good lass. Let's go inside." Kileen made an exaggerated bow and ended his sweep with his hat in his hand pointing toward the door.

She snorted her defiance and stepped onto the boardwalk. Kileen followed, knocking three times loudly on the bolted door. Inside, shuffling and urgent whispers erupted, and then it was silent.

"Jes' a minute, I'm a'comin'."

Marshal Dillingham opened the door with enthusiasm.

"Oh, I see yo-all been ri't bizz-ee." He touched the brim of his hat. "Evenin', Mrs. Hold-un. Sorry to see yo-all hyar."

She burst past him into the yellow-lit office and stood beside the desk, looking for her husband. A lone gas lamp was doing its best to provide light but losing to the corner shadows.

"Be that one cell open?" Kileen demanded, following her inside.

"Well, yeah, I guess so."

"This lass be under arrest for murder and rustling. Just like her man. Put her in it." Kileen's glare was more than Dillingham wanted.

"B-but this ain't no place fer a wo-man."

"It be now. Do it."

From the back of the cells came a haughty command. "Ranger, you've done enough to me—and my wife—today. Put up your hands." Dr. Holden pointed a long-barreled Colt through the cell door. He pushed it open. "It's your turn to get in here."

"Don't be thinkin' that's so," Kileen said, almost smiling, but his mouth was closed.

Marshal Dillingham's own grin vanished with Kileen's

330

response. He took a step toward the open door, keeping his hands close to the belt gun at his hip.

"And why not?" Dr. Holden demanded.

Jessie shouted, "Remmy, you fool . . . the other Ranger—Carlow—is outside somewhere."

"Not somewhere. Right here."

Dr. Holden turned his head toward the back of the cell. Through the small barred window he saw Carlow's face. His hand-carbine was shoved between the iron posts and aimed at the physician. "Drop the gun, Holden."

"What be takin' ye so long, laddie?" Kileen said.

"Couldn't find anything to stand on." Carlow glanced down. "Had to use my horse. He isn't as good as Shadow at doing what he's told."

"A good hoss it be, though. 'Tis lucky to stand upon a horse. Make a wish. Ye must tap the bars three times. Do it, me son."

Dr. Holden frowned and let his gun bounce on the floor. In the uneven light, his purple and swollen face looked like a carved pumpkin beginning to bloat. His mouth trembled with rage, but there was no courage to back it up with action. He stood for a moment, then retreated to the back of the cell and sat on the cot.

Picking up the keys from the desk, Kileen directed Jessie to the open cell, then closed and locked the door behind her. He walked to Dr. Holden's cell, picked up the dropped gun, locked his door, and turned back to Marshal Dillingham.

"Looks like we be needin' to let this fella full o' fine drink go free," Kileen said, nodding his head toward the cell with the drunken cowboy.

"Wh-why?"

"Ye be needin' a place to stay until the judge gets

here." Kileen's right fist held up the doctor's pistol by the barrel.

The big-eared lawman gulped his surprise. "B-but I—I didn't do no-thin'. Nothin' at-tall. I-uh didn't know he had that. H-honest." His ears wiggled as his agitation grew.

"Honest? Don't want to be hearin' that word from ye, Dillingham. It be hurtin' me ears."

Kileen walked over and yanked Dillingham's pistol from its holster with his left hand. With a nod of his head and holding a gun in each hand, the big Ranger indicated he wanted Dillingham in the cell.

The marshal's chin fell to his chest. He began to blubber and his ears wobbled. "I—I'm s-sor-ree. I—I d-didn't know w-what to do. Th-they w-were gonna kill me."

"Aye, so ye be spittin' on your badge." Kileen grabbed the star pinned to the lawman's shirt and yanked it hard. Cloth ripped and the badge was released to the big Ranger's fist. He looked at the sleeping cowboy in the cell. "Get up, laddie. 'Tis time for ye to be back on the streets."

Slowly the bleary-eyed cowboy with long sideburns and a scraggly mustache sat up on the cot. He stared at the big Ranger and Marshal Dillingham and decided the town constable had brought in a state lawman to take him away.

"Come on, Marshal, I didn't mean to break that window. I said I'd pay for it. Really." The cowboy's mouth pulled down at the corner when he spoke. It was permanently misshapen by a scar; the drop was not whiskey induced.

Ranger Kileen said gently, "Me son, all is forgiven. Ye be leavin' now. Go an' sin no more."

"Really?"

"Aye. An' don't forget to be payin' for that window."

"Well, thank you, sir. Thank you, sir. I will, sir. I promise." The cowboy jumped to his feet and hurried past Kileen and Dillingham, nervously opened the jail door, and vanished into the night.

As Kileen turned to watch the cowboy leave, Jessie reached through her adjacent bars to scratch at his face.

With practiced skill, he dodged her attempt and pushed Dillingham into the now-empty cell. Just out of range of her hands, he turned to her and said, "Did ye be knowin' the forefinger of ye right hand . . . aye, that one . . . it be full o' poison? Aye, the ancients say it be true. Never be usin' it for puttin' sweet salve to a wound. Nay, ye should not. Now the ring finger, ah, that fine finger can be stroked along any wound. All by itself. Soon the sore be healin'. All the other fingers be poison, but the forefinger is the devil itself. I thought ye would like to be knowin'."

She stared at her fingers. "You old fool! I wish they were poison. I'd kill you—an' cut out your heart. The spirits would like that."

"No, lassie, they would not. The spirits don't want to have anything to do with ye. Not now, not even after ye hang," Kileen said as he locked the marshal's cell.

The marshal stood, his eyes staring at the torn hole in his shirt.

Toward Dr. Holden's cell, Kileen yelled, "Doc, ye should have been teachin' your sweet wife some manners. 'Tis a pity to see such a pretty lass so poorly ready for society."

Slowly Dr. Holden raised his head. He stared at Kileen and spoke softly. "I've never been able to control her. She's crazy like her mother was. An' she was a damn witch." He took a deep breath that brought new pain to his battered face. "Whatever you want, I can pay. You name it."

"Aye, Doc. Her name be Justice. That's what me an' Ranger Carlow be wantin'—for Bea."

Dillingham found some strength within himself. After glancing at the doctor and his wife in the adjoining cells, he looked back at Kileen. "Hey, I will tell yo-all ever-thang yah wanna know."

"Shut up, you idiot," Dr. Holden growled.

"Yo-all shut up, Hold-un," Dillingham shot back, pointing his finger at the doctor. "There wasn't supposed to be any problem, re-mem-ber? It was gonna be eas-ee, re-mem-ber? Yo-all don't know noth-un'. Noth-un'."

"Have a nice chat, lads."

Behind him, Carlow stepped into the jail along with Chance. Kileen locked the cell door and strolled toward his nephew. The big Ranger's grin was as large as he was, showing the full breadth of his teeth, missing and intact. He told him about letting the drunk cowboy go so there would be room for Dillingham. He planned to offer the marshal his freedom if he turned on the Holdens. He expected that. Carlow agreed with the action and told him that Nichols and Two-Wolves were holding Holden's outlaws and getting signed confessions.

"Looks like we spendin' the night in a jail. Again, me son," Kileen said. "Will ye be all right with that?"

"Sure. We can wire Captain McNelly tomorrow and tell him what's happened. Better wire Judge Garrison, too."

"Aye, the judge be two, three days away, I be thinkin'."

Carlow suddenly felt very tired—and very hungry. He glanced toward the cells and saw Jessie standing against the bars, watching him. Her back was straight, accenting her bosom against the red cloth. Her soft eyes were free of anger; replacing the venom was a cal-

culated, come-hither gaze. Her warm eyes studied him
and encouraged him to approach.

"I can't believe you stayed to help that old German
woman. Why would you do that? You ruined everything. She was nothing. Nothing. The moon wanted
her gone." Jessie glanced down at herself, inviting his
gaze to follow. "You could have had so much more."

Instead, Carlow looked at Kileen and smiled. "Oh,
she makes mighty good sausages. Never had a spirit do
that."

"Aye, an' fine biscuits tasting like they be made by
the sweet angels themselves."

Jessie's fist slammed against the bars.

"Do you remember that frozen pink rose we saw
once?" he said to Kileen. "Three years back. There was
a late snow that spring. We were heading for the Red
and rode past a house with a little flower garden. Really something to see. That rose so pretty—but all
frozen."

Kileen watched his beloved nephew without speaking.

"Always wondered what happened to it," Carlow
finished, "when the sun came out again and the ice
melted."

"It became a stick, me son. 'Tis sad to see beauty
that has nothing inside it," Kileen observed, and put his
hand on his nephew's shoulder. "Why don't ye be gettin' us somethin' to eat? I'll stay here."

Carlow's grin was a knowing one. "There's only one
woman I'm interested in, Thunder."

"Would ye have been includin' Widow Beckham in
your wish upon the horse?"

"Well, now, if I tell you, it won't come true."

Kileen nodded his head and patted Carlow's shoulder
affectionately. "I be thinkin', 'twould be good to ride
out to the Von Pearce ranch tomorrow. I should be

telling her that all be well. Ye know, let her mind be findin' peace." He followed that by telling Carlow about Bea's shooting Viceroy and saving all of their lives. He spoke in glowing terms of her fierce courage. He didn't mention knowing the black man from his early days.

It was Carlow's turn to observe his uncle. "You old rascal. You're interested in Bea Von Pearce."

"As ye be sayin', 'tis a grand meal she makes."

Carlow laughed, and it felt good. He suggested Kileen take a wagon of supplies with him; Bea would be needing them. The big Ranger agreed and said he thought Will Nichols would make a good foreman. Carlow teased him about his original opinion of the one-handed cowboy. Kileen didn't respond but wondered if they should scout around for a few cowhands for her to hire. He nodded toward Dr. Holden's cell and said there would be some good pastureland for sale soon, as well. Carlow told his uncle that Bea would soon have him riding herd, too. Kileen frowned and said he had other things in mind.

Neither thought Bea would be interested in the Holdens' hotel or saloon. When Carlow told him that Dr. Holden also owned the whorehouse, Kileen laughed out loud.

"I wonder if the general store has any pretty dresses for little girls." Carlow stepped over to the jail door and opened it. "Or one of those dolls."

"Maybe a fine leather-bound book . . . in German, me son." Kileen grinned.

"Oh, I've got to get some cigars for Will, too. Said I would." Carlow shook his head. "An' I'll bring us back a couple of steaks."

"A wee sup of Irish whiskey would be a fine touch."

"Sure. Come on, Chance."

Carlow strolled outside in the easy night air with

Chance at his heels. He reached down to push the knife handle back into place in his right legging; it had worked its way up. His spurs mixed with the sounds of music and laughter from the saloons.

Kileen stood in the doorway, watching him, then looked up to the star-blossoming sky. "Aye, Mary Lucent Carlow. There be standin' a Ranger—or me name ain't Aaron Lucent."

COTTON SMITH

DEATH RIDES A RED HORSE

What started as a simple trip for supplies has turned into a race against time and a fight to survive. Cole Kerry almost single-handedly broke up a raid on the town by a gang of outlaws. But one of them grabbed Cole's wife as they rode off, and Cole himself was shot in the back when he tried to track them down. Now it's up to his older brother, Ethan, to find Cole and rescue his wife—if they're still alive. It's a tough enough job for any man. Ethan isn't about to let the fact that he's blind stand between him and what he needs to do.

WINTER KILL

COTTON SMITH

Rustling is an ugly business. Just the suspicion of it can get somebody hurt—or killed. And there's a whole lot of suspicion over on the Bar 6, the largest spread in the region. Old Titus Branson is missing a hundred head of Bar 6 cattle, and he's mighty sure of who did it: Bass Manko. Titus isn't about to sit still for something like that. He and his boys are dead set on seeing Manko swing from a rope. But Titus will have to face someone besides Manko first: Manko's best friend—Titus's own son!

SONS OF THUNDER

COTTON SMITH

No one in the small Texas town of Clark Springs knows that their minister's real name is Rule Cordell, or that he used to be one of the most notorious outlaws the Confederacy had ever seen. He's been trying very hard to put his days as a pistol-fighter behind him, but that's getting harder to do lately. When his friends and neighbors are threatened with losing their family spreads to a cunning carpetbagger, Rule realizes it's time for his preacher's collar to be replaced by a pair of .44s. But he won't be able to do it alone. If he's going to rid the town of this ruthless evil, he'll need to call on a very special group of warriors—the Sons of Thunder!

NIGHT OF THE COMANCHEROS
LAURAN PAINE

In these two brilliant novellas, celebrated author Lauran Paine perfectly captures the drama of the frontier and the gritty determination of those who lived there. In "Paid in Blood," an inept Indian agent has put the Apaches on the warpath, and U.S. Army Scout Caleb Doorn is all that stands between the bloodthirsty braves and the white settlers. The title story tells of Buck Baylor, who returns home from his first cattle drive to find his father murdered and the countryside in the unrelenting grip of vicious outlaws. Will Buck be able to avenge his family before he, too, is killed?

Will Henry
THE SCOUT

Will Henry remains one of the most widely recognized and honored novelists ever to write about the American West. As demonstrated by the three novellas in this brilliant collection, throughout his career he was able to create exciting, authentic tales filled with humanity, adventure, and empathy. "Red Blizzard" is the tale of a Pawnee scout caught between the U.S. Army and the Sioux in the time of the wars with Crazy Horse. "Tales of the Texas Rangers" recounts the courageous battle waged by the Rangers against any danger, from Comanches to John Wesley Hardin. The title character in "The Hunkpapa Scout" is a trail guide for a wagon train set upon by rampaging Sioux. He will be the only hope to warn the nearby cavalry troop…if he survives!

Dorchester Publishing Co., Inc.
P.O. Box 6640
Wayne, PA 19087-8640

_____5568-6
$5.99 US/$7.99 CAN

Please add $2.50 for shipping and handling for the first book and $.75 for each additional book. NY and PA residents, add appropriate sales tax. No cash, stamps, or CODs. Canadian orders require an extra $2.00 for shipping and handling and must be paid in U.S. dollars. Prices and availability subject to change. **Payment must accompany all orders.**

Name: _____

Address: _____

City: _____ State: _____ Zip: _____

E-mail: _____

I have enclosed $_____ in payment for the checked book(s).

For more information on these books, check out our website at www.dorchesterpub.com.
_____ *Please send me a free catalog.*

MAX BRAND®

JOKERS EXTRA WILD

Anyone making a living on the rough frontier took a bit of a gamble, but no Western writer knows how to up the ante like Max Brand. In "Speedy—Deputy," the title character racks up big winnings on the roulette wheel, but that won't help him when he's named deputy sheriff—a job where no one's lasted more than a week. "Satan's Gun Rider" continues the adventures of the infamous Sleeper, whose name belies his ability to bury a knife to the hilt with just a flick of his wrist. And in the title story, a professional gambler inherits a ring that lands him in a world of trouble.